ISMENE
THE NOBLE LADY

VASILY ANNA YOHAN KOUSKOULAS

ACKNOWLEDGEMENT

The Author wishes to acknowledge that in typing this book Dr. Barbara Anne Burstein made also the necessary corrections and improvements for which the Author remains thankfully in debt forever. But young she followed those who loved her in heaven before the end of the book...It was finally finished by Dr. Vasily Kouskoulas.

Dr. Nicholas Tserpes, professor of Mathematics and others helped the Author in his efforts to bring forward his ideas. Those who knew and those who didn't know are deeply appreciated for the expression of their views and contribution. Those are deeply thanked and long will be remembered by the Author...

Dr. Yanni Kouskoulas, Eng'ng, and Ms. Tamara Kouskoulas, Physics, were my ambition and inspiration in this work written to remind them that I do not have their artistic and professional talents but their wish and love have guided me on my way to express my ideas, gratitude and ministration...

DEDICATED TO :

Barbara Anne Burstein Kouskoulas
Professor of Economics
Lawrence Technological University
Southfield Michigan

"Μηδεν εκ του μη οντος γιγνεσθαι
Μηδ' ες το μη ον φθειρεσθαι
Γιγνεσθαι δε και απολλυσθαι
το αυτο καθεστηκε και αλλοιουσθαι..."

Father of Modern Science
Δημοκριτος (460–370 BC)

To remember:
Barbara,
a noble lady ...
VK.

◆ FriesenPress

Suite 300 - 990 Fort St

Victoria, BC, Canada, V8V 3K2

www.friesenpress.com

ISBN

978-1-4602-6509-3 (Hardcover)

978-1-4602-6510-9 (Paperback)

978-1-4602-6511-6 (eBook)

1. Fiction

Distributed to the trade by The Ingram Book Company

CONTENTS

1 ISMENE RAPED IN 'AGIUS SARANTA'

'Agius Saranta' is a harbor City in south west Albania.

Ismene at the age of nineteen was sitting at her large balcony facing the Adriatic Sea. She was beautiful and charming. She was attractive, disciplined and enchanting. She was day dreaming and laughing. She knew that Ismene and Antigone were sisters. Eteocles and Polynices were their brothers. She was laughing. Her green bluish eyes were capturing and love was her choice. She was not a rebel but behaving. She was not unruly but pleasant and disciplined. She loved history following those who wrote it.

But she didn't believe those who write history. She knew most of them were eventually departing from the truth. Especially the Christians who wanted a Christian State even under the rule of the Turks, were more corrupt than expected. Ismene knew that Emil Zola was the figure head among the literally bourgeoisie of his time. She knew that in 1906 Dreyfus was finally exonerated by the supreme court of France. She knew that the intellectuals were shaping public opinion and she was careful to read but not believe them all. She was so young and so informed.

She had lost her father at the age of 15, but he had left her a good wealth of money to receive when she becomes 21 years old. Her mother was Albanian but her father was Greek. Ismene was a young lady capable to adjust herself to the needs of the environment. She loved her mother, who loved her father like a God. Her Albanian mother, as they called her Denysa, the daughter of Dionysus, had learned to speak Greek to please her husband, and since she lost him, she had no eyes to see others.

It does not mean she didn't like them, but she didn't want them. Ismene, her daughter, was her goddess, and she loved her with passion but no weakness. Sergio was her son and she loved him with admiration. She loved him as much as Olympias loved Alexander the Great: Young, intelligent, well educated, noble and a fierce thinker and fighter.

She lost her Sergio to Germany when he was 17 years old. He went to study and be what he liked. He chose Aeronautical Engineering. Now she loved Ismene, who was 15 years old, with passion and no weakness. Denysa had recently lost her husband and was bitter. She knew those who had killed her husband and was living with the desire to get revenge. But the way of revenge for her was a long one and the thought was depressing. The killers of her husband were not yet punished.

The way Olympias loved her son Alexander the Great and her daughter Cleopatra, Denysa worshipped Sergio her son and Ismene her daughter. Ismene had the name of her paternal mother and she was admired by her father. She was really a real knowledgeable woman, noble and kind; determined and forceful but very legal.

Denysa's son Sergio was a gentleman admired and worshiped like a god. Ismene knew that one day he was to return when communism was to fail. Her father had said so anyway. Democracy was a Greek concept. One day all people would have some kind of Democracy: The gift of the Hellenic people to the world.

Unfortunately, Ismene lost both her father Alexander and her brother Sergio early, and with them she had lost everything but her mother. Her brother had left for Germany when he was only 17 years old. Even though she was very young, she remembered him and loved him with passion. She needed to love someone to exist. She doesn't remember why he had left. More likely to study, but she had not seen him since then. Communism was not the system he would accept. He was now a German Aeronautical Engineer with a Doctor's degree and as her mother was saying, he was unique and noble. As all mothers praise their sons and daughters and say their children are the best, why should she not? Her husband was a virtuous and noble man respected by all those who approached him and asked his assistance. He was a noble and respectful Greek. He attained the same honor in Albania.

Denysa her mother was daring, but Ismene was careful and wise. She was not an easy loser. She was legal and a thinker. She was sensual but reserved. She was not like her mother, but she loved her with passion. She had no sisters. She had only one brother whom she loved. But she had not seen him since he left when she was nearly 10 years old and he was just 17. She wanted to marry a man that she loved. She was not questioning her virtues. But how many woman do? How many woman deny their virtues? To question is to deny till you have the answer. Ismene was Sergio's sister and loved him endlessly. He was her perfection and passion. She was strangely dreaming that one day she was going to meet him; and ask him of the revenge.

At the age of nineteen Ismene was accepted in the Bank of Agius Saranta in a position of Investment Advisor for Greeks in Albania and others. She was bright, beautiful, studious and respectful. She was advising the Greeks of Agius Saranta how to invest and prosper.

It is Saturday morning in Agius Saranta in southwest Albania. Ismene, the young, beautiful and intelligent girl is sitting in her western balcony enjoying the Adriatic sea. You can tell she is of a rare beauty. You could not see and not want her. The hair is nearly blond and charming. Her eyes are dark, orange-blue, and her lips burning red and attractive. She is just 19 years old. It is time to love and give herself if she wished and they wanted her. Love had to be mutual. She had lost her father and she was crying each time he was coming in her mind.

The book she is reading is the 'Iliad and Odyssey', written in modern Greek. But it is a new one. It had not been read before. As a matter of fact, it is a new book given to her by her father at the age of fifteen years old. It was a book not read before by anyone. He had given to her brother a new one also, when he left for Germany to study. He wanted his children to grow up with the company of his heroes Achilles and Odysseus. Achilles was the hero of war and Odysseus the hero of return. He wanted his children to read and know about both.

Her eyes often cry after she looks at the sea and returns to the book. She must have been waiting for her brother who does not seem to be ever coming. She knows that her father has left her forever but his love is with her as long as she is alive. She does not want anyone to know. She is waiting for her brother. She is staring deep in the sea and waits. Sometimes she hopes more than others, and expects more.

Ismene looks as if she is waiting for someone who, however, never comes either from the land or from the sea. Then she cries, and bending reads the 'Iliad and Odyssey.' But just before the sun comes to her balcony, she gets up and goes downstairs. Apparently, she does not need anyone to tell her to go because she senses that the sun will begin to read her book. Each time she reads it, she cries thinking of her noble father. As she closes the book to go inside, she whispers: A name from Minor Asia. Then she reads his devotion smiling and crying:

> To my wise and beautiful Ismene,
> I place wisdom before beauty;
> If you have them both you are blessed!
> Your Father
> Alexander Aristomenes

She loves his name and bitterly smiling whispers: A fast man, the son of the excellent in wrath." Then with melancholy she says, "I have the beauty but I do not think that I have the wisdom." Her father believed that it was easier to have the beauty than the wisdom.

Each time she reads the handwriting of her father, she looks for him deep in the sea and cries. She never sees him coming and seriously reflects: light brown hair and light blue eyes; looking at her beauty, and making her cry. For whatever she is waiting, it never comes. It is only the sun or the clouds, and some times the blue sky is filled with birds and her eyes cry. Her brother was not coming and her father has gone. 'Aristomenes from Minor Asia,' she whispers and cries. He will never come. But her brother more likely will; to take the revenge. She thinks but never speaks of that. She was secretly in love with her father.

The book was written a long time ago in the language of her father. She was only 12 years old when she learned to read the Odyssey and had made her father proud and happy. That was when he begun to save money for her trip to the places of Iliad and Odyssey and anywhere else she wanted to go. But she lost him, and her mother since then has been dressed in light black and she is secretly crying.

Denysa almost never went to church after she lost her husband, even though that was only on Christmas, Easter and special holidays. She was following her husband's philosophy with passion: Religion was a private matter only to be respected. Those who accept it, they don't understand but believe it. It is easy for people with no much brain; or with too much fear. Man does not understand where he is coming from and where he is going. It is the same place, more likely. Democritus thought so too!

It was Saturday again when Ismene sat on her balcony to read her Iliad and Odyssey and watch the Adriatic sea stretching to the end horizon broken only when ships were coming to the harbor. This Saturday she was by herself trying to understand her father: Knowledgeable and understanding as her mother thinks of him when she cries. Ismene was showing great loyalty to her father when she was alerting him to the situations with the law. "People with the Law are either cruel or fanatics," she used to say.

Alexander didn't listen to his devoted little lady and he died. Now she is looking at the sea for him and she is crying. She remembers that she was only fifteen years old when he died. But she didn't want her mother to know. She was hiding her tears with her smiles and she knew how to do it. But she was wrong to think that her mother could not see. She was crying as she was leaving the balcony.

———————————

Ismene is nineteen years old now, sitting on her balcony a Saturday morning and studying again the 'Iliad and Odyssey". She is watching from time to time the birds flying and playing. She is employed at the Agius Saranta bank in the Investment Section. The Greeks, especially, are happy to be served by a noble young and intelligent lady like Ismene.

Suddenly, that Saturday, four men get into her house, as quietly as possible. Two of them go upstairs and block the path of Ismene as soon as she tries to go downstairs. The other two take her mother under the command of a gun and leave in a car. Apparently, they didn't want to get them together. Who knows what the hell they wanted to do. If God exists he should know; but he never tells. Some people dream what he says. They are funny; they are confused imposters! God does not speak.

One of the men upstairs kills the other, as soon as the two below leave, and he orders Ismene: "Come now, lets go," pointing the gun at her; the same gun with which he had killed the other man. Under the command of his gun, he puts frightened Ismene in the car that just came and they leave. He had just called the driver to come. He was still holding the gun that had killed the other man. There was really no question that he could pull the trigger and kill Ismene as well. So, she followed confused and trembling.

She didn't know who were those people and what was the issue: What did they want? She was though frightened under the command of the gun. It was the pistol that had killed the other man. She could be the next one. But there was no reason. That was her logic: Yes, if she didn't resist to anything he wanted! She just wanted to survive before she did anything. At that point she was just confused.

Ismene was terrified and didn't know what to do or what to say. Before she did anything, one of the men is dying and the other is ordering her, pointing his gun, to move downstairs. She is slow; he pushes her with the gun to move down and he follows. The man is well composed and calm, and another man arrives with a car. Before Ismene screams, the man pushes her into the car that he opened; gets in next to her, closes the door and says, "My name is Jack. Please call me Mr. Jack and lets go."

While they are leaving, Ismene cries, "Where is my mother; my mother please," she screams. "Don't worry Ismene, we will take you to your mother," he says deceptively. The driver takes off and Ismene is driven to a strange but very pleasant looking place in Agius Saranta. "Where is my mother, Mr. Jack?" yells Ismene frightened. "Be patient my young lady; we will get her," replies Jack. "We are trying to find her." He is now reversing his role and Ismene is wondering. She only thinks first about her mother, and not what the man is saying.

Soon the phone rings and Jack answers after listening. "We are here waiting for you. Please, come here and we will explain." "Thank you, we will be waiting for you," Jack replies. He puts the gun into his pocket and he offers Ismene and the driver a soft drink. "I do not wish to drink: I wish to be taken to my mother," screams Ismene frightened and trembling. "This is what we are trying to do, lady," responds Jack.

"I am sorry, I had to use the gun to be effective. I had no other choice but to bring you into safety. I had to be sure that those people didn't bother your mother. You cannot trust them, of course." He sounds very worried and protective.

Ismene is thinking confused. "I am sorry, but I don't understand you," whispers Ismene looking at Jack terrified. The driver finishes his drink with Jack and says, "I am sorry Jack; but I have to go now." Then, looking at Ismene he adds, "Be calm young lady. Everything soon will be fine." He thinks that Ismene is just like the women he has met in his trade. Then he leaves rapidly. She didn't know who the driver was and what role he was playing. She looks very confused and terrified. But she has to wait frightened.

Mr. Jack remains with Ismene who is trembling. She thinks of her mother and loses her strength. She has to think before she acts. She has to pay. That is the fate of different people. Some like Ismene pay anyway but at the end they may win. She does not believe what he says, nor she trusts him at all. She wants him to be finally punished and she is not thinking how to escape, but how to crucify the bastard. She is terrified but thinking. She does not know what to say or what to do.

Ismene is not to win or lose. But to win or die, no matter what happens. She is not a loser. She wants the law to punish the bastards. She wants the criminal to be punished no matter how much she may suffer. It is very strange. She looks at him with hate. She wants him punished no matter what happens to her. She looks at him and cries. The weakness of hers she wants to be always strength.

"Miss don't cry. The fellow will come and either should leave your mother free or he will die. I know that he has to leave her free, if he wants to live." "And if he does not leave her free, what will we do?" she asks terrified. "He will pay the consequences," he replies. She looks at him frightened and knows the consequences. She begins crying again with no hope. She wants to kill the man but she can only cry. She looks at him terrified and feels paralyzed.

The time passes, Ismene is crying and the other abductor does not show up. Jack lifts his phone and pretentiously mad calls the scum who had kidnapped Ismene's mother. "Would you please come tonight as you promised?" he asks. Here he stops and listens. "You know, I have her daughter waiting." None knows what the man answered and Jack replies, "If you do not come by nine tomorrow, you will not find me here." He listens for awhile and closes the phone mad.

After a few minutes he goes to the crying Ismene and says, "If you don't stop crying, and if you don't wait till he comes tomorrow morning to know what the bastard wants, we will not know what he has done with your mother, and what he wants. I will try to help you because I love you!" he states resolutely. This frightens Ismene.

She hears the word 'love' and gets confused. What 'love' has to do with her right of freedom. She no longer knows what to say and what to do with an imposter. She knows he is deceiving. She wants her mother and she will do anything to help her and be with her. Jack, all of a sudden, takes her by the hands and guides her to the bedroom closing the door behind him. Ismene gets terrified and tries to resist. But finds it impossible. He is too strong and she is too weak.

Her will and his strength are not comparable. He drags her, closing the room door behind, and throws her already exhausted on the bed. She tries to escape but it is impossible. Her will and his strength are not comparable. Like crazy he begins to rub her breasts, and placing his left hand between her legs continues and reaches her vagina. She could not resist his strength and his rubbing. She could no longer stand the pleasure and he rapes her. "I love you and I will make you happy," he said while he was raping her. She cried from pain and pleasure. But for long after, she was crying regretfully for what had happened. For what she had liked with pain.

"Don't cry Ismene," he said pleased. He was an accomplished rapist. Ismene had no experience or ways to resist him. She was a young virgin. Now she was young and raped. All she could do was to cry. He was an experienced rapist and pleased. Her pain was his pleasure. She was discovering that rape could give pleasure, pain and madness.

She was no longer a virgin and hated both her weakness and his strength. She realized what happened and she could not control her tears. She was no longer a virgin and he could tell. She was not the first one that he had raped whether she cared or not. You have to be trained to learn, before you kill someone. She was afraid till she surrendered. He was really experienced and Ismene could not resist and fight; he was a trained bastard and an experienced rapist. She was now a woman wishing revenge. But all she could do now was to cry.

You look at the eyes of the hurt one and you see the revenge pictured along with the humiliation and fury. But her eyes were still beautiful waiting for revenge. The weaker she was, the longer she was to wait for revenge. She was really frightened. She was a woman who has decided to die whether she killed him or not. But she wanted to kill him and go to her mother. A mixture of wishes were torturing her. Where was she hoping to go? She had no answer or will. She was also aware that she liked it. She hated her fate.

Ismene realized what had happened and was crying in pain, pleasure, rage and regret. But she could not ignore the pleasure and she was mad.

It was a forced, strange experience that made her hate the man. She was not going to forget but wanted to kill him. She was thinking of her father and she wanted the revenge. Soon however, her eyes closed with tears on her face. Next to her was resting the disrespectful pig, pleased with himself. He was a strange experience. He was not a pleasure.

Like Dionysus' daughter, she wanted to die. But her mother wanted her to live and pursue revenge for her sake. She was furious and angry. She had surrendered, weak but still hoping. She was a strange woman with pain and pleasure. She hated the rape that pleased her. She hated her weakness and herself. She didn't know what to do now.

Next morning on Sunday, Ismene awakes embarrassed and crying. She cannot look at Mr. Jack and face him. She is in pain and shameful. He has no character or shame. She looks at him and thinks of a pig. She cannot look at him in his eyes. She wants to kill him but she has no strength or means. She wants to die. But it is not so easy. She may die and he may not be killed. She wants to see her mother first, and to kill that insolent man after. She didn't care for herself anymore. She didn't want to go and leave that pig alive. But the ability to kill a man of Jack's qualities of corruption, was not an easy matter for a raped noble young lady. She wanted to be trained, learn how to kill and then try.

Jack could not trust a hurt woman. She was not his friend and she had no way to convince him. She had to be trained both in her behavior and abilities. She was now weak but obsessed and hopeful. She was hoping but her ways were icy and she could not be trusted. She had lost her parents, her brother, her virginity and female pride. Where was her brother to protect her? She was crying. Her brother was a dream no longer pleasing her. She didn't have him when she needed his support! She had no God to pray or people to protect her.

Her brother had left when she was ten years old and she didn't even know if he was alive. She was alone to live and seek her revenge. But she was always hoping with expectations. Her brother was a noble man. Now she does not know whether her brother one day will avenge her and cries. That pig didn't know why that charming and intelligent woman was crying. She was a virtuous and capable woman wanting and seeking revenge. She was not trained in corruption but she was virtuous, and virtue needs revenge in a corrupt environment in order to exist! It has to be respected by reason and force. But if reason existed, where was the force? A young lady unexpectedly being a slave to a scum! Raped by an experienced rapist! She really hated him and wanted revenge.

Soon, someone knocks at the door of Jack's apartment. It was not his, but a furnished rented apartment. He opens and two men enter. A young one, no more than thirty years old, and another one no more than fifty.

"I am sorry that your mother was unruly and she had to learn to behave. That is why we didn't come yesterday. But today she is fine knowing that she will be free," the old man says with authority. "But she had her lesson." He is really enchanted by Ismene who listens, understands and remains attentive and silent. She knew. They had done to her mother what that filthy man had done to her.

She wants to run out but she wants her mother free, and does not believe them any more till she sees her mother alive. She is the only human being to trust. But she has been raped and that makes Ismene tremble and feel embarrassed. She realizes her position and it makes her miserable. She looks at that man with hate and wants to strangle him. She wants to attack him and pull his eyes out. But how can you do that? Now her enemies are three and all are trained mongols. She is ready to lose her mind but she constrains herself. If there is a God, now he should act; but no God, no law, no police, and no humans: only victims in the hands of corrupt criminals! Where is the God of justice? He hides himself and leaves the noble victims to the rapists. 'There is no God,' she concludes and cries: There are the abusers of the innocent ones.

The young man remains silent. The old man looks sneaky, and Jack appears used to such people. The old man sits down and asks for a coffee. "Make them two, please," says the young man, and he sits down also. Jack carefully watches them and gives them coffee. Then he sits down very attentively. Ismene's hands are not trained but her mind is and remains aloof and terrified considering what may happen.

The old man tries to move and Jack's pistol sends two bullets in the old man's chest; and pointing the gun at the young man says, "Get up; get out; take your car and get the hell out of here. Go to hell." The young man terrified, leaves his coffee, gets up, and goes out watching Jack's pistol pointed at him. He gets out, and taking his car, he disappears. Ismene was ready to faint and surprised to see something happening at the speed she was thinking.

Jack calmly puts his gun into his pocket and says to Ismene, "I am sorry, but I had no choice. If you noticed, he tried to pull a gun but he was too slow." Ismene does not answer, but she is looking surprised and she is trembling. She knew that Jack had to kill him. He had no other choice. The old man, not much older than Jack, was slow.

"Please, lets go out before we are caught with the killed bastard. He came to kill me; take you, and then leave your mother without you: More likely killing her also!" Ismene is puzzled, trembling, and could not say anything. "Please let's go before they come and we are caught with the killed man. I will explain to you if you didn't see what happened." He was speaking calmly and with confidence. He takes the phone, makes a call, takes some necessary things, and gets out with Ismene. She was ordered to go ahead of him.

A car arrives in front of the apartment soon. Jack enters with Ismene and says, "The outlaw came to our place and before seeing or hearing anything, he was ready to kill me, kill your mother, take you, and make you one of his whores, anywhere he wanted." Ismene confused is listening and thinking. She could not believe anyone anymore! She wanted to know where her mother was; where they were going. The man that was killed was not a man of honor to bother Ismene. But, where was her mother, was her main concern. "Where is now my mother?" she asks worried. Jack does not answer, but he is worried. He realizes the crime and he is concerned and frightened. He has to run away.

Of course, he could kill Ismene as well and claim that the other man could have tried to kill him as well. But that was a problem; and Ismene was a charming young lady of his taste.

She decided to stay and not be killed. She became aware that Mr. Jack was a trained man knowing how to kill and protect himself. She decided to stay hoping that she was to survive next to him and see what happens after. So, she followed hoping to exist next to him. Her chance of survival was as good as his. He had the skills and she had the hope. She followed him quietly and obviously sad. But she was secretly hoping that they would capture and kill him.

"Ahmet," Jack talks to the driver. "Please, drive southwest to Ksamil and tell none whom you are transporting and where we are going. "Yes Sir I will," he replies seriously. Ksamil is a small southwestern Albanian place across from Agios Stefanos in northern Corfu. It is charming and resourceful. Jack chooses to go there. He could escape from there to the Greek island of Corfu. He seems to know the places. How and when he has known the places, he is the only one that knows to describe or explain.

Originally he is from Tirana and even though young he has known many places and he is the best in the use of guns. But he will either pay now for his abuse of the young lady or he will trash her somewhere on his way. He is trained and experienced in such cases.

Jack is trying to be nice to Ismene who is unique in charm and noble in extraction. But he is not apparently for her, and he knows that. At times, he feels embarrassed but only for special moments. Even though many women would like him, he was not for Ismene. He was attractive but not suitable. She was a young beauty and he was a tough and vulgar middle-age man not compatible to the refinement and fine beauty of Ismene. She was an aristocrat and he was a proletariat.

Finally, Ahmet finds a nice hotel as instructed by Jack with its balconies covered above and looking across to Corfu on the little harbor of Agios Stefanos, near the north. "Ahmet, please, get me a room for two in this hotel, facing the harbor," says Jack, relaxed and comfortable. He was a good actor that you could not forget to admire. Ahmet goes to arrange the hotel room, and Jack says to Ismene holding her hand, "I am happy to be with you. Please, don't worry, soon we will be fine." She listens but says nothing wondering. Soon Ahmet comes with the reserved hotel, room number and gives it to Jack.

They are good friends and serve each other at times of need. They are honest and trusting each other, but Ahmet cannot be innocent. He knows that he is dealing with a bastard and need is the criterion of trust. They must have been working together before.

Then Jack says, "Ahmet, I will stay here for a few days with Ismene, before I return to Agius Saranta. Please, leave my car and take a bus. I will be here. Give me your cost, up to now, including everything. If I need you, I will call you again." Ahmet gets serious and knows that Jack is always honest with him and he is always honestly paid. Ahmet gives the keys of the car, gives the cost, receives the reasonable amount and leaves content. Ismene realizes that Ahmet was driving Jack's car and understands that he is guilty as well. He had left his car at the place he picked them up. Now he was going to go with a bus, but he is well paid: Two people are always honest to each other no matter what they were; if they were at peace. But they could not be honest to the laws of a country. They were to be honest to each other as long as they could; and betray each other in the future, if they had to.

Jack realizes Ismene's position and orders from the room a nice dinner for two including a glass of nice wine for each one of them. Roast lamb with rice was a special that night. He and Ismene were hungry, even though he was exhausted and Ismene disgusted. He knew that Ismene didn't want him. She was not a whore! But he was treating her as one. He wanted her to be one and he didn't care. He was playing his game hoping to see the results. The man will fight and the woman will wait for the time. He may kill her and she is intelligent to know.

A principled woman is more difficult than a principled man to handle. She has lost her honor and nothing is left with her but the wish of revenge. Jack is a trained man and knows better. But Ismene's charms disable every man that goes next to her, except those already in love but still free like Dr. Zhivago: In love with the one, but captivated by the other; loving the one, but dreaming of another.

That night was not beautiful anyway. He wanted her and she was hating her fate. He was experienced and knew, he will never tame that wild female: Beautiful and durable if not a capable beast. She was not trained for his life, and he was ready to face her. But what man has ever captured a wild female beast? He can kill but not tame. Anyway, after dinner, he brought Ismene in from the balcony. He was polite and serving to make Ismene feel pleased. They had shower, and after that he forced his way as before. She liked that at the start, but she hated that at the end. He was aware of the situation.

Sex was not her love even though she could not say no at the start. Each time, she wanted to kill the man after, not caring for herself. She was the enslaved whore of a man and she hated her fate. He was abusing her honor and she could not excuse him. What she was going to do no one knew, but she was thinking of revenge and she was crying waiting for the chance. She was a woman and that was her fate.

The Police in Agius Saranta were furious, and the gang of the murdered Yousuf was ordered to find and kill Jack and his girlfriend Ismene without fear. One of his co-workers sent Jack a message telling him to be careful, wherever he was with his girlfriend, because the order was to kill him and her with no fear. Jack knew those people but they didn't know him. But so what? He might have been able to kill one or two, but not always three and four. Besides, as the number of the people you kill grows, your days of life are reduced. For this reason, Jack had to be careful if he wanted to survive.

The third day at night, Jack decided to leave Albania as the people of Yousuf were ordered to kill him no matter with whom and where he was. He was not a skilled man in the use of weapons, but a clever one in handling people. "The people of Yousuf have orders to kill us for they think we killed their leader together," says Jack to Ismene. "I have to let you know for I don't want you to think that I betrayed you. They killed your mother and now they want to kill us," he says seriously. Ismene looks at him not believing what she hears and tears run down her cheeks. He might have been saying the truth. You can never tell when you listen to one who does not accuse the present ones.

"Why didn't you tell them that I am innocent?" she asks. "I didn't have the chance to tell them anything. You remember, the gangsters came to kill me and take you," he replies. "I had no chance to tell them anything but only to let him kill me, so he can have you!" he says and he was sincere in this case. But he didn't know whether her mother was actually killed, though. Ismene was not going to believe anyone, anymore, besides her eyes.

The man that kidnapped and raped her mother was killed earlier; and she was hoping. She had to kill now the bastard and go to find her mother. But so far, only the bastard was raping her, using his force. She was desperately weak but hoping. Apparently, Ismene had no chance with a man of Jack's qualities. But she was hoping, like anybody else, not some times but always.

From the small town of Ksamil, Jack and Ismene bought some clothes and decided to go to Greece. He was following her with the knowledge that he was going to kill her if she tried to escape. That was his perfect excuse: She had killed Yousuf! He was telling her that he loved her but she didn't have confidence in anything he said. In the morning of the fourth day, they left.

According to Jack, they could not go to Greece through the usual roads because the people of Yousuf were alerted and were watching the check points and border, and they wanted the reward. But Ksamil was not watched. So, Jack convinced Ismene to go from Ksamil of Albania to Agios Stefanos of Corfou. Then, from Agios Stefanos to drive to the City of Corfu. From there to go to Igoumenitsa and then drive south to Preveza. Then, his advice was to go from there to Patra through Messolongi. Ismene listened and agreed hoping eventually for a solution.

Ismene listened to him but she was unhappy and depressed. He could see that, but he could not change it. None could understand what she wanted. Fortunately, Ismene was depressed without even knowing anything about her mother. He had raped and he was still raping her. Therefore, she didn't believe Jack anymore. She was, though, afraid and deeply unhappy but not believing that her mother was dead. The man who had her mother was suddenly dead! That was encouraging.

Her mother was an innocent noble woman so that anyone who knew who her husband, her son and her daughter were, he would respect her. She was hoping to meet her mother some time even though she was depressed. She was Albanian and anyone who had met her husband was amazed. Ismene didn't know the whereabouts of her mother for sure. But she loved her freedom and wanted to honor her father and her mother.

The bastard who was using and raping her, had to die. If not he, at least she. It was her oath! She had to defend the name and the honor of her parents. She didn't know where her brother was and she was crying, but always hoping. She started thinking about the revenge. Easy to think, but hard to accomplish without punishment.

When you are raping or screwing a woman unwillingly, you are not humiliating her but yourself, was the thinking of Ismene. She knew because she never slept with the bastard willingly. She could not stop the pleasure but she had no choice. She was human.

Ismene had lost her brother that she loved, the father that she admired and respected, and her kind and virtuous mother that she was admiring for her kindness and generosity. And now, she was innocently crucified for a crime that she didn't commit. She was now left in the hands of a man she could not trust, believe, respect or tolerate. She was innocently accused for a crime that she didn't commit. "I will follow you anywhere you go; why not?" she answered him when questioned.

"Yes sweet, lets go south and find our place," he said. He didn't understand her answer. An intelligent, honest and beautiful girl can be screwed and be killed, but not corrupted. He was afraid because she was innocent and with time innocent people die or find their strength to win.

"Well, let me go to a bank, before we leave, to get any money that there may be to survive till I get a job," she said to him. "Of course," he answered happy finding out that she had some money. She could get it, but he could not. It was not for him to convince or confiscate with his myriad of techniques, unless he robbed the bank or killed Ismene. There was no benefit in such an act. He had to wait and learn before he acted.

They went to the Bank and she got some money that her mother was depositing in her name. She also found that her father had the account in American dollars from which she could not withdraw, till she was 21 years old. She had not said anything about it, to anyone, even though she and her mother already knew.

She had the picture of her parents in a silver pendant that she was kissing them when she was alone. Fortunately, it was silver and none was willing to steal it. Often, when she was alone and thinking about them, she would open her silver pendant and kiss them with passion and tears. She had no other way to hope and exist besides her brother. But he was so far a lost opportunity. She was, however, strangely hopeful. "Your brother will be living forever," her father was used to say and smile. She had never forgotten to remember her father's beliefs. He was her real educator in love with her.

The picture of her brother was in her mind. She was thinking about him and she was having a conversation of her own choice. But at the end, each time she was crying because she looked at his picture and he had never said anything. She only remembered him looking at her. She was talking to him but he never spoke. He was looking at her smiling. She was growing but he was the same. She was wondering if he existed.

He was now in Germany married to a beautiful German lady that she had never seen. It was painful, but he was happy knowing that soon he would be able to come and see them in Agius Saranta. The communist system was failing and changing. It was saving him, and he wanted to see his mother with whom he was lately corresponding. But didn't he know she was dead? That was a real question; a real hope with negative expectations. Ismene could not say anything.

Jack and Ismene went to Corfu and from there to Igoumenitsa. Then they drove south to Preveza. No one had seen or noticed them. Jack's car windows had dark glass and none had seen Ismene. It was hard to see that beautiful woman and forget her. After their stop in Preveza, they continued on to Patra through Messolongi. Patra was attractive for Jack but confusing for Ismene. She didn't like the setting of Patra and the sea was good only for the ships and the boats. She had read about Kalamata. She loved to be by the sea and be able to swim and enjoy its theaters. She was forgetting and dreaming. When she was swimming she was inspiring. She was not a woman but a fish: A professional swimmer.

Ismene did not like Patra. It was too busy, too provocative, and unruly in the center. But Jack was enchanted. He tried to convince her but Ismene was not charmed by the refugees from many lands trying to reach Patra; and from there to settle somewhere in Europe. She was not feeling comfortable and safe. She was feeling Hellenic and honest. She was hoping to prevail and from there in peace find justice. Of course, she didn't know but she was hoping to learn without being killed.

In an environment of peace, Ismene was hoping to find justice and more noble people. All of a sudden she felt more free in her father's land. She remembered how her father liked that land. She could not forget now that she was there. She was feeling more comfortable. Going south she was going to the sea that was warm and friendly.

"Too many people from many different places, ready to see and ready to run," Ismene said irritated in Patra and Jack was surprised. "Too many immigrants, too many whores; ready to sell themselves," she said upset that Jack was amazed, irritated and pleased. For him it was a place for action. For her a place where she could get lost. "Where should we go and not die?" he asked. She looks at him and replies: "We should go to

Kalamata. It is quiet and pleasant. A harbor to swim. A place to die." He was surprised, he objected but finally he agreed. His objective was to go to Athens where he can act and not be caught. But he knew how to go there from Kalamata as well!

"Too many immigrants, too many dealers! Lets get away from here," says Ismene, the sister of Sergio, the daughter of Denysa and Alexander. As expected, Jack listens and wonders. "Where we are, from Patra to Athens, or from Kalamata to Athens, it does not make any difference," he states. But for a peaceful and capable Ismene it does. She is an intelligent woman who can make it work no matter where she is! But not for him. He wanted to abuse and rape. "If it does not make any difference, lets go to Kalamata," she says sternly. He loved the gambling places of Athens. But Ismene's mind wanted to work, wanted the sea to swim and play with the waves.

They take the road from Patra to Kalamata and Ismene is peacefully resting and reflecting. While she is trying to escape the time of misfortune, she believes that she will be welcomed by the time of peace. She expects to escape the capture of the scum and enjoy the freedom of the innocent. She heard Jack speak of her mother's death but she is hopeful. She expects to escape the scum and prove her innocence. She wants freedom or death. But not enslavement for long.

Besides, her mother is an Albanian respected by all those who have met her on their way. She thinks of her father and says: "I am what my father was." She is recovering and no one has yet met Ismene: "If I do not punish Jack and get my freedom, I should not live," she whispers. It was her terrifying thinking.

Ismene was now going to be in Kalamata. Alexander's smile was not going to be in error. She was waiting for the opportunity to revolt. But how a woman is to win? She knew nothing, but she was an intelligent young lady ready to learn and fight. She was daydreaming.

Those who learn are better than those who revolt. Those who are trained, are better than those who dream. Ismene was the woman that she was to learn. The bastard who raped her when she was young is not a bad lover, but she is one to have him pay and not placate her with his force. Ismene wanted a noble knowledgeable man and not a bull.

She is really confused but still hoping for her revenge and freedom. She didn't mind his sex but she was expecting a noble man as well. Sex was not for Ismene the Christian concept but a pleasure in life. She had to enjoy it not by a vulgar criminal but by a noble man. If she was going to persist, she was going to find him.

Ismene is hopeful and revived. She recalls the stories narrated by her father about the slaves rising and adores the freedom of the Greeks. She had learned that the Greeks had been civilized before the other people and they could not fight united. When they did, none could enslave them. They were not suspecting that one day the barbarians will think to enslave the free Hellenic people. When they woke up were already Greeks and not Hellenic people. The slavery of Christianity could not fight the barbarity of the Turks. The Hellenic people had died under the peace of the Christians who were using the Cross when the others were employing the Sword and producing the gunpowder.

They had to use the French, the English and the German Kings to rise in that period. And when they foolishly rose, they were abandoned by the Kings and defeated by the Turks. A government by Bishops was not a Government by the Kings. The democracy had to ripe from a tradition of Kings and not from a Christian slavery. Christianity was the result of the Kings and not of uneducated Christians. Any Christian power was to be temporary or a discipline to Kingdoms. And the King at the end to be just a figure and not the governor...

———————————

2 ISMENE IN THE CHARMING HARBOR

'Kalamata' is a southern city in the gulf of Messinia in Greece.

Jack is driving and with Ismene hopeful are approaching Kalamata after Asprochoma. If you go straight and you turn right at the end, and go along the river south, you will eventually hit the sea. If you turn left as soon as you hit the sea, you are going along the residential part of the harbor. There you can find everything, whispers Ismene excited and forgotten. Jack thinks of everything but he knows that everything will be only in Athens. He did as she said and not long after they were driving along the sea. For Ismene it is fantastic. For Jack it is wondering. The blue sea enchants Ismene; and impresses Jack. Kalamata looks as a peaceful place, in reality a dream. It is a harbor with ladies that have 'Good Eyes': Kala Matia = Kalamata. One can assume and if he is wrong, people who think they know better will protest and explain.

They drove along the beach a few times between Faron and Messolongi, west and east, and they were enchanted. It was charming for Ismene, but challenging for Jack. She was thinking of playing in the water; and he killing his undisciplined servants on the sand at night. Ismene thought never to go with Jack at the beach unless she wanted to be killed. She knew already that Jack hated the sea. But the beach, it was a place to discipline his unruly disciples. Ismene frowns as she thought what she was to suffer. She smiled thinking and hoping to have Jack killed by any of her people. She knew already the value of money; and she was thinking how to use it. She was not Ismene any more!

They were in Kalamata but Ismene was in wonderland; and in the evening they walked along the harbor after they took a room in Haiko Hotel as a married couple. There was no doubt that Ismene was a puzzle for the hotel and the people on the promenade as soon as they saw her. A young beauty with a middle age bull. The walking people were Greeks and assumed that she was a beauty that found a rich man, or a whore captured by a bull. She was too young, too beautiful and too charming.

They had dinner, they walked along the promenade of the beach and sat in a luxury coffee house at the corner near the intersection of Akrita and Navarinou streets, at the end of Akrita. Their room was on the Iron and Rosa crossing roads, and the people in the coffee house were young and well dressed. It was clear to anyone who paid attention to Jack and Ismene that the relation of the couple was not friendly, or what a man should wish. She more likely was not his daughter. She was a charm hard to find and difficult to forget. That is life, quite often disappointing for the young and the old. The young don't have the money and the old the strength or the appetite.

Who knows? In any case, the couple didn't look happy or cordial. The relation of the couple was not a friendly one. No man with pride would have liked to be next to a woman who loved the environment but not him; neither a woman with the beauty of the lady would have liked to be next to a man that she didn't like or want. The drama was obvious, if anyone decided to see the case and observe the couple. The place was beautiful but the couple incompatible. They could not communicate or laugh. They could not enjoy the serenity of the night. Definitely, there was a problem that anyone could see and guess if he paid attention: A story of life often repeated.

After the unpleasant communication between the couple, but pleasant for others, they left and went to the hotel. They were both tired and after a light shower in their room preceded by Ismene, they fell asleep. It was probably the first time, since he abducted the lady that they didn't have sex and it was a relief for her. She wanted to get up and go, but it was not easy. He was never in deep sleep and he had been continuously with her since she was abducted. She could not live in peace and she wanted to kill the man before she went to her place. She knew and she was right. If a man decides to kill you, he can, unless you disappear. But she couldn't. He was in strange love with her.

She wanted her mother and her home in Agius Saranta. Where was she? She would ask herself and cry. It was her ability to cry that had saved the beautiful young lady. She was Ismene, the young lady waiting for her chance to kill and not be caught. To go back to her home and find the mother that she loved. And her brother? She was crying each time he was coming in her mind.

She knew that her brother would have killed the bastard, if he was home. But if he was home, that would not have happened! Her brother apparently was a noble man. But to be noble, it does not mean to be abused by any scum. It was her fate to suffer losing slowly with time what she had, what could have protected her: The pride and the courage. She was an intelligent, innocent and timid young lady.

It was the first night that he had not raped Ismene and she was thankful for this relief. In the morning they got up still tired and with no fear that someone was going to kill them. They were far away from Tirana, Istanbul, Smyrna and Athens. She could not escape and not be killed. No one knew where they were. They went for breakfast and Ismene spoke to him. "This morning I will look for work and in the afternoon for an apartment. Do what you like. I will take care of you but I need some freedom." She meant what she had said.

"In the afternoon, I will look for an apartment around here by the beach. I will not run away from you. You do not have to worry about that. But you are free to go wherever and whenever you want," she added. She looked into his eyes to see his reaction. He tried to understand her but he was confused. She was calm and sincere. It was not what he wanted, and she was intelligent enough to know. He wanted her to be his wife and a whore! But he was hoping in vain. A woman of Ismene's upbringing was never going to be a whore. You are what you are supposed to be, or you die.

"It is too early to do that: It is not?" he claimed. "I don't understand why it is too early," she asked wondering and knowing. "You may start whenever and wherever you want. My place will be open for you to come whenever you want and do what you wish." It was her decision to kill him and die with him if necessary. She was not going to live like a whore. He listens. Then, Ismene bends and whispers, "Even to rape me without I refusing." She wanted to make it clear that he was free to do as he pleased. He didn't answer but remained thinking. And she didn't say that she was willing to kill him if he didn't have the courage to leave. None could read the thinking of a hopeful Ismene. She had decided to live without him or die!

He realized that Ismene was an independent young lady, very capable and beautiful. He realized that they were not going to pay her enough, as much as he needed and wanted. So he didn't say anything but chose to wait and see. He was, however, dreaming. If Ismene wanted to go with him to Athens and play in the casinos next to successful gamblers whom he could have pointed them out, she and he could be rich. She would be screwed and he would be screwing, gathering and entertained. So, he decided to wait and see.

The first day Ismene returned to the hotel with a knowledge of the Flower Industry that she acquired in the morning. She also came with an idea regarding apartments by the beach. She was content with the results. At night Jack asked her what she did with her day. She looks at him and replies: Purchasing and upgrading flower shops was a good opportunity, but required money that she didn't have. However, if she had the one, she could have the others. It would be easy. She didn't ask what he did and he didn't say. She was not interested to know, anyway. Her wish was to let her free to choose. He let her know that he loved her and without her he could not be free and enjoy life. He was willing to die for her. "Doing what?" she asked smiling. She realized the irony. He was asking her to be screwed for money and he was talking about love!

This way, he was putting a harness around her head that he could pull anytime he had to. She was not afraid of death, she wanted to go to death only if he who was dragging her there was to follow, at least. "Let no man live, if he has no respect for life," her father used to say, and he was generous with the poor who wanted to work and live honorably. She was going to follow her father's wish. She was trained by her father. She wanted to be screwed but wished to remain honorable. But he didn't know with whom she wished to be screwed.

She was hoping to let him know: She was a rebel. But he was violent and at moments of depression and fear, he was terrified becoming aggressive and with no respect for the life of others. One had to be better to fight with him and it was not easy. So, she had to wait for the opportunity and not the hope. She had seen him already and she was not afraid any longer. But she wanted to be sure that he was going to be eliminated. She had to think how to cope with a man who was capable, afraid, a scamp and a scum.

Fear and capability were making him dangerous. She was convinced that she had to kill him in order to be free. But she had to learn how to kill. She was alone and a stranger in a strange place even though she was Hellenic. She didn't know any people. She cried as she thought of her father. "You read the Iliad and the Odyssey to understand," her father would say, and she would burst into tears.

She tried and in a week's time she found a job in a florist shop on one of the corners of Faron street. The money was little but her knowledge and experience were extensive and expanded. Her contribution was impressive. But one morning the old owner laid her off. She didn't understand the reason and she left wondering.

The excuse the gentleman gave was ridiculous considering his benefit and cost relations. But she left smiling without uttering a single word. She was certain that Mr. Jack had played one of his games. The man was surprised that the lady left with a smile. The man saw the lady leave with no complaint. She only said, "Thank you Sir; for the chance!"

He was staring her leaving with no regret and he was surprised even though frightened. He really liked Ismene, but he didn't say a word. He had never seen a lady not to complain or accuse in the process. He was probably hating his fortune and his old age. But he needed peace to exist.

Jack wants first to know Kalamata and damp Ismene somewhere if he does not find a solution. Of course, a solution of his own. It was easy for him; he had no other choice. But he needed some money before he could dump her. As it was then, she was not making enough and he was not doing well in his casino and roulette games. He decided to be more demanding and more careful in his games. But before anything else he decided to be making more, from Ismene, by demanding more. So far, he was not successful but he was thinking and hopeful. Kalamata was not the place for him, but for the mind of Ismene and her noble ways it was perfect. Anyway, he decided to start with Ismene and drag her to Athens.

Ismene was not an easy trap for him but one hard working to accumulate power and attack the gentleman if he finally decided to force her. She was not going to do anything till she knew that she had no choice, or that he wanted to ridicule her more than what he was already doing. He would have been happy if he could have her in Athens as a whore. But he was a fool for he was gambling and would never have the money, no matter where he was.

Ismene knew even though she didn't like him. He was not the noble man for Ismene. She had decided to get rid of him. It was he or she. Ismene was crying since she lost her mother and her honor. She was hoping that one day her brother Sergio was to punish the filthy raping man. But when that was to happen?

Jack decided to know the area of Kalamata along the beach and along the center where women were flirting and fishing. He was trusting that he was good. So, he started with the area along the beech from Akrita till Messolongi. He was middle age and women were flirting. But he was not the man to catch a lady by virtue. Many women like to be captured by force. This is fine if the man is fine as well. So he decided to know the area of the shore. It was enough deserted for him, in winter time especially: He could play his games.

He takes a long walk to the left from the end of Faron to Messolongi where the Navarinou ends. There is also the hotel Filoxenia. On his return, he stops to take a cup of coffee with white biscuits at a restaurant by the name of 'Avra'. It is only about 100 meters from the intersection of Navarinou and the end of Cretes. He is very thoughtful and concerned about things of his own. The man is corrupted and wants the women next to him to be obedient whores and the men hungry beggars serving and pleasing him. But what he wants, it is not easy to have with Ismene.

As he is taking his coffee with the biscuits, he is sitting outside at the restaurant 'Avra' and he is looking around to enjoy the view. Further ahead, to his right and left, are the capes of Akritas and Tenaron enclosing the Messinian gulf. Jack is enjoying the view and his dark features are almost handsome. He must be around forty-five years old with very brown eyes and very dark hair. He is, relatively speaking handsome, but rarely laughing. While he is drinking his coffee and taking the biscuits, he lights also a cigarette and begins smoking. To his left, very close, is the mountain Taygetos and to his right, the harbor.

The sea with the harbor is pleasing and enchanting. But the sports of his pleasure, horses, gambling and women are not promising. Only if women like Ismene were to listen, he would be happy. He frowns as he thinks; but he enjoys raping Ismene every night as he takes her into his bedroom. She goes after into her own bedroom and cries.

It is nearly spring and Jack seems pleased. Groups of seagulls visit the beach across from him, feed themselves the little there is and fly away. It is approaching two o'clock in the afternoon and he makes a call using his phone. Then he calls the waiter, and gives him an order. In fifteen minutes, he gets his fried fish with a small salad, grilled bread and half a pound of cold yellow wine. In less than ten minutes or so, a young lady arrives and joins him. She sits on the opposite side of the table with her side facing the beach, says something none could hear, and soon both begin their light meal. He was serious and the lady looked sad. But as soon as she lets one see her beauty, he is sure to say that she was too much for anyone. She was too beautiful!

She was Ismene. Her eyes were large dark green-blue and her lips inviting. Her teeth were charming white and no one could miss them behind her red lips, so inviting and tempting. Near the end she said kind of loudly, "If that is what you want, you will have it tonight." He looks at her and says imperatively, "Yes, I will have it tonight." He pulls his flat gun and puts it on the table. She looks at the gun and says, "Yes, if I find the man. If I don't, what will you do? Will you kill me?" He does not know what to say and looks lost. "If I do not find the man, what will you do? Kill me?" she asks again wondering.

"It is not what I want but what we need," he says mildly. He takes the flat gun, puts it in his pocket again and repeats, "It is not what I want but what we need; and what I need is what we want and what we need. We are not separate but one thing, and the one lives for the other." She understands what he wants. But she was not born to be anyone's whore. No matter who he is. "Why? If I work and you work, it isn't enough to make a living?" she asks wondering.

"But your work is valuable, and if combined with mine is most profitable," he says. She looks at him and replies, "You think I do not understand you?" "No, I know you are very intelligent; that is why I asked you to come with me to Athens and leave like a queen." She looks at him, understands what he wants, and replies, "No, you have the gun and you can kill me. I am not coming to Athens. But, I can serve you here if you let me free. You can go to Athens whenever you want and as many times as you please; and you can stay there if you wish." Jack didn't say anything.

"Ismene, how we will live in this boring place?" he asks wondering. She looks at him and replies, "Each one has his or her own choices. I can't tell you how you will, but I can tell you how I will." She got up and left. Later he walked to his car and left also.

So, the night of that Friday at 12 o'clock when she returned home, she was free to cry. An hour later Jack went home and found the lady crying. She tried to hide her tears; and to distract him. Then she said, "I brought you enough money for the first night; the next one will be much better." She smiled and he asked, "Did you like it?"

She looked at him surprised. She didn't believe what she heard and decided to look happy, as happy as she could; and kill him, as she was planning to do. She was sure she was supposed to enjoy it. "Yes, honey; I did not like it, but I can take it. Is it clear to you or it isn't?" She knew where her positive answer could lead.

Here she was determined to get rid of him and she didn't tell him anything more than what he liked to hear. He wanted her to be screwed, to give him the money, to pay his gambling debts, and say she liked it. She knew that; after that, he could do anything he liked. He could even kill her with the excuse that she was his wife and was screwed by others, or that someone of her lovers killed her!

Ismene was a beautiful and charming young lady. She was intelligent and could entice and trap any man she wanted, anywhere. "My name is Alice; and if you use another, you will not hear me," she said to him and went to sleep. He didn't care what she said. He cared that she brought him what he wanted: Money to pay his debts!

But she knew it was not enough and tried to cover it with empty promises. She was using the money she was making from the flower shop, and soon she was going to get the money that her father had left for her by the beginning of the next year.

Alice didn't have the child to resist, but the hope to kill the bastard before she died. So, she kept practicing shooting after she bought a gun and hoped. Her beauty was changing with her becoming the beauty of what she was. She did not know that and people loved her no matter what she was. Only God could resist that woman and restrain himself from loving and raping her. Men could see that, women admired that, and Ismene remained humble and kind. No Zeus could ever resist that woman if challenged. No God could resist if he met her.

Farther down on the same avenue of Faron from the shop that Alice was fired, there was another flower shop. This time she goes to the shop and finds that the owner was a nice but business unimaginative and poor young lady. She looks at the shop and sees that it is adjacent to another place at the corner empty and available for rent. Alice sees that if it was rented and the flower shop was expanded, a combination of the spaces was sufficient for an impressive flower shop with many flower and other decoration accessories. The site across the street was a small park with a house. Ismene is impressed!

The existing flower shop with the space on the corner would make an excellent shop. These two spaces would provide the best flower shop on Faron street in Kalamata. She left and at home at night she didn't say anything. But the pig asked when he went home and Alice didn't say she was laid off. She was hoping something better. It was on the table. She was an imaginative and persisting young lady. She was enchanting and charming. She was trained and nice but poor, noble and inspiring. She was beautiful but not conceited.

In the morning, Alice goes to the young lady and speaks to her. Alice said that the flower shop was nice but it was too small with limited supplies and humble service. The lady agreed that her shop was in a nice place but needed some renovation. She explained that she knew the problem but she had to either die or become a whore to expand it. Ismene laughed and replied, "I understand; but look for someone who neither wants you to die, nor to become a whore; nor to use you! I am sure this is not your fate." "How should I do what you advise me to do when I have no means?" she asks earnestly thinking and charmed with Alice's beauty. Alice, looks around discretely, and politely remarks, "If I was a man, I would have asked the same: First you; and next your business." The lady smiled at the real humor of Alice.

Alice looks around and continues, "First, you have to find the person; second, to become sure that he or she needs to cooperate; and third, to deal with the one that knows and needs to work." Alice is smiling and captivating. "Of course, he or she would have to know something about the business," she adds. "Yes, to find one that needs to work and not just screw," says the lady smiling and Ismene laughing. "Yes, wishful thinking. Please, find me the one that wants to work and not screw," says the young lady looking at her with admiration.

She smiles and replies, "In that case, please let me talk to you tomorrow while you are thinking."Alice leaves but she is too charming to be ignored or forgotten. She was too attractive not to be followed as she was leaving. "I will see you tomorrow," she said while she was leaving. "It will be my pleasure to see you again; if possible," said Louise. Alice left smiling.

Louise was enchanted by Alice's simplicity and honesty. She had not seen before a woman of charm and convincing as Alice. She was certain that she was not from Greece but she didn't say anything to that graceful young woman. She was a charm and attractive. Whether you were a man or a woman, she knew how to charm you.

The next day in the afternoon, Alice goes to the young lady's flower shop. The lady was happy to see her coming again. She moves to her and greets her with a natural smile. "I have not seen young beautiful ladies visiting my shop twice, for long time," she says smiling. "Thank you, but I don't think that I still look young and that I am beautiful," replies Alice entering Louise's shop. "Yes, it is a matter of opinion," says Louise. "But in your case there is no man or woman to think otherwise." "Yes, there is no man, but there may be a woman," replies Alice smiling;"Plus those who have what they want." Louise smiles, agrees but she does not reply.

After some spiritual conversation, the Louise smiles and brings two teas and two sweets of her own to treat Alice and herself. "Louise, I found out that the space to our left is empty. I talked yesterday morning to the gentleman and he said that it is available for rent." "Yes I know. He asks 400 euros per month which is a lot," says Louise. She looks at her and smiles. "Yes its a lot; but it is negotiable, and if it is unified with yours, it makes a large shop where we can market many goods and please many people," replies Alice.

"I believe that being on a nice area, on a large street, and offering many things, it will satisfy many tastes and people. But it has to be presentable, spotless and unique," adds Alice talking with animation. "It should have pretty flowers, nice little and large; suitable statues, and small paintings, original and good copies of small and large sizes. Nothing should be something cheap and not worth admiring," she adds further. Both laughed content, but Alice was wondering. Louise was intrigued with Alice's fertile imagination. She was really impressed and fascinated. She changed to an expecting woman.

Alice had the gift of articulate speech that magnetizes. "The employees should be trained and know how to behave to their customers, supervisors and suppliers. It is important never to let a customer leave dissatisfied," says Alice. "Yes, you will be selling and I will be collecting," says Louise and looks at Ismene wondering. Then Alice replies smiling, "Yes, we all will be selling, but you will be the only one selling and collecting," says Ismene and touches the hand of Louise. "In that case; I agree," replies Louise smiling. "And who will be training me?" she asks. "Anyone, any time you have a question," replies Alice laughing. Louise is pleased with Alice, touches her hand and asks, "You know what do I have now Alice; don't you?"

"I know what you have now, but not what you will have tomorrow," replies Alice smiling. "Thank you Alice, as long as you know that what I have now is what I am capable and willing to give." Alice smiles and adds, "Plus, good character and plenty of labor." Louise smiled but said nothing more. She was looking at Alice with admiration. Alice was an inspiring and trusted young lady: Something that Louise had not experienced before. She was indeed, surprised with the young lady, who was intelligent and sharp.

Alice looks at Louise and says seriously but always in a charming way: "Louise, this is going to be fifty per cent to each one of us. You keep working and I will keep preparing the addition. Anything you have is ours and anything that comes and goes with the new part is ours also. If it ever goes to fifty per cent from the time it is finished, it is yours and I will go; but anything above is ours," says Alice smiling. Louise thinks and replies, "No, any time, it is fifty per cent for each one of us, from the time we start to the time we finish." Alice looks at Louise and replies, "As you please, but we can discuss it, if it ever gets there." Louise touches the hand of Ismene and says, "Please, do as you like; I trust you." Louise and Alice had passed the test.

Alice touched the hand of Louise but said nothing. She left and Louise kept thinking and working. It was Alice's choice to act and Louise to cooperate. She was filled with hope and she was a noble woman to be trusted. Alice could tell because she was very intelligent; and in spite of her age, very experienced. "Good brains, have to think and be trained quickly!" says Alice pleased and smiling.

Alice rented the place, found the construction workers, modified the space that she rented, and out of the 200 square meters was an office of 25 square meters facing opposite from the window the yard of the old large house. Next to the office there was the payment counter of the shop. The space of the new room was to be filled with precious decorative articles of small and large statues and paintings. The atmosphere was inviting and pleasant with comfortable seating. The atmosphere was new and attractively well designed. The old room was filled with garden articles and posts, along with small and large bouquets of fragrant, colorful and ordinary flowers. The rooms were decorated and comfortable with space to rest and read for waiting customers. Louise was fascinated when the place was finished with the care and direction of Alice!

There was also a basement for storage and flower preparation. Louise was enchanted with the space for working. She was really excited and pleased. She did not know how to thank Alice. She decided though to be a new lady following and devoted. Let alone that she was an intelligent lady depressed before. Alice with the working mind directed the relations of the personnel.

A new atmosphere was developed that customers loved and visited again with friends. The people were trained to please and not to bore. Alice was really admired. No man or woman visited the place without at the end remaining enchanted. The men were attracted and the ladies were charmed with Alice.

In a month's period the 'Garden of Art' was a place for the people who went to find what they wanted for weddings, name-days, holy-days, birthdays and gifts. For weddings, people were offered the unusual and the inexpensive; the decorative and the charming. Alice was bringing from Greece, Italy, France, and Spain what was needed for celebrations. Louise was really grateful to Alice who was an inspiring friend.

There was nothing that Alice had not thought to provide when it was needed. She was admired, respected and asked. She was always friendly and not even once bored or annoyed. She was one so much needed for a place like that. Alice spoke besides Greek; English, Spanish, French and Italian. Louise was surprised and faithful to Alice. She was a young and intelligent manager with unusual artistic abilities.

Two girls were hired by Louise and trained by Alice. Louise needed a third girl and her sister, a graduate from Panteion University wanted to work. Louise had to talk to Alice following the rules. Alice smiled and said, "If you think the girl will be pleased, bring her. I will try to help her." "Thank you, said Louise who was happy to have her sister in her place to work. The remuneration was not small.

Alice and Louise wanted to pay their sales people what they were making on the basis of experience in the business. The girls were surprised and happy as their salary was increasing rapidly. None was to leave from that place displeased, whether worker or customer. It was the principles that operated and pleased everyone. Louise was impressed with Alice's marketing skills. "She is a business woman and an artist to admire," she used to whisper. She was extremely satisfied with Alice's ways. She was the first woman that had inspired her.

The money was not a lot from the 'Garden of Art' but enough for Alice to pay for the apartment that she bought, to have her car and clothing, to buy the necessities and to give Jack each time he asked for his gambling money. But the fortune was not his friend anymore. He was losing and borrowing. He was having enough for his basic needs, but not for his gambling habits. She was not able to feed a wasteful parasite constantly demanding and abusing. He was insolent and wasteful.

Alice was not making enough to satisfy his loses and save. She was growing desperate. Fortunately, Louise was nice and understanding to help. But, there was so much! Alice could not do it. But she was her young partner and her faithful friend. "What Alice wants she has my consent," used to say Louise and was always helpful.

Alice was five years younger but many times wiser. "She is a noble woman," Louise used to say to anyone who asked her opinion about Ismene. "Let me know, if you know a more noble lady," she used to answer when asked about Alice. People were impressed and were always asking for Alice's advice and contribution. Alice was always prone to respond with pleasure. She was never conceited or tired.

Alice was always pleased to discuss anything, and supply people what they were asking. Anyone who ever met her, remembered to ask for her again, for many things. People were content with Alice and grateful. She was one to be asked and please. "God blessed her," used to say Louise and the customers who ever met her.

One day, Jack goes to Louise and asks her to lay Alice off if she does not want to see her business become dust! Louise looks at him surprised and waits to hear more. He does not say more but waits for her response. "Thank you for telling me. Try and I will make your head dust: no matter who you are. And I know who you are, if she doesn't." He was surprised with the answer which was calm and firm.

"My answer is 'no'. She will work here and none should tell me what to do with my help. It is my business!" He left immediately while Louise was watching him leaving. He didn't want her to know his car license number. But Louise knew it already as she informed Alice always about everything. She was her best friend never to do what she wanted without her agreement. This was a surprise that Louise wanted Alice to know. But Louise got prepared and was waiting for the gentleman. The 'Garden of Art' was doing well and Louise was every night guarding their place. It seems he realized that and quit threatening.

Not long after, Louise calls Alice and she tells her what happened. "If you want me, we can chase the bastard. I can only wait for your command. You know you have our love." Louise does not know the mentality of the bastards. They involve you first, they protect you after, and they use you at the end. Then, they kill you or your friends if they cannot keep you as their slave. "Louise, I do not involve people that I love. Try to protect yourself from those fellows that have bothered you. I am sorry but justice will come for me one day. So far you are doing well and I love you more than I can say." "Fine Alice. I want you to know that I love you."said Louise.

Alice was now waiting for her turn. She was waiting to see what the imposter was going to do. She was crying each time the imposter was screwing her to boost his ego and assure his supremacy. She didn't want to die before him. She wanted to see him dead and then everything was acceptable. He had sullied her honor.

"I know you may kill one or two men; but you cannot kill three or four. So be careful. I will not be your whore in Athens!" she told him. He was surprised but smiled. "I will kill you, but I will not give you, because I love you," he said sternly. He was loving a whore!

The next day, she goes to the shop early in the morning and asks Louise to go in the office. She greets her and begs her for a tea. Louise is happy to serve her a tea with biscuits and join her. After they discussed some business with pleasure, Alice says, "Louise, you know that I love you. And just for this, I have to inform you that no man will be able to kill Jack in the open. If he knows the man, he will kill him. If the men can hide, they may kill him. If three or four men hide and trap him, they will kill him. Please, I love you, and I want you to know." She is slowly drinking her tea and thinks.

"Please, let me solve my problem first. If I fail or succeed, you will survive." Tears flow out of Louise's eyes. She keeps quiet, thinks and replies, "I will do as you say. But I need only two hidden men and ten bullets." "I think you will not need anything but my love which you have, anyway," replies Alice smiling. She was a noble woman; hard to find and hard to win. But Louise had to learn and wait. She loved Alice and she promised to wait.

After that, the two friends discussed a number of problems and questions and Alice left content. Louise was pleased and thankful because she didn't know that capable and guilty people are inscrutable and very dangerous. Only very capable people may rescue the innocent ones in a dishonest manner. She needed two good men to kill him.

Alice had to look now for the men to be paid to kill the filthy and crazy wolf. She was not placing any limits but she needed the men and the money. She could probably find the money next year when she was going to be 21 years of age. Her father had left her enough money to get it at that age. But next, she had to find the ones to be paid and kill the bastard! How was this to be done? She was thinking and terrified.

Alice was desperate. She decided to kill the pig herself, and die if she failed or was caught. She was innocent and she had the right to live if she couldn't find others to do it. It was not an easy job, but it was easier than living with a corrupt human. You could hurt him and not kill him. He had said that he would kill her and whether it was true or not she had the right to defend herself. The defense was to kill the bastard.

Many nights alone Alice was staring deep in the Messenian gulf and torturing herself. She had decided to kill the bastard herself. She knew that each night he was coming home after he had two simpletons walking with him: One to his left and the other to his right, being sure that no people were waiting for him. One could kill those people but he didn't care and he was no longer afraid of Alice. He had done the best to be sure that no others were to kill him while he was coming home.

The only one he was afraid of was Alice. But he had decided to get rid of her before she could do anything. He was ready to kill her but she was too sweet to kill. She would have been able to survive, if she was to be his whore in Athens and play his game. But that was not a life for an honorable woman. She could not be anyone's whore; she had to kill him and be free or die. She wanted to avoid any embarrassment in public. She could not stand the corrupt policemen.

But that was not her solution and she decided to find the assassins. First she decided to search for the assassins. Second to find the money needed, and third to have them kill the bastard. She was not going to be his whore and she had to kill him first. She needed the courage to start and know that she was to die. There was no other solution.

The ladies from Souli died not to fall in the hands of the Turks. Why should she not fall trying to get revenge for her honor and that of her parents? She had already been raped and her victory would be to kill him and not go to jail, unless she failed. But failure was not in the book of the noble ones. She could not be helped not to be raped, but she can sure kill a bastard and not go to jail!

It was Sunday night and the sky was dark blue. She sits at her table to watch the sky and the stars. To her left in the yard and on a tree she sees a huge Owl watching the harbor. She smiles and the Owl turns her head and looks. Ismene surprised smiles but the Owl does not respond. Many times the Owl turned her head to watch. It got late but the Owl was resting. She was serious, looking once in a while to her left to see Alice. She was reading Alice's mind but she was enjoying also the night which soon removed some clouds and left the sky blue, filled with stars.

Not long after, Alice went to sleep. She was very tired. In the coming September she is to be 21 years old. It was the time that she could use the money from the Bank of America given to her by her noble father. She had to get revenge without punishment.

But Alice had no other choice. She didn't believe in God to prey and hope. She had seen and she knew that Jack was a vicious bastard. If God existed and he was what they say, he would have not allowed the existence of such a brutal wolf: Never kind to anyone, not even to his whores. Alice was not his whore, she was an abused young lady as soon as she lost her brother, father, mother and honor.

3 POLLUTION IN THE BEACH OF KALAMATA

"The beach of Kalamata can be polluted but not corrupted."

Simon a young man, is walking alone on the big long square of the city of Kalamata going home from the City Service. He had been there to ask the City to demand from the renter below his apartment to move the fixed top awning. It is not allowed there by any law or logic. The owner has rented the space below and the renter fixed the awning above horizontally, level with Simon's floor. Simon requests the renter Mr. Pig, as he used to call him, to move the awning because it was illegal. Simon was polite and explained: Nothing below 3 meters high could extend beyond the wall. The awning was placed fixed at 2 meters just above the ground at the floor line of Simon's apartment.

"Please take your awning and place it elsewhere, following the law," he had said politely to the Pig. "Tell the one responsible to do that. Not me," the renter had replied angrily. "I will sir," Simon had said and left. He was thinking to burn everything including the bastard below. He was mad, and also a man with reliable friends, hard to find anywhere. He decided to push his request as suggested. He checked everywhere to be sure. He was right. The renter below had no right to place a tent at the line of Simon's floor just 2 meters above the ground.

He had talked to the lady Manager responsible and she had denied her responsibility. At the same time, she was demanding money from the residents to maintain the building. After that, Simon had said, "If it is not your responsibility to keep the place safe and clean by prohibiting illegal flat awnings at 2 meters above the ground, why it is your responsibility to keep the place clean by cleaning floors?" She bullshitted all she wanted and Simon replied politely, "I will not pay to clean anything, if you do not clean my wall and the view of the gentleman's garbage accumulating on the awning."

After that, Simon tried the City Office again with no result. He was now going home unbearably furious. The awning was horizontally flat and was holding all the trash blown on by the wind and thrown by the rascals. It was beyond doubt illegal and flat. It could not be cleaned, closed or folded. But in any case, why please the bastard in any way? Simon inherited an error that he decided to correct. He has two noble friends: Jason and Stuart on whom he always depends if there is a need. But now he had the right to act. It was a simple and clear place where Simon was right as usually.

Simon is upset and he has to do something anyway. Tomorrow, he has to meet Stuart at 9 o'clock at night for fun, and for an easy dinner with Jason. He calls Jason and cannot get him. He calls Nicholas but he cannot get him, either. He must be somewhere in Patras lost, he thinks and smiles. He calls Stuart and tells him that he will be little late. "Please, try to be there by 9 o'clock. If I am late wait for me. I could not reach Jason to let him know." "Yes Simon, I am used to you. It's fine if there is no problem. Jason is better for laughing anyway." "Yes Stuart, there is no problem. If there is, I will let you know," replies Simon seriously and hangs up the phone. Stuart knows that Simon has a problem with the bastard below and smiles. Simon is aging to be waiting any longer for the bastard below to learn and behave properly. He decided to burn the illegal tent.

At about 9 o'clock at night, Simon goes to his apartment at Faron street. He goes upstairs and pours gasoline on the Tent below from the middle to the end. He stretches a cable from the start at the entrance to the middle on the Tent and puts fire on the cable from the start.

From the other side of Faron street he was watching the burning cable. As soon as the cable finished, the poured gasoline was instantly inflamed, and the old tent cloth blew up in flames.

Simon happy, turned left from Faron to Nikitara street and went to join his friends at Pete's Bar in the harbor. It was about ten o'clock in the night. As usual, Simon was on time. Neither Stuart nor Jason could complain much. Simon was content and happy. The bastard below was unbearable and a coward bully.

The three friends ordered their special hamburgers with tomato salad and beer and laughed for the rest of the night with jokes and funny events. After the time and the light beer with the hamburgers and the tomato salad were slowly consumed, the three friends laughed with anecdotes and events of the day. The process of burning the tend of the gentleman below was humored by Simon and the three friends laughed that night. Soon they left laughing with jokes of Jason who was the most humorous and pleasant of the other two.

Next day, late in the afternoon, Simon was alone walking through the Central Square of Kalamata going towards the beech. A beautiful lady was also crossing that time the Square going in the same direction. Simon reached the lady as he was walking faster and the lady smiling said, "You always walk fast. No time for reflecting?" Simon slows his step and asks, "Have you seen me many times?" "Not many times, because I have not been for long here, anyway," she answers wondering.

Simon looks at the lady and he does not know what to say. She is really young, charming and enchanting. Her smile is attractive and Simon gets perplexed. She is staring at Simon wondering. As they walk together, Simon asks the lady to join him for coffee or something in the corner confectionary. "If you relax, I will join and treat you as well," she says with a tempting epicurean smile. "Oh! No," says Simon surprised trying to understand the young lady. "Anyway, I will join you," she adds with a pleasant expression.

After they had a night desert and a very pleasant but reserved conversation, she gave Simon her phone to call her any other time he liked for another meeting. She explained that she could not stay any longer after midnight. The lady was Alice and Simon was surprised. She sensed the reserved nature of Simon and smiled. She was attractive and enchanting, but Simon could not freely relate with Alice. She looked very sophisticated to be a woman of the night. She was elegant, very charming and beautiful.

Simon promised to call her, but he was reserved and awkward to approach that woman. He could not believe that she could be of free morals. But she was one who could magnetize any male. Alice wanted to know Simon but he could not believe that she was of free morals.

She was beautiful and charming. She could be anything and Simon was uneasy. It was hard to believe that she was of free morals. He didn't believe that Alice could be anyone's lady. "Thanks for the treat. Call me any time you feel like," she said leaving after an hour or so with a thoughtful smile. She was very young and very attractive.

Another time, not long after, Simon went to have his coffee and pie in one of the confectionaries on the western side of the Square. It was Friday evening and a young lady, very attractive and pleasant was working. She was reserved with a charming expression. She was a middle class girl with easy behaviour and very pleasant features. She smiled and Simon asked for her name. She gave him her name. "Norma," she said absorbed and smiling.

Simon was fascinated with Norma's figure which was charming and attractive. But after that, Simon could not ask for anything else. That is what happens when the female figure excites your interests. Norma is an intelligent girl and let Simon realize that she liked him also. However, Simon was lost absorbed by the pretty features of Norma. He was awkward and Norma could see that with her female tastes.

Simon that evening left early to avoid his awkward behaviour. But his tip to the young waitress was generous. Simon left thinking of the beauty of Norma. She was really charming with that large dark eyes. He could not help it though being attracted with the charm of Alice. She was an aristocrat that kept people at the distance she wanted. Both though were charming and attractive. "Don't forget to see us again," she whispered as Simon was living.

Another night, Jason was going towards the sea to relax. Alice again was going at her apartment by the beach. She was walking slowly and reflecting. "Its a beautiful night for dreaming; it is not?' asks Jason. She looks at him and replies, "Yes, if you are alone." Jason smiles and replies, "You mean I should not disturb your loneliness?" Looking at Jason she answers "Why? Are you interested in young ladies?" "Shouldn't I be?" he asks smiling.

She smiles and replies, "If you think you are an exception." Jason smiles and answers, "It depends on you." She reaches her purse, takes out a card, gives it to Jason and whispers, "Take the card and give me a call any time after tomorrow, if you please." Jason takes the card and wonders, "May I call you?" "If you please," she replies smiling. Jason reads the card, "Alice in Wonderland." He looks at her and smiles. After awhile they separated laughing. Jason was impressed with Alice and kept thinking looking at the card. " She is charming," he whispers. "Blessed is the one who has her!"

Simon with Nicholas went again to flirt with Norma the following Sunday. The temptation was really annoying and the desire inexplicable. Simon is also handsome. And what a young woman would not give to sleep with him? Just fear and the conception of a child before marriage! Then you are in the penal colony of Franz Kafka; the Jewish writer in Prague of Bohemia, writing in German; to a German? Nicholas who had lived in Germany before whispered, "Yes Gentlemen, to a German if you meet one!" Germany was filled with immigrants who went to work, after Germany's defeat, and remained there. The German's were killed.

There are many ways that men want to be protected. Alice was a goddess but Norma a Greek charm that made Simon happy. Perhaps his Jewish background was content with human charm. Norma had it with grace that charmed Simon. She had the penetrating intelligence of Greeks after Christ. It was a natural learned behavior: You condition the man till he can no longer resist. As they were leaving later, Simon smiled and said, "Keep the change please, you deserve it." She smiled and thanked Simon. "Please, come back," she said smiling with pleasure. Simon looked at her enchanted and replied, "If we are invited, we will certainly see you next Sunday." She was happy and smiling.

The temptation was really annoying and the desire inexplicable. He is also handsome, relatively speaking. And what a young woman would not give to sleep with him? Just fear and the conception of a child before marriage! Then you are in the penal colony of Franz Kafka; the Jewish writer in Prague of Bohemia, writing in German and charming all future people. No writer who has read him can forget.

Jason was charmed when he met Alice. He had never meet before a woman so young and so charming. On Wednesday, early in the morning, he called her. "Will I see you tonight?" he asked. "If you wish you may see me at Pete's Bar at seven o'clock. "Sure, I will," he answered excited. She hang up and at seven or so she met him at Pete's place. They had something light with good wine and by nine they left. "Where shall we go now?" Jason asked. Alice looked at him with the same question but different answer. "We go to Filoxenia, if you please," replies Alice. She looks at Jason in the eyes and tears run on her rosy checks. Jason does not understand, but Alice's eyes run without explanations. Jason thinks that Alice is a whore and she cries without explanations. But he is one of the many who think so.

Once they get to Filoxenia and get their room, Alice looks at Jason surprised. Jason kisses her politely. She touches his hands and Jason's lips get involved in Alice's passion. She kisses him with such a force that both fell on the bed and forgot to get out. "I was thinking about you since I met you," she whispered. "Don't forget that."

This surprised Jason who could not resist the temptation of her body. It was fire. Suddenly, her hands got pinned on Jason's flesh and tears of pleasure began rolling. Then her hands tied on his body and Jason surrendered. It was for him and for her an unusual pleasure while her tears wet her face. She was a charm.

"It was amazing," whispers Jason after while. She does not answer but asks, "Do you want more?"Jason looks at her and replies, "No. Thank you." "Did I please you?" she asked smiling. " Yes, you did," he replies confused. She grabs his face and kisses him like crazy. Jason surprised couldn't say anything. He was again the victim and when both finished again, they surrendered. He was wondering with the beauty and the passion of the woman. He was surprised but chose not to say anything more. He was really confused.

"Will I see you again?" he asks. "Of course," she answers with an exhausted voice. Her eyes had a charming surrendered expression. Jason was surprised. He was lost in the lasting orgy of Alice.

They got dressed and Jason asked, "How much do I owe you?" She looks at him and does not reply. This leaves him surprised. "It is not possible," he whispers. She does not answer but slowly gets dressed.

This woman is beautiful no matter how she fixes herself. Her beauty is her weapon to leave any man begging for her attention. Jason smiles, gives her more than she expected (she didn't expect anything but knew what they were asking and taking). Jason smiles, gives her double of what the others were given and says, "If you told me this before I would not have come. Please take it."

She looks at him, refuses the money he gave her, and replies, "If that is the case, don't call me again." She goes to bathroom, washes her face, gives him a kiss and goes. Jason remained surprised. He realized that she meant what she said: She was not a whore. Or she was? No, apparently she liked the man. But she didn't know him; it was strange!

Jason that night left confused and intrigued. The lady was not giving herself at night for money. She knew how to make money and she didn't want any. But why was such an intelligent woman a whore? The answer was probably simple. She was not a whore! Who knows?

Some man wanted her to be a whore and be able to move, anywhere they wanted her to do so. Her guard was a gambler and he was addicted to gambling. Why was she not going to the Police to seek her freedom? It was not easy. With no protection but only potential prosecution, she was forced to serve a bastard or die. Who knows?

She was followed by two bastards ordered to abuse her if she didn't behave according to the gambler's orders. She didn't want to die, but she preferred to kill the bastard. He was abusing her with no remorse of conscience. There was no answer to the question. Jason was puzzled. He was though convinced that the lady was not a whore. He was also enchanted by her beauty, charm and intelligence.

She didn't hope to live but she wanted to kill him for sure before she died. Jason was confused and unhappy. He wanted to know the lady. He was a noble man respected by anyone who happened to know or work with him. In his encounter with Alice, Jason remained enchanted and surprised: She was a miracle unexpected. She was sharing and not selling. And she was sharing with one she loved and wanted.

Alice learned to love Jason but she didn't believe that she deserved him or that he should die for her. Jason could not understand all these circumstances and wanted to sleep and forget. They were really torturing his mind and heart. Jason was not the man to go with a whore. He was simply attracted and captivated by Alice. He was really wondering and amazed. No woman had ever attracted him like that.

Jason wanted to pay and Alice was feeling insulted. She was not going to have him if he insisted and Jason could not take it. She could not explain to him that she was not a whore. He had to understand that. So when he called and they met in one of the outside places of the main Kalamata square, she simply explained: "I am not a whore and I cannot meet anyone who thinks so." Jason was surprised, confused and hard to believe anything. Alice got upset and said smiling, "There are many whores anywhere if you want. I am not one!" She got up and left.

She never accepted any of his calls anymore. He was surprised and confused. Alice was a riddle for Jason; and Jason a petty bourgeoisie for Alice. But she was awaking and rising by the principles of noble Jason.

She needed a moral support to rise. She was learning but she could not surrender. She was rising with the sun since she met Jason. He was a charming man of liberal and known principles. She was impressed.

Simon and Norma decided to go one night for fun to a bouzouki taverna on Navarinou. They enjoyed their night and Simon thought that he deserved her love. After leaving the taverna, Simon took Norma to his apartment. They had their glass of wine and after, Simon wanted to make love with Norma. She smiled and said, "Simon, you don't know how much I love you. But sex is an act of virtue after marriage; not an act of exercise before. Please let me love you and take me home. It will not cost you anything." That was an embarrassing surprise for Simon. He didn't know what to think, what to say or what to do.

Simon was not inexperienced, but he was someone who had found his love and wanted to live it. He was surprised but also awkward with Norma. The pleasure he was expecting was just a dream never to be reality before marriage. Norma sees Simon suddenly depressed, awkward and deprived. "Simon, don't you know I love you? Don't you know I live for you? Don't you know that I am dreaming about you every day?" she said crying. All that was an insult to Simon.

"Okay Norma, let's go at your home, as you please. It does not matter, don't worry." Thus, Simon took Norma at her home. He said good night, and he even forgot to kiss her. She was devastated.

She experienced everything and she was crying all night, till she fell asleep exhausted with half her clothes on. Who was right? Simon or Norma? Norma was right if sex is a holy ritual; and Simon had to be respected if sex was to be a mutual pleasure to be kept! But that was not the case. The Christian was right and the Jew was wrong!

A few days later, Jason and Simon meet at the place Le Garson on the walking section of the street, in the center of Kalamata. Simon tells Jason what had happened between him and Norma a few nights before Easter. Jason smiled and said to Simon, "Please, screw the others and keep Norma if that is what she likes. She is yours; the question is what do you want? If that is what you want, don't worry, we will take care of her." Simon shook his head and said nothing. Jason understood that his friend was in love and in error. If he was going to have her, why not wait? She didn't prohibit him to screw another woman. She wanted to give him herself with virtue. But, he could not wait!

"Listen Simon, I want you to meet a girl by the name Alice, says Jason to Simon. She is fantastic but I cannot really win her. She attracted me because I think she is very special; and if you forget the bourgeoisie criteria, she can send you in heaven," says Jason. Simon was thinking and as soon as Jason stopped, he said, "Yes Jason, I met too a beautiful girl, prettier if not better than Norma. She invited me for sex but I was not ready; and to tell you the truth, she terrified me. I will show her to you when I have a chance to do that. She puzzled me." Simon was again thinking.

"Simon, I want you to meet the lady I am talking about, and if you escape, let me know." Jason now sees Simon lost and almost screams. "Simon, aren't you listening? I am not talking about Norma!" Simon looks at Jason and says smiling, "I know Jason; you are talking about the lady Alice; and I am thinking about Norma. I am sorry; but I heard you and I wish to meet that lady." "Yes Simon; you should, and I will arrange that. Alice is captivating. She is an exception to the rule. When you meet her; either you run away or you love her! You know I love her." Simon looked at Jason smiling and wondering: "Was she Alice?" he asks. "Yes; that is Alice," replies Jason.

It is again in the coffee house on the Aristomenous street where the friends meet. While Jason and Simon talk, Nicholas is passing by, and

Simon rushes to catch him. "Nicholas, Nicholas, come here," he shouts. "We are waiting for you!" Nicholas hears and sees Simon. He walks into the place smiling as usual. Nicholas, once upon a time, was a charm for every woman. Now he had forgotten but he was not forgotten. However, he was a man. "Where the hell are you going without looking?" asks Simon. "Oh! Well, I was going to find you Simon," he replies recovering with a smile.

"Okay, sit down and have a drink," replies Simon. As soon as he sits down in a chair, he adds, "Simon, you are okay with three Ladies? Shame on those with one." "Well, Nicholas; don't you think that is a subject for debate?" replies Simon, wondering what to support, what to debate and what to reject. It was really a subject for anyone to debate.

Jason laughed also, and Nicholas who always agrees with the one that speaks, said, as usual, "Yes, yes; but if you have three and you lose one, you are still happy!" This time Simon laughed too amused. He knows that Nicholas in your absence can always say things that everyone can hear; in your presence he can only say things that you agree; and he knows what to say. "Of course, if only the one is good for screwing, then what do you do?" asks Nicholas laughing and closing the subject. He was fine if the woman who wants you is also the one that pleases you. In reality the problem is yours.

"Jason, I was told that you have quitted teaching business; is that true?" asks Nicholas. "Yes I did; it was already too long and frustrating. Besides, with friends like you I don't have to worry; should I?" "No you should not. You know the Stock market and it will be fascinating. Besides, your friends will be happy now. It was waste of your talents after all. Now we know where to go and what to say." "Yes, yes Nicholas, there is money but you have to know how to get it. Of course, you have to get working with officials and money; you have to see where the market is going and drive them there." "Well, Simon is our friend anyway, and you should teach him how to make money also."

Jason looks at Simon and says, "I am sure that with Simon we will make a lot of money. He has to learn, being an Engineer, how to bribe the others and make it for himself. I am sure he will be our good source." "Yes, yes, you have to get to know them," replies Nicholas thinking. "Of course, you have to get to know them, and be generous with them," adds Jason. A smile was finally formed on the face of Nicholas certain that Jason was a very intelligent man.

Simon was listening trying to understand. He didn't believe that you could do much if you didn't get away from school after you know the wheeler-dealer. Nicholas and Jason agreed. No one seemed to disagree when Simon said, "You have first to get inside, and then be trusted by any of the known ways of connection." Jason looked at Simon and said, "Yes Simon, I will guide you in the ways of making connections. I know all those people." Simon smiled indicating his trust on Jason.

The three friends understood each other and Jason continued: "I will call and take care of Norma, Simon; don't worry." Simon said nothing but he smiled. He was very respectful of Jason and Nicholas. He knew that neither one would ever think of doing or saying something that didn't honor Simon. Both were admiring the Jewish Greek people. Nicholas and Jason are people who know how to honor friends like Simon. Nicholas is an Ilyrian Greek but he hides it. Who knows?

"Gentlemen, I have to go," says Jason and gets up. Then he turns to Simon and Nicholas and says, "I really want you to meet Alice. But be patient. I am sure, you will be surprised to see and know her. I really want your opinion. She is really a charm." Neither Nicholas nor Simon said anything but both smiled content with their friend's excitement. After leaving, Nicholas said, "If Jason likes the lady so much; she is not for you Simon. But I trust she is for Jason and you know what to say."

A few days later, Simon receives a call from Jason at his apartment home. "Simon, please come and join us at Pete's Bar on Navarinou. Alice will be glad to meet you. She is a fine lady. By the way, I could not reach Nicholas. I don't know where the hell he is now. I will call him again, though." He didn't say more and hung up. Nothing more was said but Alice felt uncomfortable when she heard the word Simon. Soon after, Jason called Stuart. But there was no response, either. Alice also called somewhere. Jason heard the name of Jack and noticed how the face of Alice changed color. "Okay, okay, don't yell; I will be there as soon as I can," she replied. "I am at work now, and I can't be elsewhere." The man was angry and wanted her to go right away.

After a few minutes, Alice says to Jason, "I am sorry, but I have to leave." "Can you wait for a few minutes? My friend is coming," Jason says begging. She understands, holds his hand and says, "Next time Jason; please, next time. Try to understand." She gets up, gives him a kiss and goes bitter with the sweetest kiss. On the way out, she looks at Jason and feels upset. She wanted his lips and not his sadness or money! No one could understand that lady yet. She was though a temptation hard to escape, if she wanted you.

Jason stays upset and thinks of Alice's kiss and lips. No matter how she gave them, they were sweet and hypnotizing. Her eyes were in his dreams. Not long after, Simon arrives smiling. He greets Jason and asks "Where is the girl Jason? I was afraid I was going to be late." "No Simon, you are not late. She just left. The bastard called angry, and the girl had to go." They ordered ouzo and they got it soon without any delay. They were both upset and no words could be said.

They both put water in their ouzo and Simon said, "Okay Jason, to our health. These things happen. Next time we will make it." "Yes Simon, we will. But tonight she was a charm and the bastard made her a whore." "No Simon; don't say that. We have to fix the bastard. If the woman doesn't want the man, he has no right to keep her." Jason gets his glass of ouzo and drinks it with passion. "I swear to his God, if he has any, that I will break his teeth with my bullet. If he wants to know, he will!" says Simon. He knew Jason was a noble man, to be trusted and loved. He knew Jason was proud.

Simon was upset with the bastard that was using whoever he could as a package. He looks at Jason and says, "Don't worry Jason. I will meet her next time. If the bastard doesn't know to behave like a gentleman, he has to learn. If you like her so much and if she wants to see me, he has to respect her wish like a gentleman and not like a pig."

Simon drinks his ouzo and continues. "If you like her so much; and if the feeling is mutual, you have the right to see her! Please be patient." "I am too patient with the whore," replies Jason in a moment of frustration. "Don't call her a whore, Jason. If she was, you should not be worrying now. Please be calm and each is tested. Sooner or later we will know who the filthy pig, and who the noble man is." "Okay Simon; I am sorry. He becomes unbearable and I blame the lady. I know I am wrong." "Well, you know. I am sharper with Norma."

"Oh, yes, let me talk to her first, please. Also, I will bring you in contact with the design and construction people next week. I know them and they are nice with me. I know where the people's money should be. The politicians are stupid and should be ignored. They all pretend they are pious and know, and they all are actually corrupt."

This was Jason's view. People's money should not be touched. The bastards take it, invest it, and make it theirs; strange consciousness. Someone has to teach the investment people respect for the investment money of the others. Jason is serious as he speaks.

"Monday, I will talk to Norma, and when I see you next time, I will let you know. We have to take her from that pastry place. She came the other time and asked for work. I will find now when she is available and I will arrange for her what she wants," says Jason. "Yes, and don't forget to let me see Alice," says Simon. "Fine, either way we will meet again. But be calm." He was pleased that Jason was going to talk to Norma! He was in love with her and Jason knew. She was a woman to be loved and trusted. She was not a woman to deceive. Jason knew she loved Simon; and Simon was loved and respected: Such a noble man hard to find anywhere!

On Thursday night, Norma was home from Athens. Friday, she was going to work in the pastry place. But she received a call from Jason who wanted her to see him. He called and left a message to see him on Friday in the morning. She was happy to hear from Jason; she thought about Simon and cried. But anyway, at about ten o'clock on Friday morning she went to see Jason. At about ten thirty she met him. She was so happy that seeing Jason she thought she was seeing Simon. After exchanging the trivial information of news from Athens and School, Jason called Nitsa and asked her to bring Norma what she had and what Norma wanted. "Let me bring you what I think you would like," says Nitsa. Soon she brought her cold water and a fresh delicious 'banana biscuit'. Norma was delighted! She could not have anything better. She was pleased and very thankful.

"You called the other time and you asked for work. I know that you are studying at the School of Economics in Panteio University. I think that you made a good choice. What do you want me to do now for you? You know that I know Simon loves you, and what you want me to do for you I will do, as long as I think it is good," says Jason. She looks at him smiling and says with tears, "Thank you; I am in need of money and I want something better than what I am doing now in the Sweet Coffee shop." He looks at her and says, "Okay, we will settle on that."

He thinks and asks, "Do you like the Analysis of Stocks?" She looks very intelligent. "Yes, if I know," she replies smiling. Jason thinks and laughs; then he says, "Okay, we can teach you, and if you like it, you can continue and learn more. If you don't, we will find something else. So, you come to work as many days of the five, as you want. And any days you do not come, I know you are studying." He smiled with her because he was assuming that she was so disciplined. He was not really making a mistake knowing the discipline of Norma. Jason is intelligent and friendly.

"You will get more than any high school graduate with zero experience going to college. If the money you are making is not enough, you let me know," he adds with a smile. While he stops, she thinks. Then he says, "This week, Mr. Argyris will show you the different places in the Firm; and your work starts next Monday. Nitsa will be delighted to help you."

She was so thankful that no one could imagine. She was in need and almost cried. The city of Kalamata was not a place for young and intelligent women. But Jason's place was a national one and challenging. Jason was planning to extent it anyway. He had the charm, the mony, the experience and the knowledge.

"Come with me," says Jason. He takes her to Mr. Argyris, introduces her to him and says, "This is Ms. Norma Orfanidou that I mentioned to you before. Please, take care of her starting tomorrow. She is a noble woman." Jason looks at her and says. "Now I have to go. From tomorrow, Nitsa and Mr. Argyris will guide you anywhere you need." He left smiling and Norma remained surprised.

She came depressed and she left happy; and she was cheered by the prospect of a job. Only tears of happiness one could see after. When she went home, her mother learned what happened and was hopeful. "This is what I and your father were expecting from Simon. But I knew that Jason had to see you first and know your character. That Jason is amazing, as they say." She was so surprised that she loved him after Simon. She made her cross to thank God for Norma's luck.

Norma didn't say anything but she was thoughtful. She was also wondering. She loved Simon, why did she care for anything else? If he didn't care that was his problem. Of course, she wanted him and she wished to know that the love was mutual. But that was never the question. She decided to give herself to a man that loved her and she now was above nineteen years old! She had to make her own decisions now and live with them. If she loved one, she had to enjoy him and laugh. If he didn't, that was his problem: Good selfish thinking!

Now Jason wanted to find some better work opportunities for Simon. He was working and people loved him. But the place where he was working was small. He decided to find something better for Simon. He called Stuart and asked to see him sometime next week. Stuart was working now in a Structural firm and found his work interesting and rewarding. He was also respected and Jason knew that. He called Stuart and decided to see him sometime in the middle of next week.

Jason told Stuart that he wanted to find a bigger place for Simon. That was fine for Stuart. "Yes Jason, I was thinking about that all this week. Simon is special and needs some help. We shall meet for sure some time on Wednesday or Thursday next week." "Thank you Stuart; till next week," said Jason thinking. Everything was perfect for Jason and he was happy. He knew that Stuart was going to do what he could. Those were not just friends but better than brothers.

On Sunday, Simon called Nicholas for tea and pastry. They decided to go to the coffee-bakery where Norma was working. Jason had talked to Simon and told him about Norma. "Do what you want Simon and do not worry about women. It is only necessary that they love you." Norma had decided to sleep with Simon because she loved him. And if he didn't love her, so what? She felt tired of the game. She was waiting for the opportunity to give herself to the man she loved and not to the man that loved her. Of course, if he loved her as much as she did love him, she was lucky and happy!

She knew that Jason was a noble man respecting the wishes of his friends. He knew that Norma was a noble lady with her own principles. He had asked Simon to try to understand and not judge. Love was more important than religion. Religion was a mater of tradition that you inherit from your parents, usually. Think about this and decide how important it is: As the knowledge of the clergy! All they know is to screw the young boys and girls that offered themselves; and both find the excuses later!

When Simon and Nicholas sat down, Norma came smiling. "What shall I offer you today?" she asks Simon. He looks at her and says, "Your love after my coffee and your pie." "If that is what you want, you will have it," she says smiling. "And don't ask if I ever had it before. You are a man and you should know." "I want you to know Norma, I love you." "Not as much as I do," she replies. "And if you cannot tell after, it does not matter; I will still love you!" Then she turns to Nicholas and asks, "What about you, Nicholas?" "I want a tea and something of your choice but not so sweet as your lips. And don't forget a cold glass of water?" She remains flabbergasted. She recovers and says, "Thank you, I will try. I will do my best."

With her blushing look, she was very charming. Simon was looking at her with admiration. She was free, noble and charming. But she was also so young! She was closing her eighteenth year. She came back with the tea and the pastries. "Tell me if you like it," she says to Simon. "Fine; I will," he replies with his eyes melting as he is looking at Norma's youthful breasts. She was aware, but she had surrendered. She was youthful and wanted Simon. Soon after, Yannis asks for his special. Simon was wondering if he knew what it was. Yannis knew how to enjoy it and leave the others wondering. When Norma came back, Simon said, "You are perfect Norma; the sweet was amazing but not as sweet as you are." "Thank you Simon," she replied burning with the desire for Simon; and looking in his eyes and lips.

On Sunday Simon called Nicholas for tea and pastry. They decided to go to the coffee-bakery where Norma was working. Jason had talked to Simon and told him about Norma. "Do what you want Simon and do not worry about women. It is only necessary that they love you." Simon smiled thinking of Norma's lips and flaming youthful breasts.

Norma had decided to sleep with Simon because she loved him. And if he didn't love her, so what? She felt tired of the game. She was waiting for the opportunity to give herself to the man she loved and not to the man that loved her. Of course, if he loved her as much as she did love him, she was lucky and happy! She knew that Jason was a noble man respecting the wishes of his friends. He knew that Norma was a noble lady with her own principles. He had asked Simon to try to understand and not judge.

Love was more important than religion. Religion was a matter of tradition that you inherit from your parents, usually. Think about this and decide how important it is: As the knowledge of the clergy! Never deep or charming but always naïve and frightening.

Simon was wondering if he knew what it was. Yannis knew how to enjoy it and leave the others be wondering. Norma smiled and Simon got lost in her beauty. She left to continue her work but Simon was looking at her as she left. Nicholas was certain that Simon was in love with Norma. And sure that Norma was thinking of Simon. Nicholas was an experienced man and he knew: A professor of Mathematics with a specialty of women in his knowledge'. Yannis was an Architect with music in his passion. But he gave his time in Architecture and never in music. But he had to say that he loved something besides drawing lines.

Next to Simon's table was another table with three other young girls of free morals, wishes and tastes. They were all charming but not ready for anything. The men were all attractive and young. They liked and laughed at Simon's flattery and looked in his direction. They saw him blushing and laughed. Nicholas turns to the side of the three girls next to him, and smiling says, "My friend is deeply in love, but I am not." "Why not?" the girl asks. Nicholas thinks and says, "I fall in love not with the words but with the woman's deeds." "That is very interesting," she says looking curiously at Nicholas. "Yes, my name is Nicholas and we are all workers and hunters."

She smiles and he adds, "It is very nice to have talked to you," "But I have not," she says. "That is why I said so," Nicholas replies smiling. She gets the message and laughs. "But you will, if you give me your phone number; will you not?" She smiled, took a card out of her purse and gave it to Nicholas. He took it and thanked her profusely. Then he gave her a card of his own. She looks at the card and asks, "Are you a Professor?" Nicholas smiles and replies, "That is what they say: A Professor in Women."

The girls who were listening smiled. Nicholas was an artist when he was with women. He knew how to flatter and enchant them. He knew how to drive them crazy. They wanted but they could not have him. He had a Mexican lady that she was crazy and charming. She liked him but she could not have him. She was attractive but for some reason she could not get him. She was charming but not experienced to deceive.

Nicholas was certainly difficult and the ladies could not get him. Or, the one's who met him were not so lucky. They gave him what he wanted but that was not probably enough. Who knows better than Nicholas to say what was enough?

Next Sunday, Simon and Nicholas went again to the place where Norma was working. She was no longer a waitress. She was sitting at a table drinking tea. She sees them, gets up smiling and calls them to join her. Both Simon and Nicholas see her and smile. "Don't you work tonight?" asks Simon. She does not answer, invites them to sit down smiling, asks them what they want, they order their tea and coffee, and Norma says smiling, "I knew you would come here to see me, and I came to be sure you don't miss me." Simon smiles, Nicholas is thinking and Norma is wondering if she impressed Simon. In reality she did as he went to see just her, besides having his special coffee.

"I am glad you came Norma; but don't you work tonight?" asks Simon the work cholic. She looks at him, as a new waitress is serving them what they want, and says, "No Simon; didn't Jason tell you that he gave me a job at his office?" Simon is surprised and wondering. "Do you mean that he asked you to quit school?" "Do you believe that Jason would ever do that?" she asks surprised. "Of course I did not," he replies. Nicholas did not believe that Jason would ever do that and he would never ask that question. So, he was waiting to hear more. He wanted to hear and enjoy his brother's noble ways.

Norma, aggressively, touches Simon's hand and says, "You didn't kiss me like before!" Simon looks at her and replies embarrassed. "I am sorry, I didn't mean that." She smiled; she knew the truth and answered his question. She knew that he cared and replied, "Simon, Jason was fantastic. He allowed me to go to work any time I wanted from Monday to Friday and arranged for me to work with Nitsa and Rose! They were happy to teach and guide me whenever I was there."

Simon was waiting to hear more and she was embarrassed to do that. She bent, kissed him on the cheek and said, "My parents were happy!" He looks at her and she replies smiling, "So am I." "I was sure he would do something that you deserved," said Simon content. Nicholas smiled and said, "Was there ever a case in which Jason didn't do well with money and people?" Simon smiled and asked, "You mean not with women?" "Wait and you will know," replied Nicholas. Simon laughed and Norma said softly, "Have you had Dinner?" "No, but we were waiting to see what you wanted to do after work," replies Simon. "After work I want to be with you," she replied.

Simon knew how much he was attracted. He wanted now to know how much Norma was. She looked at Simon and said smiling, "I am hungry." He looks surprised and says, "Nicholas, do you mind if we go to Pete's Bar?" "Of course not; there we can always have something light and pleasing," was the reply. Soon Simon decided to drive and all three went to Pete's Bar by the harbor. As soon as they got in, they see someones calling them. They were Jason with Stuart. They walk there and they were happy to meet their best friends.

Simon was surprised and greeted his friends cordially. They were pleased to see him and Nicholas who was always welcome. "Nicholas, stay with me. I want your warmth next to me. Norma now has Simon," says Stuart. Nicholas smiled and sat next to Stuart. Norma was now between Simon and Jason. "Now I feel great," says Norma and everyone laughed. She either was glad next to Simon or pleased away from Nicholas. "Don't worry Nicholas. She does not know what you were in my age," whispers Simon. Norma smiled knowing Nicholas.

That night was pleasant. Norma was different and relieved of all pressures of the future. Her mother took down from the corner of the dining room the candle, lighted it using oil, and made her cross. She knew that Simon was not Christian. But she didn't care, if her daughter and Simon were happy. Her husband was not a devout Christian, anyway. She knew her daughter was free to choose! She knew she was happy and she was praying. But she knew also that Simon was not a devoted Jew, anyway. His mother and father were liberal people.

They were both born in Greece, and that was their country. That night was fun for all and at the end they left content. Simon left with Norma, after Nicholas was taken to his car, and Norma agreed to meet Simon again for dinner at Pete's Bar, next Tuesday. It was a new start! Simon was never so much happy before.

Next Tuesday at seven o'clock, Simon went to Norma's home. Simon met Norma's parents and happily took Norma for Dinner. They went to Pete's Bar and sat by the window looking at the landscape outside. It was really romantic looking at the trees and the grass next to the Bar. The music was pleasant and the meal especially tasty. Nothing was out of place, known for its good draft bier and hamburgers with round fried potatoes, good cheese and salad. It satisfied the taste of both and there was no need for special praise.

They talked about Norma's new job and Simon was sure that she was happy. It was what Simon wanted to hear. He wanted Norma to be happy next to him. It was the thing that was making him also pleased. He loved Jason more than any brother that he didn't have! Stuart was generous with two brothers and a sister already married. He used to say he was lucky and busy. His sister was willing to die for him if ever was a need. Everyone was happy to hear that: unusual and interesting.

They talked about many things and Norma asked, "You don't live with your parents now; do you?" Simon looks at Norma and says smiling, "Why? Does it matter whether I do or not?" Norma looks at him and smiling says, "No, for me it does not matter; I just want you and nothing else!" Simon continues his smiling and wonders. "I asked because I want to see the place where you live, and not anything else!" she says smiling. Simon looks at her trying to understand and replies, "I have had my place apartment for three years now, and I do not wish to disturb my parents. They love me and I see them often. Don't forget that they are Greeks."

She smiles and says, "Simon, anything you do I like. I want to know and not to order." "Okay Norma, do you want to see my place tonight?" he asks. "Of course I do," she replies. This made Simon happy. He touches her hand and says, "You know I love you!" She smiles and replies, "I know that; but you have to know that I feel the same about you also!" Simon smiles but says nothing. He was emotional and happy. He knew that Norma loved him. He could say that.

Soon after, Simon pays for the meal, greets the people who knew him at the place, and leaves. He drives to his apartment. It is not very large but very pleasant. It is facing the sea and it is very comfortable. Norma is restless and has decided not to say 'no' to anything that Simon wants. She is certain that he loves her as much as she does, and does not worry. But she is virgin and does not know how to act. She runs to the back doors facing the sea and says, "Simon, this is fantastic!" The apartment was at the top corner and could see the sea from the front and a park from the left side. There Simon had placed his dinner table. "I like having the good view; not only when I sit in a certain way, but always," he says. "It was the present I got from my parents when I received my C.E. degree from the Polytechnic School, in Athens," he says smiling. Norma looks at him and says, "Simon, I love you; but the things your parents buy for you are admirable."

She stops, looks at Simon and bashfully whispers, "Remember that I love you, and I love you naked," She said that bashfully and her eyes fell on the floor. She was wondering if he understood. That moment she was thinking what her mother had said: She was supposed to love her husband naked and share the rest. His mother was a nice Jewish lady who was married to his father who was Jewish also. He met his mother in Greece when he was a student at the university of Athens. He was an intelligent Jewish fellow that loved his son and his friends. He was friendly and humorously admiring Jason. Each time he met him he used to say, "Jason don't forget to love Medea and don't lose you sandal." Jason used to laugh and reply, "No, I love Medea and I will not lose a sandal!" After this, everybody used to laugh.

Simon lifted the face of Norma and kissed her. She looked at him and said with a smile and tears, "I am sorry, I know nothing more." Simon understood that it was his work after. He kissed her, he caressed her, he took her clothes out carefully, he put her on bed, and after started taking his clothes off.

He realized that she was virgin and he started trembling. She was really a beauty to see and never forget. He took off his clothes as well, fell next to her and started caressing and kissing her with passion. Not long after both were excited and uncontrolled. None knew what to do and what was doing. Simon felt that the woman was virtue and passion! He was really surprised and happy. He had found an intelligent and pure Greek lady. He loved her so much that tears flooded her eyes.

Once they were in bed naked, Simon was surprised: She was wild and uncontrolled. She wanted to have Simon and she was strong. He knew she was a virgin. She did not care what he thought as long as he knew she was his. The smile that he saw on her at the end, he will never forget. "I want you to remember that I will love you till I am dead; and I will never ask you to marry me. I wish to be the one to go with you in my arms." Simon understood what she was exactly saying and he knew that she loved him.

Jason is happy that Norma enjoys her studies, her work and Simon. She would probably reverse the order of things, but that is her choice and not his. She is a very intelligent girl, she loves her work and the Greek way; she has identified herself with Simon. "I want to be what Simon prefers, whether I know it or not," she had whispered. No one could argue with her, otherwise. "I am Hellenic and I want to be what my husband is," she used to say, if people tried to question or negate her choice. She wanted to be with him when he could; and wanted to be alone when it was necessary.

Norma had the talent not to interfere with what Simon was doing. When he could and she could, she was happy to be with him. Her husband was happy and Jason very satisfied. He was happy, he had done something so successfully. Jason was pleased and happy and people very content with Norma's behavior: Always willing, capable and pleasant. She was a pleasure to watch and never to regret. Jason was happy with Norma and proud to work with and rely on her participation in anything he was doing. He was indeed open minded and respectful.

Jason, Stuart and Simon, the three Musketeers, got together one night to discuss Simon's work opportunities. His friends loved him and wanted him to stay. Jason and Stuart thought that it was time for Simon to open his own Mechanical Engineering company. It was the starting point. But as soon as the two engineers with whom he was working learned about Simon, they approached him and asked if he would like to be the third partner. "I will discuss this with people who are my friends and I will let you know," he said. "Of course, you should know that I appreciate the offer, but allow me to discuss this with my friends," he added with a pleasant smile. Simon had a pleasant business smile and he was an intelligent Hellenic fellow of Jewish principles.

They were happy and told him to answer whatever it was convenient for him. They let him know that they all participate at work and there is no job for lazy, unproductive partners. They expressed their pleasure to have him with them, with no reservation. They knew Jason's good character, who Stuart was, who Nicholas was and who were his friends. They had known him for four years already and he had also a master's degree from England. He was serious at work and dedicated.

Simon was happy with Norma and she was still going to college. But he thought it necessary to discuss the case with his friends. He told them that they had to enlarge certain sections and they were happy to do that as soon as he joined them. He was besides an intelligent man with intelligent and successful friends.

Both Jason and Stuart were happy and they knew that both of the partners were appreciating their functions. They discussed the case and they concluded that it was to the interest of Simon to be a partner on an equal basis after the expansion. "Emphasize that you have the money, the connections, the experience, and the people to participate and deal with any problems in the business," said Jason. "Yes, let them know that you have the business connections to contribute and thrive," added Stuart. Jason agreed and Simon impressed said to his friends, "Thank you my brothers, I will do that." "And don't worry Simon, it will be fine no matter what," said Stuart. "Remember that friends are for always, and for all problems." Jason and Stuart loved Simon. He was a noble and devoted friend they could rest on as well.

The morale and the courage of Simon were boosted and he was encouraged. The three friends laughed and the rest of the night was filled with jokes and pleasure. Nothing could have made Simon happier. Besides, he was a unique friend hard to find anywhere. Simon was flexible and Stuart more strict; but Jason unique and brave. In life the carefulness of Stuart and the caution of Simon were needed. The three Musketeers: Stuart, Jason and Simon were really happy.

---

4 VIOLENCE IN THE PORT OF KALAMATA

"The harbour is separated from the shops by a Plaza"

The marriage of Simon and Norma was not something that Norma or Simon demanded, but what Simon's parents wanted. It was not a religious but a civil one. It was what Norma's parents were pleased to have. It made life easier for Simon and Norma.

He is a man and I am a woman, Norma used to say. She wanted Simon to feel that she deserved him, his friendship and his life; and nothing more. She had learned that if noble people are your friends, you will be noble and happy. Anywhere you go with them, in any case, you will be welcome! Norma used to say that and she was respected. The needs of her friends were hers and all they had to do, was to ask her politely. She was kind and tough.

Norma was a charm and she welcomed any friend who went to her. Simon could not find a better Greek than Jason, and he was always happy. But neither you could find a better friend than Norma. Next to her, you were always someone respected. Jason was happy with his choice. Norma was not only noble, but an easy pleasure as well. Jason was free to depend on her, whenever there was a need. He used to say that he was lucky to have friends like Norma!

Alice was doing very well with her first flower shop, and had located another place in old Kalamata also. She had mentioned and shown Louise the second place that she liked and she was moving carefully to eliminate Jack, before she could act and buy that as well. But fortune was not favoring her because the gentleman, as she called him, was not doing well and was turning his demands to an easy victim. But he didn't know she was only believing that with force one can achieve nothing, in the final analysis. That is how Jack became an expert in the use of guns and with no fear was pursuing his goals.

But neither he, nor others could measure Alice's philosophy. She had the natural feminine weakness but she also had the female persistence of surviving, winning and living, but not losing. The outside people thought that she was a whore, but the inside knew that Alice was a noble and intelligent woman. Jack really didn't know what to do. The solution was to leave her and go. But he didn't believe at that. The struggle was to be continuous: None was to be a winer with her. She might die but not lose. It was an insult to her intelligence and existence.

However, after he spent all her money in gambling, he demanded that she had to sell her beautiful body to support a gambler, as well. For him it was an easy job to have his money when he wanted. But he was thoughtless. He was asking the impossible from Alice. She was the daughter of Alexander Aristomenes: a man for her to think and cry.

And her brother? Her mother was thinking of him and she was crying. Alice had learned to wait for him since she was 10 years old and watch the streets North and the sea West. None ever asked what she was looking for, at the sea far. It was only the sky at the end of the horizon.

There was no way for Alice to do what Jack wanted. If he did not release her, she had to die a winner or kill him and be free. But she had to find the way to do that. He had raped her and she was crying every night after she realized her fate. No man was found for her to deserve her knowledge and abilities. She believed and hoped but as time was going on, her morale was decreasing, till a man, young, handsome and able was found. His name was Jason of the Argonauts. He was liberal but she was conservative and honorable. For him, love was a virtue.

She did not believe that she deserved Jason, but he gave her freedom because he was honorable and loved her. She did not believe that she deserved a man with so many virtues, and never told him that she loved him. He was patient and enchanted. The others were resigning but he was insisting. Her beauty and intelligence were her weapons. You could not see Alice and not think of her beauty, charm and intelligence. She was not Greek but very Hellenic and flexible. You had to be next to her to understand. She was Alice in love with Jason. She was Medea loving Jason. She was not going to punish but love him; no matter what he did.

However, she changed from a slave to a rebel, asking for freedom and revenge. You could not meet Jason and not revolt. His confidence and abilities were inspiring and charming. You could not go with that man and not become a rebel in pursuit of freedom. She realized that it was not just her beauty that trapped the man, but his virtues to see who and what she was. His friends were conservative but their respect for him was immense and worthy. If you needed something that you didn't have, he was quick to try to learn, to acquire it, and give it to you. He was a man to be admired and his companions were the Argonauts.

Jason's woman was beautiful and clever; and his advisor was Nicholas, a noble man hard to deny his advice and wisdom. He was not a man of force only, but one of brightness as well. His force was retreating to wisdom as he was growing older. It was a pleasure to be his friend whether you were a man or a woman. Alice was a woman.

It was one of those many Thursdays that Jack was to go to Athens to have his treat with his money and her money. With time he was expanding his activities in Athens and he was going more frequently there. Alice was still his choice but others in Athens were replacing her. She was a woman and not a fool. And if one assumes that she was also very smart, then he knows that she knew and she was praying that he stayed there. She was afraid that he was planning to take her to Athens by force and she was planning her negative final response.

With time, Jack was getting disrespectful and violent and this was forcing Alice to her final defense: Freedom or Death. She didn't know how to use the gun as well as he, but she was getting more effective with training and practice. He was not like Stuart and Simon either.

Jason was making money and becoming their leader. But money, when you gamble, comes and goes. You never know what you have and what will you have, unless you know there is a source to rely on or hope. Jason was not a gambler but a thinker to be respected. If you asked him, what he was doing, he would reply smiling: I am a Commodities broker playing music and loving women.

This Thursday, Alice was to be guarded by Miroslav and Vlasok. They were supposed to support her and be her friends, besides what else they were doing. Alice didn't care. She knew though that they were watching her and she realized that Vlasok didn't have the money and the charm to approach her. Miroslav was dutiful. She knew though that if she resisted as she was planning, he was thinking to be violent. She didn't care though, and she didn't believe that he was such an idiot. But there was always a possibility to consider. For one to get her, he had to have the knowledge, the youth, the money and the talent. None did as she defined that. She belonged to Jason and he didn't know.

Second, the cost was rising with age and decreasing with youth and beauty. It became obvious though that she was faking. She was making her money from the flower shop with Louise. But she was milked by Jack. So, she could not complete her second shop that she was planning. She was remaining though determined and hopeful. She had to play the whore because the bastard was either to take or kill her. She was not going though to fight him; but kill him. She had the female patience.

Vlasok decided to go first by servitude, then ask for her love, and then apply force and get her. Alice had decided that the only way for him was the alternative of money that it was going to cost a lot that he didn't have. They knew already that she was practicing shooting which did not bother the experts. Jack thought he was the best and he did not bother with such qualities. However, he had to be careful. He thought he was the best but he didn't know the story of the guns so well.

No man would risk his life to fight with Jack knowing his skill. Yet, the gun is a weapon for all, and all can kill you! Alice had seen that truth and was getting ready. But she didn't want to kill a bastard and go to jail. She had to wait for her chance. She would take it if she could; and waited. It was already almost a year and she was getting frustrated. She was really suffering. She wanted to kill him without being punished. She was going to need more money and she was going to have it. She was trusting her father's promise. His word was his honor.

As soon as Jack left, the master plan of Vlasok was put into action. He served Alice with servitude all Thursday and Friday morning. But Friday afternoon, Alice realized the awkward behavior of Vlasok. She put her gun under a handkerchief on her bedroom table on Thursday afternoon, as soon as Jack left. On Friday night, Vlasok was expecting Alice outside her house. "Ms. Alice, this is Vlasok. How are you tonight?" he asks smiling. Alice realizes who this man is and asks, "Hi, Mr. Vlasok; is there something that I can do for you?" "Yes Alice; Mr. Jack called me and said that he probably forgot a sealed addressed envelope on one of the tables in his room; and wants you to find it and give it to me to mail it tomorrow early in the morning; if you find it." It was not the first time that he had forgotten something.

Alice looks at Vlasok, sees him waiting and replies, "Just a second please." She goes in, looks around and comes out. "I didn't see anything left. I hope he didn't lose it," she replies seriously. "I know that he was not serious, but he wanted to check and be sure he didn't forget to mail it," he replies with a smile. Alice didn't reply but he continued. "He goes to Athens with all those ugly whores, forgets things and asks a beautiful lady to find his junk," he says pretending seriousness and sadness. "He leaves a beautiful lady, and fools around with her money in the casinos with others." Alice knew those things and was not surprised but she didn't answer and he continued with a confession of love that turns into portions of need for sex.

He promised to make her happy. He didn't care if she loved him and he didn't know how awkward he was. He only cared that she understood his passion and his wish to have her love and make her happy. But she didn't believe any of the things he said and she knew his objective. She was an intelligent woman worthy to be trusted with the truth or be left alone. She was not in need of any man. She wanted to get rid of Jack!

Alice looks at him surprised and gets terrified. "I understand you Vlasok, but you know that I am with Jack, and people who can pay me a lot. But not with ones who are paid to watch me," she says to send him away. She could not say that she loved Jack, no matter what happened to her. She was in love with Jason whom she would never betray, even with words. Vlasok was young and wanted Alice. He was also stupid not to realize that a woman has to reflect her passion before or after a noble act, unless she is a whore to be paid what she wants.

There was nothing shown for Vlasok who believed that any whore that he loved would sleep with him and follow him up on his offer. She couldn't say that she was in love with Jack or that Jason was her passion; and she knew that Jason was a choice for any women.

Vlasok, however, was really stupid, thinking that any whore would like him, if he wanted her. He was relatively young and ugly for a woman of Alice's qualities. He was not even as good as Jack. But he was much younger and that was where he relied. He had the deception of youth not being aware of Alice. That was normal and Alice understood.

Vlasoc approached her, confessed his love and tried to kiss her. She retreated to her bedroom and he followed her. His logic and his passion for Alice got mixed, and a fight began in her bedroom. As she refused and he tried to kiss her, she escaped and grabbed the gun from the table next to her bed and pointed that to Vlasok. "If you do not go away, I will empty this loaded gun into your stomach," she screamed. He stops, and she continues. "Get out before it is too late," she says bruised.

He stops and says, "I love you Alice; don't misunderstand me." "I said what I have to say: I have Jack and I want no others," she said strenuously. "Please, get out before it is too late for both." She didn't want to kill the bastard and go to jail. She wanted him to go away. "Please, get out and let's forget what happened. I will not let Jack know," she said hoping. He retreated slowly terrified and she breathed freely. She was more relieved than him. She was afraid what might have happened. He was really stupid. She was determined!

While he did not mean to hurt but just screw her, he only left when on her face blue bruises were to stay for some time. After that, Alice called Miroslav to tell him that she was sick and will not be out till she feels well. Vlasok heard that too and he didn't understand that he had left rough marks on the face of Alice; even though he suspected.

He left and called Alice to apologize to her for his daring. It was only his love and passion for her and nothing more. But she let him know that if Jack noticed, she would not be able to explain otherwise. "I advise you to leave the place; please," she said irritated. "You did the crime, you should try to correct it. Just leave, please."

Vlasok did not leave. No one could explain the small damage. But Alice had not learned to lie if she was asked. While Vlasok was worried, he didn't leave. The place was small, but he stayed. That was his big mistake. He was going to pay because Jack didn't mind if Alice was screwed for money; that was work and not prostitution.

Jack had developed his own philosophy on prostitution. God could save Vlasok from Jack. And none believed that Vlasok could fight Jack. He was too young to fight a beast. None knew where this would lead.

The following Wednesday, Alice came out and both, Miroslav and Vlasok played their role as instructed. When they saw Alice, they could tell the difference. Miroslav looked at her and said, "Alice, what happened to you? If Jack sees you, he will ask." "Well, who knows? By the time he comes, he may not be able to see and may not ask," she replies to him. "Wishful thinking," he whispers and smiles. Alice realized the problem and was resigned to telling the truth, if asked. If Vlasok could play with Jack, that was his choice. He knew though that it was her choice as well. She was not a vindictive woman with anyone. But some times she had no choice. She had to face the bastards and the romantics. Yet she was one, and much of everything.

Alice suffered but she had also the pain of knowing what was going to happen. It was nice: One of the two bastards was going to go, and she was going to have half of her revenge. The mentality of Alice was hard to understand. But she was professional now. She had given herself to Jason with passion, but to Jack unwillingly and now suffering with pain, patience and calculation. The question was: Does she really go with young people who have a lot of money and are her age?

She was really confusing and Jason was frustrated. But he loved her with passion and patience. He tried a few times to find out if she was really a whore but she did not like it, and he almost lost her. He was now patient to learn in the process. People in love are often confused.

Next Friday night, Jason came and saw Alice. He saw her and asked, "What happened to you Alice?" She looked at him and she said embarrassed, "Someone decided to screw me because he thought I was his sister. I miss you Jason; and I came to be with you. Please, don't ask what happened. Wait and you will hear." Jason and Alice, after more than a week, enjoyed their night with dinner and love that lasted till eleven o'clock at night. She wanted her guardians to report well on her behavior to Jack on his return. Alice was nervous and Jason wondering. He knew it was not a way to live and after leaving, each time afterwards, he was wondering and suffering.

But each time was his choice to be served by a beauty that wanted just his love. She was not accepting any money but Jason was attempting. So, this time she told him, "If you think I am a whore, don't come to me again." He apologized and remained, and never asked again. He was really a gentleman to be remembered and loved. He was a noble and above human pettiness and criticism.

The two friends of Jason were the ones to hear his complaints every time. Both Stuart and Simon were thinking and wondering. They knew that Jason loved Alice; and she did not believe that she deserved Jason while living with Jack. She had decided to die but not go to prison. It was too long now that she knew she belonged to a young man of the qualities of Jason. But what else could she do? She didn't want Jason to face Jack. But Jason knew that he had to face him and be free; or let him be free. His friends didn't agree with him on this and he was not allowed to face Jack. Simon and Stuart were asking him to wait.

All things happen when the time comes. He had two friends and the order to wait. "Be patient Jason," his friends used to say. But, he could hardly be. He was thinking and talking about Alice each time he met them. His friends had once to listen: Let him fight Jack and die or take the case themselves. There was no other solutions to honor Jason.

Sunday Jack arrives from Athens. He had missed Alice for more than a week. As he goes home, he sees Alice with signs of abuse healing. He looks at her and wonders. He smiles and asks, "Who did that to you?" She pretends that she does not understand and asks, "What are you talking about?" He smiles mischievously and asks again. "Who messed and bruised your face?" She looks at him curiously and asks, "Why, is there something wrong with my face?"

He looks at her and says, "Whoever has done that, he must have paid you a lot and I want to know him." She stares at him and with bitterness and tears replies, "Yes, but he had no money." "Then you should not have gone with him," he says. "Oh, Yes, I didn't go with him. Where were you to protect me?" she asks him crying. He feels embarrassed and says, "You have to tell me who that bastard was." She cries wondering if it is worth living with that decrepit creature or die. "It was your guard, Vlasok! What are you going to do now? Expose me and leave me unprotected?" He thinks and says, "Yes, I will leave him unprotected!" That night, he left and went to sleep. Alice cried and laughed with the bastard. He had no knowledge of honor. He wanted her to be a whore!

A few days later, Jack calls Vlasok to go together for dinner by a place at the beach. They go to eat and he tells Vlasok, "After they bring the service and we eat, I will tell you who is the man. Find an excuse yourself to hit him, and leave. But come later after an hour and wait for me across, down at the beach. In the mean time, I will come and meet you there." Vlasok listened carefully and after awhile, he gets up and hits the waiter. The nose of the servant was bleeding and Vlasok left.

The establishment owner came and Jack explained, "I don't know what happened, the two gentlemen quarreled and they had a fight. I think your server was wrong. He has to be polite and careful to your customers. But anyway, let's forget about it." The owner apologized and left with a bitter smile. There was no reason to get into details. They were useless and creating problems for all. The owner chose to forget. He realized that he had to do with an imposter. Only God could find a peaceful solution to Jack's problems.

Not long after, Alice came. She had eaten and accepted only a juice. After finishing her juice, she and Jack went down to the beach. There they see Vlasok waiting. He was surprised but he could do nothing. Jack, to be certain of winning, pulled his gun and asked, "Do you remember Vlasok who she is? "Of course I do," he replies terrified. "I told you Jack, not to take the case seriously. I was with a lady that I liked. She refused and that was it. Of course, in such cases you can't always control yourself and you become careless." "Otherwise, the man just liked the woman," says Alice. "Did the woman like the man?" asks Jack. "Yes, that was it and nothing more," says Vlasok terrified. Jack smiles bitterly and puts two bullets in Vlasok's leg. "Next, the bullets will be in your heart. You can ask a lady, but not demand using your filthy hands," Jack replies. He left the man and he walked on the promenade; and from there, he said to Alice, "You go now to work."

Terrified, she left hoping that Vlasok was just injured. Nothing more happened after. She left wondering what to say, if someone was to bother her. She was certain that she was seen by others as well, but nobody bothered her after. Jack realized that Vlasok was one of his own.

Vlasok was taken to a public hospital and everything was forgotten for a while. No one knows what happened to Vlasok after that. But Jack had to replace him. Two men were watching and wishing her, but none dared to bother her. She was not a whore to play with the bastards.

She was really a noble lady if you could forget anything else. This was a problem that Jason had to solve.

Alice was terrified realizing that punishment was not the cure to eliminate vices. The awareness of the vice and its elimination was the solution. Alice was a just woman and justice was not the punishment of the guilty ones, but the creation of the noble. The solution of the problem was difficult. You do not punish but create the right people.

Alice loved Jason; and Jason was wondering if she loved him. She wanted to die rather than not be with Jason. He was virtuous and ready to die for justice. One night, Alice spent it with Jason from seven in the afternoon till eleven thirty at night. They had their afternoon dessert, they made love in Jason's place and quite late, they met Stuart and Simon in Pete's Bar for their light supper. Alice had the opportunity to meet Jason's friends and impress them.

Norma met them there later and she was happy to see Alice. She was very conservative but happy and pleased to observe that young lady. "My wife must be bitching now; but it is not the weekend," said Stuart smiling. "I am sure she knows that the pleasure of kids replaces many other pleasures," remarked Norma. Alice smiles and says nothing looking at Norma with admiration. Norma saw the marks on the face of Alice but she was not surprised as if they were expected. "I am sorry Norma. It was not my choice." "No Alice, I understand that your beauty makes people unruly," said Norma with a smile and tears. "Yes Norma, makes them insolent and daring. They are distorted not knowing their strength. They think that all women are the same."

"The pleasures of Anna; only married women understand," says Jason looking at Alice. Anna was Stuart's wife smiling. "Yes, the others imagine them," replies Alice looking at Anna. "Can they imagine them?" asks Jason. She looks at him and says, "Of course they can. But who knows if they ever experience them before they become mothers?" says Alice wondering. "What do you think about fathers Alice?" asks Stuart wondering. Alice smiles and says, "Stuart, you should tell us; even though the opinions will be many." Stuart smiles and replies, "Is there anyone who will tell me that I know anything about children?" "Of course not," replies Alice smiling. "It is your wife that knows everything." Everybody agreed, laughed and Jason said, "I remember my father who was contradicting and condescending about anything my mother was saying or doing at the end." This made them all laugh. They seemed all to know about Jason's mother except Alice. She used to be a strong willed woman. So was Jason, and Alice smiled. She knew that Jason was not trained but he was a very noble and capable man to new ideas and behavior.

The time was about eleven thirty at night and Alice said, "You will excuse me; but I have to go." Jason got up as well and asked them all to wait for him. "Sorry ladies and gentlemen, but I have to leave for half an hour and I will be back." They all smiled but Norma was the happiest. She could not hide how much she admired Alice. When they left, Stuart said, "We must solve the problem with Alice." "Stuart, the problem is not Alice; the problem is the bastard. This is unacceptable to me. It is as if we live in slavery; and Jack is the master!" said Anna who was watching Alice with admiration. She was a strong willed married woman; and she had a massage that they all had to understand. She was a Greek lady and well educated for her children and others.

In half an hour, Jason arrives with a pretentious smile. "This is unacceptable to me and I have to apologize for my behavior," says Jason. "No, we have to think before we resort to such extreme measures," says Stuart. Everyone wants to do something, but nothing concrete has yet been proposed. "Give us some time, and we will find the solution," says Simon with a smile to Jason. "Please Jason, give us some time," adds Stuart thoughtfully.

They all left with a mixture of pleasure and hope. Stuart's wife was, however, the one more upset and suddenly sympathetic to Alice. She was not confined or bound with Alice's constraints. She was the Greek woman of violence when her rights are abused: Even to kill yourself like Souliotissa, dishonors your existence," was Anna's choice.

When Jack put the bullets in Vlasok's foot, he left knowing that soon Vlasok would be taken to a hospital. He didn't care; as if nothing had happened. Vlasok yelled for help as soon as Jack left and he was taken to a hospital by the police immediately. In four days after Vlasok was out, his brother came to take him back to Tirana. Although he was guilty, Vlasok wanted to avenge his injury. His brother explained to him that he was wrong and he had to forget it. "You were assigned a job and instead you decided to screw another man's woman; the woman you were protecting. Were you not wrong? asked his brother.

"No; I asked, she refused, and I left." "No, if you just asked, her husband would not be able to see nearly a week later what you did!" "Yes; but he didn't have to shoot me for that!" "I am glad he didn't kill you," replies his brother. "He asked you and he paid you to protect his wife, or whatever, and you decided to screw her or do whatever came in your head. Let's forget it and go back home. Your father is waiting for you; and he has the right to love you. I have the right to tell you the truth."

This brought tears into Vlasok's eyes and the brother said, "Okay, let's forget everything and lets excuse two fools: my brother and Jack." This was taking place at a table out in a Coffee house on Navarinou street. "Don't think that we cannot kill him, but he is not worth the possible penalties. We may lose one or two people, also; but no more. I do not think that he is worth it. We know that the woman was nice; but he was a fool. She didn't even complain. Let somebody else do it." Vlasok was sad but he didn't say more. His brother was an intelligent man: Not many now days are. Vlasok's brother was a rational man to be respected and admired. Justice was his virtue.

Not far away from Vlasok's table, there was another table. At that table a young man, no longer recognizable, came and sat not long after. He was holding three books and he started reading after ordering his coffee and pie. He emphasized also that he wanted a glass of iced water.

He was also taking notes while enjoying his reading. After more than an hour and a half Vlasok and his brother left. The young fellow watched them discretely but not carefully to betray that he was there waiting for something. He was just reading his books and taking notes.

Of course, Vlasok and his brother noticed him but left without suspecting anything about the young fellow. Indeed, no one could say that he was doing anything else besides studying and keeping notes. Ten minutes later, after the Vlasok brothers left, he closed his newspaper and note book and left. He was clearly one watching the Vlasok brothers.

Later at night, the three friends, Jason, Stuart and Simon were again at Pete's Bar eating their normal supper. "What was the result?" asks Jason, "The fellow that followed the Albanian brothers told me that Vlasok must have excused Jack and go with his brother back to Tirana," said Simon. "They recognized that Vlasok was in error and he must have excused Jack." Jason wonders looking at his friends. "So, we have to get Jack with a hidden man that will be waiting for him. This means that Jack will pass or be there where the hidden man can kill him." Stuart agrees and Simon is thinking. "Do you agree with that Simon?" asks Stuart. Simon is still thinking and then replies, "Yes I do. That is the best way for us." The three friends agree and decide to do that: To find one that will kill Jack.

Alice through Jason has proved to be a noble woman. Males and females have been admiring Alice. She is really a pleasant woman and a beauty to admire. Everyone was sad thinking of her fate. Jason was in love and loosing patience.

The next step is to find the killer; to have Jack there and kill him without any one seeing the hit-man. "But someone of us has to find the man who will kill Jack; and someone must force Jack to go through there," says Jason. No one could say 'no', but Jason says, "I will be the one to do it; I am the one responsible." "No; you will not do that!" says Stuart. Jason smiles and replies, "I will never accept a friend of mine to take my inalienable duties." The three think and Simon says, "No; none of us will do that. But only one of us will know who will do that.

Certainly, he will not be Jason. So it is: I or Stuart. But Stuart has a wife and two kids. It follows that I will be the one."

None could argue about that. Simon was determined and pleased. He was not to kill anyone, but to know the killer; and it didn't matter: None could argue. Simon smiled and he said: "It is one thing to know and another to do. None of us will do that. There is no much to say. Jason is our friend and our brother. We will do it and he will know nothing. Please, lets not waste any time on that, now."

However, Jason was doubtful and begun to argue. But Stuart said, "No Jason, you should not even be known." "That is right. So, it is my fate and my pleasure. I hate that bastard," insists Jason. Simon smiled seeing his friends arguing and said, "Stuart, you have two kids and a marvelous woman; you should know but not bother with the case. I am the one left. But don't argue yet. Stuart and I are better with guns and most qualified. Jason, please; leave the case to me and Stuart." Jason tries to argue and Stuart says, "Yes Jason, when you learn to shoot as well as I and Simon, then we will discuss the case. Leave it now to us." Jason tried to argue more but Stuart was smiling, making Jason think. Simon was remaining quiet.

Next day on Thursday, Alice called Jason and she said, "Jason, this is Alice; may I see you on Friday?" "You ask me? Of course you can see me; any time you wish." "Thank you Jason; we can go for dancing, if you want to." "That is perfect Alice; I will be waiting for you at my place." "Thank you," she answers and feels happy and restless.

She is thinking of the day, if it comes. When will she be free to see him whenever he wants? She gets lost and wonders if Jason knows how much she loves to be with him and talk and do many things. Before she goes to sleep, every night she looks at her mirror and wonders: Does he know that it is my choice to please him? Does he know that I can wait for him all night till he comes to kiss me? Then she feels her tears coming, and rolling down her cheeks. She was a woman in love that could not be ignored. She was not only a woman, but a gifted one also.

That is the time when she becomes a rebel capable to die in pursuit of her freedom. Now in love with Jason she hopes and can fight. Now she has a reason to become one of the best, in everything she does. Then she wonders, if he loves her; and her eyes close. They are beautiful and Jason is aware. He knows it is not her choice to be with a ruthless scum.

Stuart and Simon meet in one of those coffee houses on Navarinou looking at the waves in the late afternoon. Simon tells Stuart that he is the one to take care of the case. He knows the men that know how to shoot but wishes Jason to disappear and have nothing to do with Alice till everything is finished. "I know the people and I ask you to resign and temporarily disappear. If I need you, I will let you know," says Simon to Stuart. The eyes of Stuart focus on the eyes of Simon who replies, "Forget about it, and trust me. If I need you, I will call you. You know my voice." He does not appear to expect amy problem.

Stuart is surprised with Simon's persistence. "If you want me to be silent, I will," says Stuart. He looks into the eyes of Simon who is smiling. Nothing more is said and the two friends keep drinking their evening drink. Always, these people get into business after seven o'clock at night. They are honest with each other and there was no doubt.

They know that people change when they are caught, but there is no possibility for anyone of the three friends to do it. And they are certain that none will be tested. Besides, they love each other and Jason is willing to die anytime for them: They had to have the reason. Stuart tells Simon that he will call Jason to let him know where they are. He will ask him to join them if he can. "I am sure he will come," whispers Stuart smiling.

Not long after, Jason comes as always thinking and wondering about commodities and stocks. He joins them and happily starts his predictions. Stuart and Simon listen while Jason speaks. "Gentlemen, next week is our week. Cocoa is going to go up all week. We will buy it on

Monday and we will sell it after next week on Friday, the latest. I am certain that it is going to be the best."

Stuart and Simon ask a number of questions that Jason answers with pleasure. He tells them that he may sell the half on profit and keep the other half raising the limit price of sales. He was speaking with certainty that surprised his friends. After while Simon asks, "How is Norma doing in Commodities?" Jason looks at him and replies, "Simon, she is very sharp. I plan to have her work on commodities. She is better in what requires simpler thinking. I assure you that she is doing excellently. She is really amazing."Everyone is content with Norma: A beautiful and serious worker: Beautiful, capable and respectful.

Simon is happy, and smiling says, "I am happy Jason; she enjoys her work and I am pleased to hear the same from you." Stuart smiling says, "Mine is good in making the house, taking care of the kids and cooking as you know." Jason smiling says, "Don't forget Stuart that she is the best housekeeper I have witnessed and the best cook I have tasted; and the most capable, and you know what you are!" Stuart smiling asks, "Do you think I should keep her there Jason?""If I was, that is what I would do. But I assure you that she can do everything!"

"Why not Stuart? asks Simon. "Oh, don't worry, she knows how to take care of you too and she is proud also. She is really Greek," says Jason smiling. "Having a perfect home is better than having a perfect job," replies Simon. None disagreed with Simon. But Simon was young and they all laughed. "That is what you think if you are young with a beauty," says Jason. They all laughed. It was really the truth, let alone that Stuart's wife was intelligent and always available if there was a need. People were respecting Stuart and his wife. She was one not to be surpassed by anyone, once she was challenged and trained.

Norma just got in and as usual sat between Jason and Stuart. Then looks at Simon and says, "Wait Simon, and I will show you too." "I didn't complain sweet. I know you are precious and I realize that you will need a servant when you get your degree," replies Simon. "It's up to you Simon what I do; and I will be happy," answers Norma. She will be happy as long as he is content. He could not find a better woman.

Anyway, Simon reports that he will be in Athens next week, and hopes not to cause any problems to his colleagues. So he casually reports to his friends that next week will be hell, but after that, everything will be fine. Jason informs him that his partners are happy with him and he should not worry. He mentioned to Simon that both of his partners who visited him in the office were excited about his presence and impressed by his knowledge. He doesn't think that there will be a problem. "Simon, both of them admire you, and you should not worry," says Jason. "I am so happy to hear that," replies Simon. "You know, at times you wonder." Jason smiling replies thoughtfully, "Yes Simon. Don't you know that Norma is a Greek gift to admire?" Simon thinks and smiles content. He was certain that it was the truth.

Anyway, they left that night pleased and Stuart was wondering looking at Simon. He loved him so much that he could not hide it. "When you come back, my wife said that she will call you and Jason a Saturday night for dinner." "How could we expect something better?" replied Simon smiling. Jason heard that and said to Stuart, "I am sorry that I always have to treat you out in restaurants." "Better late than never," replied Stuart smiling.

Simon looked at Jason as if he wanted to say something and avoided that. Jason realized that but he also said nothing. A smile of Simon perhaps answered his question. Simon was the creation of Jason whom he always respected. He was a brown Jewish diamond respected and admired. The Jewish pride of flexibility, humility and persistence.

Simon was amazed. Norma loved him and when a woman loves a man she knows what to do. Simon had no other choice with a woman crazy about him. Norma was a jealous woman and loved Simon with passion. You could not wonder if she will kill the one who would take him away from her. She didn't look like, but you were sure that she would like to die next to him. She had a way to convince the man she loved. She had the art to transform her love to passion.

On Tuesday night, Simon met Stuart at their normal place in Pete's Bar. There Simon let him know that he was going to Athens for work on Thursday afternoon, to work on Friday and Saturday morning, and be back on Saturday night. Soon after, Jason came, and as usually, his head was filled with Commodities and Stocks. "Gentlemen, tomorrow we will have our results. I do not know how much will be our profit, but it will be substantial. On Friday we will know. Both Oil and Cocoa are moving substantially in the favorable direction. Friday afternoon we will take part of our profits and Saturday we will know." Jason was smiling and he ordered more beer with ham and the delicious round potatoes.

"In that case, Saturday night, I will know the news," says Simon. "Why, where are you going to be?" asks Jason. "The following Friday and Saturday morning I have to be in Athens to discuss some business on a new building. Stuart wants an estimate so I have to be there, this and the following Friday and Saturday. But I will be back on Saturday afternoon, both times, and I will see you here, as I said to Stuart; of course, if you can, be here as well." "Sure I will," replies Jason. "A night with my best friends makes life worthwhile." It was a pleasant remark that pleased both, Stuart and Simon. Anyone loved the presence of Jason in their company. He was physically imposing and mentally dictating. He was always considerate and pleasing. Ready to sacrifice himself for his friends. He was not an artist but capable to get rid of many and excel.

Not long after, Norma arrives. She was so pleasant that all three men got up to welcome her. They offered her a chair and she sat between Stuart and Jason. "The gentlemen know my place by now," says Norma. "Of course they do," replies Stuart smiling. "But in the beginning they didn't know," says Norma looking at Simon with passion. She was certain that she had made the right choice in the beginning and that remained her choice there after. "I know you will not try," says Stuart bending towards Norma. "I know and I will not try," she replies.

Stuart captured the double meaning and smiled. "But if Simon goes to Athens this Thursday, I will join him, if he wants," says Norma. "That is perfect," replies Simon smiling. "And Friday night, we may go to the Theater, if it is possible," says Norma. "Sure, we will," answers Simon content. He was happy that he was going to be with Norma in Athens. She was going to pick up the tickets and he was happy. After school she could go and be with Simon.

Simon's friends were delighted; both he and Norma were conscientious workers of rare species. Norma's parents were thinking where she was a year ago and where she was now, and they were thankful. Simon was their immortal god! Jason was Zeus always imposing and neither Stuart nor Simon ever minded his initiatives. They were always expressed when they were needed. Jason and Stuart were impressed with Simon's willingness and skills. Such a friend was hard to have! He was the youngest and the brightest Jew, Stuart and Jason had met. They didn't tell him though because they knew he was feeling Greek.

Simon knew that Alice was going out of her home after six o'clock in the afternoons. Then she was going into one of the coffee houses for her orange juice and tea on the square of the city. After that Simon didn't know and he didn't care where she was going. So on Wednesday, he went very early to work and just right after six in the afternoon he went to follow and talk with Alice. He sat inside in one of the luxury houses on the square of the City and was waiting. Not long after, he sees Alice coming in his direction. He gets up and goes to her as she is walking. "Good afternoon Alice," he says smiling. "Good afternoon Simon," she replies. "Is there something I can do for you?" "I admire your memory," says Simon. "You see, I am very young," she replies and both smile. It was as if they had a meeting.

"Anyway, what can I do for you?" she asks. "I want to talk to you, if you allow me." "Of course; if you have to pay," says Alice smiling and tears come into her eyes as she looks at Simon and thinks of Jason. "Sure I will," he replies. She looks at him and says, "If that is the case; lets meet, please, at the Elite Hotel on Navarinou street at about seven thirty tonight." "Thank you Miss," says Simon and leaves thoughtfully smiling and happy. It was as if it was planned and scheduled. It didn't escape Simon's attention. Alice smiled with a bitterness but said nothing. It was hard to think and say what she was thinking about. She had, probably, her own plans of liberation that Simon wanted to avoid.

Alice continued on her path to one of the special confectionaries and sat there thoughtfully for her juice and tea. After an hour she crosses the square and takes a taxi for the Elite Hotel.

Alice knew that she was a slave to Jack looking for her freedom; and she didn't want to do anything that would endanger Jason's life or success. She was not feeling happy with Simon but she knew there was no possibility of hurting Jason. She was respecting Simon and Stuart but she was in love with Jason. The evil floods the mind with evil thoughts.

Jason told his friends that they were right: He had to do something else! And he was intelligent enough to know what to do. He received his master's degree from Anotati Emporiki. He started to teach Basic Economics while he was working for his Doctorate in Economics of Trade. It was not getting him anywhere and he chose to trade in Stocks and Commodities and forget the glory. He was bright and decided to open a Trading Office in Stocks and Commodities. Those who knew Jason were very enthusiastic and encouraging.

Simon had studied Jack's art in shooting and he was certain that he would rarely lose but he was also certain that it was many times a matter of luck. He was convinced that it is stupid to let one shoot hoping that he will be slower than you. He wanted to have the advantage of killing his target before it could kill him. But he was fair, never to shoot at one who was not going to shoot at him. He knew that with the gun in his hand, he could fight for fairness. He hated Jack who was dictating justice holding the gun. Neither he, nor his friends had ever used the gun out of the shooting range or the hunting place. But he was an expert even though not as competent overall as Stuart. He was very capable, very meticulous and ready to defend his friends. Simon was a special type of man to be admired and wanted. He had the Jewish genes of not ever loosing because of pride or fairness. He could not be fair to an unfair!

But now, Simon was determined to kill that bastard who had no sense of freedom for others. He was a good fighter if challenged, and he knew that Jack could not use the gun to dictate his ways. He was anxious to teach him the justice of the gun if he could not accept the justice of reason. Simon knew that Alice was a noble woman abused by a rascal creature. He was getting mad seeing how Jack was using his gun to exploit people and satisfy all the antisocial habits he had learned.

Jason was brave and courageous. He was a brave fearless man. Simon was careful and brave. They were two friends ready to die, the one for the other. Between them, was Stuart: little older and capable, a man to be trusted! You could not debate this evaluation. But he had two beautiful children and a courageous woman hard to find. She was a noble Greek to be admired.

Anyway, Simon at seven o'clock in the evening goes to the hotel, gets his coffee and cookies and waits for Alice. He notices that ten at most minutes later a men comes and sits at one of the tables. Soon Alice comes and joins Simon. Soon after, another man comes and joins the man who came earlier. Alice tells Simon to rent a room, after a short period enough for their tea and coffee.

Simon did, and soon after, both got into the elevator. Simon preceded and Alice followed after five minutes. They got to the room rented by Simon and Alice. As soon as she got in the room, she hung up her coat and sat on the couch. She was looking at Simon wondering. He and she were never before alone in a hotel room. They smiled at each other. "What can I do for you Simon, if I can do something?" she asks politely.

Simon joined her smiling and said, "You know you are tempting Alice, don't you?" Simon sat on the other end of the couch. "Of course I know Simon. You pay and I will not say 'no' if you wish," she says wondering. Simon agrees, looks at Alice and smiles. Then he explains that Alice should meet Jack in the Hotel. "If you were not my friend's lady I would not be able to say 'no', but you know I didn't come for that." She is listening smiling and he explains:

" I want you to help me get rid of Jack for the sake of Jason, me, you and the rest. Next Friday night or Saturday noon you should go with Jack in the beach at the Elite hotel. After your dinner on Friday night or after your late breakfast on Saturday noon, from the inside of the hotel Elite you cross the street Navarinou to the promenade. There you either walk east on the promenade or preferably you go down the stairs on the beach. In either case you challenge Jack to run going east. That will be his end. Then you walk and take the buss to go home and wait for a call at night.

Alice smiles and replies, "Then, Alice and Jack will be dead!" Simon thinks and says, "No, Jack will not have a chance to shoot!" Alice smiles and answers, "Alice may not be dead, but she will be at least injured." Simon thinks but he does not answer. He lowers his head.

Then Alice says, "Fine Simon, let me meet you on Wednesday at the Elite hotel at seven o'clock to see the place." Simon lifts his head, thanks Alice and says, "Alice you have to know that you have captured all those who were lucky to meet and hear you." Thank you Simon she replies with bitterness.

The discussion was diverted to other things for an hour to pass. The last question of Alice was straight: "Will I be allowed to carry a gum during that time?" "Of course not," answered Simon. "Jason does not want you to be accused of anything." Tears run down the face of Alice.

After an hour and a half they left, and Simon was assured that no one would know their decision to construct and know about the crime. Neither he nor she knew who was to shoot Jack. He assured her that no one would know who she was. None knew with whom Simon was communicating; and Alice was wise not to ask or know.

5 TRIAL OF THE ABUSER AND GAMBLER

"The Trial of the Lumpen Proletariat by the Noble"

Monday, Alice was not working and her objective was to condition Jack. She had nearly two weeks to work but she could not have the money she knew he wanted unless fortune was to bless him all of a sudden. She was bitterly ashamed, after being sweet and tender to Jack. On Tuesday she met Jason for love. "I can no longer exist," she tells Jason on Tuesday evening with tears. "Since I met you, I want to either die or get rid of the pest. However, I do not expect you to take me. Please, try to understand: I love you but I don't deserve you." Jason is listening and thinking. He wants to act but the promise to his friends that she does not know, keeps him away for some time. She didn't know and she was supposed to listen and obey.

"If you are patient I will solve the problem," he says. She grabs his hand and begs him. "No Jason. It is my problem. Give me some time." "I am not doing anything," he says wondering. "Thank you Jason," she replies with tears. He gave her some money and she said, "Thank you Jason. I can no longer have a man touch me. I am sorry. But that is the way it is. You can see me Saturday after next. You will have your money back by the middle of September."

He looks at her, smiles and leaves wondering. Jason was puzzled but what could he do? Apparently, Alice had decided to finish the story herself: Either win or lose the game. Jason didn't know and he had to trust and wait for Alice.

The week passed and Alice was doing everything possible to please Jack. She was happy, and that Friday and Saturday were his days and she was not going to bother him at all. But next Friday and Saturday she planned to be demanding. She knew that Friday will be difficult, but Saturday was to be certain. She was no longer seeing Jason and this made her want him all the more. Jason was not seeing Alice and he was missing her also. This was making him mad and flooding him with frustration. He had to get rid of the bastard.

While Simon with Norma had an excellent time in Athens, Jason met Stuart and his wife at "Signal" and enjoyed the meal and the music of the place. The kids were left with a young lady at home to play as long as they wanted and after to sleep in the guest room. A discussion was started by Stuart's wife about Alice. "Jason, it would have been nice if you had brought Alice as well. From what I have heard Stuart saying, she is a fantastic woman." "She is a strange woman to be able to define," replies Jason smiling.

Stuart looks at his wife surprised and replies, "Anna, do not take Jason seriously. He does not understand. The woman loves him and she is careful. She loves him so much that she is willing to take for his comfort any punishment with no protest. She is involved by a criminal so that she is afraid something wrong may happen to Jason. I sense that she prefers to lose anything but not hurt Jason."

His wife looks at him and seriously replies, "Stuart, why don't you break his head so he understands?" Jason laughs and Stuart replies, "This is what we are going to do, my dear. But we have to think so we don't pay for that." His wife looks at Jason thinking and smiles. "Jason, be patient. Something is going to happen with only one head broken!" she replies smiling. Who knows? That woman must know.

Stuart is lightly reflective. "Yes Anna, we have to be careful so only one specific head breaks," says Stuart. Both Anna and Jason remain silent for a few seconds looking at Stuart. They really do not understand why it takes so long. They have no experience with people of Alice's qualities and problems and with Jack's corrupt morality. Alice wanted to kill

Jack and he could kill Alice with no remorse. He is a trained bastard in protecting himself.

The discussion continued lightly so they all remained pleased and Anna was convinced that something was going to happen. Jason was thinking wondering seriously. "Something must happen with that bastard soon," says Jason. "Only after we think," replies Stuart with a sweet smile. Anyway, after awhile they left pleased and Anna said holding Jason's hand, "I am sure, Alice is a beautiful and clever woman. That is life: The good things come hard." Jason felt more relaxed and was also more determined. But Stuart knew that Jason was idealistic and aggressive, while Simon and he were very careful and determined. They believed that they must win.

People complained that foreigners were intruding Greece corrupting the standards of the people. Athens and Salonika were corrupt: Patra rapidly and Kalamata slowly were now degrading. The Greeks were going into the University and professional schools; for professional work, business offices, trade and sales. But the foreigners were planting and harvesting and raping their land and their women. The Greeks were young but avoiding hard work. Jason used to say that they were unorganized and incapable of providing for the aging people who had the land but not the strength to cultivate, consume, save and live a noble old age.

Jason was upset that he could not have the woman who wanted him, and whom he desired, and a bastard was corrupting both! Jason was to act and be destructive unless a bullet was to stop him. He had to be careful dealing with people of Jack's qualities of vice. He had devoted his life training his body to use and respond to the needs of his gun. Jason could not hurt a man of Jack's qualities with guns. Alice had seen and was afraid to see again Jason face the filthy pig!

Sitting with Stuart outside at a table and staring into the Messinian gulf, Jason says, "The week after next we should try to bring that bastard around here and beat the hell out of him. We should not give him a chance to complain. You, Simon and I should approach him, and I will give him a lesson. I will take care of him while you and Simon are watching. Then we leave him there and we come here to take our coffee and pastry." Stuart is listening, smiling and wondering. Then he says reflecting, "Twenty to thirty years ago, I would have done that Jason; but not now. You shoot him and his little fellows disappear; if he is the leader." After hearing that, Jason remains thoughtful and Stuart is watching. "If I knew that you could use your gun, I would say, okay Jason, let's get rid of the bastard. But now we have to think."

Jason smiled. Stuart said seriously, "Now you are not the man for me to say that. Of course, if you want to be the loser, you kill him and you go to hell. Be patient please. We will find the man. You know how much we love you. So we hope to win. Wait till Simon comes and we will discuss that. Times have changed."

Jason has no other choice but to wait. He loves the revenge but he has to obey things that he and his friends agreed. Stuart and Simon trust him so much in everything else. But in this case, it takes thinking and patience. Jason has no patience. But you have to be calm, smile and shoot. Its the philosophy of the men who can and know.

Jason remains thoughtful and too embarrassed to speak. But he understands and says nothing. Stuart remains thinking and contemplating. "Jason, you must remember that someone must kill that bastard and the others who follow him will disappear. We must know whether he is a leader or a follower to act accordingly. Be patient, we are trying to find the right hand. I am sure we will." "I am sorry Stuart. I understand but I am frustrated and I want to kill the bastard," replies Jason upset. "I am sure we will get him wisely as you deserve," says Stuart with a smile to ameliorate the case. "After a week; you, I and Simon we will talk and we will finish the bastard. He is getting clever and insolent with the useless policemen we have. I am more frustrated than you are to have to watch anywhere I am going or standing. This is my land," whispers Stuart betraying his own frustration.

The two friends smiled and left. Each was expecting that the time was coming. But each had his way. Anna was now convinced that something was going to happen. She knew and trusted her husband. He was a man never to lose as far as she had witnessed. As they left, she smiled at Jason confident that Stewart was to act. She was sensing that time was approaching.

On Wednesday night, at dinner time, Stuart's wife after their dinner, fixes coffee and tea, for her husband and herself, and offers sweet dates with cold water. "This is the best I ever had," says Stuart after trying a date. His wife smiling says, "You know, I give you always the best when I want you to use your best efforts too." Stuart looks at his wife and smiling says, "Yes, I know. Please tell me, what it is now?" Anna was chewing her dates and drinking her tea. Then she asks, "Why is it so hard to take care of that bastard?" Stuart looks at his wife and replies, "Do you refer to the bastard who is pestering Jason?" "No Stuart, I am referring to the bastard that is torturing all three of you." She stops and waits for an answer.

Stuart thinks and replies. "Yes my dear, I am referring to that bastard that tortures all three of us. But be patient." "How patient can I be?" she asks seriously, apparently without worrying. Stuart looks at her and thinks, but he gets lost in his thoughts and his wife is ready to laugh. She was right because she has being waiting too long. She could no longer tolerate the situation. Things were really getting confusing and everyone was suffering. Anna could no longer understand. She was a real Greek woman. She can die but she can no longer wait and suffer.

Stuart looks again at his wife and says, "Yes dear, I understand. You are a Greek woman. Saturday night, Simon will be free and we will discuss the case." His wife laughs and says, "I am sure that if I and Norma were Jason's friends, we would have solved his problem." Stuart looks at his wife and asks irritated, "Why don't you do it my dear, you are not his friends?" "Because you do not keep the kids yourself, to surprise you!" she replies calmly, drinking her tea and chewing her dates. Stuart remains puzzled and thinking. But he says nothing and his wife laughs. He could see she was bitter. She got up and left. He didn't answer her question. Apparently he didn't know enough about educated Greek women.

"Anyway, do something and help your friend," she says smiling. "If you think that we could not have done something, you are wrong. You may be stronger but we are more resilient and lasting." Anna had never talked to Stuart with such a spirit. He said that he was surprised, and she smiled contentedly. Soon after, Anna got up and left. Stuart was left alone wondering. His wife was right and Jason rightly frustrated. But no one knew what Simon and Alice were going to do something. Of all people, Alice was happy and unusually expecting success. "That bastard has been taken kindly for too long," whispers Stuart thinking of his friends' frustration and torture.

For Jason, enchanted with the beauty and wisdom of Alice, what excuse would he have to ignore her? How if she killed his children later like Medea out of fear from Creusa's charm and other virtues? Jason could not abandon Alice like Medea. Jason didn't know but he was afraid. He was afraid that he would not wish any glory from the killing of his children by Alice and her escape to Agius Saranta in Albania. He had to do something to free Alice and enjoy her love and share her virtues. If she wants him, and he is crazy about her, why anybody else has any reason to interfere? It is just human and Jason had to learn.

If anyone had seen her, he would have concluded that she was desperate because she did not believe that she was worthy of Jason. That was true, but she wanted him and nothing more. The young lady had found the noble man she was dreaming for years. But she didn't deserve him. At least that is what she was thinking. She was really a Hellenic woman. She didn't have any faith in any system that was killing. She wanted to be noble.

She wanted something only if she thought she deserved it. She preferred to kill Jack if he was to bother her. But this was to happen if he didn't disappear. That is why she wanted him to disappear.

But it was not easy. He was a pest that he wanted to live on others. The idea only was making her life miserable because she was a capable woman without boundaries. But Jason? He was a noble man without limits. He was admired and respected. If her pimp was only aware of Jason, he would have committed suicide. She was not in need of a man, but one that resembled her father. But now she didn't deserve one: She was a whore that she could have anyone as long as he paid. These thoughts were not true but were making her resign and cry. "I am a whore!" she was whispering and crying. Perhaps she was hating herself because she had accepted a scum. But she was deceived.

She was raped! Now he had to pay. She didn't want to be responsible for any crime. But she was Alice and had to be rough to survive. She had to be free and find her mother. Alive or dead she had to see and kiss her noble mother. She had lost her brother and she was now responsible. She had to find her mother and tell her that the man who had raped her was dead now. She had to find her and let her know that she was indirectly her revengeful daughter.

On Wednesday late afternoon, Alice was to meet Simon again at the Hotel for a tea. Simon was there, sitting behind the main entrance. Alice arrives a few minutes after and smiling joins Simon. After ordering their tea with biscuits, Simon smiling says to Alice, "Do you see where we are?" Alice looks carefully and Simon continues. "This is the main entrance of the hotel." He stops, takes a sip of his tea, and continues while Alice is looking around casually. "Do you see where we are?" She looks ahead at the beach and replies,"Yes I do." "Please, tell me what do you see?" She looks ahead, thinks, and Simon continues.

"Do you see the street walk? The street with passing white strips; the promenade, the stairs, the trees, and the beach with the waves? And as you are going down to the beach, to your left there are trees." "Yes. I see the trees," she replies. "Well, not this Friday, but the following Friday in the afternoon after seven o'clock; or on Saturday in the morning after eleven o'clock, I will expect you to take Jack to walk with you from here to the waves by the beach. But you should run towards the waves to your left as soon as he steps in the beach. Ask him to catch you if he can," says Simon looking at Alice and wondering for her reaction. "Yes; I see," she replies smiling and thinking.

Both, Simon and Alice are drinking their tea and thinking. "If he chooses to walk with you on the promenade, take him to the left, preferably; but if he chooses to walk on the promenade to the right, follow him. But keep a distance from him, if you can." She looks at him curiously and replies, "Yes, I understand," and continues to take her tea. She likes it more than Simon. Jason has captured her mind and her body. She talks with Simon but cannot help it and thinks of Jason.

Suddenly, Alice looks at Simon wondering. "And where are you going to be then Mr. Simon?" she asks. "I am sorry, but I will be in Athens. You would not have to do anything but ask him to join you for a dinner on Friday night, or for a lunch on Saturday morning." Alice does not answer but looks at Simon wondering. "Alice, don't worry if he comes with you in the beach or not. As long as he gets out of the dining room he will be treated as he deserves. The man who will shot him is perfect. But he has to get out from this door," he says and points out the door with his eyes. It was the main door that all people were coming in or going out from the hotel. As a guest she had no other exit to get out. He is calm and determined.

Simon was certain that he was talking with a very intelligent woman. She was certain that Simon was intelligent and one that deserved Jason's friendship and attention. With a smile she said, "Simon, Jason must be proud that you are his friend." Simon looks at Alice and replies, "Yes Alice, I am so proud and fluttered to be Jason's friend." She remains thoughtful and Simon adds, "Lucky are those who win Jason's friendship." She looks at him with admiration. Simon has won already her admiration because he has Jason's friendship. She cannot help it to hide her tears. Simon can see and understand that.

After some trivial discussion, Alice left content that Simon was Jason's friend. She was now wondering whether Stuart was to be for Jason as valuable. If you know the friends of Jason, you know they are noble and capable. This meeting with Simon, left her content and hopping: She was feeling now to be respected by the friends of Jason. They were noble and trusted. She left pleased and inspired by Simon.

She extended her appreciation to Stuart as well. She remembered what she was told by Jason about his friends: They were noble and trusted; and if you questioned their friendship you were denying their values with no reason. They sat with him on the same desks, listened to the same teachers, read the same books, and played the same music.

Alice had to be nice to Jack till Friday night and or Saturday morning. She had to help others kill him; she had to kill him; she had to kill him and herself, or kill herself also. All he wanted was money to gamble and screw her. He loved to screw Alice as long as she was bringing him money. Otherwise, it was for him to kill her. This made her sick. It was not worth any longer!

She had to bring him money. It was her only way to control him. It was not the only way to please him. She had to enjoy his sex as well. This time she wanted to be successful. She could not get away, and he would not let her alone. She had to be with him where she lived. She had no choice. She was constantly watched. He or she or both had to disappear Friday or Saturday. Of course, all was planned but not executed. Alice smiled bitterly. She had to rely on others!

Two men were watching her when Simon was going away. He didn't tell her, but she knew. She cried more and her eyes were getting dry. She had to kill him or kill herself. But she had no more her gun. She calls Simon to ask for her gun. But she was told that he was in Athens. She resigned and cried more. She decides to follow what she had agreed with Simon. She called his girlfriend; but she did not have and could not give, if she had his phone. She no longer tried. She didn't care if she died. She decides to follow Simon's orders.

She really liked the orders but she was afraid. They were given her the opportunity to see the noble Jason again with no fear. She knew he was noble and brave. She knew he was unique. But some way she formed the idea that she didn't deserve him. Was she right? She was a noble woman drawn to prostitution in order to live and get revenge, at least before she died. She knew the time was to come. Either she, or Jack or both had to go. She had met a noble, rational and brave man and she had to follow him. Who was he? Jason and nobody else. Did she really know?

Holding her tears she called Jason at his office. "High Jason; this is Alice." "Yes Alice, remember that you can always call me. Don't forget that I will always love you." "Yes Jason, I am aware and I will always love you. But now I need $500 to give it to you by the beginning of September. Can I have it?" "Of course you will," replied Jason. "You will have it in fifteen minutes. But call if you need anything else. "Thank you; Jason," she replied and hang up crying. Jason put $1000 in Alice's account wondering. He knew that Ismene was not feeling well. She was frightened and ill maintained. But he could do nothing.

Alice was to be nice to Jack till Saturday noon at least. Jason loves her and she is going to die for him before he tries anything and possibly fails. She wants to die for him, but wants to live till she kills the man who is torturing her. She hopes that Simon succeeds and she will do anything he wants. She hates the man that all he wants is to give him money and screw her. He was a male whore; an imposter. All he wants is more money, to screw her and nothing more.

Was he the whore? It was the question. Yes, he was and she was. He is a suspicious man and drastic changes will not help any. Sometimes he has a lot of money and others he is broken and dependent on Alice. None understands Jason, but all love him because he is noble. She was crying for a noble man. He had never met before a lady like Alice. Her virtues were capturing. She was her lost father.

"He is very capable and honorable!" said Simon. "I know that better than others and I love him. I can say that to you." "But I don't deserve him," she answered to Simon with tears. He looked at her and replied, "Alice, our man is not a simple man. If the pig comes out from the hotel with you, he will be dead; if he comes out with you and tries to walk on the promenade, it will be easier. If he goes to the beech we will have an easy game. But he has to come out from the front door alone or with you!" That was her duty.

She went upstairs to a room five minutes after Simon and left after about an hour to be sure there was a record. But she had seen Simon so little and she had good reasons to doubt. She left depressed but determined: That bastard had to die before she did. All he wanted her, was to be screwed, to give him the money, and to screw her: He was a male whore! How else can one call such a man? He was distorted mentally and physically. Alice was determined to be a whore. But, was she? Yes, unless she was to die. It looked that the time was approaching. She could no longer live like that and she had accepted Simon's plan because she was convinced that no noble man was in danger! Was it true? Nobody knows to say.

The following Wednesday morning Alice took care of Jack as it was appropriate. The breakfast and her love were as perfect as at the start, after she had given herself to a gentleman. She was already an artist if she wanted. She was thinking about that and she wanted to kill him and then herself. She hated to know that such people existed. On Wednesday night at her home, she made excellent dinner and said, something like this: Jack, I am sorry every time I make you feel sad, saying improper things. I want to make you happy and I fail. That is the time I want to kill myself. To love someone and not being able to please him and make him happy, it is a good reason for one to die. For this failure of mine, I don't care if I die. I know, I say lately improper things. And I know you don't understand. I want your child. Am I asking you too much?

Jack is listening and while tears run on her eyes, he says, "Alice, you should know I love you." He said that wondering. "Yes; I know. Now that I am young, I can bring you what you want; but tomorrow? How will I show you my love? I will be a useless whore with no money." Tears run on her cheeks as she cried. She was not crying for him but the truth. She was thinking to do anything that Jason wanted and demand nothing.

She was sure that Jason was never to violate the honorable will of any woman. She was wondering why he wanted her. May it have been that he was seeing her situation? It may, but she could not excuse herself. She loved him and she hated herself. If she had a knife, she would have committed suicide. But that was not noble. She had to kill the bastard first, without paying anything. Not to pay for the death of an impostor. But that was life and she had no choice other than what Simon was pointing out.

Jack looked at her today, as usually possessed by the truth; to forget her tomorrow. But this time he said, "Don't cry Alice; soon we will pay our debts, as we have done before, and we will be able to save." She looks at him and says, "Thank you my Jack; and don't forget what you promised me long ago," she says with tears. While he was thinking, she kisses him with passion and drags him back to the bedroom. It was still early in the morning and she made love with him.

It was still early and none could say what she was feeling. She cried more, anyway, before she kissed and caressed his hairy chest. She was sure that he was going to forget, but she had to try. He was a gambler and then a lover and then an exploiter. Alice was trained and capable now to deceive anyone. She didn't like that game but she was a charming artist; one to be admired.

Anyone who is a gambler should be aware of the passion that dominates the brain: That drives one to the ugly table with the men, the women, the drinks, the cigarettes, the coffee, and the cards when you are in the club or the casino; and if not that, it was the horses with the young women in Athens. Alice was the whore watched by two paid men in Kalamata, while he was enjoying the women and the horses, as well, in Athens. It was unbearable to live. She must have been a bitch!

But it was hard to say. She was abused and could no longer behave. She wanted to kill Jack! But a wish is not always a possibility. It takes more that Alice didn't have it yet. She had to be trained and then to kill.

But it is not an easy process to kill as it is to injure. Any one can injure but not kill without being captured. You had to know how to do it.

One of the men, watching her in the City, approached and tried to rape her when Jack was in Athens. He didn't succeed but left her with slight bruises. She locked herself in her house and two days later, when Jack returned, he saw her with the marks. She explained to him what had happened and one night he shot the man in the beach with four bullets while she was watching. "Tell the next one who will try, that he will be shot like a filthy horse," he had said. He liked good horses. He took her back to his car and left the man die. She was trembling and he said, "That is what he, and anyone else who will try to rape you, deserves." He said that looking ahead and at the mirrors in the back as he was driving. He was indeed afraid. But the man was not from Kalamata and none knew what happened to his body after. She was feeling miserable but the man should have been careful. Each one is at the end rewarded for his actions and their results.

"You know that he did not manage to rape me," she said awkwardly. "You know it is better to die than to let any bastard touch you," he said while he was driving carefully. When he said that, she was thinking of Jason. "It is one thing to work and another to make love," he said convincingly. She didn't say anything then, but she was crying. She was still then with the black marks on the face. It was evident that she could not hide them. Those that were to protect her, were the ones that could not many times protect themselves from the attraction of Alice. She was a unique temptation. She was a woman to be admired by the wise and be wanted by all and especially by the young and the scums.

On Thursday morning, Alice made again excellent breakfast for Jack. She took him for love again in the bedroom that made him forget everything. "I want you my honey, to have you again tonight and have a child with you; of course when you are ready and you want one," she added relaxed and thoughtfully. He looked at her, he felt her caressing his hairy chest and he said, "Yes, we should have one as soon as we have paid our debts, honey." Staring to the past and thinking about his debts that were pushing him to more gambling, was only making him hope. "Well, I understand. But Saturday we may go in the morning for breakfast and in the afternoon to work," she says thoughtfully. It takes time for him to answer; but finally, he answers while Alice was caressing his chest and was waiting.

On Friday night, Alice is waiting for Jack reading a book, as usually. Books are her company and comfort. They make her forget. She lost her first chance of Friday. She feels depressed but books make her forget. At about midnight Jack arrives. The expression changes on Alice's face. She becomes filled and pleasant. She gets up and kisses him with a smile. She could be a marvelous actress. But she didn't like the profession. "Do you want something?" she asks. He takes off his coat, hangs it, looks at Alice and says, "Yes please; can I have a coffee with water and a glass of wine?" "Yes Honey," she replies and goes to the oven. She makes a cup of coffee, fills a glass of wine of his choice and a glass of cold water.

"Do you want something else honey?" she asks. He looks at her and replies not so pleasantly. "No honey; I had just a bad day today." She is sitting next to him in the table and waits. "Six hands were so bad that I had to leave by the seventh," he replies very upset. She delays to answer; lets a smile form in her lips and says, "Honey, I was lucky today. A business man from Athens met me at the Coast Hotel. He looked rich and after three hours everything was complete. Next time will be your turn." She got up, and gave him 500 Euros. She knew it was the sweetener. But, it was very bitter for her mouth. One could see her bitterness, but not the bitter Jack.

Then she continued. "He was so enthusiastic that he called me for breakfast tomorrow. But I remembered our plans for tomorrow morning and I said that I will call to let him know." He looks at her and asks, "What time in the morning does he want you?" She thinks and replies: "I bet you any time; he will be happy. But to get any money, it will have to be very early. I gave him though my phone to call me next time. I also promised to see him in the morning for breakfast at eight, only if I could." She was a talented actress by now. She was a good student for all teachers; and a good teacher for all students.

He looks at her again and says, "Well, you may go and see him any time you want, and when you are done, you give me a call. I will be ready by ten thirty and you can call me any time after." She listens to him, smiles and says, "Okay honey, I will go to see him and by ten thirty, I will call you." She kisses him and goes to sleep. He was very tired, but he went to sleep much later. She was wondering if he knew what to expect. She had no choice. She had to do something before she hated herself. She really wanted to commit suicide. She fixed the alarm and fell asleep. She was very tired and frustrated. She was feeling to be a whore. But she was still hoping.

In the morning, she got up and didn't want now to make any mistakes. She left at eight, and at about eight thirty, she went to the hotel. She was an artist and she was beautiful. She had no problem to find a place for breakfast alone or next to another gentleman. She was pensive that morning and sat alone for a light breakfast. She was sure that she was not followed by anyone. None knew what she was thinking. But that morning she was very different and looked determined. None could tell the decisions that were made in her mind. But she appeared very peaceful. She was a capable actress. Soon she would do something that she hated but she had to do if she was not going to commit suicide. She smiled thinking of her crime. She was not going to do it, but be innocent. It was very hard for her.

Alice gets absorbed now in her own fate. She is alone and if she attracts anyone she knows to let him forget but not stop him admiring her. A gracious smile is enough to disarm any man no matter what the age could be. After that, anyone was convinced that Alice was in her own world: Concentrated and pleased.

She was not a conceited female, but a noble young lady concerned with her own problems; and her problems were not the ones of a young charming girl but of a knowledgeable, educated, attractive and informed lady. People were pleased to see and admire Alice. It was not strange that Jason was fascinated by that young lady. She was the product of her father.

She was certain that she had no weapon and could not be guilty. She knew she was either to be alive or dead. Jack was not going to make a mistake and forget about her if he was to be shot. The sound of the gun of the killer had to be faster than the ear and the motion of Jack. She was sure it was going to be, if not seen before by Jack; and if it was to be accurate! She smiled at the thought and she no longer cared. The killer had to know and be accurate. Otherwise, it was to be a matter of luck. She had no gun and decided to relax. It was impossible to assume that she was peaceful. But she looked like. She was a charming actress.

While she was resting for the time to come drinking her tea, she notices a young man getting in the breakfast room and looking around. He sits by the glass-wall opposite of Alice looking at the beach. He orders his breakfast and opens a newspaper after ordering. He could not deceive the eyes of Alice. He was charming and attractive. Alice lowers her eyes and remains thinking and drinking her tea. As she looks at the sea she sees the left of the young man put behind a newspaper. He was able to see Alice, as he was unfolding his newspaper and reading. Nothing seems to bother Alice as the young man is charmed. Alice plays the attracted and smiles.

The young fellow catches the eyes of Alice and sees the attraction. Alice gets up, takes the bill to pay and goes towards the young man. As she was approaching the young man gets up and invites her to join him. "I do not have much time but I will join you for a few minutes," she says smiling. He offers her the chair opposite of him and she accepts. She sits down and a conversation begins. She was charming to the man and she started a communication.

The waitress comes and Alice accepts a juice. None can hear the conversation but it must be pleasant. After a short exchange of normal discussion, the young man offers her a card and Alice accepts it with pleasure. She reads it smiling and puts it in her purse. He had brown hair and dark blue eyes. He was young and charming. Alice liked him and he was fascinated by her femininity.

Not long after, Alice gets up, greets the young man and smiling whispers, "Who knows? We may meet again some time." Smiling he replies, "Yes, you have my phone number but I do not have yours. It is difficult for me not to ask you to give me a call when you feel." Alice smiled, said something and left. She was sure that she was not going to meet the young man again. He must have been little older than Alice.

6   EXECUTION OF JACK THE RASCAL

"Execution of a Rascal beautifies Life."

At about ten in the morning of Saturday, Alice parks and enters the Elite Hotel on the beach. Immediately she calls Jack and she tells him to come to the restaurant. She is sitting on the table behind the door at the entrance. It was a nice place because none could hear their conversation, whatever it was to be.

She knew it was not going to be pleasant. She had to meet Jack the rascal. He was already sentenced to death alive. Alice and Simon had committed him to death. But that was not their legal or moral profession. It was though liberation for Alice and Jason, or death for Alice and freedom for Jason. It was to be freedom for any of the possible victims of the scum. She was convinced she was noble.

At about ten thirty in the morning, Jack arrives smiling. He sees Alice, gives her a kiss and sits at her table. "How did it go honey?" he asks. "Let's order our breakfast first and I will let you know," she replies smiling and giving him a kiss. She knew how to smile when she was to cry. She knew how to cry when there was no hope. All Jack wanted was Alice to be screwed and he to be entertained.

This time she was different. They both wanted something light and after giving their order she said, "Everything was fine, honey, but he was ready to go when I arrived. I joined him for breakfast and he promised to see me next time when he comes. He was really a pleasant person and one to rely upon. He will be my customer when he comes; for sure." It was a story that Alice could expertly transmit.

Jack looks at her and says, "Its fine honey; to have reliable customers." He was thinking of regular customers and regular income. She smiled bitterly realizing that he thought she was going to be his whore slave forever. But she didn't care anymore. She knew that she was to be his slave forever if she didn't finally either kill him or die.

"Yes honey, he is married and reliable," she said confidentially and content. She was sure he was repulsive and she didn't want to live anymore that way. It was today the day of execution of a rascal. She was getting optimistic, smiling and convincing. She was a strange young lady as always attractive and as she wanted to be. But this time she was to be the loser or the winner. She had no other choice.

Death was better than life and his company. She thought of the noble Jason and almost cried. She knew that one day Jason would kill him anyway. But she barely held her tears. Her thought was her hope. The time was getting shorter and Alice could no longer live in slavery. She knew how to kill him and then commit herself suicide if there was a need. But that was not enough or certain. She wanted to kill him and then run to Agius Saranta. She wanted to kill him and then be free: It was noble but difficult.

Jack was irreparable. He had dark hair, average height, brown skin, and looked rough. "It's nice that you came," she says touching his hand with the rings. Both he and she are well dressed and nearly the same height. She is beautiful and young. Jack is not ugly but rough and middle aged. His eyes are brown in contrast to the blue-green eyes of Alice. They are talking for awhile till the light breakfast comes. Alice is smiling while Jack is serious. As soon as they finish their breakfast he gets itchy. Alice cannot understand.

You could not hear what they were saying but as soon as she holds his hand asking him something, he pulls his hand and gets upset. She wonders why the hell he gets upset all of a sudden and why he is so angry. He was probably expecting more money. He was probably thinking of his debts. He had already screwed Alice or wanted to screw Alice again. Whatever it was, it had nothing to do with Alice. But it was Alice to bear the insult and offense, never knowing what it was. Certainly, it was not for long pleasant. If she had said to follow him in Athens, everything would have been, probably, fine with promises.

Who knows? Why the hell he is so upset, she wonders. But not like other times, she is patient looking at him and wondering. "I can never come to you; and you can never leave me in peace for the last year," he says. This was surprising and unreal. But she didn't leave like other times to go to her filthy job. "I am sorry Jack; I never thought that I was so rude and annoying. I just love you," she says. But she didn't leave like many other times. He is thoughtful for a while and Alice is smiling wondering. She could not understand.

He looks at her and says, "Let me pay and go with you to the beach as you want." Apparently, he didn't like to go to the beach; and had no reason to say 'no'. It was still early before lunch. He had promised to go to the beach with her, to walk along the edge of waves and laugh before going back at home, and after to go to work. It was Saturday morning, anyway. The critical time was approaching and Alice was getting nervous but pleased. She had no other choice.

She didn't know how better she could do, to be natural. He was restless and uneasy as usually with her. Only the devil could explain. But in any case she was not a machine constantly producing money. She had decided already to die. Soon he was going to know if any God exists. But does he exist? That is the question torturing the mind.

The man had problems that could not control. She was not really his problem, but he wanted to be alone. He wanted to know how to be free. But freedom is not the gift for people of his type. He was a gambler and more money was the solution. After while she tells him before they leave that she has to go to the wash room. She kisses him and says, "Don't worry Jack; everything will be fine. Wait five minutes please."

She was really acting, but she was always the same pleasant spirit. She goes to bathroom and in ten minutes she comes out smiling. She was as always attractive and provoking. "Don't worry Jack, I will help you more. We will pay our debts and be free; we will make it. Do you promise? Don't worry," she concludes smiling.

He looks at her; she smiles and says, "Do we go now?" "Of course," he replies with a smile. He believes that she will help. She is really an artist. She had to be, to live with that man. To be his slave, lover and whore it was unbearable. She was not his fate but his fault. She was a noble woman to be left free or dead. He was now sensing a change in the charming behavior of Alice that he was trusting more.

Both get up and go out from the front door. Alice goes ahead tired and upset. But she knows how to hide it. She proceeds and he follows. She is silent and really afraid. But she does not leave him till they cross the street. As they walk on the promenade she tells him something and continues on taking the stairs as naturally as one can do. He follows her down the stairs carefully. It is his habit to do so. He is instinctively careful. She realizes that and gets afraid. But her smile can hide the truth. She is afraid but he cannot tell. He was flattered by Alice an artist in flattery. She could be anything, but she wanted to be herself.

As soon as they step on the sand she looks at him, says something and playfully runs towards the waves to the left. Between her and Jack to the left, near to the side behind, there are trees at the edge of the promenade on the sand. But nothing is obstructing the views on the beach. A fellow was sitting on the bench of the other side of the promenade enjoying the deep sea of the beach and reading. He was not the only one communicating with nature. It was still cold though, but very pleasant. None could see who he was and what he was doing. But none was interested in knowing, anyway. He was a stranger none to pay attention to. He was reading his newspaper and on the bench he had his books. Nothing interesting to attract attention but still chilly.

Alice begins running to the left as you look at the beach. "Catch me if you can," she says to Jack smiling and peacefully. "I will show you who can run fast." He advances slowly. He looks to his left carefully; then to his right. He looks again carefully to his right and loses his forming smile. He sees a man coming and rapidly pulls his gun and shoots at him as the man is falling down screaming, "Alice, fall and be careful." Then Jack turns his gun towards the running Alice, but he receives three bullets before he could shoot. It was amazing. The man that was shooting was unknown and expert: No more bullets, but exactly three as they found out later. He had two bullets in the heart and one in the forehead. Jason had two bullets in the knee as he fell.

None could see who was the man that shot Jack. He was better than Jack and professional. It was proved that two bullets hit the heart and one the forehead as he turned to hit Alice. He was very slow to aim anywhere; he didn't know where as he was surprised!

Jack fell, the gun stopped and none knew what had happened. Probably Jack knew. Jason and Jack were wooded or dead? Alice was not hit but had stopped. She turned around and crying she went straight, running to Jason. She was doing what she was not supposed to do. She was supposed to be running and leave. None was supposed to see her or speak to her. She was not supposed to be known before or after. That was Jason's wish. He didn't want to see her involved in anything. My God! What a noble man and blessed he was. Three bullets: Two in the heart and another in the head. The man that shot Jack must have been an expert. But Jack had hurt Jason and none knew his fate.

Alice saw Jason and she run to him. Jason saw her but he had an expression of pain. Soon Stuart came running to Jason from the promenade, after Alice was holding Jason not knowing what to do. Stuart looks at Alice, takes the things that she is offering and says sternly, "Please, now go to your car and drive home. Answer the phone when it rings. But you don't know anything." Alice wants to know and kisses Jason. "He will be fine," says Stuart looking at Alice and expecting her to do as he was saying. Alice afraid gets up, goes to her car and drives home crying. She was stern and hopeless.

She wanted to know but she had to obey Stuart's order. She knew and trusted him. He was a gentleman. He didn't give a damn for Jack, but he was concerned about Jason. Alice was certain and read it in his eyes by the concern they were expressing. She left crying. She could not resist what she saw. But she had no choice. Jason was certainly hurt. But none knew exactly how and where he was hurt by Jack.

What happened exactly none could say. A pedestrian said that a lady was approaching the waves and a man was following. In a moment he looked to his right and sees a man coming on the sand. The man looks carefully, and for some reason of his own, he pools a gun from his waste and aims at the man coming on the sand from his right. He aims at the man, shoots at the man, and the man is falling. He looks at the woman who tries to come towards the hit man and tries to kill her; but another man hits him with three bullets. The other man left and none knew who was he, where he came from, and where he went.

The lady did not stop but screaming and crying goes to the hit man. She realized who he was or she already knew. Soon after, another man comes running to the wooded man where the lady was. After that there was confusion and none could say anything. Many people walked to where the two men had fallen. Everyone was surprised. The shooting man had not missed but the man had instinctively dived and was injured as he was falling.

Did the man that killed Jack wanted to kill also Jason? None can answer. But he killed only Jack and wooded Jason. Was this certain? None knew, and none could tell, who was the man that killed Jack. Was he the same man that killed Jack the one who also wounded Jason? None knew and none could say. None had seen more clearly to be certain.

The wounded man was really Jason and the killed man was really Jack. Alice saw that Jack tried to kill Jason; and then was aiming at her; but she didn't see who killed Jack and saved her. She ran terrified at the place where Jason had fallen and she embraced him with passion, kissed him with tears and was searching for his woods. None could miss that he was her man. Her confusion and love were mixed and terrifying.

This was another description given much later by Alice and many others who approached Jason. Things were confusing but nearly the same, in both cases. Yet, none could say anything with certainty. Things were perceptions of people who run there to be informed; and every one gave different information. As time goes on, the confusion grows.

The people, who gathered there quickly, were rapidly kept away by the Police called by Stuart, the friend of Jason. He came running to Jason. Alice was terrified by the wounded Jason who saw her and smiled. But none saw who killed Jack and hit Jason. All people there were kept away by the Police. Most left not wishing to be among the witnesses. Stuart, after seeing Jason, he threw his eyes on Jack but he didn't go there. He realized who was the gentleman and chose not to go there, even though he was very close. Apparently, Jason the injured man was Stuart's friend as he was terrified not knowing for a few seconds what to do, till Alice gave him some bandages. After that, everything was confusing and terrifying. None had a complete story to tell. There was confusion after.

Stuart identified the crying Alice and he told her to go before the Police come so not to be involved with the case. She didn't want to go. Stuart said, "Please, go home and if needed we will call you."

She left terrified not knowing the state of Jason. Apparently, she didn't bother at that moment about Jack. And none could tell if she ever bothered about him, anyway after. He was a stranger and remained so. He could not say anything after, anyway. He was really dead. The man that shot him and saved Alice was apparently an unknown expert. None had seen him.; and none could say anything after. "God bless him!"whispered Stuart.

Jason had fallen as soon as he saw Jack; and Jack's bullet had hit him in the leg. Jack fell as he was aiming at Alice; but fell before he could pull the trigger. This was what Jason had seen; but nothing more. Stuart ran as soon as he saw Jason falling; and Jack falling right after Jason. He didn't care about Jack even though he was careful about his movements. Apparently, he was not trusting Jack. It was clear by his movement and indifference.

But Jack fell with three bullets. None could tell which one killed him and who shot those bullets. None run to him when he fell, but only after Stuart was already calling the Police and the Hospital. If any of his people were there, they were with the crowd and none approached them. If they knew, none spoke and left with the others when they were told by the Police and the Hospital people, to leave immediately and leave them to do their work. No more information was also given.

If Jason didn't respond with the movement of Jack, he would have been dead. Jason's movement saved him from a bullet in the head. Jack was fast. Both fell down and none knew what had happened to him except Jason; more likely. He knew that Jack was hit with the bullets and saw Jack falling as soon as he tried to shoot at Alice.

Jack was missing the strength and he fell down. He was not approached by anyone, for none wanted the responsibility, anyway. He was taken by the Hospital Service along with Jason. None was interested to know. But Stuart was concerned about Jason and followed the Police. The case was really confusing and puzzling. Alice left confused and terrified: Jason had been shot and none knew where and by whom.

As soon as Alice realized what happened, she went to Jason crying. She ignored what might happen to her or what had happened to Jack. Jason's friend Stuart came running, looked at Jason, received some bonding strips from Alice and said to her, "Please, take the car and go home. You know nothing of what happened." Hearing that, she was wondering if Stuart knew anything. But she knew nothing as Stuart had said. Jack had shot Jason and someone had killed Jack. None knew anything more. Jason was the only witness.

Alice had seen a man seating on the edge of the promenade looking in the sea, but none knew if he had anything to do with the case. Besides, they knew nothing more about him or others who stopped to see what was happening. People were not allowed to see the shot men, anyway. Nobody knew, if anyone had seen, who had done what.

Alice terrified was crying but she left as she was told by Stuart. She got into her car as she was told, and she was supposed to know nothing. Indeed, Alice didn't know anything; and this it was what she said later and as expected by the police. When they came, she was not there anyway; and she didn't know anything.

––––––––––

Alice with tears and love was thinking about Jason whom the nearest Hospital took along with the incomprehensible gambler. She called Stuart, because Simon was in Athens. She asked about Jason and he told her that fortunately he was not badly injured. He told her, to wait though till next week when Jason was to come out. She thanked Stuart but she was also thinking about Simon. It happened the way he had told her and she didn't know how to thank him. She never understood who killed Jack. But she knew why.

She was not allowed to ever mention the name of Simon as it was agreed between her and Simon in the Hotel. But she was thankful and obliged to Simon forever. She was even afraid to think or mention of Simon. She was crying knowing that she didn't deserve a man with the qualities of Jason; nor a man with the qualities of Simon. She wanted to die, but what she had done wrong? It was Jason injured and she was crying. She was thinking how noble was Simon, and how accurate was the man assigned to kill Jack. She knew nothing else to cry for. She was not supposed to speak to anyone about the events.

Alice wanted to go to the Hospital and be sure that Jason was not in danger. She wanted to go to the hospital, to see him, to thank him, to kiss him and leave. She was free and he was wounded. Who is going to understand how noble he was and how thankful he was that she was now healthy and free? A slave of yesterday was free today. How she could excuse herself to be free while he was in pain?

She was pleased end she wanted to make him happy. But, did he know? He was now wounded and she was free. Why she could not go there now and be with him? She loved him so much but she could not go and see him. All people, and all his friends were cruel. They did not know how much she loved him and wished to share his pain. But if he really loved her why didn't he asked her to be with him? She didn't know how Jason was thinking about Alice's innocence and need to be unrelated to the crime.

Simon knew how much she loved Jason. Why didn't he ask her to be with him? Because she didn't know how stupid the law people are. Apparently, it was Jason's wish not to involve the lady and not to involve themselves. The problem was his, because Alice was his. Both his friends had to listen. And both loved him because he was a noble man to be loved and be trusted.

They knew when he was right and when he was wrong. They knew when to listen and when to object. But Alice didn't know. She had suffered in the hands of a scum for long and could no longer think straight. But she was an abused lady in love with Jason: a noble young man trusted and admired.

Alice wanted to see Jason. She no longer believed Stuart or Simon. Not that they wanted to fool her, but that they didn't want her to suffer. Monday, she found where was the Hospital and decided to go and see Jason. She didn't want to be seen by anyone. But she had to see that he was as they said out of danger. Sunday she was called by Stuart and she was told that he was doing well and not to worry. His mother had seen him late Saturday and Stuart had informed her that he was doing well and not to worry. But Alice could not believe anyone but only her own eyes. She was though happy that nothing was going to be obvious after he was going to leave the Hospital next Saturday. She could not believe anyone anymore. She was no longer real.

Sunday afternoon late, Alice decides to go and see for herself the state of Jason. She no longer cares what people will say if they see her. She is obliged to the man who gave her his love, respect and freedom. Indeed, late in the afternoon on Sunday, she takes a taxi and goes to the Hospital. He was sleeping, she looked at him and not to wake him up she talked to the nurse. She presented herself as his fiance. The nurse was nice and she said nicely, "He was lucky and so you are. The bullets missed his cup. He will be able to walk next Sunday." Alice looked at the nurse in the eyes and as tears were running on her two cheeks she managed to say, "I thank you, miss." The nurse smiled and said, "If I could not say that, my eyes would have been crying. He is noble and handsome."Alice smiled, thanked the nurse, and left. She knew that Jason was well, handsome and noble.

The expression of Alice changed as she took another taxi to go home. When she arrived home, she picked the phone, called a lady and said, "Louise, this is Alice. I just came from the hospital and I was assured by the nurse that Jason was lucky. The bullets of the filthy man missed the cup of the knee; Jason will be able to walk as before." None knows what was the answer, but Alice was happy. Apparently, Louise cried as Alice promised to see her in the middle of next week. "And don't forget to call me Alice, if you don't see me next week," she added and hung up crying.

Alice walked in the large balcony of her apartment and looked at the sky. It was blue and was getting dark. She sees the first stars coming out and whispers, "The sky today is celebrating my good fortune." She fixed her tea, took one of the pastries that Louise was not forgetting to supply, and with a smile she whispered, "As soon as I know that Jason is free, I am going to find my mother." They were cutting the hair of the wolf and he was asking which way went the sheep!

She could not believe that she had lost her mother. The last one to stop loving her was her mother. She knew and trusted her virtues. But, she thought of Jason and cried. He was the only left to rely on. She could not think of him and not cry. She knew he deserved, and she had given him her love. She needed now to give him the money she had asked. But Jason for sure was not going to accept anything from a woman he loved. But she was going to give him the money.

The Policemen found the gun on Jason's pocket when he was injured by Jack. But he didn't have the permit yet. He had though the opportunity to use it, if he wanted. But he didn't, because he had no license or because he was not fast enough. The bullet in the heart of Jack was not the bullet in Jason's gun. Why should he be punished? "Because the Judge was a pig," said Stuart and fortunately none of them were there to hear him. None knew who killed Jack, and none knew how many Jack had killed.

Jason was punished three months for illegal possession of a gun. It was probably the reason that Jason didn't use the gun that Saturday morning. None knows because Jason could not probably do both: Pull his gun to shoot at Jack, and fail to protect Alice. He had fallen to protect himself and delay Jack. None knows. But Jack was anyway an expert licensed shooter. But he didn't have to use a gun because Jason didn't try to use his. So, why Jason was to be punished three months of jail?

Who was the man that killed Jack? None knew and none could say. Alice knew what Simon knew. But Simon was in Athens and Stewart may have been. But Stewart came as soon as Jason fell and after Alice was there. Who knows? Stewart arrived after Alice was with Jason, and he was with Jason walking on the promenade before Jason was shot by Jack. None could say or prove who killed Jack. Whoever he was, he was a noble man getting rid of Jack and saving both Jason and Alice. May have been one wishing to kill both: Jason and Jack. No, that was not the case; but none could exclude it. People are crazy, anyway. Each one says what he thinks and not what he sees; if he sees.

Fortunately, the Judge had no witnesses and Stuart was mad. But the Judge was also saved for he was stupid and didn't know what was expecting him, otherwise. The people of the law are often guilty. But they have no choice if they have no brain. They depend on the law if they don't depend on the Judge's brain. Jason had every reason to carry the gun and everyone was wondering why he didn't use it: Jason was a noble man following the law even when it is stupid! "I must fight the law and win it, before I use the gun with no license," he would say, "Or kill the law giver, before I use the gun. He had his reasons. Every other noble man would have used the gun to be sure he was defending himself. They didn't know Jack, but they were right: One more reason to try to kill a stranger who was a scum! He should have killed the scum.

Jason and Stuart thought that they knew who had put the bullets in the heart and the head of the pig. But they could not tell nor wanted to prove it; and there was no reason to do so. And no matter who was or who they were, he or them, they were the enemies of Jack and friends of Jason, more likely. Jason was hit by Jack. One way or the other, Jason loved Alice, and Alice loved Jason. You could not talk with him and not fall in love, if you were a woman; you could not deal with him and not admire him if you were a man. Anyway, none knew where in Athens was Simon. But he had a ticket on Thursday going to Athens. He also had a copy of the ticket on Saturday coming back late in the afternoon after the crime. He was very upset finding everyone in the Hospital on Saturday night and not on Pete's Bar as expected.

However, that night, late for more than half an hour, Stuart went to Pete's Bar and found Simon as expected. "Why are you so late Stuart? Where is Jason?" he asked. Stuart looked at him and after thinking he said, "Don't you know, Simon, that Jason is in the Hospital?" Simon looks surprised and asks upset, "What happened to him?" he asks. "On Saturday, that pig Jack died with three woods: Two in the chest and another in the head; thank God." "My God," says Simon. "It was Jason who did it?" he questions waiting for the answer. "No Simon; it was you who did it!" says Stuart softly in a way that none could hear him. Simon looks at him and replies, "I wish, I was; lets be little careful, though. Let's not implicate our friends."

"Where is Jason now?" he asks with anxiety after recovering. "That pig Jack shot him with two bullets in the right leg. He is now in the hospital." "How is he now?" Simon wonders, after reflecting for a few seconds. "It is too early to know," replies Stuart wondering. "I don't know what the hell he wanted there that time," says Simon and tears slowly roll down his eyes. Stuart looks at Simon and Simon lowers his head. He didn't want to be seen crying. But he loved Jason. He was thinking that Jason could be dead and he could not control his pain. He had the blood of Jason a few years ago, to survive an accident, and Jason was noble and happy.

After they had some wine with roasted chicken and potatoes at Pete's Bar on Saturday night, Stuart optimistically said, "I hope nothing is finally wrong with Jason's foot." Simon didn't say anything but he was upset because he could have done nothing more anyway. Pete, the Bar's owner who knew Jason's friendship with Stuart and Simon, went to the table of those friends and said to them that he had called the Hospital and the people told him not to worry. They were certain that Jason was to be fine by the end of next week.

They thanked Pete for asking and telling them. This made Simon happy because the information given them was only a few minutes ago. Simon knew that Jason was not supposed to be there, and was very upset. He understood why Alice called the last moment Jason; but he could not understand why Jason had to go there: Don't you ever have been in love Simon?" asked Stuart.

Simon remembered what he has done with Norma and didn't say anything more. But this case was much different and Jason had done what he was not supposed to do. You listen to your friends many times but not always. He forgot it this time.

Monday, Stuart goes to a lawyer of his own to talk about the defense of Jason. They expect Tuesday after next, Jason to be tried for possessing an illegal gun. Jason who was never involved with such cases was upset; Stuart was furious, and Simon thoughtful. Stuart met Simon in a Bar and told him during their dinner that this case was his. None had any right to be involved. "Let Jason know," said Simon. "Yes I will; and if

I need any help, I will call you," adds Stuart. "Of course you will; but please tell Jason to know that and do nothing," says Simon. "Of course; don't doubt me Simon!" says Stuart and looks at Simon wondering. He really could not understand! But he said nothing if Simon refused that he had anything to do with Jack's killing. The man that killed Jack might have been another; he had so many enemies and friends. He was a scum able to placate the corrupt policemen. There was none to cry about that trained pig. apparently, others knew better. They had no reason to bother with a disrespectful creature.

Jason in two weeks was back at work, and in three weeks he was tried for possessing an illegal gun. He was punished for three months and everyone was furious. The Lawyer was stupid, the Prosecutor a bastard and the Judge an old retarded fellow. Stuart was upset and decided to appeal without leaving Jason in the jail at all. He paid everything and told Jason not to worry. "The most is going to be a month; if the prosecutor and the judge know what to expect otherwise," said Stuart to Jason a night in one of the places they used to meet.

Jason looked at Stuart and said, "Don't worry Stuart, one way or the other it was my mistake. I should not have been there with a gun." Simon who is usually listening disagreed. "You should not have been there at all; but once you were, you had to have a gun and use it if you had; because Jack was a bastard." Both Stuart and Simon thought and Jason realized that he had to be careful.

Jason was put to jail and was waiting a week for the appeal. Two days before the appeal Alice goes to jail with flowers to see him. Tears were in her eyes. She loved the man and could not have her eyes clear. As soon as she goes and sees him, tears flow in her eyes and she whispers, "I am sorry Jason; I love you and I cannot keep my tears. I don't deserve you and I do not expect you to love me. I will start working next week. So, I brought you some flowers." She gives him the flowers and as he takes them she grabs his hands, kisses them with passion and says, "God to be with you always; I thank you for everything." She could not keep her tears; turns around and leaves crying. Before getting away, she looked back to see him. He was watching her silent and serious. She was beautiful but he was handsome. He had given her life and freedom, but he could not understand because he didn't know. She was his, no matter what. You could see that in her capturing eyes. She loved him with passion.

The same night, Simon with Norma, and Stuart with his wife Anna went to 'Signal'. It was a place better for couples. They ordered their dinner and they were in sad mood. Not long after, Nicholas arrives. Stuart knows and respects the professor. "Nicholas; join us if you have no other company," says Stuart. "Yes I will," replies Nicholas and sits next to Anna. She moves little to give more space to him and he joins them. "Professor Nicholas looks happy tonight," says Anna smiling. Nicholas smiles too and reserved replies, "Not really Anna. Three months of jail to Jason is a crime." He thinks and continues. "Three months for Jason is a shame; two months is an insult; and one month is disrespectful. We should seek one week the most, which is embarrassing," says Nicholas. "Do you know the minimum penalty Nicholas, for carrying a flat gun?" asks Simon. "There should be no penalty when the gun is carried by Jason," replies Nicholas. Simon smiles bitterly and replies, "It is a different case for people who know the law," replies Simon, and Nicholas wonders. "I am sorry Simon, I have to disagree. You would have been right if we had no Judges."

"Simon, I know and I understand; and there is a difference between people who know and people who understand," replies Nicholas. The people who know and understand are a few; therefore we have to be careful about the Judges, the Prosecutors, and the Lawyers. We have to be careful about the Judges: They must know and understand. If the Judge does not understand, we should do everything to change him. If the prosecutor is a bastard, the Judge can tell him to go to hell. This is our goal. The Judge should be a sharp young fellow. Otherwise, we have to send him to go to hell." "I agree Nicholas and I am sure of that," replies Stuart. "In that case, lets be sure that the Prosecutor is a moron," says Nicholas contemplating. They all laughed and Stuart said, "Nicholas, you let me know tomorrow, when we meet them." "Yes let's now relax," whispers Nicholas.

They talked that night a lot about many things. Anna was not very beautiful but she was charming. She enjoyed Nicholas and she asked him what happened to his girlfriend that night. "Who knows?" he replies smiling. Then he added, after Anna laughed, "She had a cold and stayed home." "That's better," she says smiling and letting none know what she was thinking. After talking a lot and laughing, Nicholas says to Stuart that he would like to go with him and see the Lawyer on Tuesday. "We cannot allow a noble man like Jason for even a day in the Jail," he adds. He has suffered a lot.

"Of course we can't," replies Stuart. "We cannot allow a noble man like Jason to be punished when he takes a gun to defend himself against another; when he knows the other is a pig and has a gun," adds Nicholas. "You are right Nicholas: You have to have a gun when you know, the one you are going to stop killing another, has a gun!" Stuart thinks and says to Nicholas. "Can we go on Tuesday together and explain to the Lawyer that Jason got the gun for defense, if he had to defend himself. We should explain to him that Jason didn't use the gun anyway, even though he had one!" Stuart thinks and replies, "Yes Nicholas, we can and we should."

Thus, Nicholas and Stuart on Saturday go to another Lawyer, friend of Stuart also. They clearly explain that Jason didn't have a gun. But when Alice called that noon to tell Jason that Jack was going to kill her that day, Jason took the gun and run to catch him. He asked and she told him where she was. She could not refuse to tell him the truth once he asked. Stuart was instructed by Jason not to follow him closely. It was an order that Stuart had to follow. Jason didn't wish to involve Stuart with a wife and two children, even though he would have never refused. "If you don't see me again, you know what has happened to me," Alice had said and hung up crying. She was a woman loved by anyone who met her. None had ever heard her protect herself, more than others.

Jason decided to follow Jack and was waiting at the beech to be sure that he didn't miss him. He was certain that he was going to kill Alice at the beach by the sea, if she was going to do something unfaithful to him. Jason wanted to be waiting but failed to know that Jack was a trained professional killer. His eyes were sharp and as soon as he stepped at the sand of the beech, he saw Jason and drew his gun; and shot three times at Jason. He missed the first deadly shot; hit Jason with two others, and he had no more luck.

Three other shots from behind the trees hit him, two in the heart and one on the forehead. "God bless him; whoever he was," said Stuart thinking. "Who was he; do you know?" asked the Lawyer. "May have been one of his enemies, and he had many," replies Stuart. "Yes, we do not know and we do not want to," replies the Lawyer. Nicholas is listening but says nothing. Apparently, he wants to be sure that Jason will be respected.

"God bless him who killed that bastard as he was going to kill the lady after wounding Jason," says Nicholas to make the Lawyer think. Then he added "Why did he try to kill Jason when Jason didn't use a gun; even if he had one?" The Lawyer stops, thinks and says, "This is better: He didn't have a gun but he got one to stop another who was going to kill a slave." Nicholas looks at the Lawyer and says, "And he didn't use a gun which means he would have been dead; after killing the lady; the pig does not deserve a human name. He would have finished the wounded Jason!" The Lawyer looks at Nicholas and says, "Yes, that's it; and Jason would have been dead!" While he said that, the expression of pain was obvious in the face of both.

"It will be a natural instinctive behavior, when one wants to save another, to use whatever is available," says Nicholas. "I agree," replies the Lawyer. "Can we bring the lady, who was with the pig, at the court?" he asks. Stuart and looks at Nicholas, who has never met Alice, and after a few seconds of time replies, "Yes we will try; but may we know what we want her for?" "Don't worry Stuart; we want to let them know that Jason is noble and nothing more!" explains Nicholas. "Yes we will try," repeats Stuart seriously thinking of Nicholas' sad reaction. The Lawyer's wish had to be respected.

There were no objections and the Lawyer was content. "We will teach the old bastards to rely not on past experiences but present facts that control each case," said the Lawyer upset. He apparently knew and respected Jason. He was a noble Lawyer that impressed Nicholas, and he was feeling sad that they didn't have him to begin then and be finished now. Finally, they left and leaving the Lawyer, Nicholas said, "Yes Stuart. Everyone is not Jason!" At the end whispering he said, "When a woman honestly explains, none wonders but everyone listens!" Nicholas was the type of Lawyer that you listen in difficult cases.

Stuart called Alice and explained to her that she had to see the Lawyer when she is called and say exactly what happened that noon with Jason: Nothing more and nothing less, before or after. She should go to his office when she is called. "I am sure that listening to you, the Jury will be surprised, if not stunned and the case will be clear and convincing that the 'gentleman' was a scum." Alice remains thinking. And after a few seconds, she replies: "You should know Stuart that for Jason I will do anything; and I know that nothing dishonest will ever have his approval." This pleased Stuart because he was an admirer of Jason. Stuart was unbearably happy. He communicated his conversation with Alice to Nicholas who was content after that. Nicholas had respect and admiration for Jason. Anyone who had met Jason knew that Jason was a noble gentleman. Anyone could say about Jason that he was noble.

Stuart thought it wise to just mention to Jason that they wanted to use Alice in the court. Jason objected but Stuart smiled. "It is not your choice Jason but Alice's. I just mention this to you so you know. I am not doing what you and I want, but what the Lawyer wishes," replies Stuart with a smile. "And I told you, Jason, what the Lawyer wishes. He wants to know the lady and he will decide." Jason smiled but he said nothing more. He knew that Alice was not to object to what he wanted and he said no more. Jason smiled to Stuart who was getting serious. "This is my case," said Stuart. "I am just informing you." Jason smiled and changed the subject. There was no point to argue if Alice had no objection. She was an intelligent young lady.

The Lawyer called Alice. She went immediately dressed in light black. The Lawyer had not seen a woman with such a physical perfection. Yet, she was simple in her manners and speaking. He was enchanted with her and knew that she was Jason's woman. He didn't know more and could not think of anything to say. He offered her everything; she wanted nothing; but anything she rejected was done with finesse. After they were relaxed, the Lawyer asks, "Ms. Alice, you know why I have called you here, don't you?" She looks at him and smiles. "Yes, of course I do," she replies. "Alice, I want you to say nothing more or less than what you saw that Saturday noon when Jack shot Jason. I believe that Jason is honest and innocent."

"Yes, that I know," she says looking at the Lawyer. "So, you can say that he is honest and innocent?" "Yes, I believe that, and I will say that," she says and smiles. "So, nothing should be said about before Mr. Jack pulled the gun, and after Mr. Jack was killed. But everything in and between should be said." "Yes Sir, I will do exactly that, if you trust me," she says wondering. "Do you know who shot Mr. Jack?" "No, Sir; I don't; Do you?" He looks and smiles at her. "Do you know why he tried to kill you?" She looks at him and asks, "Can you tell me Sir?" "I cannot tell you that," he replies. She looks at him bitterly but says nothing. "Ms. Alice, that is sufficient. Thank you." "You are very welcome Sir," she says. She is very calm and looks very intelligent. The Lawyer was impressed. She was very charming and tempting.

"Not to forget, I have to inform you that Jason and his friend Stuart, do not wish you to come to the court." She smiles and replies, "In this case Sir, I will do what you want me to do." He smiles and after a short pause he responds, "In that case Miss, I want you to come and partici- pate in the court case as a noble witness." "Thank you Sir; I really want to come," she replied. "This is not Jason's case. It is ours; to show that he is honest and noble. It is a case that none has the right or privilege to deny."

The Lawyer explained some things to Alice pertaining to her knowledge. But he emphasized the fact that Jason didn't try just to protect himself. He tried to protect her as well. She was present and aware of the fact and she was trembling each time she was thinking of the scene. When Jason fell, she didn't know if he was dead or alive. She had decided to die with him, but she was hoping because Jason was not worried. He saw Alice next to him, taking care of him with Stuart, and he was wounded but happy.

Nothing was given him the hope of life. She and Simon were the only ones that knew the truth; and a noble stranger that she admired: The one that killed Jack. But she didn't really know who had killed that pig. She wished not to have called Jason and she was regretful that she did. For her, Jason was noble. He did for her what every noble man could not have done. When she left, she said to the Lawyer, "Thank you Sir; and let God be with Jason, and his noble friends. If you find another man of his qualities, let me know."

She believed that she was not to be born and loved by a man of Jason's virtues and values unless she was an unmolested youth. He was for her a noble man hard to find anywhere. She admired Stuart and Simon but worshipped Jason. They were people of different breed: You admire the Generals but you worship the King!

The Lawyer decided to get Jason out of Jail as soon as possible and not delay. Immediately he acted. He arranged for another court case within two weeks and selected another Jury to the extend he knew. People were upset with the imprisonment of Jason. He was not to stay again in Jail. He arranged to pay and stay out of the Jail while he was waiting for the court case. In two weeks the case was arranged and Jason was waiting out of the Jail. But he was not working. The Prosecutor and the Judge were embarrassed. They learned after who was the man they had put three months in prison for the illegal carriage of a gun and they were embarrassed. The new lawyer brought in a young Judge and a young Prosecutor to try Jason later. It is sad, but it is also a fact that Jason is one of the men to be left out of jail.

They let the previous Prosecutor and the Judge to know, who was the man they had put in Jail before, and they were embarrassed. The new Lawyer deliberately advertised the case, and the new young Prosecutor and Judge studied the events to be prepared. The Prosecutor and the Judge realized that Jason was a noble man trapped in the machine of legalities, prosecution and people, and was put in jail already for two weeks. He wanted to appeal now his case. All his friends in the City were excited and upset. If another one was in the position of Jason, the Judge and the Prosecutor would have suffered and vanished. The Jury now was surprised knowing that Jason was the prosecuted man.

Two weeks after his punishment in Jail, the case of Jason was reviewed. Jason's lawyer had deliberately brought people from banks, investment places, business establishments and schools, to attend Jason's case in the court and learn. The case opened on Thursday afternoon. Jason was there, Alice, the young lady whom Jason loved and tried to protect, as she deserved, was also there; and five other witnesses were there as well. The room was uniquely filled.

---

7 JUSTICE TO JASON THE "NOBLE MAN"

"One can be knowledgeable, powerful and rich but not Noble."

We are often convinced that the courts are a waste. It would have been the case if we had no right to Appeal and pursue Justice. Therefore it is important for the loser to be able to evaluate the results of his trials and decide whether to pursue Justice. We cannot always have fair trials because the Prosecutors and the Judges are not always, not to say in most cases, fair and capable people. They are just human and many times careless and unfair.

And not only that. People like jack have the talent to deceive the police by giving them the illusion that they are virtuous. Stuart swears that if his friend is punished he will be the rebel to kill all scums till someone gets him. He knows it will be difficult but he will get rid of many of the scums. His wife sees him mad and she is afraid. He is the man that will kill many if challenged. He swears that if his friend is punished for being a noble man, he will exterminate all those bastards once he knows them. He does not believe that he is the only one. But there is Jason also, the one whom he knows.

He lifts his phone and asks his friends Simon and Nicholas to meet him for a light supper at the intersection of Navarinou and Akrita by the beech. They agreed to do that, the following night. Simon, Stuart and Nicholas got into an outside coffee house on Navarinou street facing the sea and with their bier, hamburger, potatoes and salad they started their night. It was a night of the Spring, cool and pleasing. The flowers were budding and the friends are aging now to suffer. "Why the hell, don't they see anything?" Stuart wonders.

Nicholas and Simon are ready to listen. Stuart is upset. He is trying to find out how to face the imbeciles of the court that put Jason three months in the Jail to justify their existence. "The Policemen, the Prosecutors and the Judges should be kicked to learn to respect honorable people like Jason," whispered Stuart. "We cannot trust anyone to kick them," whispers Nicholas. "If they do not catch you, everything is fine. But if they catch one, they catch them all, unless we are lucky," said Simon who was silently thinking. "Yes we cannot trust anyone," whispered Simon. "If they abuse one he will betray everything." "But if he knows nothing, whom should they catch, besides him?" asks Stuart. "Yes, that is the point. But how one will hide himself?" whispers Simon thinking. "That is his problem and abilities, says Stuart. He cannot make a revolution and win by himslf.

"Gentlemen, I swear to God that I will give them one more chance. After that I will give my own justice. I will kill as many of them as I can while I am living. Jason is innocent!" Simon and Nicholas are listening carefully. Stuart is really mad. After a few moments of silence they agreed with Stuart. "But lets plan together and act alone," whispers Simon. He is the wise and able voice. Nicholas knows and respects Simon; but he is afraid of Stuart. He looks at Stuart and says, "Lets now decide together and tomorrow act as we please alone."

After a long discussion they concluded that an Appeal case with new Lawyers, Judges and Prosecutors must be pursued. A public interest was to be generated long before the court case was set. But this was to be done as soon as possible; so Jason does no longer stay in Jail. The public was to be invited and the case advertised so that the prosecutors know who is the convicted man. Jason had the respect of all those who had ever met him and he should be invited to the court the day of the Appeal. The Lawyers, the Prosecutors and the Judges to be informed by all people about Jason and his honorable social standing. They didn't know who those were; but if all possible ones were informed, the ones to prosecute and judge Jason will one way or the other be informed also.

The public was to be informed, including all those who admired Jason, by articles in the local newspapers. This was not to be done by lawyers, and respectable reporters in the best public newspapers. Jason was already known in the financial newspapers and to investors in the Stock and Commodities markets. Simon, Stuart and Nicholas were also known and capable to inform the public. Before the Appeal case they were all to be informed and demand a place in the court. The Prosecutors and the Judges were to know who was Jason and realize that they had put him in Jail for three months with no reason: He had to defend a noble lady. He had no choice.

The Lawyer understood and agreed that Jason was a noble educated professional with a degree from Anotate Emporiki in Athens and with about ten years of experience in Stocks and Commodities. He knew and respected Jason and was surprised that he was involved by bad luck, but noble to his estimation. He assured Stuart and Nicholas that there was not going to be a problem.

Jason's Lawyer was thoughtful. He wanted to make this case a success knowing that the respect of the crowd was for Jason. He realized that the decision of the previous court was ridiculous for a noble man. It was painful for him but he had chosen to be calm. He knew he had not made a mistake but he had no way to show that. The laws are often incomprehensible and the people have to realize that it is up to the Lawyer and the Judge to violate the Laws and give justice to noble people. He could not see how a man like Jason was to be put in Jail for any reasons. Those reasons had to be just and with people like Jason they were not. But the Lawyer and the Judge had to see! It was now their objective and reason to be what they were assigned to be.

The Lawyers strategy was to select the Judge and the Prosecutor and inform the public of Jason's standing. Apparently he advertised the case and many customers of Jason were informed of the injustice which Jason had suffered. Casually he begun a conversation with Jason's customers who had missed him and casually invited people to go to his trial and listen. "I do not understand the noblemen of our society to be punished by Prosecutors and Judges who are cockroaches, not aware that our society rests on some people that stand up at certain times, to protect the just men, who defend the noble men and women, at any cost."

When they were asking more questions he was mentioning the case of Jason who was punished in his pursuit of protecting a young lady. If he was not there to protect the young lady she would have been fucked and killed by scums, let alone they were all foreigners with no respect for justice. Even the policemen were their collaborators and victims.

The Lawyer knew to speak at select people who knew the noble and respectful behavior of Jason. Selecting that type of people to go to listen, was embarrassing the court for they all knew that Jason was a noble and intelligent young man not to be punished by the court while he was protecting the just and the noble ones.

The visiting foreign workers had to respect the order of the Greek society. They have no right to be abusing the respectful ones. Three weeks after his punishment in Jail, the case of Jason was reviewed. Jason was out after a week waiting for his appeal. None could believe the three week punishment of Jason and were all upset. If it was not the peaceful appeal of Jason, problems would have been created by the unjust punishment. None would have known then who were the true guilty: The court or the public knowing Jason?

Jason's Lawyer had deliberately brought people from banks, investment places, technical business establishments, entertainment and schools, to attend Jason's case in the court and learn. The case opened at two thirty in the afternoon. Jason was there, the young lady whom Jason tried to protect was also there, and five other witnesses were there as well. The room was uniquely filled.

The Lawyer wanted the court to lift the punishment of illegal armament of Jason in the beach of the City near the intersection of streets of Navarinou and Crete; about a mile from Messolongi running along the mountain of Taygetus and continuing along the sea after, at the hotel

Filoxenia. The street of Navarinou runs along the beach and terminates at the street of Messolongi in Filoxenia.

There, a few weeks ago, Jason was arrested injured, carrying a flat gun without license which was not however used. Jason was arrested and punished for three months imprisonment. He served already the minimum of two weeks and requests now the remaining to be cancelled because he believes that under the circumstances he was entitled to carry the gun that he, however, didn't use.

This will allow Jason to leave the jail, as the two weeks of minimum punishment will be finishing the following Monday. "Jail for Jason is a social insult by the court," said the Lawyer. "Under these conditions we need no courts to insult justice." The Lawyer had known the Jury and did his best to inform them about Jason. They were upset and the Lawyer was pleased to have conditioned them.

Simon, Stuart and Nicholas had decided to pursue the case legally to the end. Nicholas was to help them with the courts. Simon was to help him as much as he could; and Stuart was to act independently till they succeeded. None was to know what Simon and Stuart were doing. Nicholas was to be the dexterous of legal actions.

Stuart had selected the best Lawyer and was certain that in the case of failure, Nicholas was to pursue the court case farther. Stuart and Simon were not supposed to do anything that Nicholas was to know. There was no problem with money to bribe and please, said Stuart. Simon knew Stuart and was afraid, but certain. "If a capable and noble man is insulted the bastards have to pay," whispered Stuart.

Nicholas decided to follow the Lawyer. He talked with him and promised that they were to be paid what they asked and deserved. They agreed to spread the case and make the court aware of the consequences of failure. They were to advertise the qualities of Jason and be at the court the day of appeal. The response was encouraging and promising. Professional and business people were to be at the court of Appeal and protest if the Prosecutor and the Judges were to forget the justice of the case and play with their rules.

The case was to be tried on Thursday afternoon. The Lawyer has excited the people who know Jason and all can talk about his integrity. They were all there. On Thursday afternoon the court case was the last one to start at three o'clock. The court room was filled by two thirty. It was a surprise for the Judge and the Prosecutor. The audience was a mixture of people of all sorts. Among them were Stuart, Simon and Nicholas sitting together at the back. They were not talking but carefully watching. They looked at the people and they were surprised. Jason's lawyer had decided to free Jason by Monday. They were wondering if he was going to succeed. Nicholas was enthusiastic, Simon hoping and Stuart waiting. It was not going to be an easy case. It all depended on the Prosecutor, the Judge and the Lawyer. Jason should not have been punished at all. That is why we have the Lawyers and the Judges. It was a violation of Justice to punish a noble man without being careful.

When the Lawyer had to speak, he looked at the audience and noticed that the room was filled with many of the people he knew.

"Jason is an honorable man," was the Lawyer's expression. "He is not worth of any punishment but worth of any reward that a man can have. He had a gun that he didn't use; and exposed himself to a dishonorable stranger who had the audacity to use a gun when Jason tried to protect himself and a noble lady, projecting himself and warning Ms. Alice."

Content as he was to see the audience and make the court authorities aware that they were treating a noble man, he continued. He wanted the court to lift the penalty of illegal armament and see the noble wisdom of Jason: He had exposed himself to save Alice. He had exposed her to begin with and he was feeling responsible. She was first and he was second! She was innocent and Mr. Jack was an exploiting gambler."

He was by now dead and none knew his killer. Jason had already served the minimum of two days and had to be left free. "No society can be respectable with people of Jason's qualities going to jail," the Lawyer said. The people got excited and applauded. The Judge could only ask for discipline. "Please, listen and be calm. Justice will prevail," he said seriously.

"I want to lift the penalty of illegal armament and let a noble man, as noble as Jason, to go home in peace as he now deserves," says the Lawyer. He looks around to be sure that the audience heard him, believed him, and continues. But he takes his time. He is peaceful and upset that the court had made a mistake.

"Circumstances forced my client to seek a weapon to defend himself, if he had to. He was going to save the life of an innocent and noble young lady." "Why didn't she or he let the police know immediately?" asks the Prosecutor. "I do not know about the lady, but Mr. Jason can tell us." He turns to Jason and waits for an answer. "I did call; but the police didn't come till after the drama!" replies Jason. "Then I was wondering why; and now I ask them to answer. But none was there to respond except the court guards. They had bull sheeted with him when he called and he knew they were not going to come.

"They never act responsibly; what did you expect me to do? To go there and die without at least having a defense? Or not go and know that I have a lady be killed? They were and they are irresponsibly indefensible! So, I took with me a gun to use, if I had to. I decided to defend a lady and die; and survive only by lack." Hearing Jason speak, Alice cried silently; not wishing to betray herself. Everyone, however, could see her eyes flooded with tears. She was a charming beauty deserving everyone's respect and admiration. If she was guilty, none was innocent or could be respected!

The Lawyer turns to Alice and respectfully asks, "Please, tell us, why didn't you call the Police, if you were afraid that he might have killed you?" Alice smiles, and bitterly replies, "I had done that before, a number of times. They didn't do it the first two times, and they never came after; but if they had done it the first two times; by the time they came, he would have killed me, and run away. After that, they never came and after that, I never called. But I called Mr. Jason not to come and know. He came and saved me; and another one, God bless him, saved me and

Mr. Jason. Whether he wants me or not; of course, it is my choice." Ismene was honest and surprising.

"Your Honor, you know now that such an act was useless and signing her death. If she is alive now, she is because of Jason and the Stranger. Whoever he was, God bless him!" says the lawyer. "Mr. Jason and Ms. Alice are now alive because of the Stranger. God bless him." Stuart looked at Simon; and Simon was looking at the Lawyer surprised. Jason was remaining silent and was suspicious. Few were those with the steady hand that killed Jack; and none of those was caring for Jason that much except Stewart and Simon. Jason knew this fact. But Jason didn't know how many others hated Jack.

Anyway, Alice and Jason said the truth as it happened. She finished here and was asked to sit down till the case was closed. She was innocent. She was intelligent! The judge was impressed by the beauty and the truthfulness of the lady. He looked at Jason to be sure he was alive. Alice was so honest and beautiful, that you could never doubt.

"Yes, the beautiful ones become the victims of the ruthless and the hungry," whispered the Judge. The tears run down on the Lawyer's face. He smiled but he said nothing more till he was called. The Judge in this case was young and noble. He knew the law and its authority. If one has a gun, the other has to have one also; and the scum should be punished anyway. "The application of the Law is the duty of the noble and not of the scum," he whispered.

The Judge examines the papers, and soon after calls Jason. "Why didn't you use the gun Mr. Jason," he asks wondering. Jason looks at him and answers. "If I could, I would have. But I was slow. The only choice I had was to protect the Lady." The Judge looks at him and comments. "You know that if the Stranger was not there, both the lady and you will have been dead now?" Jason thinks and replies with bitterness, "Yes, that would have been, most likely, the outcome."

Jason realized that the young Judge was an intelligent man. He looked at him and saw him thinking and smiling.

The Judge looked at the papers, talked to the two Judges to his right and left, and not long after he said: "It is one month of Jail for Mr. Jason. He was carrying a gun before the permission was issued. Even though he acted right on the basis of the facts and circumstances, he was not allowed to carry the gun." He didn't believe what he said, but it was appropriate. Jason had served already nearly two weeks. The rest was to be paid and arranged by Jason's Lawyer.

After that, the case was closed and the groups in the court happily were discussing the case; some in the Justice room and others as they were leaving. Stuart and Simon were talking with each other and with Nicholas who was happy and smiling. Stuart could go now home and rest peacefully. He had enough tortured the intelligent and aggressive Anna.

Alice was allowed to leave and left inconspicuously the room; and Jason was to pay for the two days he was to leave before the end of his sentence. He followed his happy attorney and thanked him as much as he was allowed. "I am sorry Jason; many people are not wise," said the Lawyer smiling and proud of his victory. "I know you are a noble man hard to find," he remarked. Jason thanked him as much as he could.

Jason's friends were happy, and the solution of the case was just. Jason's friends Stuart and Simon with Nicholas were very pleased, and Stuart invited his friends for a beer in one of the bars. But Jason was asked to go to his home with his sister as his mother will now be waiting. "I was very pleased with the Lawyer, said Stuart to Jason. "Tomorrow we will think about. We will be more relaxed thinking about everything. That bastard gave us trouble for long." Jason smiled, thanked his friends and left happy with his sister. "Saturday, gentlemen, I will see you," repeated Jason leaving with his sister and dropping the mask of agony. He really wanted to go home with his sister and make his mother happy. She was certainly waiting to hear. She wanted to see her son free and not to be told.

As they left, Irene said to her brother, "Tomorrow Jason, I will go with Norma to get some flowers for our mother. She didn't show it, but she was depressed. I hope she will be at least little happier now." Jason was now looking at his sister, who was driving carefully, and replied, "Yes Irene, some flowers, fresh, beautiful and charming will make her happier." Irene was smiling and replied that she was going to get her a small vase of basil that will be awaking her every morning with its perfume. "If you find one like that, it will be at Alice's flower shop," said Jason. She smiled and was pleased that her brother had no objections to supporting Alice. He was really a noble man!

At the end of the court day on Thursday, Alice left embarrassed. She left quietly crying. She was the guilty one and Jason had gone to the Hospital and then to Jail for her sake. A noble man had suffered for a whore. What a shame for anyone with some dignity! Alice was thinking not being able to see a noble man. He gave her the freedom to revolt and the freedom to know.

She was thinking to leave and not see Jason anymore. Another women deserved him, and Alice much less than any other. For a year she was a whore to a bastard; and now that she is free, she wants only Jason and no other. But she does not deserve him. He is a noble man and she was a whore. But why he still wants her? Because he is wrong, was her conclusion! But she was wrong and people, intelligent like Jason, knew better. He had to be patient. Now he had to smile.

Alice went home, sat at the table looking at the sea, got her tea and began reflecting. She is free and so is Jason. That makes her happy; but also, unworthy of Jason's virtues and kindness. She cries thinking her fate, her love, her torture, her mother. She is so tired, so confused that she no longer wants to think. Eventually, she goes to sleep. She is so confused that she no longer wants to see anyone including Jason. Alice was too tired and went to sleep. She got up on Friday very late.

Jason gave her the freedom to revolt, and the freedom to know. She was thinking to leave and not see Jason anymore. A few women deserved him, and Alice much less than any other. For a year she was a whore to a bastard; and now that she is free, she wants only Jason and no other. She is free and so is Jason. That makes her happy; but also, unworthy of his virtues and kindness. It was nice of him to celebrate and for her to cry. She didn't know how much she was admired and wanted!

Alice was too tired and went to sleep. She wanted probably to forget. She got up on Sunday very late. As usually she got her tea and biscuit. She sat at her table facing the sea and began reflecting. She decided not to see Jason. It was not his fault. It was hers. She didn't deserve that man. She had to find a way to keep her mind away from Jason. She got dressed modestly; she knew how to do that. She was thinking being not able to see a noble man. He gave her the freedom to revolt and the freedom to know. She was thinking to leave and not see Jason anymore.

A few women deserved Jason, and Alice much less than any other. For a year she was a whore for a bastard; and now that she is free, she wants only Jason or none. She gets home, sits at the table looking at the sea, gets her tea and begins reflecting. Any reflection was confusing for the young lady. She had the youth and the beauty and she didn't know what to do.

She is now free and Jason healthy. That makes her happy; but also, unworthy of his virtues and kindness. She cries thinking her fate, her love, her torture, her mother. But her mother was killed by the bastards. That thought wakes her up and depresses her as well. She is so tired, so confused that she no longer wants to think.

Monday morning, after her usual tea and coffee cake Alice goes to the City Bank to find the money her father had left for her and pay her debt to Jason. She was to use it only if she was a free woman. She decided to be, by being free, by being independent. The beauty of this woman was a mystery. You could not make her ugly for anything. You knew she was acting, you knew she was unusual; but always attractive.

At the City Bank everyone was anxious to help her. She was led to the manager who was shocked but also stunned. There she finds that her father had left money for Ismene to get it any time she wanted after she was 21 years old. That bastard Jack had taken her and Yusuf had killed her mother, as Alice knew, before the age of 21. It was in the form of dollars that she could pick it up any time out of Albania. She was thinking of her father and her mother, and she was crying. They were noble people and she lost them both when she needed them most.

Alice provided all the papers they asked and they gave her a book with her account. She was going to find her brother and mother. She had grown not to believe when she saw; and not to trust till she touched and experienced their love.

When Jason's sister went to buy flowers for her mother with Norma on Saturday, it was Louise who served her. She knew who Irene was and was extremely happy. She gave her enchanting flowers and smiling said, "If there is someone who does not like these flowers, bring them back and ask for other or your money. You will have it back with no explanations." Irene smiled and said, "We no longer have smelling flowers." Louise didn't say anything but smiled. "Yes we do," she said.

The flowers were really perfumed better than roses and carnations. The following day, Irene went back to thank Louise for the beautiful flowers, but Alice was not there again. Louise said, "I am sorry, Miss Alice is not here but I will let her know."

Alice decided to incorporate the shops and leave. It was more than a year already in Kalamata. So, she got herself and her suitcase in her car and went to Agius Saranta. She knew by now to capture and disarm any people. She got into her car for Agius Saranta with Jason in her mind. She was not planning to come back. But she wanted to be sure first where to live. She was certain that she could find something to do.

As she was going through Patras and Ioannina she was getting emotional and crying. She tried though to keep her posture. It was not long time ago anyway. Just little more than a year had passed since the bastard had kidnaped her. But after they had taken her mother, she was an easy prey. They enslaved her involuntarily by the time she was twenty years old; and the bastard was keeping her by the force of fear.

It was Jason that had given everything to save her. Of course, he loved her but he was not forcing. He was noble in everything he did. If she didn't love him, which was not the case, it was fine. He could do nothing even though he loved her and lived with her image.

His friends knew but didn't believe it: They were surprised but that was the truth. They could not see the reason besides Stuart and Simon. Of course, Nicholas was wondering: Jason was going to either find Alice or look for another. He was still young and attractive.

Alice has done her best to honor and please Jason. She went and gave him flowers as soon as she learned that Jason was in prison. She went and as a witness she gave Jason freedom, and even as a noble man wanted to maintain the feminine dignity of Alice. He does not know that she feels now like Ismene. Jason is now free and working in his place. Alice loves him; she wants him, but she does not believe that she deserves a men as noble, as strong, and as understanding as Jason: Worshiped by all those who ever met him.

Tuesday morning, all of a sudden, before leaving, Ismene went out. She was simply, but as usually, beautifully dressed. She went in one of the flower shops and ordered flowers. "I want a bouquet of roses and carnations, and I will pay what it costs. It should have six white and six red; with some green leaves of both. Put them in a light green vase. I will come and pick them up in the afternoon at six o'clock. Can you do that?" she asked. He thought and said, "I will, but the cost?" She looked at him and replied, "The best but reasonable."

She was always charming whether she answered or questioned others. She was leaving and the man said to the lady at the desk, "My god, she was a charm, hard for anyone to say 'no.'" She looks at her as Alice was leaving and replies, "I would not say 'no' either, if she asked." "That's impossible," he answers smiling. Both laughed as Alice was leaving. Then, Alice turns around and replies, "Tell the gentleman it was impossible." Both the man and the woman were surprised! She heard them and they were embarrassed. They didn't know however that Alice was a noble humorous lady, as well.

At six fifteen Alice paid and picked the beautiful bouquet. She looked at that carefully, went to the lady at the flower desk and said smiling, "If you were a man, I would have refused." The lady blushes and remains staring at Alice as she was leaving. At quarter to seven, Alice goes to the office of Jason. The young lady that opened the door was surprised to see Alice. She had heard about her, but not seen her before. As soon as she sees her, she realizes who she is and surprised, with a condescending smile said, "Welcome; I suppose that Mr. Jason has been waiting for you. Please, walk into the middle office." "Thank you," she replied smiling. That woman was a mystery: she could laugh and cry, smile and frown any time it was necessary and expected! None saw, observed and forgot Alice.

Alice walked slowly into the room and as Jason saw her, he got up surprised and smiled. "I am happy to see you Jason; and see that you are well as I expected," she said. "Yes Alice, I was lucky and I am happy to see you again." Alice walks to the low reception table, unfolds the small package that she was carrying, gives it to Jason and says with tears, "Please, accept the flowers of my freedom. They are the flowers you were bringing to me, each time we were seeing each other. All together gave me my freedom. I am thankful for your generosity." She is staring at him crying. Inside the vase of the flowers was an envelope with the money she had borrowed from Jason.

She grabs his hands, she kisses them and says, "Simon loves you and you love God, if he exists." Before he did or said anything, she leaves his hands and goes. He was surprised and moved. He remembered her tears. He went and sat back to his table watching the beautiful flowers. They could not be as beautiful as she was. Nothing could match the beauty and the perfume of Alice. Whether she is smiling or crying, she is captivating. If one saw and had that woman, he was in heaven praying for her.

White, red, green in a polished greenish vase, were the flowers elegantly placed! You were hypnotized looking at those buds that were to open and enchant you. Sensing their scent, Jason whispered: "Whoever was the man that sold her the flowers, he was enchanted by Alice!"

Alice left with tears running. The dark was falling soon and none could see the face of Alice. It was watching the harbor with the ships and the boats as Ismene was walking along the promenade. It was probably the last time Ismene was seeing the calm harbor of Kalamata. She wanted to go and forget. She wanted to see her mother and her father now both dead and find her brother later.

She wants to kill those who killed her parents. The smile of Alice is now erased but her brother must be alive. She knows his wife is German and wonders: Will she let him be the son of his father? Tall, handsome, educated and proud?

Early in the morning, well dressed in light blacks Ismene locks her apartment by the sea, gets into her car and goes to Patra. There she gets a light lunch and goes straight to Albania following the international road. By late in the evening she gets to Agius Saranta. She goes to the hotel above her old house. She wonders if it still exists.

She was tired when she got there and went straight to sleep. In the morning she got up early for breakfast, and after she drove up and down the street where her house was. Early in the morning a young fellow was working who noticed Ismene, and as she was walking for the third time in front of his house, he opened the door and asked her if he could help.

"I like this area and this is the third time that I pass by," she said smiling. The man was young and looked at Ismene with a strange interest. "If you allow me, may I ask you where are you from?" he asked. "I am from Greece and this area is charming," she said with her eyes pin in the eyes of the young man.

Then, he opened the outside iron door and smiling said, "We are Greeks too. Please pass if you please to see my mother. She will be excited to meet you." He yells for his mother and invites Ismene to follow. He looks Ismene in the eyes and she precedes while he follows. Soon the interior main door opens and a lady about fifty years old opens the main door. She sees Ismene and walks carefully towards her. She approaches her and in the last five meters she runs and embraces her with tears in the beautiful eyes. "My Ismene!" she screams and falls in the arms of Ismene. Then Ismene turns around, pins her eyes in the eyes of the young man and whispers, "You must be my brother Sergio!" she whispers and falls in his opened arms. "I have been dreaming about you for the last ten years," she whispers and cries.

Ismene turned again and embraced her mother. They got into the house while the mother and the daughter were crying. The son was smiling with tears in his face and surprised with the beauty of his sister. As they entered, a young lady was coming down from upstairs and embraced Ismene. "I am your brother's choice," she said with a smile. She was an attractive young German lady! Her eyes were also dark blue.

Jason had not seen Alice after his release. He was not saying anything but was missing her. He was getting pensive and idle. He lost his mother and was now left just with his sister. She had finished her school in England and was married with an Englishman. The marriage didn't work and Irene was in Greece disappointed. However, it was Norma her friend that made everything for her a pleasure. She was also aware of her brother's misfortune and was trying to please him. He never discussed his pain with others. His young sister was his only consolation.

It was only Norma her friend who took her in Jason's place and trained her as a broker. Jason was thankful to Norma who was patient and made Irene an excellent broker. Since Irene did not have the skill, Norma was clever to push her to just be the Broker for some knowledge-able traders. Jason was thankful. It was a solution to a serious problem. Irene had the education to learn and she did. With intelligent people she was capable to work and communicate. She learned to respond and be appreciated. Jason was aware and thankful. He was never forgetting his obligations. He was a character to admire and respect.

If there was a problem, she was directing the people with kindness to Jason. It was a pleasure for those people to work the difficult problems with Jason and continue after with Irene. With time, she became an appreciated Broker and very helpful for Jason. He was a man that knew how to express gratitude and guide them after in the care of Irene. He appreciated also the help of his sister. It was an appreciated help provided by Irene. The friendship of Irene with Norma was respected by Jason who was that period disturbed. The relationship was appreciated by all people. Irene had found undisputed support from Norma who was an excellent worker with responsibilities in the company. Everyone was thankful and Irene was accommodated to be pleased and please others. She could satisfy Norma in many issues of human relations in which she was trained.

But Jason's love for Alice was at times suppressing and affecting his performance. His friends realized that and decided to help. But it had to be done carefully because Jason had also grown arrogant. It was natural considering his continuous success in all relations: Human, business and arts. His support of Norma for the sake of his friend Simon was an invaluable asset for she proved with time to be an invaluable Financial Analyst: one trusted, believed and successful. Jason was thinking of Norma and was happy because she could communicate with him in many difficult cases and be reliable. Norma was making Simon happy, and Simon had the Jewish gift of being a good one and easy professional with humor playing his Bouzouki. Stuart was his partner.

Stuart and Simon got together a night at Pete's bar and had a long discussion. First, they agreed that Jason's performance was getting marginal. It was not vital and vivid as before. A number of times, Norma's advice proved more wise and thorough. Second, they agreed that they had to relieve him of the pain of Alice. He had to find what she was doing and make a decision: Either she had to go to him or go to hell. Third, it had to be done carefully because Jason had grown more defensive and arrogant. But his friends loved him with no reservations. Each one has a place and we should search to find it," he used to say, and he was firm about it!

Stuart called Jason at Le Garson, on Aristomenus street, with Simon. The three friends were more comfortable now than before. Jason had overcome the trauma of his sister who would prefer to die than go back to the British fellow who wanted her. "He is a scum," she would say and refused to talk about. She had the art to avoid talking about him. Anyway, the three friends got together and both Stuart and Simon asked about Irene. I am sure that Norma can tell you everything: "She is doing fine," said Norma. "If Norma says that she is doing fine, I am sure she is excellent," said Simon who liked Irene as much as he liked Norma. She was the sister of his best friend that he respected.

After ordering their drinks and joking about women Stuart said to Jason, "Jason, you know we love you; that is why we use the freedom to be expressive with you." He smiled listening to Stuart; but Stuart ignored the smile of Jason and continued. "You and Simon should go to Agius Saranta and find out what Alice is doing." They concluded that Simon was more trusted and loved by Alice; and Simon was to go with Jason, find Alice and decide. They agreed that Alice was easier with Simon and essentially more loving him after Jason than any other. "She will do anything for Simon out of love. He would refuse that, but Stuart knew why, no matter how. Simon would refuse anything that had to do with the killing of Jack. Two were the people that did it, Simon and Alice; and two that knew it, Jason and Stuart.

But none could prove anything. All could conclude anything but not on solid basis. All could be wrong not suspecting the cooperation of Simon and Alice. She was a noble woman beyond comprehension: Ready to give her life for Jason. It was agreed that Simon who loved Jason like a brother for many reasons, should go with Jason and find Alice to solve the problem.

"Who knows? She may have been married and that would solve the problem," said Stuart. Simon looked at Stuart and said, "Yes, that will solve the problem. But you don't know Alice! That is why, we should find out and make Jason screw all the woman who are dying for him; instead of wondering. We all understand love but with limits." "Are there limits? Do you know them?" asked Stuart smiling. He had the experience with Anna. Simon looks at him and says, "Yes, we should find them and let Jason know. We have listened to him and he should listen to us at least once. I know that Alice loves him with passion, but she is embarrassed with him and she will never marry him."

"Don't say that," said Stuart. "I will say it again and again till you know," said Simon. "It is probably true, but not well said," replied Stuart smiling as he was drinking his wine with Simon who was thinking. Simon was of Jewish origin and could give a hell to Christians about Christ. "If you say that Christ is God why should I refuse it? He was Jewish, wasn't he?" he would ask and laugh.

Stuart agreed with Simon that they were going to do it. "This will give the answer to Jason who wants finally to know," even though he was going to do what he was supposed to. Now that his sister is settled at the firm, Jason looked also more relaxed and determined. He was unbearably thankful to Norma. Now she was his choice in everything. Jason was not one to make one a favor, if that one didn't deserve it. "Jason you will go to Albania in Agious Saranda. There you should ask to see Alice. You should go there and find out what she is doing. Then you come back." Jason smiling asks, "Why should I go to her and not she come to me?" asks Jason very relaxed and smiling. He was looking at Simon and Stuart was waiting for the answer.

Tears run out of Stuart's eyes that surprised Jason. "Because, she was wrong and you were right. And I think that you should go with Simon. She knows him better than anyone else." Stuart was very serious and Jason begun thinking. "What should we say," asks Jason looking at Stuart. "Anything you like. You can say, for instance, that you were passing by and you thought it wise to stop and see an old friend." Jason looked at Simon and asked smiling, "And you should come with me Simon?" "Of course; unless you don't want me to," replies Simon seriously. It was clear to Jason that it was a demand of his friends that he could not refuse. It would have been absurd of the Three Musketeers otherwise. Jason could not refuse the demand of his friends.

Jason realized what was going on, and smiling he said, "Okay, when do we do that Simon?" "Tomorrow if you please," replied Simon seriously. Jason thought for a few seconds and replied, "Okay Simon, I will be at your place at seven in the morning. We should have some light breakfast and go." "Thanks Jason; I will be waiting for you," replies Simon smiling pleasantly. Stuart who was listening, he was delighted and smiled also. However, he did not say anything more on the subject. It was getting late and the friends decided to go. Smiling they greeted each other and left.

It was not as bad as Stuart and Simon were thinking it would be. They were convinced that Jason was getting tired and wanted to rest also. They were happy though that they were to know, even though Simon, who knew Alice better, was certain that she was not going to be with another man. She loved Jason and she would be also thankful. She was not deceiving. Simon was certain: Alice was a miracle for Jason.

It was late at night but Irene was waiting for her brother. He finally came and she cordially welcomed him. "You are little late Jason. I hope you don't mind that I was waiting." Jason smiling as usually replies, "Of course I don't mind, as long as you don't feel that you have to wait," replies Jason. "Oh, no, I don't. I just wanted to see you," she replies smiling. Jason sits down and says, "Irene, I have to tell you that tomorrow morning I go with Simon to Agius Saranta for work and we are going to see Alice, as well, if we can." "Ah! I am sure she is very pleasant as Norma tells me. Please give her my greetings as well. Tell her that I am your sister and I would like to meet her when she comes this way."

He looks at his sister and replies, "Of course, I will, if I see her." She looks at him and remarks, "Norma keeps telling me that she is very intelligent and charming. Please, don't forget to tell her that I will be happy to meet her." There she stops. Then she adds "I am very happy working for you now," she added smiling. "You should thank Norma," added Jason. "Yes I will," she replied seriously. She knew that it was true.

Jason looks at his sister pleased and replies, "Yes I know. Norma for some reason is attracted by Alice and wants to be her friend." "I want to be also," says Irene and looks at her brother wondering. He looks at his sister and replies, "I know her; she is very charming. But to see her; we may some day when she comes this way." His sister looks at him and replies wondering, "Why not get a visit some time and see her as well?" she asks wondering. "Of course, we may," he says surprised.

"Jason, I would fix your things the way mother did. So please, let me watch so I can try next time." "Of course Irene, I will call you as soon as I am ready," replies Jason. His sister looks at him and gives him a warm kiss in the check. Soon after, Irene carefully watched her brother to be sure she knew how to prepare his suitcase. They were going to load it in the morning in his car. She was unbelievably very happy. She was thankful to Norma.

When Stuart got home, his wife said, "You are late again and I am not going to wait for you next time." Stuart looks at her and says, "I didn't tell you to wait, did I?" She looks at him and smiling says, "I forgot to tell you last time that Alice was a charm. So don't think that I was not attracted. I say this so you invite her or me again so we get together when she comes." "Sure I will," replies Stuart stunned.

"By the way, I know that tomorrow Jason and Simon go to Agius Saranta, and they may see Alice, if she is there," he adds. Anna smiled and asked, "You mean, they are going to look for Alice, or they are going that way and they may look for her?" she asked curiously. Stuart looks at her and says, "Well; you may ask, if you please, Irene or Norma. I know they will tell you." "Okay Stuart; I will ask if it is so hard for you to answer. I like Alice anyway. She is a devil!" Stuart smiled but said no more. He knew that his wife was sharp and right. However, it was not the time to enter that late in a conversation.

Anna called Norma and said, "Norma, I asked my husband but he was tired and secretive. What do you think Jason and Simon go to

Agious Saranda for?" "I think Anna, they are going for Alice. But she is pleasant anyway; why do we care?" "I think so too sweet, but let them feel that they are secretive. We love her anyway," "Okay sweet; let them think that we are so naive. I will be happy to see her again. She is so charming." Norma already knew that her teacher Jason and her husband Simon were to have early breakfast before leaving. She prepared herself not to be surprised. Jason was her teacher and supporter. She was glad each time he stopped at her place for breakfast, before going somewhere with Simon. She was in love to do that and please Jason anytime.

In the morning, Jason and Simon had a nice breakfast and as usually Norma joined them. "When are you coming back?" she asked. Simon looked at her and replied, "When we are done." She looks at him and replies, "Well, I knew the answer." "We are planning to be back by Monday," says Jason smiling. "If we are done," replies Simon. She looked at her husband smiling and said, "Remember, if you see Alice, tell her that we have all missed her." Jason smiled and said, "I am sure to tell her that, when I see her." Norma laughed, and happy as ever, she made sure they were pleased. Just before an hour, Jason and Simon left. Norma always knew how to have Simon ready. Now, Irene was doing the same with Jason. He was pleased and Irene happy to please her brother.

Jason and Simon left at eight in the morning from Kalamata to Patra. There they met Nicholas. He treated them at the intersection of the Suspension Bridge. They had their coffee and biscuits and drove north for Ioannina. Nicholas as always was fun. "Gentlemen, if you need help remember to call. But I am sure; with Jason's car you will need no help," he said smiling. "And remember to call me in your return," he said again smiling. "If you need to see anything on your return, please don't forget to call. I wnt to be ready."

Both Jason and Simon laughed with Nicholas. For some reason of his own Nicholas liked Patra and had kept his apartment since he got retired. None knew the true reason. More likely was the medical service he was receiving after retirement. But it was not the best solution.

However, it was one satisfying Nicholas: A good man and an appetizing professor of Mathematics highly respected by his students.

Later, Jason and Simon arrived at Ioannina. They had early dinner at a place by the bridge and then drove back to Epirus. At the border of Greece with Albania they checked and were instructed in the morning to go to the police station in Agius Saranta and make their entrance for whatever period they wanted. Anyway, they arrived late in Agius Saranta and rented an apartment at the new Butrinti Hotel. They were tired and decided to rest and Saturday to search for Alice's place.

They were very busy and they had to be effective. They were sure that the place was not so large. Jason was, besides, a man that had collected all the information pertaining to Alice's place.

They were hoping to enjoy Agius Saranta on Saturday night and Sunday till the afternoon. At night of Sunday they could go to a good restaurant and enjoy a real Albanian meal and music.

8   JASON AND ISMENE IN 'AGIUS SARANTA'

"When in Love you think of pleasures and not duties."

Stuart, Jason and Simon have their night break at the 'Garson' on Aristomenus street. Stuart and Simon have to request Jason to search for Alice. They know that Jason is falling apart and justifying his failures in the present by his successes of the past. Jason knows that Simon had met Alice before and defends now himself offensively.

In defending himself aggressively Jason asks Simon, "Why didn't you then marry her when she wanted you?" he asks. Simon smiled. "First, I was afraid to have any relation with a woman like Alice. Second, I could not approach her." It was Simon's answer, so wise. "But you don't have my problem, do you?" asks Simon and waits for an answer. He knows there is no answer to a stupid remark.

While he was filling his glass with wine, the reasonable Jason asks, "You mean, you have not seen me do what one who loves should do?" "No, we do not think so, and we have not said so," replies Stuart. "We believe that something has happened in Alice's mind concerning Jason and we should find out. Then we should quit," answers Stuart. "Then we should know how wrong we are, and quit," replies Simon. "Then we should know and it will be your choice what to do. We will be free to let you do, what you think is right. Don't forget we are your friends." added Stuart; "and you know our meaning!"

Simon and Stuart remained thinking. "I quit, but I trust you more than the devil. I should not be intransigent. Tell me what I should do and I will do it," says Jason peacefully. Stuart and Simon look at each other. Jason waits to hear. Then Simon says, "I will go with Jason to meet Alice, see what she is doing, listen what she says and come back. Then Jason should know what to do." Simon waits to hear what Stuart and Jason think. "We leave Friday morning and come back, as soon as Jason decides," adds Simon. Stuart looks at Jason and waits. "That is fine, gentlemen," replies Jason with a smile of doubt and disbelief. Stuart accepts this as agreement and smiles.

The three friends remained thoughtful. "Thank you Simon; thank you Jason," says Stuart catching the hand of Jason. Simon smiled looking at Jason and added, "In that case gentlemen, Jason and I should leave early tomorrow morning. I will be ready in my apartment waiting for Jason." There was no objection. Stuart paid and the friends left. Each had his own thinking but none was speaking. But they were laughing though diverting their discussion. The three Musketeers loved each other; but they remained skeptical.

Early Friday morning, Jason got into his car and drove to the harbor apartment of Simon. Norma welcomed him and offered them, including herself, a nice small breakfast. Soon, early Friday morning, Simon with his small as usually suitcase got into Jason's car and left. They drove through Patra where Nicholas met them for coffee at one of the places, near where you turn to cross the bridge of the strait and drive north to Greece. Jason and Simon were very happy and friendly.

"We are going to get a woman," said Simon to Nicholas smiling. "If you need help, don't forget," said Nicholas. He wished them good trip and good luck as they left. They stopped at Ioannina for something light to see and eat, and continued their trip. At night about eight o'clock, they were at the border. They got some papers with some delay; they were instructed what to do next morning, and they left.

Jason and Simon arrive at night about nine o'clock. They go to rest at Butrinti Hotel, and look for Alice next day. Each gets a room at the hotel, they have a nice night dinner, and after resting for awhile go to their rooms for shower and sleep. They get up early and Jason arranges everything about the hotel and other visit issues. Their problem was to find Alice and know what she was doing. Neither Stuart, nor Simon believed that Alice was ever a whore. Disrespectful men may have raped the young lady, but they were not to live after.

Jason and Simon asked first for the names of Mr. or Mrs. Aristomenes. They spent all morning and the conclusion was pleasant: Mr. Aristomenes was the Economist in the Bank of Agriculture. He was killed almost six years ago. His daughter had escaped to Greece, about two years ago, and his wife had survived and kept her house partly with her husband's salary, and the help of her son Sergio. They didn't know anything about the return of the daughter. They gave them the address of the house as well. Jason and Simon were happy. The morning of Saturday was wisely spent; and Agius Saranta was a pleasant Albanian city. You could not go in that place and forget its history and art.

Jason and Simon decided to spy on Saturday and Sunday and see what they were to observe. They saw a young man working on Saturday morning at the yard; and an old attractive lady who went shopping in the morning of Saturday and returned after two hours. There was no sign of any other people. In the afternoon they saw a lady in the house working but it was not easy to make any conclusions. She was young and they thought that she was a maid or possibly the wife of the young men or the wife of some man or his sister. They had to be careful because they didn't want to be observed or fail.

They decided to observe on Sunday and Monday and get more information before they visited on Tuesday. It was too early to call before they had some information. It was still cold for swimming but the hotel was pleasant with many services and good entertainment. They could relax in the bar and be served anything they wanted. "I hope they serve some of the nice ladies too," whispered Jason smiling. "I do not think there will be a problem," answered Simon. The ladies were young and tempting.

The place clean and not expensive. And the services very liberal; in a politically conservative land.

On Sunday morning Jason and Simon spied the place before their visit to the museum. It was a pleasure! Jason and Simon decided to spy on Sunday afternoon, as well, and see what they were to observe. They tried to be very discrete in their search and appear at most as two friends walking casually through the area.

They saw a young man on Sunday morning working at the yard with a young lady. An attractive older lady was working in the morning of Sunday in the kitchen and beautiful music was coming out of the living room. There was no question that both young gentlemen enjoyed the music. Who was playing the music? There was no sign of Alice or any other people. Who knows! They were to find out. They were hoping but they left to see the museum and spy again in the afternoon. They had no time to waste. Besides, it was sunday and any people that time were to be home. They had no time to waste.

In the afternoon of Sunday nothing was to be observed or concluded. Only the music was playing from the living room. It was quite far and not well heard as before. Jason and Simon went late for lunch and after that they went to rest. They were disappointed but still hoping. However, it was still early afternoon on Sunday and Jason with Simon were still hoping. After their afternoon spying, they were disappointed. None was working outside on Sunday afternoon. Jason and Simon decided to go for dinner in the evening in another place and at night visit again the Butrinti bar for some fun with wine and the ladies. They could watch but not touch. Simon was the one more likely who could watch but not touch.

They really wanted to relax. Simon was sure that Norma was his passion and his friend Jason was hoping to finally decide about Alice. He could not believe that she had forgotten him, anyway. But who knew to let him finally be free and his friends content? Men are easily confused but women always want to know and expect. They are more determined when men fail. They are more confident and persistent. They know how to exploit the weaknesses of man and many times win. Do they succumb? No, they wait for later. Yes, sometimes they lose.

On Sunday morning, Jason and Simon spied the place before their visit to the Museum. It was a pleasure! Jason and Simon decided to spy on Sunday afternoon, as well, and see what they were to observe. They tried to be very discrete in their search and appear at most as two friends walking casually through the area. It was beautiful to walk in Agius Saranta by the beach at the center.

They saw a young man on Sunday morning working at the yard with a young lady. An attractive older lady was working in the morning of Sunday in the kitchen and beautiful music was coming out of the living room. There was no question that both young gentlemen enjoyed the music. Who was playing it? There was no sign of Alice or any other people. Who knows! They were to find out. They were hoping but they left to see the Museum and spy again in the afternoon. They had no time to waste. Besides, it was sunday and any people that time were to be home. They had no time to waste in a place they knew.

In the afternoon of Sunday nothing was to be observed or concluded. Only the music was playing from the living room. It was quite far and not well heard as before. Jason and Simon went late for lunch and after that they went to rest. They were disappointed but still hoping. However, it was still early afternoon on Sunday and Jason with Simon were still hoping. After their afternoon spying they were disappointed. None was working outside on Sunday afternoon. Jason and Simon decided to go for dinner in the evening in another place and at night visit again the Butrinti Bar for some fun with wine and the ladies.

They really wanted to relax. Simon was sure that Norma was his passion and his friend Jason was hoping to finally decide about Alice. He could not believe that she had forgotten him, anyway. But who knew to let him finally be free and his friends content? Man are easily confused but women always want to know and expect. They are more determined when men fail. They are more confident and persistent. They know how to exploit the weaknesses of man and many times win. Do they succumb? No, they wait for later or for another one.

Jason and Simon left and went to a place for dinner. Each one was immersed in his own thoughts. Simon was calm and resigned in his own logic. Jason was stoically concluding the outcome. But he loved Simon and said, "You know Simon; I have you to always hope." Simon looks at him and says, "It is a relaxing place Jason and the Albanians are friendly. I am really glad to have this experience." "Yes, we have always the bad ones. I really don't know what to say besides the fact that the bad ones are always looking for the better in life." "Yes Jason; but that was not the case with Alice."

Jason thought but didn't answer. He knew he was wrong. He loved Alice and he could not believe that she was going to drop him like that. Nothing so far was encouraging or promising.

Sunday night Jason and Simon sat in the Butrinti Bar each one to have a glass of wine and relax. A young lady serves them their choice of sweet red wine and she gets enchanted with both. Ten to fifteen minutes later, another young lady, very attractive, passes by and distinctly looks at Jason and Simon enchanting with an attractive smile. "She is a charm," says Jason looking at the young tall lady as she passed by slowly looking around. "Yes she is," replies Simon lost in his own thoughts. But she was not better than Norma. Of course, not with his own criteria and preferences! But not with those of others!

A few minutes later, the second lady passes again and bashfully looks at Jason. "She is charming, is she not?" says Jason looking at the lady and smiling. Simon looks at her and answers, "Jason, she is really a charm?" He was looking at the young lady who this time passes looking at Jason embarrassed and lowering her eyes. "They seem to select their service for their beauty first and everything else second," replies Jason. "Then, if they like and if they can, select their lover!" answers Simon.

Soon after, the second young lady comes back and asks, with a smile, looking at Jason, "Gentlemen, is there something else can we offer you?" Jason looks at her and smiling replies, "We would like another glass of the same, for each one of us." The lady smiles at Jason and leaves. Soon the first lady comes with their wine drinks. Jason feels embarrassed as he is looking at the second lady. The young lady looks, and she understood Jason's search for the other lady. It was not that the first young lady was not charming, but the second one was amazing and enchanting. She was little taller and capturing, yet embarrassed looking at Jason who sees her and gets enslaved. She was really a charm to want: Tall and brunet but obviously much more difficult and composed. This was an evaluation hard to forget.

She sees Jason, approaches the table and shyly asks, "You look challenging. Where are you from?" She wonders looking at Jason's large long fingers and large sliding blue-green eyes. Jason smirks and replies, "I had the same question looking at your dark hair and your dark charming and burning eyes." She lowers her eyes, then raises them again and answers, "I am from here, but I have spent the last six years in Istanbul with my father." "Do you have those charming and inviting eyes from you mother or your father?" asks Jason looking at her with admiration. She smiles and replies, "My father is an Armenian but my mother is a Greek and has blue eyes; not blue like yours of course." She remained enchanted with Jason's attracting large blue-grey and expressive eyes. He was searching with his eyes her physical charm. "I am from Greece," he replied. She was really attractive and magnetizing. But she left whispering, "I hope to see you tomorrow, again." She was enchanting and Jason was really attracted and charmed. The young lady, was enslaving and knowledgeable!

Jason looked at Simon smiling. "Women are tempting; aren't they?" said Simon watching the lady who was leaving. "Lets go Jason to avoid the temptation. No woman can compare with Alice," said Simon. Jason left a good tip to the young lady who was serving, flirting and tempting both young men. But she was lucky. Simon was captured by Norma and Jason enslaved by the charms of Alice.

He had come from Kalamata to Agius Saranta for Alice and not for any other woman. But Jason was not Simon. The mind was attracted and the body was given. He really liked the lady who was not Alice but she was attractive and intelligent. Neither Jason nor Simon could both be wrong. She was intelligent and charming, beyond doubt.

Sunday, Jason and Simon, very relaxed, had their breakfast at the hotel and they decided to see if the people in the place of Alice were working. They passed by the place of Alice but they were not lucky to see if she was there. Another lady was working with the man who was charming to work with. This was a surprise for both. But Jason said, "This is a German lady." Simon remained thinking. She might have been the wife of the young man, concluded Jason, but he didn't say anything. "I wonder if there is another lady also," said Jason.

"I am sure though that this is the address I was given, but I don't know what happened to Alice," said Jason annoyed. Simon didn't say anything because he expected to learn soon. Jason was really upset and looked disappointed. He wanted to be right but he was afraid that he might be wrong. The Sunday night was relaxed and both did not see any other woman besides the German lady, as Jason thought. Simon was pensive. He knew that Alice was a precise lady: Not deceiving or lying.

For two days, Simon had not seen or heard about Alice. They were both wondering and kind of disappointed. But they could not say; and they were both questioning if they were looking at the right house. Jason was already tired and wanted to leave. He was getting depressed and wanted to abandon the effort. There were not many like Alice, but there were enough ladies like Flora. Jason wanted to escape from the grip of Alice. But it is one the thing that you want and another the thing that you get. And there was no God to tell them.

Simon was getting upset and said disappointed to Jason, "We have a plan and we have to follow it till we can say what happened. I will not say what you are saying till I have the answer. Our women are enchanted with Alice; Stuart is waiting for a reliable answer, and Nicholas would like to know as well. You know how you feel, but you don't know how

I do." Simon was still waiting to see. There were only two days left including Sunday. Simon was certain that Alice could not deceive. She was a noble and trusted lady. She was not a Greek lady who had lived in England and knew how to flirt, lie and deceive.

Jason remained thinking, wishing to drink more and follow what the hell Simon was expecting and wanted. He was of course wrong but he had not finished what they had come for in Agius Saranta. He knew that Alice could not lie! Soon the beautiful dark eyed lady comes again and smiling says, "Would you like something more?" She smiles with admiration that she cannot hide. "Bring me what you think I want," replies Jason and waits for the answer.

She looks at Jason, smiles and responds, "If I knew you, I would." It was a whisper with a charming smile. But she could if she wanted and she was not shocked with the serious charms of Jason: A man was really charming if you watched his blue eyes in the setting of his face. Jason looks at the young lady surprised and as she left, Simon whispers, "What she wouldn't give to have you Jason, if she had." Jason smiles slightly and whispers, "The most beautiful woman wants me when I am already enchanted with a whore!"

Simon bitterly smiles again, but he says nothing drinking his wine. Simon does not seem to agree; smiles but says nothing. "Of course, we cannot do anything," Jason whispers. "It will be wise if you think that Medea will destroy you with the consent of Athena" whispers Simon smiling. "Yes if I cared more for anything else besides Alice." "Yes, because Alice is Medea." "Don't course me Simon. I do not want the fate of that Jason. Medea was charming but that Jason was ambitious." "Well, you are not?" asks Simon surprised.

The young lady brought something that Jason liked, but Flora had ordered. When Flora came back, she asked calmly wondering, "Did you like what I thought about you? You don't have to pay if you didn't like it; and do not say you did, in order to pay!" "No, I liked it," replies Jason looking with admiration at Flora. "In that case, you must like me too. Blessed is the woman that will have you," whispers Flora with a shy smile. Jason looks at her surprised and answers, "No woman has me now." Flora leaves thinking and wondering with his charm. "If it is not Medea I would have been happy," she whispered leaving. She was really a charm attracting and puzzling; a good posture and modest. What Jason would not give to her in Istanbul. She was really the goddess of flowers with charming and enchanting black sparkling eyes!

In less than half an hour later, Jason was sitting in his hotel room so far reflecting about his life. One woman had attracted him and he had to chase her for she was so noble and so unfortunate that she believed she didn't deserve him. So many young and beautiful woman wanted him but he was enchanted by Alice; a bastard's whore. Tears run down from his eyes regretting his whispered expression. He hated his expression but Alice was really the slave and the whore of a bastard. He could not understand himself and his fate. He could not understand his attachment to Alice and his desire. But he was right. She was charming!

Jason looks at the young lady surprised and as she left, Simon whispers, "What she wouldn't give to have you Jason, if she had." Jason smiles slightly and whispers, "The most beautiful woman wants me when I am already enchanted with a whore!" Simon bitterly smiles again, but he says nothing drinking his wine. Simon does not seem to agree; smiles but says nothing.

The young lady brought something that Jason liked but Flora had ordered. When Flora came back, she asked calmly wondering, "Did you like what I thought about you? You don't have to pay if you didn't like it; and do not say you did in order to pay!" "No, I liked it," replies Jason looking with admiration at Flora. "In that case, you must like me too. Blessed is the woman that will have you," whispers Flora with a shy smile. She had seen that she liked him and she didn't like to lose the opportunity if he did. She was a charming young lady.

Jason looks at her surprised and answers, "No woman has me now." Flora leaves thinking with a wish. "If it was not Medea I would have been happy," she whispered leaving. She was really a charm attracting and puzzling; a good posture and devastating. What Jason would not give for her in Istanbul! She was really the goddess of flowers with charming and enchanting black penetrating eyes.

In less than half an hour later, Jason was sitting in his hotel room so far reflecting about his life. One woman had attracted him and he had to chase her for she was so noble and so unfortunate that she believed she didn't deserve him. So many young and beautiful woman wanted him but he was enchanted by Alice; a bastard's whore. Tears run down from his eyes regretting his whispered expression. He hated his expression but Alice was really the slave and the whore of a bastard. He could not understand himself and his fate. He could not understand his attachment to Alice and his desire. He was probably right but he could not explain.

Flora was a charm but he wanted Alice. His mind and eyes were attached to Alice. His friends could not understand him but they were also captured by her virtues. They had no choice. She was a charm of beauty and knowledge that they could not find in their own woman no matter how they searched. His friends knew it but he could not admit it. Alice knew being enchanted and captured but not surrendered. She had chosen to respect Jason, no matter what he was thinking or what she wanted. She was a noble woman abused by a disrespectful scum.

As he was thinking and contemplating the beauty of Flora, his door is knocked three times. He listens, wipes his tears, goes at the door and asks, "Who is there please?" "She is Flora; the Manager of the Service in the Restaurant," was the answer. "Just a second please," he replies. He wipes his tears, opens the door and sees Flora blushing and smiling. He smiles and before she says anything, Jason asks, "If you please; come in; the truth is that I am thinking of your service, your beauty; your youth and I am enchanted." As she is smiling embarrassed, he adds, "Please, come in; your visit is an honor and a pleasure for me." The door is widely open and inviting.

Flora enters slowly and timidly. Jason adds, "Please sit down. It is my honor and pleasure that you came" She moves fearfully and Jason realized that she is inexperienced. "I can offer you what I have; and if you don't like it, you have my apologies." "No, no. I just came for a few minutes to hear your opinion about our service," Flora replies wondering and really afraid. You could easily see that in her smile. But, she was really enchanted with Jason. She was looking at him wondering. Jason had the expression of the enchanted customer.

Jason smiles genuinely and replies with calm as he was going to the little refrigerator of the room and brings almonds, cashews, coke and sweet wine. "Speaking for myself and my friend we were enchanted. The beauty of the serving women was amazing." "But we were only two," she says smiling and more relaxing. "Yes, we were two and you were only two; but why should there be a difference if we were or you were more?" replies Jason smiling and offering Flora a glass of wine.

Flora refuses and Jason offers her a glass of coca pointing to the cashews as well. "Thank you," she replies taking the coca timidly and smiling with fear. Jason's service is really enchanting. Flora is charming and looking at Jason with surprise. She can see that Jason is a noble gentleman to be trusted.

"Well, if you ever decide to invest in any Stocks or Commodities with our Company, I will be able to help you. I promise you success," says Jason smiling. The bright Flora smiles and responds, "Now that I know, I will not escape your capture." She thinks more and adds smiling, "But anything else was not necessary." Jason thinks and says, "I know that, but you came and I have to express my pleasure in case there was the least doubt of your physical and professional charm."

"If I had the least doubt of sincerity, I wouldn't have come," she replies looking at Jason carefully in his large blue-green eyes. "If that is the case, and you have no objection, I can bring a glass for myself as well, to join you," he says as she keeps looking at him enchanted. Of course,

Jason was smiling as he sat at the couch at a distance signifying a dignified professional dialogue to follow.

Flora is looking at him and bashfully replies, "There is no need, but I will join you to trust me." Jason didn't miss her bashful smile. He entered a conversation that was pleasant but could not last long. "I am sorry but it is too late and I wish you good luck for whatever you are in our place. I am thankful that we have pleased you; and we hope that you will remember us, each time you pass by our place," she says, and slowly, unwillingly gets up to go, forcing a smile.

"Thank you for coming," replies Jason and gets up as well. The young lady smiling says, "I know you have been enchanted and so I have been." She wanted to emphasize that and smiled waiting for a response. Jason looks at her and bashfully says, "Something that is mutual it is also hard to hide. But I am a serious Trader in Stocks and Commodities and I would like to serve you." She looks at him and replies, "I cannot say no after I have seen you more." Jason smiled content that the lady was really young.

"Thank you Flora; can I see you if I can?" She looks at him, thinks and replies, "Yes, you can bring Simon and I will bring Alexia, and I will treat you," replies Flora mildly smiling. Jason thinks and quickly replies, "That is noble! But give me your phone in case there is a problem. I will call you anyway just before six o'clock tomorrow; and I will see you anyway." Flora gives him a card to call her. Flora is enchanted, touches Jason hands, as if she knew him from long ago, and goes pleased and blushing. Jason was made really happy. He was sincere and pleased. Flora was really a beauty with no problems.

Flora was really pleased and Jason closed his door amazed and thinking: God, you didn't make many woman charming and inviting; and you gave us only one to be pleased and thankful. You are very brutal. You are ruthless if you exist. He knew God's answer if he exists: You have a choice, but this is the choice for two or more that you cannot afford! Jason thought of it and smiled.

He realized that Alice could be indifferent if he chose. But what about the others? The more stupid they were, the more they were demanding! Alice was noble and no other could replace her. Her beauty, her knowledge, and now her experience were rare qualities. But Flora was one of the few exceptions. Jason knew and could tell.

At about six o'clock on Monday, after their search for Alice with no success, Jason bitter and convinced that he was not going to meet Alice, decided to call Flora. She was happy to receive Jason's call and asked if there was to be any problem if she brought the beautiful Alexia along for Simon. "That will be great," replied Jason and Flora was happy. She wanted to be sure it was fine with Jason. "We may meet you anywhere it will be a pleasure for you," added Jason. Flora thinking asked Jason to meet them at the hotel and relax for Monday in a nice place that she was going to take them.

After their failure to find Alice anywhere, Jason and Simon were at the hotel waiting to meet Flora and Alexia. Simon was not flexible and happy but he had to follow his friend. "I think you are wrong Jason to think that Alice got another man. That is the fear of a man in love and ready to revolt." But they had the obligation to know first where was Alice. Their enchanted friends with Alice's charms were waiting. They want to know and wish to see her.

After their failure to find Alice on Monday, Jason and Simon were at the hotel waiting to meet the ladies. Jason was hoping that Simon was to be entertained at least by Flora. He didn't know yet Alexia. At five after seven o'clock, Flora comes with Alexia. The one is prettier than the other and the gentlemen were impressed. "A confident charm does not choose an ugly friend," whispers Jason. Simon smiles and adds, "Unless she is at least beautiful if not intelligent," adds Simon. Alexia had dark blue eyes and both, Flora and Alexia were charming and attractive. Both, Jason and Simon realized that; they looked at them with admiration but they said nothing. It was a good policy because the ladies were the one prettier than the other. Alexia was a Greek from Salonika studying in Istanbul.

They ordered each one a glass of sweet wine and soon Flora said, "We can go anywhere you wish; but if you choose, because we know, we may take you to a nice Seaport place with popular music. If nothing else, it will have very charming music and tasty food. "Yes, if the music will make the food tasty," said Jason smiling. "But be careful of Medea," said Flora smiling. "Yes if you are the Kings daughter," said Jason. Everyone laughed and Flora responded, "No, no; I am not." Everyone understood and laughed including Simon. Finally, they all agreed to let Flora make the choice.

Jason and Simon look at each other and Jason smiling says to Flora, "If you will, we trust that it will be perfect. We are sure you are and you know." Flora looks at Jason with admiration. But at the end she says, "Okay, I will. I have been here with my parents. Good food and music, and," looking at Jason and Simon she whispers, "good company will make our night a feast." They all wondered and laughed. The night indeed, started and finished with smiles and humor.

Not much later, they all get up and leave. In the front of the car sat Jason and Flora. Jason is driving his car. In the back, sat Simon and Alexia. In ten minutes they arrive little north of Alice's place. The place outside and inside is a charm. It is Monday and there are no many people. But this with the light pleasant music, to which Jason and Simon were fascinated, was a charm. When they got inside, Flora says something in Albanian and the man takes them in a table of four with good inside and outside views. You could see the boats near the restaurant and hear the light inspiring music that made one feel it was coming from outside, soft and sweet, charming and inviting.

The ladies were both speaking English and the company was easy. Flora who realized the impression of enchantment of Jason and Simon, touched the hand of Jason and whispered, "Jason, we both speak English very well." Jason smiled and Flora added, "But neither I nor Alexia understand love in English." Jason smiled and said, "But you can learn that too; it is not true?" She touches his hand, looks in his eyes, and he sees two tears coming down from hers. It was a surprise, but she answers, "No, you will see!" It was really a surprise for Jason and Simon could not plug his good ears. "Now may I order?" she asks again and proceeds. Alexia was listening with a pleasant smile but she was not saying anything. She looks at Simon and whispers, "I am sorry but Flora is noble and free." "I suppose," he replies smiling.

While Flora gives the order to a young and pretty waitress, she stops and asks, "Is there anyone who would like a red wine in place of yellow? None said no and she proceeded to order yellow wine. By the end they all had what they wanted: light wine, fried chicken with round potatoes; okra, squash and egg-plan, tomato and lettuce salad with oil and vinegar; and toasted bread. The dinner was tasty and plenty.

"Ladies and Gentlemen, we have nothing more to offer you on Monday," says Flora smiling. All were surprised and pleased. "It was more than enough," says Simon. "Next time in Istanbul, it will be my friend Alexia to order." "And in Athens or Piraeus it will be Jason," says Alexia smiling reserved. Jason and Simon were impressed with the freedom of the ladies and had no time to interfere. These ladies were free and the gentlemen were looking at each other with a smile impressed and eyes enchanted. Their eyes were sparkling.

After their excellent dinner and pleasant conversation, with light music, and ladies trying to free and please the men; all pleased and fascinated, they get up to go. Jason tries to pay the bill. "Sir, neither you, nor I have a choice. When you get out, please, try to convince Miss Flora," says the head waiter. Jason apologized but he was assured that there was no way for a different solution. He was surprised and impressed with the unexpected behavior. Flora's father had the Armenian spirit given to Flora: friendly, humorous and witty.

"I wanted you to be sure of my strength and not my weakness," Flora replied to Jason when he tried to complain. "Please, we are honored to be offered your company tonight; but tomorrow; when you have our permission, you will be free to do as you please." Flora smiled, Simon listened surprised; and Jason was convinced that the Flora and Alexia ladies were ones of honor. So, he chose to just smile and thank them. They were charming and well educated young ladies. They were not dancers in a harem of Istanbul.

After their dinner, they go to a place for desert with nice light classic music that all enjoyed. The girls felt more comfortable and the men more free. They all forgot, all their reservations and the night turned out to be pleasant. The pastry with the ice cream were tasty and all felt relaxed with the music. "When are you leaving?" asks Flora wondering and holding the hand of Jason all of a sudden. Simon thinks and Jason answers, "We hope to leave tomorrow by eight in the morning and plan to see at night the city of Ali Pasa in Ioannina."

"Nothing to keep you here any longer?" asks Flora tying Jason's hand with force and concentrating her eyes in Jason's. Alexia's eyes drop on the floor and Jason gets surprised. She knows something more about Jason. "I am sorry Jason, I know that you can have only one," and let her eyes run. Jason feels the girl and he can only smile sadly. He didn't know that he could have only one! But now he is learning; Simon smiled thinking.

Anyway, Alexia had to go and Jason was asked to take her home, if he didn't mind. "It will be my wish and pleasure to take you home, Alexia," whispers Jason looking at her with affection. It was the truth that made Jason and Flora happy. Apparently, Flora wanted to be longer with Jason. They took Alexia home and leaving she said to Simon with a smile, "It was my pleasure to have met you. And I hope to see you sometime in Istanbul." She gave him a kiss in the cheek, she greeted him and said, "Flora is a noble lady, Jason; not possessive like Medea, and not hungry." She looked at him with respect and added, "Don't forget to give us a call when you have a chance." She smiled and run away at her house, not far from the sea. Jason and Simon were looking with respect and admiration at Alexia as she run in her house.

They knew already that she was a woman deserving their honor. Flora was smiling with respect and admiration for Alexia. Jason drove back in the hotel with Simon and Flora. Jason and Simon had a glass of wine each and Flora her special fruit-drink. Not long after, Simon asked the excuse of Jason and went to sleep. He was made really tired by Jason's instability and agony in finding Alice.

It was not easy for Jason and Simon. "I hope you understand," he said to Jason. Then turning to Flora he said smiling, "Jason is young, but I am not; so I will say 'good night' and go to rest." He gave to Flora a kiss in the cheek and expressed the desire to see her again. She was happy, but Jason knew the truth. Simon was in love with Norma and she wanted no other man! She was in love with Simon and a respected member in Jason's place.

Jason and Flora were left alone and each ordered a second drink of the same. Flora was happy to be left alone with Jason and said, "Your friend is a noble man; is he not?" "He is not just my friend, he has my blood," replies Jason. "Once he was injured and I told the Doctors to give him all the blood he needed from mine." She touches his hand and Jason looks at her surprised. "I am happy that you feel like that. My father is Armenian from Greece and my mother is also Christian. There was never an argument between them." Jason looks at her with admiration and asks, "When are you going back to Istanbul?"

She thinks. "In the beginning of September," she replies wondering as Jason is touching her hand. "You know you can come and meet me in Istanbul, if you wish," she adds smiling and wondering. Jason does not give a promise, not being able to decide. So, he thinks and soon replies after thinking, "I certainly will. But I don't know when." She bends and kisses his hands covering her own. Then looking at Jason's eyes, she whispers, "Thank you Jason." All that Jason could do was to smile certain that he was not going to see Alice. Flora didn't ask for that, anyway. She was just admiring Jason, and he was already tired.

Jason was already influenced by the nobility of Flora and his failure to see Alice as he was expecting. "If you wish, you may come to my place tonight. Of course, I am not expecting you to come, but I am obliged to invite you so you don't think that I am not attracted. But whether you come or not, my heart is yours and my admiration of your virtues is not small. I have to admit that you are an irresistible charm." Flora looks at Jason and whispers, "I was told not to ever go with anyone to anyone's place unprotected and I didn't. But I was not told not to go if I wished. That is why I came."

She lowers her eyes to be sure she was correct to give herself to Jason. She didn't seem to care more than what she was all of a sudden. She wanted Jason! He thinks, looks at Flora and whispers, "Thank you Flora!" She looks at Jason and wonders, "I am more than twenty one years old; I am not Medea and you are not Jason of Colchis." Jason saw the eyes of Flora filled with tears and felt his tears rolling dawn as well. She was hard but he was easy! His eyes were blue-green sparkling, but her eyes were large black diamonds cutting anyone's heart.

Jason and Flora leave the Bar of the Restaurant and go to his room on the Hotel. They were both thinking as their eyes were crossing. Jason's were charming and serious, and Flora's black diamonds wet and surrendered. The room was comfortable and Jason made two glasses of sweet wine, one for each. The drinks were strong, sweet and hypnotizing. This made Flora less resisting and more tempting. Jason was tired and not so much excited; but Flora's charm was attracting and with the drink she was tempting and charming. She liked the drink and said touching Jason's hand, "It is amazing; it makes you feel free; but I will not ask for more." Jason smiled and being very close to her, he gave her a polite and tempting kiss. She wished to be wanted.

Jason's kiss was enchanting and irritating. Flora liked Jason's kiss as much as she liked his wine and fixed his hands! Jason realized that she was a virgin, as she claimed, not knowing what to do. He takes her tenderly by the hand and leads her to the bed. She followed willingly but at the same time afraid not knowing what to do and how to behave. But this was the charm a man has to remember. This is the passion he and she had to experience. She was a virgin and he probably had learned from another non-virgin what to do: He had probably learned from another young lady more likely experienced when he was venturing in music at his early youth. Who knows besides him? Everyone had his own experience.

Flora was the first virgin that Jason was experiencing and he was not much better. But as he takes out her little blouse and sees her beautiful breast, he thinks of Alice and kisses her nipples tenderly. He caresses the nipples of her breasts, kisses them mildly and gets excited, with her tying her body on his with some fear but strong excitement. He softly caresses her vagina and with reserved passion he penetrates her; he gives her a pleasure stronger than the pain. First time Jason felt the pain and the blood of a lady. She had painfully surrendered.

She ties herself on Jason's body and soon she faints in pain and pleasure. Jason and Flora both melt in a mutual passion that neither one was to forget. Both melted and finished together in the excitement. Flora caressed Jason with a smile that he was never to forget. Floral and Jason felt so strong that they were never going to forget her painful pleasure. Jason was surprised but he could say nothing. He was wondering while Flora was happy with the pain and the pleasure. She tied herself on Jason at the time of the magnificent strong pain and pleasure. She was smiling pleased and Jason enchanted.

Not long after, the charming Flora recovered and surrendered with passion to enjoy and share in Jason's pleasure. She gave herself again and Jason was surprised. In spite of her pain she surrendered to Jason and both were drunk with passion. The second time Flora was burning fire. Jason was not going to forget Flora; and when both finished together, the second time, Flora said smiling; "How happy I would have been if you could bite me and leave a mark on my breasts to remember you forever." She looked at Jason, and with passion she was kissing him. But after the second time, both Jason and Flora closed their eyes to rest for a while. It was a strong and delicious ending to remember. The smile on the face of Flora was charming for Jason.

In the arms of Jason, Flora was expectedly happy, and she knew that next time with the pleasure and not the pain she will be in heaven. "Now I know to love you and not to expect more, if you want me." It was really a difference for Jason that he was not going to forget. That was at least what he was thinking! A musician in love with Alice and fascinated with Flora: A real blooming flower! He didn't know more.

Jason is strangely pleased and wonders. Will another woman ever want him with the passion and strength of Flora? Will she try again to please him and herself with her passion only? Alice was probably the only one. Flora didn't tell Jason about her pain but she was hoping he knew. With no fear she was going to love him. He was the first man that gave her the pain and the pleasure.

"Will you ever come to Istanbul to give you my love again?" she asked smiling, wondering and wishing. I know that I am Greek and Armenian; but will you ever come to Istanbul to see me and give me your love again? I know you are Hellenic, but I will always wait for you to come. I have everything, but I need your love."

Jason was listening and comparing. He loves Alice, but Flora is a beautiful charm, a miracle of worship. She is passionate, mentally excited and given to Jason. He is certain that she is the first woman he only had. She is sane, understanding, passionate and given to Jason! "I know I will love and want you forever. But it is up to you whether I will be with you, or be forever dreaming. But please, come and see me in Istanbul. If nothing else, I will be waiting for you."

She was hoping to impress him when he was going to be in Istanbul. She knew that it still had the beauty of the Greeks who only knew to live and create with others but never to conquer and kill. Those who did it, were not Hellenic people. She was respecting, as most people do, that the Hellenic people were noble conquerors of mind and body. They could do well with the word but not with the whip.

Jason walked slowly back to his hotel room from the parking place as soon as Flora left. He fell on his bed to think and closed his eyes. But as soon as he fell to think and closed his eyes, he fell asleep. Alice was his passion and Flora his desire. But passion is stronger and more destructive! Desire is demanding but controlled and directed with pleasure. Jason was always considerate and respectful. This had impressed Flora. He was not a man expecting to take and not give.

Tuesday early in the morning, Jason and Simon were having breakfast. It was the last day that they had to look in the morning and visit in the afternoon to find out what happened to Alice. "I will be surprised if we find Alice free," whispers Jason, resigned and liberated. Simon looks at him and smiling whispers, "And I will be a fool if I see her with another." He looks at Jason and continues, "I thought, after I got to know her that she is an enchanting woman in love with Jason; and Jason in love with Alice." This made Jason smile. "You don't know Flora, do you?" asks Jason. He is tired and Simon whispers, "I didn't say anything about Flora; we came here for Alice and I spoke only about Alice," replies Simon. "If you want to speak about Flora, you may and I will listen. But let me know: I know she is a noble lady." "But no more virgin," whispered Jason.

Jason smiles and realizes that they came to Agius Saranta to meet Alice. He is certain that his friend is probably right and he does not want to hear about anything else but Alice. Of course, Flora is another case, but his friends do not want to hear or talk about. She had to live secretly in his dreams. Alice was his passion and Flora his love. He was dreaming of Flora but he was seeing and thinking of Alice. Jason decides to change the subject and shut his mouth. He is aware that he is enchanted with

Alice. They are no longer kids in love, but lovers to conquer each other. God give them the strength to love.

"Yes Jason; but that was not the case with Alice." Jason thought but didn't answer. So they changed the subject, as a young lady, dark but sparkling like a diamond comes to their table smiling. "I know this was to be your last day here and I thought it was wise to share this morning with you and your friend Simon," she whispers. Jason and Simon look at the lady surprised and get up to greet her. "Please, sit down," says Jason content seeing Flora unexpectedly. She sits down and whispers to Jason, "I was thinking about you and I thought it was wise to see you again." She sits down smiling, looks at Simon and whispers, "I correctly thought that Jason was not going to have with him a lady this morning and I decided to come and meet you again."

"Thank you," replies Jason. "I am sorry if I am impolite," she says smiling to Simon. "I was sure Jason was not going to have a lady this morning; and I was proud to be the one." "Yes, yes, that is true," replies Simon to Flora looking with admiration. He was surprised that the lady was a charm hard to miss or forget later.

"Will you have breakfast with us?" asks Jason smiling. She holds his hand and whispers, "Yes; a glass of grape fruit juice, a cup of my chocolate coffee, to wake up, and a glass of cold water." "If this is all, you will have it immediately," answers Jason smiling, while Simon was admiring the beauty of Flora. Fortunately, she didn't know the charm of Alice, if Alice was the Medea! "But, I will love Jason more than Medea," said Flora looking at Simon who was enchanted. She didn't know anything about Alice yet.

Flora was a charm and in the conversation she mentioned that her mother was pleased to have them for dinner on Wednesday. She explained to her that they were leaving late in the afternoon; and smiling she was claiming to be the first one in line for their next trip in Istanbul. Jason and Simon were pleased and both promised to see her again in their next trip to Istanbul. She was in love with Jason and Jason was not indifferent. He needed a woman like Alice and a woman like Flora. But you cannot have legally two women. Of course, you can have as many women as you can but not be legal. But why they have to be legal? Only the women can answer!

After an hour or so, Jason and Simon greet Flora to go to continue their business. Flora never learned why Simon and Jason were in Agius Saranta. But she was pleased and happy with the kindness and artistically talented character of Jason. He was a man she could associate and love; if she only could have! If she chose to love she must have taken the responsibilities as well. Flora was aware and happy if she could have the man whenever he could. She was really an independent woman that she wanted to have the choices of her will. She knew what she had done and she was happy to have the man whenever he could! She was not weak to be demanding.

---

9 LIBERATION OF CHARMING ISMENE

"There is liberation of mind and slavery of body."

On Tuesday early in the noon Jason and Simon went to see what was going on in Alice's place and then buy presents for their ladies. Simon looks at Jason and says smiling, "The young lady playing the piano is Alice, the young man is the husband of Alice, and the old attractive lady is the mother of Alice." "That is what I thought too," says Jason. He is really concerned. "Where is the German lady?" asks Simon. "Who knows?" concludes Jason. Simon did not believe it. He smiled ironically. "The lady playing the piano is Alice," says Simon smiling and Jason wonders. How the hell Simon knew? Simon was not in love with Alice. But he was surprised when he had a chance to know her. She was also a bright woman not easy to be deceiving or deceived.

Simon smiles and says, "I don't believe it, unless the young man says that." "Well, I am surprised with your optimism," says Jason without looking at Simon who does not respond. After thinking, Simon says, "We will see late this afternoon and we will know." "And we leave after," replies Jason. "Yes, if you please," says Simon smiling. But Simon, for some reason and experience, didn't believe it. Something had convinced him that Alice might not be there but she was not married to anyone. Simon knew! But none could say convinced that Alice was not anyone's but Jason's. Simon could!

The friends left and went to a place for late lunch. Each one was immersed into thinking. Simon was calm and resigned into his own logic; Jason was stoically concluding the outcome. But he loved Simon and said, "You know Simon; I have you, to always hope."

They were relaxed and by two o'clock in the afternoon, they returned to their hotel. "I want to rest," says Jason. "So do I," replies Simon and both friends went to sleep. By five o'clock they were up and by six thirty they were ready to visit and see if Alice existed. They were disappointed already but still hopeful. Alice could not have fooled them. She was not that type of woman, and lies were not at her door.

Simon was confident that they were if not see Alice, find at least where she was unless they had the wrong address. Jason had resigned that he would be free to forget. They had to find the truth and not call. Both put their suit and both were a charm. But Jason had the freedom that Simon was losing depending on the case. They got dressed and each was a charm: for Norma, Simon; and for Alice, Jason, if she existed. But Jason was really an exception: The leader of the Argonauts ready to capture Ismene.

They get into the car and by six o'clock they were at Alice's place. To their surprise the young man was working. They knock at the door to attract the working young man. He turns around, sees the two men waiting, leaves down the ax and goes at the door. "Yes sir, what can I do?" he asks politely. "On the way back to Greece, we thought to stop, give our greetings to Alice, if she is home, and then by tomorrow morning, continue our trip after we have seen the Old Greek Town," says Jason. He was not precise as to whether they had seen or were going to see the Old Greek Town.

The young man, almost the same age as Jason, smiled and said, "I am sorry Sir but there is no lady here by the name Alice. But you speak Greek don't you?" "Yes we do," replies Simon smiling. "Then, please come in," says the young man and opens the door. Jason and Simon are looking at each other and smile. "Please come in," says the noble young man opening the door with an inviting smile. "This is a Greek house and you are invited," says the young man smiling.

Right away, the young man turns to the house building and shouts, "Ismene, please come down, I have a surprise for you. Would you like to come down, please?" Two windows open, the left and the right, as they were looking at the house. On the second top floor in the one to the left was the lady that they had seen before; and in the one to the right was Ismene. The one to the left window kept watching and the one to the right put her right hand to muffle the sound of her surprise and disappeared running down. Jason and Simon didn't know what to do. They waited surprised. The lady was Ismene but not Alice.

The down door opens and Ismene walks out slowly watching Jason with tears. She walks to him slowly, catches his hands and kisses them crying. She sees Simon and goes to him. "I am so happy, so pleased and enchanted to see you," she says. Then, turning immediately to Jason she whispers, "Please follow me." She moves and sees her mother waiting at the entrance of the house. When she gets close with Jason following, she says with tears, "Mother, this is Jason; I have talked to you already; and this is Simon, I have no more to say. He is my brother." The mother greets them with affection, shaking both hands of Jason; and with admiration greets and embraces Simon.

"I am so happy that fortune brought you here; from whichever way you come. Please, honor our place with your presence," adds the mother. Before they sit down, she introduces to both Sergio who followed in, as Ismene's brother. He was a relief for Jason and pleasure for Simon because he was right! Soon after, the German lady was coming down and the mother says, "This is my son's wife; a grace hard to avoid. I am so lucky to have both of you: Ismene's fortune, company and salvation. My God, you love me!" The old lady was crying from happiness. Jason was calm and thinking. Simon was relieved and smiling. Tears run down on Simon's eyes. Sergio remained composed.

Simon was right in his estimation of Alice; and Jason was surprised to be confronted with something he didn't expect. "Simon, I will not say why you didn't bring Norma with you. But give her my love and sent her here with Jason's sister at least once; my mother will be happy." Simon smiled and said, "It has to be summer." Ismene smiled, agreed shaking her head, and said nothing more on that. But Jason was looking at Ismene's mother in consternation. She was dressed in light black, her hair was a mixture of black and white, and she was graceful deserving Ismene. She was an elegant woman.

They were offered cold water and ice cream coffee cake. Sergio said, "Allow us to take you for dinner tonight because our mother didn't expect anything and we were to go out anyway." Jason tried to reverse the invitation but Sergio smiled and said, "When we come to Kalamata, we will let you do that. Please, don't refuse now." Jason realized that Sergio was right and didn't argue at all. He was going to follow. Simon was not to interfere. He was moved by pleasure and watching. All six were a charm that neither Jason nor Simon could ignore: The brother was young, healthy and noble!

At night Sergio took them all to a nice place with excellent food and Greek singing. It was a surprise for both Simon and Jason. Ismene with her mother was a pleasure to watch. Sergio with his charming German lady was attractive. Six of them were a party of serious beauty. The singing was an experience that neither Simon nor Jason were to forget. In the process of enjoyment Simon announced that he has to leave early in the morning for Athens and Jason was to drive later, at his convenience, carrying also the presents. "That is what happens when you have people expecting," said Simon.

They all laughed and Jason replied, "It will not be hard Simon; I will take care of the gifts. Besides, don't forget, Nicholas will be expecting me in Patra anyway; for a rest and his present. "The Illyrian?" asks Simon smiling. "Yes, the Hellenic Illyrian," replies Jason and everyone laughed. Ismene had not met Nicholas and she was pleased to hear about him. They told her that he was professor of Mathematics at the University of Patras. He was an older gentleman.

The night was beautiful with excellent food, beautiful singing and charming dancing. Sergio asked for an Illyrian song and dance that Alice performed with Sergio to anyone's surprise. "I will never forget this," said Simon impressed. Alice was an unusual beauty and the leader of the music group came to thank her. "You were fantastic, young lady; I have to congratulate you," he said being enchanted by Alice's eyes and beauty. She thanked him with a charming smile that left the man surprised.

After, Alice tied Jason's hand looking at Simon. "I ought to you everything," she said with a sweet smile. Her mother who knew everything, looked at Simon with admiration. "Thank you Alice," said Simon with a smile. "I hope to see you back in Greece." She smiled and tied Jason's hand as hard as she could. She knew Jason's virtues better than anyone could think. She loved Jason with passion. She adored Simon with her trust.

Her experience with those men was amazing. She loved Jason but she worshiped Simon. She could die next to Simon with pleasure but sacrifice herself for Jason. Her trust on Simon had given her freedom and her love for Jason resurrection and liberation. She had experienced something that none expected and none could be surprised if she ever sacrificed herself for Simon or Jason.

The Greeks of the town were friendly and inviting. But Simon had to go and Jason was begged by Simon to stay. "Please stay with Alice and try to understand. I listen to you; you have to listen to me also once. I will explain to Stuart everything as it happened, when I see him. She is yours if you want her!" Jason thought and let Ismene know that he was going to stay in the hotel including Friday. He was going to leave Saturday morning.

Alice was happy and that is what happened. Simon let Jason stay and he left very early with the boat for Corfu and with the plane from Corfu to Athens. From Athens airport he took the bus to the bus Station in

Athens; and from there he went straight to Kalamata by the bus. Ismene was happy because she loved Jason and she would have him alone for two more days. Saturday morning Jason was leaving also. She was so excited that none could miss her pleasure and her brother knew.

Thursday morning, Ismene went to Butrinti Hotel at about nine o'clock where Jason was waiting. They already had their breakfast and they sat at the bar. Both ordered cold sweet-bitter coffee. She touched Jason's hand and he gave her a kiss. She smiled. "When are you leaving Jason?" she asked. He looks at her and replies, "Saturday morning." "Well, why don't you make it Sunday? My mother and my brother want to see you more, if possible." Jason smiled and replied, "That is fine; I will do that. I will leave Monday morning. It will be my pleasure." She touched his hand thankfully and kissed him.

He realized that it was Ismene's wish also to stay and decided not to request anything; not also to stay at their house. He never told her that he had come for her and she didn't expect it either. She was a very intelligent woman and eventually she figured that out. The willingness of Jason was expected. It was the start of Ismene's liberation.

"Well, now I am free till August and I want today to be ours in my mother's house with my brother; tomorrow it will be ours to see the museums; and Saturday at night we will be together again to do as you please. Sunday we will have our meal at my mother's; and Monday, I will say to you good buy till we meet again, if you wish."

She didn't say where, or when, but Jason understood anywhere she wanted. She looks at him and asks, "Jason, can you tell that my mother loves you?" "That is nice to know," replies Jason. "But Medea is what I want." Ismene looked at him, thought and smiled; but she said nothing. She was probably waiting to see. It's one thing to expect, and another to experience! Ismene was in haven unexpectedly. When she was with Jason, the world was hers. She made you forget the existence of anything else. She was a charming beauty.

Soon after, Jason and Ismene went to his room on the hotel. Tears run on Ismene's face when he kissed her. She looked at him and after his first kiss, Ismene turned wild. She was as never before. With passion and tears she gave herself. Jason was surprised. She was fire difficult to extinguish. She was a magician hard to escape. He forgot and surrendered. Her passion was her love and she wanted nothing more than Jason to exist. She was a slave in the arms of Jason.

She forgot everything and Jason got lost. She was a magician. Hard to resist and think of anything else but her body. It was youthful, warm, beautiful and charming. When she was finishing her first pleasure, the next would start, and the third would follow to let her finish with Jason. She was finishing with a smile of pleasure that Jason would remember. Every part of her body was touching Jason's to remind him that he was hers. He didn't believe that perception was to be possessing and her tears of passion to make him surrender. Ismene was in the process of liberation. She was an Illyrian not wishing to conquer but to posses.

No words could describe her holy pleasure and she said, "I wish to die after this in your arms and only you will be able to tell." Tears were flowing from Ismene's eyes. Then she asked him with a smile, "Now you can tell: Did you have Medea?" He looks at her and says smiling. "Yes, I had more than expected and Medea has the choice." "Thank you Jason, you know Medea never wanted to leave; but men are thoughtless." None could deny what she said and Jason was remembering his friend Simon, "He knew the truth but he could not describe it." Alice was pleased and smiling with tears.

"Why are you crying?" asked Jason curous. "Because I am not Medea and I will always love you." "Ismene, you should know that I will always love you." All of a sudden she replies, "I know but you will never know," she whispered. Then she caressed and gave him the most passionate kisses. She knew probably something that he did not.

Jason had the opportunity to know Ismene's mother and brother better. Sergio's German wife was not very pretty but very attractive. She was working with devotion when she did, and she was not talking a lot. But she was smiling and thinking when she heard or talked. She was though a serious German woman of a Greek mother.

Ismene's mother was gently imposing but very respectful of people's wishes. "Mother, I love him but I do not deserve his love," said her daughter Ismene. "Well, you are Ismene, you are not Alice. She got your revenge and passed away. He left you noble as you were not with him but with Jason that deserves you," replied her mother smiling. "I know he is a noble man and will remain so. He knows the truth and he will never be concerned; and none will dare think otherwise. You are, my dear, the only one concerned." Ismene smiled but remained the same. However, Jason never called her 'Alice' again.

Ismene could not stand next to a man with the virtues of Jason; and Jason didn't care if she did. She said to her mother, "Yes, but he knows what I am." Her mother looked at her with tears and said, "I was raped too, my dear; do you want me to die? Kill me, if you please, to go with your father. I was living and waiting for you. Don't deny me now." Ismene saw her mother crying, caressed her and said nothing more.

Sunday night, Jason was invited for dinner by Ismene's mother. It was also the wish of Sergio and his wife. They had used Ismene's mother, to be sure that Jason's presence was a pleasure for all. Sunday night the ladies prepared a nice dinner and everyone was excited. Among them was an Albanian lady Eva with her son Emilio that were helping Ismene's mother when she was alone. She was of pure Albanian origin and happy to help Ismene's mother when she needed her help. The dinner was Jason's choice, pointed out to the ladies by Ismene: Egg lemon soup was Jason's choice with lamp and baked potatoes separately. Ismene could not forget. She wanted every moment of Jason in Agius Saranta to be one of pleasure hard to forget. Jason was relaxed and entertained.

At the end of the dinner, Ismene brought a basket of presents at the table in the living room and said smiling, "Jason decided to tell everyone how happy he was to be with us by bringing a very small present for each one." She started with her mother, then her brother and went down to the Albanian lady and her son. Ismene's mother went to Jason, kissed him and said, "We are so happy, you are with us; it is our honor to have you; and don't forget that Ismene loves you." Jason looked at her and said, "Thank you Mrs., it is my pleasure to know that, and I love to have been with you."

Not long after, Sergio's wife approached him and said smiling, "Jason, remember we love you!" "Thank you Mrs." replied Jason looking at the German lady who was thoughtfully smiling.

Emilio received a copy of 'Odyssey' in Albanian and was immensely pleased. His mother, a nice pleasant lady remained thankful and always helpful. They all loved her, and she loved her present bought for her by Ismene. She didn't expect such an appreciation. "The Hellenic people are noble, the Europeans selfish," said Eva smiling. "Remember, there is no difference between the Illyrian and the Hellenic people, said Ismene's mother. They grow up together and they were brothers long ago and for long." Everyone smiled and was happy.

Finally, it was Ismene who kissed Jason in the lips and said, "Thank you Jason; you and my brother and your friends brought to life a dying family. I am so thankful to you and your beloved friends. I will never forget them." She passed her right pointing finger through his mouth and let two tears roll down her cheek. "Thank you Ismene," he said, respectfully. Everyone was pleased with the presents, and surprised with the freedom of Jason's ways. He acted as if he belonged to those people. His love for Ismene was unquestionable.

You could see everything in Ismene's eyes: Blue and grey under natural charming eye brows, and any tears that rolled under them were diamonds! Her mother approached Jason and whispered respectfully, "You should never forget that you are the only man that Ismene has loved. No man has touched her heart and mind." Finishing this, her eyes had the expression of admiration and love. Jason understood, knew and believed her. But he chose to say nothing. A stranger to be there his way, was condescending. He was really impressed. He loved Ismene and her people were all attractive and considerate.

The Albanian lady with her son left first pleased and surprised. Jason was so friendly and relaxed with them that they will probably never forget him. All people finally greeted Jason who was pleased.

"You should visit us in Colon Germany with Ismene," said Sergio's wife, shaking Jason's hands and smiling. "You should not forget what my wife asked," said Sergio smiling and looking deeply in the eyes of Jason. "Thank you for what have you done for us." His mother looked Jason in the eyes and said, "We all love you; but none like Ismene. Please, don't forget this." "No, I will not forget that," said Jason to the mother who embraced him with tears. She really loved her daughter.

Finally, Ismene escorted Jason to the outside door. There she kissed him with the usual passion and said, "Thank you Jason for the honor you gave to my mother and brother." She kissed him with tears that no longer were surprising to Jason. He was aware of the suffering of the people and the fortune to be with them.

Then Ismene said smiling, "I will see you tomorrow morning at eight o'clock." Jason looked at her and replied, "Please, do so. I will be waiting for you." He knew that it was a pleasure to be with a woman like Ismene. He wanted to remember. She was not an ordinary woman. Gods had competed for her favors.

Next day in the morning, Jason was waiting for Ismene at the bar. She arrived and both went for breakfast. An hour later, they went to his room upstairs and they did what they wanted. Ismene was as always in the beginning careful. But she was turning wild in bed with Jason. He was each time surprised but always satisfied. To convince her he said, "You should know that I will always love you, and I will always think about you." "You may always think about me, but I do not know if you will always love me." He looks at her and replies, "Yes, I will always want and love you, but I do not know for how long I will be able to."

She agreed and smiling kissed him. She didn't want to think about it anymore. She knew that they could always be wishing but not always be capable to fulfill their wishes and please. They might not be able to please physically always but satisfy spiritually! An appreciation was always expected from Jason: He loved Ismene.

Jason kissed Ismene again and left. "I will be waiting for you," he said as he was leaving. He remembered the wish 'be careful,' and he tried to be. But his passion for Flora was not satisfied yet: and her charm of independence and certainty were puzzling. She certainly was not as bright and knowledgeable as Ismene, but she was trainable and excellent in the things she was competing. That was Flora.

It was about noon of Monday when Jason called Flora. She was excited to hear him. "I will meet you at about one o'clock at your hotel," she said. "Please, wait for me at the Restaurant Bar," she begged. Jason smiled and agreed. He knew she wanted what he was dreaming. But it was mutual. He went to the bar and waited. Near noon she was there. She was so excited that she could not resist his kiss. She was kissed, and not waiting she said, "Jason, I am not Medea. You should be what you want to be. My mother is expecting us for lunch at two o'clock. You cannot deny that," she added smiling. "Of course, we will be joined with my beloved friends Nitsa and Saul." Jason smiled because he had already paid the hotel including tuesday.

They sat at the bar for an hour and talked about many things. Flora was ready to talk and listen. She didn't have the charm of Ismene. But she had the beauty and was more calm. She had not suffered in the hands of any scam and she was revolutionary. Her Armenian father had eloped her mother from Greece and he had come to Albania. Flora does not remember her mother to ever quarrel with her father. She was educated in one of the best schools of Istanbul in Business and she was calm and thinking always.

Her mother was Greek eloped by the Armenian and brought to Albania. "People will always be hungry and will need my help; cheap or expensive," her father used to say. He had his import-export business in the International City of Istanbul. Flora was now working for him for a year after receiving her master's degree from the Business School of Istanbul. "She is now in training but she is running fast," her father is used to say.

At about one o'clock, Flora is asked to drive. "I have to drive tomorrow for hours alone," whispers Jason. "Please, let me relax for a while today." Flora had no objection but smiled. "Yes, I will let you watch as much as you want at the city of Agius Saranta," she says smiling. Jason gave her a kiss and whispered, "You are a temptation never to forget now that I know you." Flora smiled but said nothing.

In about twenty minutes they arrived at a house built on the mounting and looking at the sea. It was really spectacular looking southwest. Jason was trying to see if he could recognize any of the places. But it was difficult for him to say. "It is charming, is it not?" asks Flora. "Indeed it is. All these houses are charming and inviting with their southern yards for the tourists." Flora is listening and smiling. "Does Istanbul has houses as charming?" asks Jason.

"Istanbul is a city of history built by the Greeks, the Armenians and the Jews," replies Flora. But they all had to be Turkish. "When you come to Istanbul, I will let you know." Not long after, they arrive at Flora's house and her mother with Nitsa and Saul open the Garden door for Flora to enter. "You are now in the most prosperous place of Agius Saranta," says Flora. "I am sure you realize that everything is not everywhere like this. This is an area protected by all regimes and governments." Jason smiles and does not say anything. He knows and he is bitter about the Greeks. They gave the city to the Albanians.

As soon as they enter, Flora's mother and friends welcome Flora and Jason and they are really happy. The help of the two ladies at the table are Albanians but they share in everything. This impresses Jason who always wants to forget the pseudo-aristocracy of Athens who wanted always to separate their help and play the master. Flora's mother approached Jason and said in Greek, "We all speak Greek but in honor of our help and guests we will speak in English." Jason was impressed and Flora's mother smiled.

The environment was pleasant and the meal to honor Jason was Greek. Jason was placed between Flora and her mother, and across from Saul and Nitsa. The conversation was liberal and Flora's mother wanted to know as much as there was to be known. She recognized the charm of Jason and was very happy. She knew that everything was to be her daughter's choice. She realized that Jason was a noble man to be trusted by all people. "Jason, I will need to use you help in investing; and I trust that on your travel this way you will not forget to honor us with your presence. I am sorry that Terry is not here now that Flora is learning the business. But I will be pleased to talk to him about your visit. I am certain he will be elated!" "Thank you, madam, I will be honored to also help you as much as I can with you investments." The mother was impressed and happy, the more she was hearing about Jason. She realized that he was not an ordinary man.

At the end of the late lunch, the mother asked her daughter to play her Lyre. Flora smiled and positively decided to please Jason. She played the Lyre and Jason was shocked. She was charming and experienced. "Now you will play your Guitar," said Flora smiling and brought Jason the instrument. He could not refuse but he was wondering how she knew that Jason could play. She smiled but didn't explain. She thanked him and everyone was animated and thankful. Jason was handsome and when it came to guitar he was a charm. He was always getting lost in his songs.

After two hour's of conversation, playing the music and talking, all were pleased and Jason was taken to the hotel to rest. While he was leaving, Flora's mother said, "Jason, it was our honor to have you with us today. But in Terry's return, I will contact you to help us with some investment." "It will be my pleasure, madam; and I thank you for the honor of having me with you for lunch. She was happy to know a man of Jason's skills. Soon Flora drove Jason to the Hotel and they arranged to meet at night for dinner and pleasure with Nitsa and Saul. It was an honor for Flora who was always polite and content.

At about nine o'clock at night, Flora with Nitsa and Saul drove to the hotel where Jason was waiting for them. Flora apologized that on Monday she had no better choice than a restaurant with good meal and fascinating music. But she promised that in a weekend night in Istanbul she will be Jason's guide in belly dancing with excellent food. It will be her treat for anyone to remember. Nitsa laughed and said, "I will certainly treat you," in the Greek place of my choice; and I tell you now to remember then with no arguments." They all smiled and promised to remember. "And I will have a pretty girl for Simon!" she added smiling. "But Jason should remember to bring him along, even with a lady of his choice, if he prefers," she said staring at Jason. "I promised to do that one way or the other," he replied smiling and convincing.

Flora took them to a place facing the Adriatic sea next to the water. It was Monday and all they were offering was beautiful recorded music next to the beach. The water was playing, breaking on the sand, and sea birds were flying making the beach with the small boats a charm. Jason was often absorbed and Flora liked to cares him occasionally. He was impressed with Flora's skill in playing the Lyre and remembered the charming sound and the pretty lady that was playing it.

As she was caressing him each time he was absorbed, he said, "Flora, I am fascinated with you playing the Lyre and blessed will be the one that will have you." "My father says that only the deaf ones will not respond; but my husband will more likely be a deaf one." Jason laughed and agreed. That is why he trained you in his business." She caressed his knee and said, "He was alright even though I do not agree." "Yes Flora you are alright too." "We love you Flora more for the money you make and not for the music you play," said Saul smiling. They all laughed for the truth said. "I hope I am not included in the group," said Jason. "Yes, to every rule there are many exceptions," added Saul.

The dinner was excellent, the music attractive and as Jason was paying the dinner, the boss brought four CD's, two from Flora and two from Nitsa for Jason and Simon. He had no choice not to accept. From there, Flora took them again to another place with special ice cream that they all enjoyed. "We do not have many places like this but it is from Tirana and we all like it," said Flora. It was really unique in making ice cream pastries. It was a place with pastries, ice cream, and sweet drinks. After their dinner it was really a place for fun and pleasure. Flora really knew how to please her friends and remain pleased. Jason obviously was pleased, and Flora was really a flower.

After this, they went to Bitrinti hotel where Nitsa with Saul left and Jason was to take Flora. They were all pleased and Nitsa said to Jason: "Do not forget to come to our Istanbul. Flora and I will surprise you!" She kissed Jason and left smiling.

It was getting late and Jason was enchanted with Flora. She was excited and happy. She knew how to love and remain free. The mind was trained and the body was learning. She really could not remain indifferent next to Jason. She was free but nervous for some reason.

"I love you Jason but something frightens me," she whispered. Jason brought two glasses of sweet wine and shared it with her. "I love you Flora; you are a charm and a beauty. No deception and no confusion." After their second drink, Jason takes Flora on to the bed and unfolds his passion. He takes her clothes off first and he follows after. She didn't know what to do and she was trembling. It was passion and not fear as the first time. Flora was in the process of learning with passion. She loved Jason and was looking at him naked.

Flora gets frighten and unites her body with Jason's. She is really excited and Jason tense penetrates Flora with force. They become one and Flora free lets her passion be expressed with no pain and fear. She wants Jason and with him inside her, moans and ties his body. It was strong and enchanting. Both are drunk with power and both are moaning and whispering. Their passion grows and their desire is expressed with pleasure. Their bodies united are violently moving to absorb the hedonism. At the end both fascinated with pleasure cannot be separated. They stay embraced and Flora cries listening to Jason's passion. The first time was learning and the second fearing. Whatever it was, this time she was pleasing and frightening.

"I love you Jason, and your passion is my pleasure; and I wish to give you my passion and make it your pleasure, when you are inside me," she whispers and ties Jason with her arms. She is violent and expecting Jason to rape her. Flora the tender business woman was a restless violent lover. Both, Jason and Flora were looking each other at the end with fascination. They could not leave and be satisfied.

But time was fleeting and Flora had to go. She was thinking of Jason and was afraid of a child. It was better to be his than any other's. She thought of this and found peace. She had the money and could now be what she wanted and not what other demands were dictating. It was after one in the morning when she got ready to go. "I have the pleasure to know that I will see you again. I don't know what it is," Jason whispers. "You will see me in Istanbul," she answered. "Nitsa will be waiting for you also. Don't forget." Jason promised to remember. But knew that Ismene was his already. He was confused. Both would be a blessing of Gods if not of people. It is not that they object; it is that they cannot afford it. They all learn one time or the other later.

Jason with Flora holding his hand she went down to her car. It was not too late, but it was respectable. Flora's parents were expecting Flora to get marry and run her father's business later alone or with her husband. Her mother was Greek and was expecting; but her father was Armenian and hoping. They eloped each other when they were students at the University of Salonika. Her father had a degree from the University of Salonika and her mother was the daughter of a rich Greek. She went to Albania when her lover obtained an assignment in Agius Saranta. He was a bright student and she was fascinated with him. No more was known.

Flora was educated at the university of Business in Istanbul where she also met Nitsa. Starting in September, Nitsa will be working for Flora in Istanbul. As they say, Istanbul is a Greek City run by the Turks. As usually the Greeks were always liberal and they didn't want the responsibilities of Government at a time when killing was the solution to every problem. It is the fate of people who don't wish to kill. It is not a Greek desire to kill but to live in peace. For any crime, death or exile was your choice in classic Athens: No slavery in prison!

Wednesday morning Jason went again for his breakfast and was waiting for Flora. She was little late but it was fine. As usually, Jason was polite and offered to Flora a chair and a kiss. "Thank you Jason," she whispered. He offered her what she wanted and after looking at Jason she said, "Jason, I will transfer $50000 dollars in the Bank of America in Kalamata, in my name and your name. I wish you to trade stocks and commodities. I will have the right to draw out any of that, but not you, without my permission." She stops and looks at him. "Sure I will, if you trust me," he whispers smiling and wondering. "You realize that I respect, I trust, I love and I want you," she says seriously.

"The money will be deposited in September, and you can start trading in October." "That is fine with me if it is fine with you," says Jason. But he is wondering and Flora can tell. "That will be for our son, if there is to be one," she said softly smiling." Jason was surprised with Flora's expectation. But he didn't say anything.

After their breakfast, Jason says that he has to go before it gets warm. Flora looks at him and whispers, "Jason I love you and I want you. Can you have me before you go?" Jason looks at her eyes and senses they are asking. He sees her lips slightly trembling; and her hand touches his leg. "I don't know when will I see you again; and I am afraid. I want you!" she says and her lips are trembling. Jason thinks and responds. "Yes Flora, please, lets go. You know I love you, and I want you also. Your passion is a challenge."

They go upstairs on Jason's room and with no delay this time they had an orgy. Flora tied her body on Jason and she didn't want to go. Jason screw her with a passion that he will never forget. Flora was another woman. After their orgy, Flora begins to cry. "I am sorry Jason, I love you!" she whispers. She ties herself on Jason and keeps crying. She kissed him, she screwed him and tied herself on Jason. She was relieved and Jason terrified. She separates herself and smiling whispers, "If you think that I will ever forget you; you are wrong!" Jason is pleased and surprised. Flora was a woman of a gentle wish and a flaming desire. She knew how to get drunk with pleasure.

Jason stopped at Ioannina for a new experience. Then, he arrived late in the afternoon in Patra. As expected, he called Nicholas who was waiting for him reading his mathematics at the same place. "Rion or Antirion the name of the place at the Railway Station. But Nicholas took him for a dinner and later for a special coffee. They laughed when Jason gave Nicholas his present. "I was expecting to see a lady and you bring me a book. Thank you anyway," says Nicholas laughing. The book was on Stocks "But you knew the lady," says Jason. "No, I knew neither Alice nor Ismene." "Yes, you are right. I will introduce them to you when we have a chance." says Jason smiling. "I hope so," said Nicholas content. Each lady is a charm that he never forgets. He knows the good taste in Jason's choices.

Jason was persuaded to sleep at Nicholas place. In the morning, at about eight, Jason and Nicholas went for breakfast. Soon after, Jason took off. Both enjoyed their meeting and Jason arrived in Kalamata early in the afternoon. He was tired and went straight home to rest.

At about six o'clock in the afternoon, he was at the office. He worked for about two hours and then the phone began ringing. He chose to see Simon and Stuart for a light dinner and the news at Pete's Bar. Jason was tired but he had no choice. Seeing his friends was always a pleasure and an obligation. Stuart and Simon were always the two of the three Musketeers. To see Jason they were seeing the leader of the Musketeers and were reviving. The three Musketeers were physically and mentally cooperating.

They met and talked first about Ismene. Jason told his friends that Alice was dead and Ismenne was raised. She had chosen to stay with her mother and teach at the school languages. He could not convince her to come with him sooner or later to Kalamata. Her psychological problems were still pressing. It was not her mother, who was charming and lovable. It was her morale low. She had to recover next to her mother. Soon after, she was for sure to come back. He didn't know though exactly when.

Her mother was to be alone and Ismene was still afraid. But she was already in love. Jason had a question: It was love or sex? His friends didn't have to agree. But they could wait. Both Stuart and Simon were disagreeing with Jason. Ismene was afraid that she might lose Jason. She could not be decisive like Norma or possessive like Anna. She was an idealistic woman. Her love had to be perfect. But you are never right when you think of perfect love. You cannot know and control, or ignore the transformation of emotions.

His friends understood her problem and were sure that she needed to become again normal. They realized that she was psychologically hurt by a bastard. They agreed that she needed her time to recover. "Who knows? She may need to find one easier and less demanding to feel comfortable," said Jason. Simon and Stuart didn't agree and laughed. "She needed to gain real confidence with her mother and she should be given the opportunity," said Simon thoughtfully.

"Yes, she should," said Stuart. It was not an easy process of adjusting to all these changes for a young lady. They all considered her suffering and agreed. But it was hard for Jason to do the same. "A man in love is always in doubt and questioning," said Stuart. "Let's be once wise and considerate." Stuart and Simon agreed. Both watched Jason wondering and hoping. But he was feeling safer and normal. He knew that Ismene loved him but she needed her mother's stability and affection to exist. Her brother was something to admire: A noble and capable man. Jason and Simon were really appreciative of Sergio.

Jason reminded them that he will ask the ladies at his office to distribute the presents. "They are all expecting something, anyway," said Stuart. "All those not involved, do not understand and they are excused," said Simon. "The way you were," remarked Jason. Simon looked at him and replied, "Yes, you are absolutely right. But please, do not say anything more." Jason was surprised with Simon who knew.

Anyway, other things followed the process of discussion and the friends said to Jason their success in stocks and commodities. Jason was happy and looked to his friends more normal and content with Ismene that proved that she loved him. He only had to be patient for no other woman could match his knowledge and intellect. They didn't know about Flora. But Jason knew that she was capable but she preferred to wait for years. Of course, none could speak about her besides Jason. He knew her wisdom and patience.

They were also informed by Jason that he was going to get some profits for this week and put some stops in others. They didn't say much on this anyway. But they were pleased and thanked Jason. He knew better than the others and he didn't forget to thank his friends for their support and contribution. They didn't say anything about their uncontrolled support since they knew, but they could not prove anything. Jason smiled and said, "When we win we should be taking and never waiting. Of course, it depends how much!" "Yes, there we need some strategy," whispered Stuart.

Jason reminded them that he will ask the ladies at his office to distribute the presents. "They are all expecting something, anyway," said Stuart. They were also informed by Jason that he was going to get some profits for this week and put some stops in others. They didn't say much on this anyway. But they were pleased, and thanked Jason.

He knew better than the others and he didn't forget to thank his friends for their support and contribution. They didn't say anything about their uncontrolled support since they knew, but they could not prove anything. Jason smiled and said, "When we win, we should be taking and never waiting. Unless we know. But when do we know?"

Not long after, Anna, Stuart's wife received a glass statue of a Dolphin jumping out of the ocean. It was mailed to her by Alice from Agius Saranta. Near the same time, after the visit of Simon to Agius Saranta,

Norma received a good wood carving of two naked young people making love. Anna's present was challenging for young and old. You were watching it and you didn't know what to say. You wanted to be in the sea and compete with the Dolphin. It didn't matter where you were. Norma's present was a wish to be with your young lover and enjoy your solitude. Anna and Norma called each other and talked about their presents. Both were thanked with Ismene for their moral support. Ismene was an intelligent woman to know.

Anna didn't talk. She took a piece of paper and wrote to Ismene that she and her friends Norma and Irene, wished to invite her in a party to be celebrated by her, Norma and Jason's sister. To express their desire to have her with them they were inviting her in the party. "I know you do not need any financial support but to express our pleasure that you are our friend, we will send you a ticket as well and we will be expecting you at the bus. We do not wish you to drive. We want you to be with us. Soon you will receive the ticket. It is only an expression of our gratitude to have you with us." Anna signed and send the letter to Ismene. She was happy when she received the invitation.

Anna told Norma and Irene what she had done and they were happy. They knew now that Ismene was free and they were pleased. Anna requested that she does not wish Jason to know. They will be happy to surprise him. They knew how much Jason was loving her. Ismene received the letter and cried. She could not refuse. However, they knew that she was now teaching and they arranged their party to be on Saturday while she was to come on Friday and leave on Monday. They let her know that they were ready to make any changes if she wished. There was no problem for them, but anyway a pleasure.

Ismene wrote and thanked Anna accepting the invitation. "My tears on the letter witness my pleasure," was the last sentence on the response of Ismene. Anna received Ismene's response and she was happy. That woman is an exception, Anna said to Norma and Irene.

It was only eight weeks after Ismene left that she was invited for the party. The ladies were excited to receive Ismene's answer. None was supposed to know about Ismene's invitation besides the three young ladies. Anna was happy and pleased that Ismene was not even the least concern. She was always noble and easy. "My God," she whispered.

Exactly eight weeks after was the party. Stuart was surprised with his wife's preparations but he could not think and say anything. Many people were invited but none could refuse and say anything. Nicholas only said that it was to be the best party for Anna, after seeing the preparations. But he could not explain. He only said to Stuart that it was the best party he was ever for long. "It is a women's," whispered Stuart. He knew his wife's expertise.

It was the beginning of November, Friday evening when Ismene arrives at the bus Station in Kalamata. She looks outside, takes her small suitcase and sees Louise waiting for her. She is excited. Embraces and caresses Louise with tears. Louise takes her in the apartment in the Kalamata beach. Ismene gets in her apartment and gets surprised. Outside and inside it is perfect. "Is it made just for me?" she asks. "If it is yours; it is made for you by all those who love you," whispers Louise with pride. Tears run down the face of Ismene.

Tonight, we will have a nice dinner says Louise and we should see people that do not expect you. But you should rest little before we go to see them. "It is six o'clock. We have time till then." Ismene laughs and Louise offers Ismene what she wants. "I will be back by nine thirty, to go for our dinner," says Louise and leaves. She is very happy and surprised that Ismene is great and well composed. At about nine thirty Louise returns and Ismene is ready. They go to one of the restaurants for dinner by the beach and they find a table ready for them. It was a real surprise for Ismene.

The three Musketeers and their wives, Jason and his sister, Nicholas and a new woman, they are all seated and wait to be served. As Ismene and Louise enter the place, Jason's eyes see the face of Ismene and gets frozen looking at her. He does not know what to say or do. Everyone gets excited and gets up to greet Ismene. Everyone is surprised and waits.

Ismene goes to Jason, he gets up, kisses her and waits. Everyone is excited and feels restless. Ismene was an irresistible temptation.

Louise guides Ismene to a chair next to Jason and Jason has been confused. He does not know what to say or do. Louise puts Ismene next to Jason and brings Anna to Ismene. The smile of Anna is tempting and Ismene rushes to embrace Anna. She is happy to see a pleasant lady. They embrace each other and feel their tears. "You are welcome Ismene, I am delighted to see you being with us. We have made this party to get to know you and let you know how much we love you. We should have gotten rid of that bastard much earlier. The problem was Stuart and Simon who delayed. He was a coward. When Louise told him to get the hell out of her place before, she blow his head out, he didn't do anything but hid himself." "Yes, he was corrupt and coward," whispers Ismene. The corrupt are usually cowards.

———————————

Saturday in the afternoon after six o'clock, Norma called the attention of the people. "Ladies and gentlemen, we are now in the place of Stuart and Anna. It is my pride and pleasure to introduce to you Mrs Anna, before she begins feeding us." They all smiled and applauded. Anna lifted herself, to please the people from a place at the table next to Stuart. Everyone, including Nicholas, was there.

"Ladies and Gentlemen it is my pleasure to introduce to you tonight Ms Ismene a close friend of our honorable guest Mr Jason of the Argonauts." Every one looked at Ismene and Jason and applauded smiling. "We are here to celebrate the defeat of 'Jack the scum' and the victory of Ismene and a noble Stranger. We are here to celebrate the victory of the noble Jason and the lady Ismene. We know nothing more to say than that the Scum perished when the noble Jason and Ismene survived honorably in the Field and in the Court." Those who knew smiled and applauded, and those who didn't know were surprised and applauded. "We are here to applaud and celebrate our victory with good food, good drink, good songs and singing. Thank you." The people applauded and serving begun with the help of young and noble ladies.

** There were many things pleasant to try and Anna, as if she knew Ismene for long, said softly, "Please, try it yourself first and give our men to try also my delicate 'keftedes' with little sweet wine." Ismene smiled, tried what Anna recommended, she liked it, and proceeded after with Jason and the other men to have them try. None said 'no' and Anna said to Ismene, "You see the men? They like everything a beautiful woman will serve them." "Yes, I see," answered Ismene smiling. Then Anna says, "You know Ismene, next time I will serve the gentlemen with beautiful women!" Both laughed and everyone was surprised seeing Anna and Ismene laughing. Jason who loved Ismene and respected Anna was laughing. He knew that Anna was a unique woman with casual humor. She was a Greek woman that could not be easily ignored. She knew how to defend herself and how to attack.

The big surprise happened near the end when Jason brought the Guitar to play. Simon and Stuart were excited and participated. They knew that Jason was playing the guitar and singing; but others were surprised. He ended with the song:

> Two eyes behind the tree are watching the sky
> The chords are ready to play, tremble and cry
> She wants to forget, to care, to love and play
> But her eyes to capture, to love, sing and say:
>
> I remember your tears inside hazel-blue eyes
> Plays the guitar, she sings, he drinks and cries.
> I remember diamond tears rolling on your face
> I play my guitar, you listen and I love the place
>
> My songs and passions were somewhere hidden
> Love was betrayed, stolen, raped, but not given.

It was a song written, composed, played and sang by Jason. After this song, Ismene was crying. She never knew that Jason was playing the guitar so well. She never thought that he could sing. It was money that had captured Jason's mind because nothing else could please the people. At the age of 23 he had quit the music and the singing and had devoted himself in making money. He proved to be very good at that. But he played and sang for the people he loved or liked to please. He was an artist that could sell his songs for a lot of money in the market. He tried but he could not wait. He had to quit and try the commodities and the stock market. There he was fantastic. But, was that the truth? It was for the time he tried so far, anyway.

The people were impressed even though Jason had not written or played music for long. He was applauded and thanked them all. However, that moment Jason said: "Ladies and gentlemen, we should now be thankful to listen to a real artist who is tonight with us. She is 'Ismene' sitting between myself and my sister." They all applauded and Ismene was embarrassed. However, she got up, thanked them all and said, "I will play for you two pieces. One of Illyrian love song, and another of Hellenic origin by Xarhakos. The songs were played and performed by Ismene. The people were amazed. She was a professional. She was unique and Nicholas was surprised and impressed with Ismene. "She is a miracle hard to ignore and difficult to forget," he whispered to Norma.

She was fantastic and the people surprised. She was amazing when she played and sung the songs by Xarhakos. At the end of the second song, Norma got up and embraced Ismene. It was fantastic. They were all convinced that Ismene was a real artist. Jason was little embarrassed but he was feeling great and proud. Stuart's wife came and kissed Ismene as if she knew her for years before. Ismene was also little embarrassed, knowing that it was short time during which she had played and sung the songs.

Anyway, the night was fantastic and Anna was excited and grateful with Ismene. She was a pleasure for anyone and especially to Anna's children. She talked to them and made them happy. But, happier than anyone, was Ismene. She talked with the children and made them conscious of their importance and participation in the party. Norma sitting close to Ismene made her comfortable and happy during the night. But Ismene was an exception and Jason was happy.

They all left pleased and Ismene was excited about Anna. She was really the exception. Jason was happy that Ismene was comfortable. This party was for everyone an exception, and this had made Anna very happy. Ismene was just a pleasure for everyone and she was thankful to meet and talk with Nicholas as if she knew him for long. She realized that Nicholas was a noble man. "I am jealous of your knowledge," she whispered to Nicholas who smiled thankfully.

Saturday night Ismene slept with Jason in her place. His sister was happy and Jason pleased that his sister was also a good friend with Louise and Norma. She was a beauty that Jason will never forget. Ismene fixed everything and in the morning Jason was surprised. He had his breakfast and he was pleased. She knew what to make and Jason was wondering. When he got up ready for breakfast he heard Ismene singing and he was stunned. In the afternoon of Sunday, Jason, Ismene and his sister Irene went swimming.

Monday, early in the morning Ismene goes to Jason who is still sleeping, caresses his hair, kisses him in the cheek and with a smile whispers, "Jason, please, I have to fix you a light breakfast because I have to leave early." He opens his eyes, sees Ismene and smiles. "Please, get up, our breakfast will be ready in fifteen minutes," she whispers and leaves. In fifteen about minutes, the breakfast was ready and Jason was sitting in the table looking deep in the sea. The sun was not yet up from behind the mountain to go from East to West by the late afternoon.

Ismene sits next to Jason smiling and they begin their light early breakfast. She is looking deep in the blue sea and says, "It is close to us and fantastic, I don't want to go, but give me some time, and remember I love you." Jason looks at her and says with a smile, "I trust you Ismene; and I love anything you do. But if I can do something that you want, don't hesitate to ask." She looks at him and whispers, "No Jason, I do not want anything, but remember I would love you always." He looks at her and whispers caressing her face and smiling, "When I see your beauty, I am enchanted; how can I refuse anything that is yours?" She kisses him with a smile thinking.

Jason smiled but he didn't say anything. He knew Ismene needed more time to recover. The punishment of Ismene was wrenching; her liberation was unexpected relief. Hard for the tortured mind to take it.

---

10   SERGIO THE EXECUTIONER OF THE EVIL

"A death given by a noble man is a punishment for a crime."

A year after, Ismene calls Jason and tells him that she is going to visit him sometime in June. Jason was happy and told her that he will be expecting her any time. Near the middle of June, Ismene arrives at the bus station and looks outside of the bus, but she cannot see Jason. However, she recognizes Norma with Areti Jason's sister. Ismene does not see Jason and terrified asks for him.

Norma and Areti smiled and kissed Ismene. Then Norma says, "Jason had late meetings and said he will be with us much later." Ismene puts her hand in her heart and whispers, "Thank you Norma, he had said that he was going to be waiting for me; but I didn't see him and I got frightened." Norma add Areti smiled expressing a sorrowful sweetness. They took the small suitcase of Ismene, they got into Norma's car and went into Ismene's place by the beech.

The place was spotless that impressed Ismene. Norma smiling said, "We were expecting you and made the house as spotless as we could." "Thank you ladies," said Ismene smiling. Norma and Areti left to come back after a few hours and take her for their late dinner. Jason was to meet them there. Ismene felt relieved and went to rest for two hours and be ready after three.

By eight o'clock Norma and Areti came and took Ismene. "We should go now and Jason knows where to find us," she said smiling. They went to a buffet place with a rich list of food exposed. There Simon was waiting and when Ismene saw him, she fell in his arms pleased. Not much later came Stuart with Anna who were to see Ismene. They were happy to see the others also and started their free dinner. Not much later came Louise who was happy to see and embrace Ismene. They both cried and Ismene said to Louise, "Glad to see you Louise, we will have plenty of time to enjoy everything from now on. Norma and Areti took me earlier and I had plenty of time to rest." "That was wise after the long ride," said Louise smiling.

They were all eating when Jason arrived by nine o'clock at night and went straight to Ismene. She embraced, kissed and caressed Jason with tears. The empty place next to Jason was reserved for Louise who kissed again Ismene and sat next to Jason. "Shall we share him Louise?" Ismene whispered with a broad smile. "Why not Ismene?" asked Louise. "He is ours; is he not?" Ismene kissed him and laughed.

"You will never be left with no women," she whispered. Those who heard Ismene laughed.

The night was pleasant and music with songs was always the tradition with Jason. Simon and Stuart were the special sympathy of Ismene. The hot June was an invitation for swimming. Ismene was the best and Jason was her company in dancing with the waves. You could not be with Jason and Ismene and not be entertained.

When Ismene was in her mood, everyone was getting excited with the music, the singing and the dancing. Ismene was a natural artist. Why she chose the flower selling none could explain. May have been Louise who devoted herself to Ismene ready to do anything she wanted and prosper in spite her misfortunes. Louise was a noble young lady attracted by the charm of Ismene, a mixture of Hellenic and Illyrian seeds. They liked it or not, the Ilyrians were always friendly with the Hellenic people; and their mixture was always an enchanting result.

Jason was pleased because this event was initiated with Ismene. She wanted to be with her mother and Jason. And the fact that her brother was to be in Agius Saranta also was exceptionally charming to see her noble brother interacting with Jason. She wanted to see Jason interacting with her noble brother and feel that she was also accepted with no reservations. She needed to forget her miserable enslavement and live in a pleasant environment with people of her brother and lover.

It was a cool evening for the beginning of July. Ismene caressed Jason after she served their sweet bitter coffee. The sun was setting red in the west but the blue was not retreating much. Then Ismene asks, "Do you remember where we are to be early in August?" Jason looks at her and smiling replies, "How may I forget what you like?" "I didn't think you forgot but I want to remind you that we may explore our return by seeing all the places that are Hellenic." "Well, we should, but it will be hard to find one that it is not." "That is fine," replies Ismene and gives Jason a kiss that drives him insane.

"I have a message from my brother that they will be in August with my mother and anytime after the fifth we should catch him there," says Ismene. "That is great," replies Jason and after that a discussion starts.

Jason expresses the desire to have some lessons from Sergio in shooting. "He is a magician!" claims Jason. "Yes, and I like to have some lessons in Illyrian dancing," states Ismene. That will keep him bussy, will not?" asks Jason. Then Ismene adds laughing, "And don't forget Jason that Denysa and Sergio's wife will also be recruited." They realized that their program is to be exciting.

Not much after, Ismene dragged Jason inside for an orgy. Ismene was an endless fire with growing peaks and a final explosion. Jason could not forget the rising and exploding fire of Flora. Blessed were those who could have two woman: One with rising explosions and another with a single conflagration. Jason knew and wished to have it with Ismene and Flora. But people cannot communicate.

―――――――――――――――

From the beginning of August Jason left with Ismene from Kalamata and went to Agius Saranta. On their way they enjoyed everything. What impressed Jason was Ismene's capacity to remember and perform anything they saw in their slow trip of more than five days, in a trip that didn't require more than two days with leisure.

After five days they were in Agius Saranta. Ismene's mother and brother were waiting and as soon as Jason was approaching, Sergio open the outside double door for Jason to enter. They embraced each other and Sergio with his wife carried the suitcases of Ismene and Jason straight to a room upstairs. "Jason; I am carrying the suitcases where I was ordered with my mother. I hope you understand." Jason smiles and says nothing. It was an order none could have any right or courage to object. Jason and Ismene were to share the same room in the same bed. None had any right or courage to object. Sergio and his wife smiled.

Everyone was happy, and Ismene with her mother and her brother were ready to serve Jason and Sergio's wife. But Sergio more than anything else had in mind to clear Agius Saranta of the exploiters and killers of Yusuf and Orlif. You do not kill the soldiers but their captains. It was Sergio's principle. He had to find and kill the captains and their soldiers would disappear if they didn't want to die.

Sergio's father was killed by the corrupt bastards in the middle of Sergio's studies in Colon, five years ago. He comes home and finds that his mother almost 50 years old was raped and his sister about 20 years old was kidnapped, for a year already. Her mother was liberated immediately after the death of Yousuf but none knew where Ismene was. She was supposed to be in Turkey, Greece or Albania. Sergio assigned to his wife the task to find out where Ismene was through the German Embassies. That is where his sister must have been recorded.

She was not in Tirana, Athens, Smyrna or Istanbul. However, not long ago, Sergio's wife Gertrud (spear, strength) was informed by the German Embassy in Athens that a Greek Albanian lady by the name Ismene was in Kalamata with her husband Jack. They were pleased to provide the information because it was asked by Gertrud, the German lady of Sergio. This was enough for Sergio to search and identify Jack. Sergio smiled and began planning the execution of Jack and liberation of his sister. He is not a noisy fellow from Albania. He is a quiet gentleman with excellent records of success in anything he tried.

While Jack was raping Ismene, his sister, he managed to come home to find who had raped his mother and taken his sister. He finds his mother but he does not know where was his sister. He and his wife Gertrud were sad but hopeful to find out and take their revenge. His wife could not leave her husband alone. She had told him that their children were with her mother and she was with him. He didn't have to worry about anything but only to take his revenge. Sergio was thankful knowing that his wife was really a German who knew how to be and die with him. They were a perfect couple.

In view of these facts, her brother was relieved but his mother was raped once and his sister abused and raped over a period of almost a year. She had come not much after his arrival in 'Agius Saranta'. He was happy to find his mother and sister but he was furious to find his mother and sister raped. He was raving for revenge.

Not much after, Simon and Jason had arrived on their way back to Greece, as they had said lying. But Ismene accepted them with tears and pleasure. Sergio had learned already the relation of his sister with Jason and was happy to meet him as a visitor in his house.

Sergio was feeling angry wishing revenge. He was sad not being able to bear the insult. He who killed his father was killed by the imposter who was rapping his sister for a year. And he was killed by a noble Stranger that Sergio could guess but could not name and wished not to involve. But he was to be thankful to him forever even though he was not the one to do that. He met him once but he did not know then; and when he decided, he was not allowed to name.

There was now no peace in the minds of Ismene and her mother. But the joy of reuniting and being safe was immense. Sergio was mad and raving, but at the same time thankful to the men that killed Yousuf and Jack; the perverts. Sergio knew, or he thought he knew who killed Jack and he was thankful. He told his sister: "Tell Simon and Stuart that I am willing to do anything they will ask."

He knows that his father was a noble man. The bastards killed him while he was arriving at his home in Agius Saranta. He was the noble man respected by anyone who ever needed assistance. His wife has been crying since his death, six years ago, and his children have him in their heart. Yousuf was killed by Jack; and Jack was just killed by his sister and a Stranger. It was now the turn of Orlif.

Jason near the end of the dinner turns to the mother and whispers, "There are people, Mrs Denysa, who revolt and lose; but there are also people who suffer, wait and win. If it was not you and the virtues of Ismene, where would have we been?" She looks at him and asks, "Do you think that a man like Alexander would still be in love with a woman like me?" "I have no doubt or question on that," replied Jason.

Tuesday morning, Sergio wanted to take Jason out, his brother as he called him, to make him feel and be aware of his friendship. So he asked his wife for a light breakfast at which his mother and sister joined. His mother was beautifully dressed as always in light black and she joined them with Jason to her right. "You look happy this morning and you make the day bright for me," he says smiling. She looks at him and whispers, "I love you Jason. You have made my life a pleasure."

Jason looks at her and whispers, "To love the ones you know is important; and to respect the ones you don't is beauty. Any other relation is meaningless. You know love follows respect." "I have appreciated your love," she says looking at him smiling.

Ismene was waiting for her turn to speak. She suggests that they go to see some beautiful places and at night, Jason with Sergio go for target practice; and come later for a late dinner. That was a good idea and they all went out to see the places of Agius Saranta.

First they see the Bulevardi Hasan Tahsimi and the Saranta Marina Tahsimi. Then they visit a Catholic Church and after they stop to the Friendship Park. Then they went for coffee and tea with tasty biscuits, and after a comfortable communication and some teasing, they went home for a light meal and rest. There was nothing special but something easy and relaxing. Some sweet wine with dates and almonds was fantastic. After that, a rest was needed. They all rested and woke up fresh. None knew their dreams.

In the evening before dinner, Sergio and Jason went for shooting. Sergio carried his two hand guns: a Revolver and a Flat. Jason was surprised with Sergio's dexterity who said, "My father used to say that you start shooting at 12 years old and if you have the skills; by 21 you are a magician." "Were you?" asked Jason smiling. "Well, I didn't think so, but my father did. Anyway, let's see," he said with comfort.

Sergio hit the target (bull's eye) with ease, three times, with each gun. Jason was surprised and shocked with the skill of his noble Hellenic friend! He was good also, but not as a killer. He was amazed to see from Sergio's guns six bullets, three through the center of each target. "You must have been the champion using both guns," said Jason after seeing Sergio's ease and precision aim. Jason was not bad but he didn't have the dexterity that his friend demonstrated. "You are a gift of god," exclaimed Jason. "And you are the skillful adventurer," replied Sergio modestly. "You can kill any man if you hide and by chance the best. You will never miss any insolent bastard."

Denysa was 50 years old but a very attractive Illyrian. None could question or deny that. She was a proud and independent woman. But she didn't respond with certainty. She wanted to go to Kalamata but for some reason she hesitated. Jason could see the hesitation but not the reason. Of course, they had different values of appreciation. Something undefined was bothering the mind and desire of the charming lady.

Sergio at about nine o'clock in the morning tells Jason that he has to do some work with some friends, and he was going to be home at about two to three o'clock, the latest for lunch. "If I am not home by two, please eat little and rest. I am sorry, but I have some work to do with some friends of mine and it may take that long." Jason realizes that his Greek Illyrian friends were precise in their instructions.

Jason was pleased because he really wanted to relax and enjoy Ismene's music that was enchanting and unique. Besides, Ismene was to be there with Gertrud by one o'clock to prepare what they wanted for lunch. Her mother didn't say when she was coming back, anyway. She was going to go shopping with two friends of hers. She was a desirable Illyrian woman speaking Greek surprisingly very well. She was respected by all people, Greek or Albanian for her sincerity, kindness and generosity. She was a healthy and pretty 50 years old lady.

Sergio was in a happy mood. He had his breakfast with the group and by ten he left. "I have some work to do Jason. Then I will return. Do what you please till I am back. But tell the ladies that we will all go for a fish dinner tonight. I love the Taverna Rupi, if our ladies have no objection." Sergio left smiling.

There was nothing to betray where he was going. But who knows? Ismene could probably tell. She was not physically capable but she was intelligent and very rational. She was something to know and admire. Her mother was noble and harmonious. She was a lady you wished to be with and converse. She was well educated and revengeful.

Sergio went to Anastas Café on feet. Anastas was happy to see Sergio and welcomed him cordially! They both got a coffee with a special sweet. "This is my treat, Anastas," said Sergio. "As you please, my son," said Anastas and they began a pleasant light conversation. Fifteen minutes later, Sergio says, "Anastas, please call someone to take me somewhere." "Yes I will," Anastas replies and makes a call. He comes back, sits down and says, "In ten minutes he will be here. Is that okay?" "Yes Anastas, don't worry. We have time for our coffee." The taxi driver comes in twenty minutes.

Anastas asks him to take Sergio where he wanted to go. Sergio orally gives him the address and he takes him there. He gets paid and leaves. Sergio didn't go straight in the place. He walked into the park and went around the building. The back side had three doors. Each door had no handle but a lock. You could open them from outside by a key.

The doors were closing automatically and there was no need for anyone to do that. Sergio went to the front. He seems to know what he wants. My God he looks trained! You can see by his behavior. Indeed, he was trained by his father whom he lost and wants revenge. "If you excuse them, they forget and commit the crime again," he used to argue with those who, under the conditions wanted to forget.

Sergio walks around the building and observes the situation. He looks wishing to realize the conditions. The building does not look strange to him. He walks at a distance around in the back very calmly. None seems to be there and he seems very peaceful. Just a man and a woman walked out of the building in the front, entered in a car and left. Sergio walks once more around the building and finally walks at the front. He is really identifying the environment, but he looks peaceful certain of the building. Three doors in the back, each leading to a room can be opened only by a key. Sergio knows but he is like verifying the situation. It is certainly not his first visit.

Sergio knows what he wants and goes straight at the front door. He reads the name Yousuf. He is surprised and wonders. Yousuf was killed at least a year ago. He stops and thinks. Then he knocks at the door and a young man, near the age of Sergio opens the door carefully. "Can I help you sir?" he asks aloof. Sergio looks at him and with surprise he asks, "I don't know if I am in the right place, but a month ago or so, I met a gentleman and he told me to come here and ask for Mr. Yousuf, if I need help." The man looks at Sergio carefully and says, "Mr Yousuf is not here now. But, is there someone else that can help you?" he asks.

Sergio looks around, examines the man with his eyes searching and cowardly says, "I don't know, but I was told that Mr. Yousuf would be able to help me." The man pretentiously smiles and says, "Oh, yes. Mr. Yousuf is not here right now but Mr. Orlif, more likely will be able to help you." "Can I come in?" he asks. "Of course sir, come in; come in and sit down." "Thank you sir, thank you," says Sergio politely, and timidly sits down.

Sergio is scrutinizing the room looking at the two side stairs driving upstairs, and three doors opposite down stairs closed. Sergio is looking and recognizes that the three rooms may be connected inside and allow one to escape outside from any of those rooms. In the back is the park all around and each room has a back door leading to the park. Easy for any one to run out to the park with the door locking as he is running out. But you can get in only if you have a key.

Sergio was looking and thinking. It was a place easy to run out and lock the door automatically as you were going out. Sergio was waiting thinking and looking around. He realized how the doors were operating. He knew from before as well.

The main entrance through which Sergio entered in Orlif's office was locking by itself from inside, as one gets in. The back door through which one was getting out to the forest park from Orlif's office was closing and locking by itself as one got out. No two people could get out unless the door was kept open.

"Sit down Sir," Orlif tells Sergio. He sits down and asks, "Is this Yousuf's place?" Yes Sir; it is but Yousuf is not here now. Is there some way we can help you?" he asks. "Oh, yes." He looks at him carefully and asks, "What is your name Sir?" Mr Orlif looks at him smiling and replies, "Mr. Orlif." "Thank you. Mr. Yousuf is your friend; am I correct?" Mr. Orlif does no reply but he is thinking. "I am sorry Sir, but I was told to talk only to Orlif who is the only friend to understand." "Oh, yes. Please relax and talk. None can hear."

Sergio pretends to be careful and looks around. "They told me that Mr. Yousuf and Mr. Orlif killed Mr. Aristomenes; is it true?" Mr. Orlif pretends that he is thinking. "Let me look and let you know," he says and tries to open his drawer. Sergio smiles; pulls a flat gun and empties it on Orlif's chest. This surprised and killed Orlif. The gun was silent and none could hear anything unless he was carefully listening. Orlif had no chance to reach his Gun. Sergio smiled, got up and went at the inside locking door to check if anyone had anything heard. Nothing had been heard. He pulled a piece of paper out of his pocket and left it on Orlif's desk. It said:

I came for his legal services. When I asked him for his legal papers, he did not have any! But he had the insolence to kill me. Thank God; he was too slow. I am sorry, but I had the right to defend myself.

He got out carefully from the back door which was locking when closing by itself. He walked on the street through the back of the park, walked naturally, called a taxi and went straight home. By quarter to three he was there. Ismene was restless but when her door was knocked, she looked, breathed in peace, opened the door, and kissed her brother. He saw her tears and smiled. She was damn, too smart!

Sergio had tried to find Orlif several times before but he was not successful. He had found that Orlif was the other one along with Yousuf who had killed his father and was trying frustrated to get him each time he was coming to 'Agius Saranta'.

When Sergio got home, he went straight to his mother. She was waiting for him to start the light lunch. He kissed her and said silently, "Mother, I am sorry, I am little late. But the other bastard is also dead." She looked at him, she thought for awhile and replied with tears, "Thank you Sergio. Your father will be now in peace.

A smile of irony was now harboring her face. She was proud of her son. She was now looking at him with a subtle Illyrian smile. At lunch, she said to Jason who was sitting next to her, "I will be glad now to come with you to Kalamata." Jason was surprised, but he was also an intelligent man that probably understood and smiled.

Jason got up from the couch and breathed freely knowing that Sergio was just late and nothing more. "You are late Sergio. We thank you that you didn't forget us," he said seriously and smiling himself. "If people do not listen to wisdom, they hear the hell," said Sergio sadly. Jason remained wondering but Ismene heard and understood. Sergio's wife didn't know anything and she said nothing. She was pleased to see her husband. She was a quiet respectful woman to be trusted. She was always lightly pleased.

But this time, she looked at her husband and smiled. She understood what had happened. She got up during lunch and brought more wine, she filled her glass with wine and greeted him with a smile: "We thank you Sergio. Now you will come with us next year." He smiled, he understood, agreed shaking his head but said nothing. He was thoughtfully smiling; so was his mother! It was not the punishment of a corrupt man but the freedom of the innocent ones to be relieved. The bad ones are always harmful and should be corrected. Jason was not happy but relieved that he could no longer wonder.

The killed man was probably the last one of those in Agius Saranta. Sergio was feeling bad but he had no choice. He knew that he would have been dead if he didn't kill that bastard. They get a gun and they think they can kill anyone. What a pity with the scums. Orlif was a scum and a vulture, and had to die like Yousuf.

Five years ago this bastard Orlif with Yousuf, and who knows who else, were waiting for Sergio's father outside of his home place hidden. And as soon as Alexander went home they attacked and killed him late in a rainy afternoon. None knew who they were those who did it. But it was winter and hailing. Alexander was killed when the fascists were in control and he was driving from work to home. They blocked the road and attacked him with automatic weapons. Everyone was sad and furious but the son had in his chest a load of pain. Time was not going to heal the pain but only revenge.

Sergio was noble but revengeful. He searched for five years the reports to determine the killers. He was at peace when convinced who were those: Yousuf and Orlif. He learned that Yousuf was killed by Jack. He learned that Jack had captured his sister but he didn't know where he was and what he was doing. Orlif was in Agius Saranta and Sergio was hopeful to get him in the office sometime. He had tried several times but he was not successful. But now he finally was informed and succeeded!

The sun was setting and the west was getting red. Sergio took Jason upstairs to the balcony to continue drinking their coffee with the dates and watch the setting of the sun. Ismene fixed the balcony and made it comfortable for both. "Please, if you need anything call me," said Ismene while she went downstairs. Sergio's wife came after and asked if they wanted something. She kissed her husband and said to Jason, "I am sorry, I cannot kiss you in front of my husband. I only cheat." She said that smiling.

Finally, Sergio had learned from his sister that Jack was killed; and from friends in Agius Saranta that Orlif was in command of the office. When he came back, he came determined to kill Orlif. It was the third time that he tried and succeeded. He was determined to do it and he was lucky. He was thankful that Jason brought him the peace: Love for his sister and revenge for his noble father, respected and loved by those who knew him. When he came home looked at Jason and said: "Thank you Jason; you are a noble man."

Jason looked at him but he said nothing. His friends who knew his goal were elated and some of those even called to congratulate and thank him. It was a pleasure for Sergio to hear the thanks of Greeks who were abused by Jack, Orlif, and Yousuf. However, Sergio always refused to accept the praise, but he agreed that they all deserved to celebrate the fall of the last bastard.

Jason and Sergio sat inside and were offered by Ismene cold water and coffee with dates. She was happy to serve them and they were pleased. Sergio said wondering, "Some bastards have their way and expect others to follow losing their freedom. I don't agree because if they want their way, I want mine, and I don't want to follow. They don't realize that we are rational animals to live with our freedoms. They expect to be free while we are slaves." "Yes, and they forget that they have no brain but a force that it is not so strong if the others object," says Jason thinking of those to whom you give freedom and they pursue your slavery.

Ismene got her tea and sat across from the pair of her brother and lover ready to serve them aware that her brother was involved in a crime that he had no choice. "You ask them to leave you in peace and they think they can make you their slave," said Sergio thinking of the rubbish with their guns, even though none knows how to use them. "Will we ever be able to live without?" asks Ismene. "I don't think so Ismene. But we have to make the best available choice and live with its flaws. That is democracy with controls," said Sergio. "Yes, we start with democracy and impose the controls," says Jason.

"But we should never allow the politicians to set their own remuneration," responds Ismene wondering. "Yes, that is a question to be answered with time and never allowing the politicians to set it themselves," replies Jason. But he was a fair man to be trusted. Should others can be trusted to be fair? It was a question hard to answer. "I don't think there should be anyone allowed to set that from any position established," said Sergio. He was absolutely right. You cannot fully trust all the people. They have to be changing and inspected.

Sergio was in good terms with the German Government, and he was helped to find the truth each time he wanted something. But he did not know anything yet about his sister. He was however to find eventually something, not long after. He had told his mother that he was not to forget his father. He had told his wife that the German authorities were helping him to find anything he wanted about his people; and she had told him, that she was his, and he was hers. Jason had said once that the German women were noble and he trusted them more than others. You could not argue with him about that. Jason was terribly impressed with Sergio's wife. She was an impressive lady.

Sergio and Jason talked about many things and they were relaxed. Jason was more open and Sergio more reserved. But he was also understanding if not agreeing. "Jason, when I come next year to Kalamata, I want to buy a house and invest some money as well. I am sure that I will have to ask your advice." "Don't worry Sergio. We will do well in both," replied Jason. "I will be waiting for you and my friends will be happy to know you." "Yes Jason, don't forget to give my love to Simon and Stuart," said Sergio thinking that he owed them the life and the freedom of his sister. She was still a virtuous and charming girl that had driven Jason crazy. She could not however have Jason the way she wanted. She didn't think she was the noble woman.

It was getting dark and the adriatic sea was magnificent. The two gentlemen were enjoying the spectacle of the coast and relaxed were watching the boats coming and going. But Jason was happy sensing that Ismene was getting detached from the ugly past, free from bastards. She was thankful to Jason and his friends. They gave her back her freedom with no demands. They were humble and pleased that they had liberated a noble woman and an invaluable friend. She loved Jason so much that with no hesitation she would give her life for his freedom. You could look in her eyes and see a world of pleasures.

Ismene was not the beautiful woman of yesterday but the charming beauty of tomorrow. Her eyes were the light that you had to be guided with on your path. The kindness was charming and all her friends were attracted. She could not speak, and not be charming. Jason was happy to have attracted such a woman in love with the sea trusting and the people admiring her skills. Jason could not believe that she didn't deserve any sacrifice and admiration. No wonder you could meet Ismene and not remain charmed. She had a virtuous way to attract and charm: To work and create; to serve and please. Even her brother could not be immune to her attraction and charm.

Soon Jason reminded Sergio that he would like that Friday night to go to Rupi' before going back to Kalamata. "Of course we will; to celebrate," replied Sergio. Then confidentially Jason asked Sergio, "What to celebrate?" Sergio looks at Jason and replies, "My mother and my sister have been humiliated, but now have their revenge: Ismene has a noble man, or no other; and my mother sees killed the bastards who killed my father and not his honor."

Now both Ismene and her mother were proud and free to worship them. No other concern was for them but the noble minds of three friends. They were free with no obligation whatsoever. The three Musketeers of Alexander Dumas!

But Sergio, Stuart and Simon were the three masters of the Gun. They used it the best way there was. With respect and dignity; they knew the consequence of the bullets once shot! Sergio was the master; Stuart with Simon the professionals. Their swords were for exercise in the Gyms of Universities and Sports Centers.

———————————

11 CALM, WAVES AND STORM IN THE HARBOR

"The Ocean is ugly without calm, waves and storms."

Eva, the attractive young lady, was pleased to go to the festival of Sergio. So Jason could easily carry Ismene and her mother, while Sergio carried his wife and Eva. At about nine-thirty at night, Jason brought them to the Taverna Rupi. Everyone was satisfied and thankful. They knew that it was Sergio to be thanked.

The atmosphere was lively and the fish was small, fresh and appetizing. The wine was "Retsina" and exciting. "Remember, you can ask for more of anything you want," said the waitress smiling. "The waitresses are pretty tonight," said Sergio and the young lady replied, "You can have me, if you can." Everyone laughed.

The misfortunes of yesterday were the past, and for all of them the time was ripe for some fun. Of course, memory is to remember and not to forget. However, with good company and jokes, many things can be forgotten and new ones can occupy the brain. Everyone was happy, but Sergio was trained to be calm, serious and alert. The flat gun was Sergio's companion and toy. He was brought up not to trust anyone. The soft music was played to make the environment easy and the conversation pleasant.

At about eleven o'clock at night, the restaurant owner came to the table of Jason, and after greeting Denysa, he tells Ismene, "You certainly do not know that your father was my best friend and I have missed him greatly." Ismene smiles ready to cry and thanks him for remembering her father. "I want to thank you for remembering my father and my noble mother," she says and points with her eyes to her mother next to her. The man gets enchanted and says, "Denysa, have you forgotten me?" "No, I didn't, but my tears cannot stop until noble people come my way." "Thank you Denysa and I hope to see you more next to your noble gentlemen," he says looking at Jason and Sergio.

They were two noble young men you could not avoid admiring. Both smiled and greeted him. "This is my brother Sergio and that is my beloved friend Jason," says Ismene. He greets them both with admiration as they get up to express their respect. "And this is my brother's noble German wife," she adds. The man smiled and greeted Gertrud bending his head. She was that night charming!

As soon as the melody ends, the audience applauded pleasantly. The owner of the place said, moved by the presence of all the members of Alexander's family and friends, "Ladies and gentlemen, tonight we are all honored by my best friend's Alexander Aristomenes family: His wife Denysa, his son Sergio and his German wife; his daughter Ismene, and their Greek friend Jason. I know Eva and I will not say anything for she is my love. I have asked his beautiful daughter Ismene to sing for us and honor my unforgettable friend Alexander. Here she is, Ismene Aristomenes, who stopped to see us while she is on her way to Greece with her mother, brother and friends." He applauded and the crowd followed, surprised by the beauty of Ismene!

Ismene was embarrassed and hesitant to sing as requested by her father's friend. But everyone was looking and expecting her to sing. She was not just an excellent singer but a fascinating dancer as well. She didn't want to sing but everyone was expecting her and was waiting. She slowly got up, with the prompting, and went on the stage.

She takes the microphone and looking at Jason says, "Ladies and gentlemen, first I will sing for you my new song that I have never sung in public before. I wrote this for my friend Jason while I was waiting for him to come and looking every day South. Now that I know he came, I will sing for him and you. 'Freedom of Ismene' is the name of the song." Looking at Jason she begins to sing with a smile that dazzled the audience. She gave to the musicians the tune to follow. They were all surprised! She was a capturing charm.

Looking at Jason, and with tears that started to roll down her eyes; looking at her mother and brother, she began singing. She was amazing: Young, beautiful and an artist.

> When I left my country
> I had the desire of revenge
> And as I return, I am sad.
> I had left my father's land
> And my own love forever.
> But when I came hither
> I find my love to claim
> My mind forever to tame
> The fear and the courage
> Close to my noble friends.
> Never to forget and fight
> Never be afraid of death
> And if it is for you to die
> Your pistol and strength
> Ever to use; don't forget.

They had never seen such a beautiful lady before and they had never heard such a song of bravery. They were applauding not to please, but they were exceedingly pleased by a beautiful lady and a unique artist. They were all enchanted and seriously charmed! Never before they had heard such a song, and they were excited as their voices were crazy and demanding more. They had never seen such a beauty before or heard such a song: Passionate and with meaning.

"Ladies and gentlemen, you must realize that I am not a professional singer. I sing to please people and friends and the song that I sang was for our friend, the owner of Taverna Rupi." He was listening to the song and tears run down on his old face. He probably remembered his friend

Alexander, for he left not to be seen that he was crying. But he learned though that both those gentlemen, who killed Alexander, were now dead and probably suspected that it was Sergio who killed them.

Ismene, as well as her mother, saw him leaving. Tears run on her face as soon as she finished the song. She could not forget her noble father, nor be content by the death of the scums. "Now I will sing another song, "The Rise of Jason." Again, she gave the tune for the musicians. "I wrote this for our friend Jason who has joined us tonight for entertainment," she says. She looks at Jason and asks, "Jason, please get up to be seen." He stands up smiling and sits down again. Then Ismene begins to sing looking everywhere, but not at Jason. She could not probably retain her pain; but she gave to the excellent musicians the tune: It was an easy on to follow.

> I was Medea, loved as much she was
> I am not Jason's Medea but I am yours.
> But don't betray me and love another
> I am not as fickle as she was, but noble
> To be faithful to music and my songs
> Dancing with singing that is yours.
>
> Don't ever be in sorrow and vainly try
> I will always be in love with you alone
> I will always be with you on the throne.
> Dressed with spring flowers and roses
> Of tempting music and beautiful ideas
> Arriving from the pantheon of Medea's.

Her listeners were again surprised and some who knew her even cried. They had not seen and listened such a beautiful and kind lady before, and they had never heard such songs. They were amazed and deeply moved, and sincerely applauded to demonstrate their appreciation of the exquisite woman, lyrics, and music.

"Ladies and gentlemen, I thank you for your kindness and appreciation. Now, if you want to hear a song by Dalaras, the famous Greek singer, you will have to ask Jason to play the music that I will sing." When people heard this, they exploded as they were joyfully addicted to the sound of Dalaras' music.

The audience began shouting and demanding more. After Jason and Ismene talked for a minute, Jason said, "I will play my best 'Yannis o Fonias Pethi mias Patrinias ki enos Messologite', but please excuse my mistakes." Ismene laughs and says in Albanian, "If we do not do that, how we would be able to say we love you?"

When they finished, the spectators went crazy: They were applauding and praising. They were singing and talking, and both Jason and Ismene were embarrassed and pleased. Jason, as usual, was thoughtful and composed, and Ismene was unusually happy and smiling. When they sat down, Ismene's brother and mother were thankful and proud as well. Sergio's wife was happy and enchanted. She was more Greek than the others besides Jason.

She kissed Ismene as she was more liberal with the good wine and pleased, while her husband was disciplined and good as usually. What could you expect from an Aeronautical Engineer? Discipline and knowledge were his gifts unmatched by ordinary people. He was a man to be admired and the German-Greek knew what she was choosing.

In a few minutes, the owner of the Taverna Rupi came with a bouquet of flowers and presented it to Ismene. "This is a gift from the young musicians to show their appreciation. They expect you to see them again next time." "Tell them it was my pleasure," said Ismene.

While they watched, she got up and sent them kisses with both hands. They were happy for Ismene was not an ordinary woman, and her friend was a respectful man, and young to be admired. The audience was fascinated and difficult to discipline. The musicians were stunned.

Ismene was not an ordinary person but a charm hard to forget. None knew, however, that she was just rising out of extinction from the hands of a scum. Now she was with Jason who loved her.

The night was beautiful and unexpectedly pleasant and friendly. They all reached home satisfied with everything forgotten, besides the entertainment songs. Saturday was the day for packing and Sunday the day of departure for all. Jason, with pleasure, helped all he could on Saturday. Ligia, the Albanian lady, came Saturday afternoon. She was sad that she had missed Jason's invitation, but she determinedly said that next time, she was not going to miss it.

Early Sunday morning, Sergio and his wife left from Agius Saranta for Tirana. They were content and happy. "I will be waiting for you Sergio," said Jason. "Your next trip should be to Athens and from there, I will pick you up to take you to Kalamata. Don't forget." He turns to Sergio's wife and says, "Mrs., Greece has many thinks and places to see. Just be patient and you will be impressed.." "Yes I will," she replied and smiled pleased. If Sergio was satisfied, she was pleased.

At about an hour later, Jason left with Ismene in the front of the car and her mother in the back. He had lost both his parents but he was happy that his sister was always now to be waiting for him. She trusted him like a God and she was ready to die for him if there was a need. Jason often thought about her and she was the only relative he had. Her mother and father were dead and Jason had their pictures in the house he inherited. They didn't like that the British who had Irene was a deceiving imposter, but when she found out, it was too late. They had left when she got divorced and it was a blessing. They loved her but she couldn't understand that he was not a noble man. She didn't know that men of the quality of her brother were rare. She was Greek anyway and she had to learn from her own mistakes.

Jason called his sister Irene and told her that he was happy and he was coming with Ismene's mother who loved him as much as she loved her own daughter. She realized that no matter how strong one is inside himself, he wants to be loved. His sister told him, "Jason, you know how much we love you. You know how much Ismene loves you. You know how important you are for Simon! We will all be happy to see you. Besides Simon, none has met your mother-in-law. You know we love, what you love!"

She hung up because tears were coming dawn from her eyes. Jason understood and didn't wish to talk anymore. But he couldn't hide his wet eyes either. He was really a strong and noble man deserving the love of those who had met him. His first love was music and his mind was enchanted with its tunes. At home, he was playing with his piano and at friends' with his guitar that he was carrying always in his car. But he knew that Ismene was a special gift for anyone, and this thought was making him happy.

They stopped in Preveza for rest and they had their drink and pastry. Jason was always strong and pleasant to talk and laugh. They took a nice walk to see the center of Preveza before they left it; and they felt relaxed. It was also a pleasure to leave without thinking that they were rushed. Jason was driving carefully and he was really a pleasure. Both Ismene and her mother were happy. One had a noble man to love and the other a capable man to trust. He was the same man Jason.

As expected, Jason arrived in Patra at about the time he had estimated. At the railway station, Nicholas was happy to see Ismene again. She was a charm and Nicholas' eyes fell down. He was more at ease though, and comfortable with the mother. Anyway, he was happy to see two beautiful ladies. "Where did you find these beautiful ladies, Jason?" he asked. "I was lucky, Nicholas," replied Jason.

They had an excellent late lunch and the ladies were enchanted with the stores and the railway station. Nicholas was aware of their enchantment and said, "I chose this place to retire. Of course, I had my successes with the subjects and my failures with the women." "I can see that Nicholas," says Ismene smiling. "It depends on what you see." "I am sorry if that is the case," says Ismene now laughing.

"Where were you when I was thirty years old?" asks Nicholas. "I was nowhere." "You see? My woman was not in my time and my environment. But she is in Jason's." She looked at Jason smiling. "I agree

Nicholas. There was no woman for me other than Ismene," says Jason. "I know Jason, you were going to be like me," said Nicholas laughing. "Now, I doubt this." They all laughed with Nicholas. As always, he was the professor attracting conversation and ladies. None could doubt that Nicholas was admired and respected.

After their good lunch they left and as they were told, they followed Nicholas. He took them to his apartment to rest, and it was as expected. Jason and Ismene had a room for themselves, and Ismene's mother had her own room but better. Nicholas realized the situation and said, "Jason, everything is clean in the bedroom, better than in the hotels. Besides, only here you can have Nicholas' company!" They all laughed because it was the truth. Nicholas was also laughing. Denysa was pleased and said, "Nicholas, if I was never married I would marry you tomorrow." "Denysa, why would you have to wait that long?" "Because I wouldn't like you to think that I am frustrated." Everyone laughs and Nicholas replies, "That is fine. I will be waiting for tomorrow. Now lets go for a rest." They all went to rest for the late afternoon, smiling and laughing.

After their sleep, Nicholas fixed them their tea and coffee, and soon they all left for the city of Patras; about a quarter of an hour from where they were. They went to the harbor at the center and they walked along Demitriou Gounari at Ipsila Alonia. It was a nice and romantic place for people in love. Much has been said and written about Ipsila Alonia. You need the time to know their military, entertaining and romantic significance. They visited also the square of St. Andrea of the city Saint and Protector. Religion was everywhere and interesting to study. The same was about travelers escaping to Europe.

They passed the Plateia of March 25, a place everywhere in Greece, the date of revolution, and returned to Dimitriou Gounari to have a rest. They got some tea and Nicholas, as usual, had his Espresso. Somewhere in the center, Nicholas took them later at night for a light dinner. It was a popular place for people in Patra that Nicholas knew about. But you had to live in Patra to know. The food was exposed and you had to look to see and choose. Anything was tempting and satisfying. They tried the meals and they were all pleased. "I must win somewhere," whispered Nicholas. Everyone laughed considering so far their impressions.

"Where are you going tomorrow?" Nicholas asked after some thinking of his own. "We want to see Olympia with my mother, if we have a chance," Ismene requested. "Nicholas, can you come with us? We will travel straight to Kalamata after that," said Jason. Nicholas considers the invitation and says, "Yes, if you have space, and the ladies like me." "I am sure certain we like you and have a place for you also," Jason assured him and the ladies confessed laughing, that they loved him. "Then I will come," replies Nicholas.

When they left the restaurant, Jason said to Nicholas, "If anything is good about this city, it is the restaurants we tried." Nicholas laughed and said, "It will be hard to say anything else. Tomorrow morning we will pass by the University going towards Olympia to see its architecture." "Is it something to remember?" asked Ismene. "Not really; but it is something to know," whispered Nicholas smiling.

In the morning, they stopped at the University and everyone was disappointed. "It looks like an old abandoned institution, with buildings everywhere, ignored from the time they were built till now," said the mother by the end of their brief tour. It was really the only thing that could be said. No one went inside to hear the classes in session and face the squeaks of the doors opening and closing. They were really disappointed with the architecture, as expected. For a relatively young University it was embarrassing.

The buildings were ridiculous, and their architecture irritating: Conventional (commercial-residential) buildings used for teaching! "What about the teaching?" asked Jason. "Nothing special," whispered Nicholas. He was Professor and embarrassed. "I should not have taken you here," he said in a melancholic way. But they had to see and leave soon, and it was a pleasure for Nicholas. "They are shameful people," said Nicholas about all those responsible for the Architecture and the Design of the University. He with others were wondering what was going on. It was an orgy of money making with no educational architecture. "Well; it is nice to know," said Nicholas. "The people are nice but their creations ugly."

Early Monday morning, they were on their way from the University of Patras to Olympia. Jason and Ismene were in the front of the car. In the back were Nicholas and Denysa, Ismene's mother, not to forget. She is much younger than Nicholas, very attractive and noble in her light-weight, and near white-yellow dress. A discussion begins and she wonders why the Greeks do not maintain their school buildings. Nicholas explains that they build and they forget to maintain. Tomorrow they have another political party and another company responsible for buildings. So what do you get?"

Jason was driving carefully and Ismene was admiring Jason's posture. "How much time do we need, Nicholas, to get to ancient Olympia?" asks Jason. "It depends on how fast you go, Jason!" Jason smiles and says, "Let's go 60 miles an hour." In that case, Nicholas answers, "We need two hours from Patra to Olympia and two hours from Olympia to Kalamata."

Ismene's mother is watching the environment and looks intrigued. "What are you thinking, Denysa?" Nicholas wants to know. She looks at Nicholas and says, "No planning in anything. You give them the car and a road and the fools start building anywhere they have inherited and find land!" Nicholas who never thought about living and construction, but spent his life in Series, Integrals and Classics, looks around and wonders. "What should they have done?" he asks. She looks at him and says, "For me to go to my friend three kilometers from here, either I have to walk or take a taxi if there is one, and if I have the money!" Nicholas smiled thinking how that could be done.

Anyway, they arrived by eleven o'clock and decided to spend two hours in the Museum and three hours in the Field. In the Museum,

Nicholas took them to see some paintings and pieces of ancient sculptures. He explained what he could, but it was not enough.

They left by one o'clock and Nicholas took them to the running field and then to some buildings. They were more interesting, as each had functions performed by the athletes in ancient times. They saw where the Sphere and the Discus were thrown and where the athletes were competing and running. It was enchanting because those athletes were noble and competing. He mentioned some athletes, easy to forget their names with time. But the running field was challenging and interesting.

By early in the afternoon, they left to have a light meal and go to Kalamata. The truth is that you forget many of the things that you experience during your visit; but you remember the surprise and connection you have when you are walking places where people, many hundreds of years ago, lived before you. The time is never enough to give you the chance to even imagine those people.

But everything was invigorating and charming. You were passing places where they competed and you were enchanted. They were real. They were running, throwing the Javelin, the sphere and the Discus. They were jumping, they were wrestling and boxing, and they all wished to return to their lands as winners. They were doing then, what they are doing now. These sports have not changed much except boxing. It was a vicious sport I suppose.

They left but they were still there. They remained silent or they were speaking in awe of how the boxing competitors could take the pain! "That I have never understood," says Denysa contemplating a powerful punch. Nicholas laughs and elaborates. It was really hard!

As they left after a small lunch, Jason put some haunting music by Dalaras, Galani, and Mitsias and conversation paused to listen and sing. It was of course Ismene who could sing better than all of them. But it was fun and entertaining. Not long after, they were passing Asprohoma. For a long time now, probably no one had heard the whistle of the train.

Soon Jason was at the point where you either take the road that you turn your car at an angle to the left and go to the center, or instead you continue straight to the end to go left or right; either to the center again or to the sea. Jason now is in Kalamata and knows better than anybody else. This is the City where he was born and raised.

"Ladies and gentlemen," announces Jason. "We are now in Kalamata. The road bends to the left and goes straight to the Old Center; or goes straight to the end at the sea. There, after about two or three miles, goes either left again to the center, or right to go to the beach; and there is Ismene's house facing the sea if you turn and go left for two miles: Buildings to your left and the sea to your right with sea-gulls flying and exercising.

It is a pleasure to watch the deserted beach visited now only by birds. You wonder what do they do as they come for five minutes and then they leave to come back later. They do not have the gift to talk but they have the gift to fly. Someone wonders: How do they communicate when to come and when to leave? Someone must be their leader that most follow and a few miss. Nicholas has not studied them long enough to know and explain. The others do not care to know, anyway. But the beech is inviting and challenging. If you think what may happen, if you go inside far in the sea, it is frightening. Either you have to be a trained sailor or you never return.

Soon Jason parks at the house. Near the road, there is a sizable yard, and farther from the road and the dust, there is a beautiful house. The yard inside is colorful with inviting flowers. As soon as Jason parks, a young lady runs down the stairs and from the right side, she embraces Ismene. She immediately opens the back door, and as Denysa steps out, embraces her and says, "I am Irene, Jason's sister." Denysa looks at her and embraces her warmly. "I know you my sweet. Ismene has talked to me about all of you, and I have cried with joy that we have added good people to the family. I love you more than you can imagine." She was by now an Ilyrian Greek woman that lost the man she adored and loved. It is long time by now, but for her it is yesterday.

Soon, another lady is running down to share in the pleasure of the reunion. She is Norma. She ran to Ismene and after hugging her, she turned to the mother and said, "A lady of charm and dreams is now real." She looked at her and didn't believe in her simplicity and charm. She introduced herself as Simon's wife Norma, as she hugged Ismene's mother. Denysa turned around to see where Simon was. She saw him coming down the stairs and she ran to greet him happily.

"My Simon. How have you been? Seeing you is like seeing my son Sergio. He couldn't come but said to tell you that he is looking forward to seeing you next summer." She looks at him, embraces him and asks "Where is Stuart?" "He will be here soon with his wife," Simon replies smiling. He sees Ismene and runs to her as she runs to him. "I will always love you after Jason," she whispers. He smiles and Ismene is happy. "I will try to keep him alive so I won't have to come to you," she said smiling. She knew that Simon was Norma's husband!

Simon smiled and greeted Jason. "We are happy you are back," he said embracing Jason. He felt the friendliness of his friend and he was confident and happy. Simon and Jason had grown together and you could not see them apart. A good friend is often better than a brother, used Simon to say. He really loved Jason and there was no doubt. He could not forget Jason's generosity and friendship.

Jason called his sister. He told her something. She kissed him and she ran upstairs. Ten minutes later, she returned, said something to Jason and Jason disappeared. He apparently went for a shower. But Simon was happy when he saw Nicholas and began an easy conversation. "I am sure Jason employed you to explain the Olympic Games," he said to Nicholas. "And with two beautiful ladies, who could say no to them?" Nicholas replied. He looks at Denysa and then looking at him asks, "Would you say 'no' Simon?" Simon is thinking and Nicholas adds, "If you didn't have Norma?"

Simon laughs and replies, "Of course not, other things being equal." Both laughed and so did Denysa who understood they were talking about her. Nicholas goes to Denysa and says, "I just told Simon that you are beautiful and you look very young." "Mother, be careful of Greeks bearing gifts," warned Ismene jokingly as she approached her mother. "Yes, I will be," she promised, blushing a little. She was really looking young and tempting for any man that he didn't know. She was once Alexander's choice and pride.

Ismene came to her mother and asked her to follow. They go upstairs to the room on the right of the building and Ismene says, "Mother, this is your room with your closet. Next to it is the bathroom. Next to the bathroom is a washer and a drier. Please feel free to come and go as you please." "Thank you my sweet, but this is now yours isn't it? Don't worry about me." "Yes mother." "Well, leave it as it is and if I ever bother anyone, I will go and live with your father in Agius Saranta." "No mother, we will go and live together there, in that case."

Her mother looks at her and says, "Then, write it to Jason because I love him." "Fine mother, I will." Then Ismene with her mother went downstairs smiling. She knew her mother was a rare woman, independent and noble. What she had in Agius Saranta was enough. Now she wanted only their love.

As soon as they went downstairs, Ismene sees Stuart at the door with his wife. Ismene ran to embrace him, "Stuart, I haven't seen you since last year? You should know how much I love you." She hugs him and cries as her emotions and memories overwhelm her. Then she looks at the lady next to him and asks, "Anna?" and falls into her arms and cries again. "I am thankful and honored to meet you. How many times we have thought and asked about you and your wife; we can't count them," she says and Stuart is surprised.

"Thank you madam. Your daughter we love as our sister and more. We have not met other women like Ismene." Then, smiling he adds, "And we love her as much as we love our wives!" "Yes, you couldn't be as noble without a noble woman, my husband used to say," adds Denysa, holding Stuart's hand tightly with force.

"You and Simon should stay next to me today." she adds. "My love may never be needed, but knowing that someone loves you; you have someone you know you can rely on, if there is a need." "It's true," says Stuart thoughtfully. He remembered how many times Jason and Simon had been next to him when he needed them and he thanked God. Anyone who realized who Jason and Simon were, learned to behave. Then they knew that Stuart was their brother.

Jason came down refreshed and sat next to Ismene. Norma and Irene were to serve and were delighted with Jason's return. Soon Ismene got up to help. Three ladies were to serve nine people including themselves. Norma goes to Nicholas and says teasingly, "I want to be next to you. Keep my place." Nicholas smiles and puts Norma's name next to his. "Nicholas, you are not clever," Irene tells him. He smiles and replies, "You think so? With Norma, the responsibility is my friend's. With you, the old man will be caught!" Those who understood laughed and Simon said, "Norma, be careful with the Professor." "Don't spoil it Simon," replies Norma. Simon and Nicholas laughed with the possibility. Irene was young and Nicholas single but old. But none of course was proposing.

Ismene looks suddenly around and wonders. She wants tonight to be next to the people she loves. Jason is watching; but he says and does nothing. He loves Ismene to do as she pleases. She is different now than the last time when they left. As usually, he wants to explain. It is Sergio who gave the courage to Ismene. The others gave her freedom, but Denysa gave her the love that she needed, and she didn't have the freedom she wanted. It was her brother that gave her what she wanted: The mother, with the desire of revenge and the freedom of love.

Ismene is looking around thinking. Something is missing. She finds it and excited calls. "Louise, this is Ismene." A voice responds very happily. "Will you come with your sister, if you can, to my house? You know I didn't forget you." Ismene listens and smiling says, "Thanks Louise: I am happy and I am waiting for you. I will surprise you. Please come." She closed her phone content and was smiling. Her smile was different. Before it was changing but now remains pleasant.

It is a smile dreaming and captivating. Not long ago it was unpredictable, now it is enslaving. Before she loved the sea, now she is capturing its waves. Jason observes but her brother knows. "My God," whispers Jason who is observing Ismene.

At about ten o'clock, Louise arrives with her sister. Both are charming but Louise is imposing and Elane calm and charming. As Louise reaches the entrance of the house and sees Ismene, she falls in her arms and cries. "I am so thankful to see you again," she whispers. When she separates herself she says, "Ismene, here is my sister." Ismene embraces Elane and smiles. Then she says, "I will introduce you now to a lady." She takes Louise and her sister and introduces them to her mother. Smiling she says, "Louise, you know who this lady is, don't you?" Louise looks at the lady, looks at Ismene, looks at the lady again, and falls in her arms crying.

"Mrs Denysa," she screams and stays on the arms of the old lady crying. She could not constrain her pleasure and surprise. Her tears, rich and running, wetted Denysa who could not constrain her tears either. "I know you and your noble character is a deep impression in my heart," said Denysa with large tears rolling down on her cheeks. Ismene was surprised by Louise's emotion. Her sister moved as well: She cried. She had heard many times her sister speak about Ismene with tears. But now she was moved. Ismene had an unusual charm as if she was brought up with the services of angels. Elane senses her own tears rolling down and wonders.

Ismene's mother was surprised to find out that all people were happy to meet her and serve her with pleasure. Yet, she was afraid that they may as easy betray her and her daughter. She was wondering if any people knew that she had been, like her daughter, abused.

These thoughts were clouds that Jason had not faced and was not considering. Nothing negative was expressed by any of his loved ones by choice or weakness. Ismene was strong in her defenses even though weak in herself knowing how much she had suffered. Jason loved a woman who had no desire to deceive or exploit anyone. She was with all respectful; and anyone who was not noble with her, he had better learn to be. No matter who he or she could be, Ismene was noble and proper. She knew how to avoid the scums and the wretched ones. She was very careful and mature. Ismene was brave but tortured and threatened for long.

Ismene was not as conscious as her mother. But she knew how to be defensive and ostracize the disrespectful ones. She knew how to evaluate people and behave accordingly. With the selfish and ruthless, she had to be careful and face them from a position of strength. There was a difference between Ismene and her mother. One was sharper than the other and more desired, but both still wanted.

Anyway, Ismene was thankful and thought it essential to introduce Louise to her friends Stuart and Simon. She knew Jason. Louise knew more about these people and she was to be polite and thankful. Ismene takes Louise by the hand and introduces her to Stuart and Simon. "This is my friend Louise. She gave me the money and the strength I needed without ever asking, and before Jason had the will," she said with tears.

Louise lowered her head to hide the truth. "When everyone thought that I was not an honest woman, including Jason, she offered to die for me. Of course, she didn't know the danger." Stuart and Simon thanked Louise. She looked at them and could not hide her tears.

She lifted her head and said, "I am the one to thank you." She was trying to hold her tears. Her sister who didn't know anything was surprised. None knew how much Ismene and Louise loved each other. More likely, Louise deceptively knew a lot more about Jason's friends than they knew about the friend of Ismene. It was hard to say. But the truth was that Ismene didn't care because she was pure and noble; not afraid of anyone and not concerned, how noble the others were. If she had no relations with others she was noble and polite. If she did, she was expecting honesty and nothing more.

Stuart was friendly and polite to Louise. But through Norma, Simon, more likely, knew more about Louise than Stuart. But both were optimistic about Louise, and Jason was happy. Why were the friends of Jason always positive about his choices? More likely because Jason was careful in his choices and depended on people who had trust in him. Once people develop very close to one, they maintain their trust with him; and if he is careful with them, they show respect.

Jason could lose, but his friends could not. This gave him freedom to succeed with others even though he could fail by himself. He was never placing his customers at risk with great probability. He was always thoughtful and considerate. He was always sympathetic like the musicians. He was a musician trained in securities trading.

Stuart was more liberal with ladies than Simon. But he was always careful. Louise attracted him and Stuart was liberal with her. Neither Stuart nor Louise were serious, but they were attracted and none realized if anything happened. But they were people experienced and liked each other. Stuart would never go with a woman who had a friend. And his wife was not one to fool with any. But Louise, liked Stuart and was attracted. There was a connection between Stuart and Louise and that did not escape Ismene's attention. However, it was their dignified choice and no one was concerned except Anna. She was a beautiful and aggressive Greek charming lady.

However, there was nothing serious although it was interesting. Stuart would never go with a woman that belonged to another or wanted to find a husband. Everyone knew that Louise was an independent woman neglecting and flirting with the unexpected. She was humorous and a respected lady who knew how to play her game.

This night she was happy to be with Ismene's company. Everyone was pleased and all invited her to join them. Louise was trained by Ismene and respected. She was also a very kind and tough woman. "Be kind and tough," Ismene used to advice Louise.

Jason knew and respected Louise. That night she sat next to Ismene happy to see her after so long and content to talk of many things. Among them was the new Flower shop at the old Section of Kalamata. Ismene had discussed the place, before leaving last time and Louise had succeeded in getting a 10 year lease.

She happily informed Ismene and everything was moving at the speed desired. As a matter of fact, Louise was happy since she was asked to sign the lease that she wanted to discuss with Ismene the current week. "That is fantastic," said Ismene. "This week we will discuss what we want; and next week we will proceed to sign the papers we need." Louise was a sharp woman who had placed her trust on Ismene. She could do things for Ismene with passion and respect.

Ismene was proud of Louise and said, "Now Louise we need the man." "Yes, if there is now one worth anything," replied Louise wondering. "Of course, otherwise, we choose what we like. Not a lazy parasite," says Ismene thinking. "Yes, one like Jason," replies Louise smiling. "Why not?" asks Ismene laughing. "He is a business man anyway; is he not?" Louise laughed and said, "Yes, a noble one as well; but he is yours." Both laughed and Louise added, "I will never dare think of such a thing against a friend, even if I am begged, even if I am attracted" added Louise. "Thank you Louise; you are a noble lady and I am convinced of that for long time." Louise held the hand of Ismene and let her look at her wet blue eyes. They were to be trusted!

Soon, the dinner was brought and started. Most of the people were hungry and pleased. Good wine with excellent food was to revive all the people. The ones that drove through Olympia and the ones who were dreaming and hoping, were all to be revived. Norma, Irene, Louise and her sister were ready to serve. The others ready to help whenever it was needed.

Everyone was wondering who made the dinner. Ismene's mother was the Captain Cook in charge of the total meal and the specialist of the beans. Norma and Irene were the cooks of the Hamburgers and the Chicken, and the other ladies were serving the table. The table was pleasing to the hungry and the filled ones. Everything was fresh and tasty. It was really a feast never to forget.

Jason was thinking and his friends were admiring and trusting him. It was the time just after the dinner made by the care of Denysa. None had seen Jason so happy from the time he met Ismene. She was smarter than her mother but never till her mother could be happy. Now he thought of Sergio. He was impressed by his mental intelligence and physical abilities.

Jason called Ismene and whispered, "I am happy that Sergio is your brother." "Why," she asked. "Because he is like you" he whispered.

Everyone was hungry when the dinner started. The cold retsina wine with the tomato salad, the fried chicken, the hamburgers and the red beans were a challenge that none had experienced before. The young ladies were all experts under the leadership of Denysa.

They brought excellent dessert in trays filled with pure Greek pastry. You could have all you wanted but all pieces were small and tempting. They were specialties with coffee, tea, soft drinks and cold water. Norma and Irene were smiling. As the trays with the food left, the sweets with the pastries came.

Soon, Irene was hitting a crystal glass to call the attention of the people with its sweet sound. After they all kept quiet to listen, Irene saying, "Ladies and gentlemen, we have to welcome Mrs Denysa, the mother of Ismene coming from the charming Agius Saranta of Albania to our beloved and friendly city of Kalamata." Everybody applauded and Denysa rose to thank the people.

"Norma will introduce all of us to a musical entertainment to thank Mrs Denysa and wish her a pleasant stay in our city," she added. Everybody welcomed her with applauds and she was surprised. She was not expecting the Greeks to be so open and friendly.

Just after the dessert, Norma brought in a Guitar, a Bouzouki, a Mandolin and the Drums. This was the surprise to the guests. Nobody knew who was to play the Bouzouki, the Mandolin and the Drums. Jason was to play the Guitar and Ismene was to sing. She of course could play the guitar as well.

But who were to play the other instruments? Everyone was surprised except Norma. She gave the microphone to Ismene, the Guitar to Jason, the Bouzouki to Stuart, the Mandolin to Nicholas and the Drums to Simon. Some people thought that Nicholas was to play the Bouzouki, but they were surprised.

Norma sitting next to Nicholas as promised, rang the crystal glasses and asked for the attention of the group. "Ladies and gentlemen, tonight we will hear the best music devoted to Mrs. Denysa for her first visit to Kalamata, Greece." Everyone applauded.

"Ismene will sing; and Jason will play the Guitar. Nicholas will play the Mandolin, Stuart the Bouzouki and Simon the Drums." They were all surprised. "Please, let's welcome them all in the house of the honorable Artist Ismene" Every one was surprised and applauded.

Finally, they were all obliged by Ismene to take their instrument and exhibit their knowledge. The others had no choice but to listen and participate, if they wished and were expected. But you could not be Greek and not participate. You could not be Greek and not sing. "Nicholas is good with the Mandolin as he is with Mathematics; and he said that he will play the Mandolin for Ismene's mother." Everybody was excited and applauded.

But before they started, Norma asked their attention. "Please, let me tell you that a few years ago, about ten or so, Jason asked Simon and Stuart to join him in making a music group and play for the students and others at the University of Athens. They started and played but the only one to be attached was Jason. Stuart and Simon had to stop to finish Engineering. But Jason wanted to continue. He learned that while others were to make money, he was going to gain the admiration of the people for which, however, none wanted to pay." She smiled and added, "That is why Jason is with us tonight." Every body laughed and the group started the music.

Everyone was impressed as Jason and Ismene dominated the scene with songs of Dalaras, Mitsias and Mbithikotses. The friends Stuart and Simon played some fascinating songs of Mitsias; and Nicholas being the correct one, played songs that brought Denysa in the years of 60's and 70's. The others were amazing members of the choir but none the listener. All were an organized and happy group or chorus! Each one wanted his favorite song to be played; and it was done!

———————————

12   SACRIFICE OF THE HELLENIC BEAUTY

"There is no sacrifice for Love by a fickle."

From the start of September, two young people, a man and a lady are always going every Saturday for swimming at the beach of Kalamata across from their house. They have been doing that for almost five years. These are Jason and Ismene.

This September the lady was a charm tempting, and the man strong and respectfully smiling. They were both friendly and charming. They were both getting in the sea that was blue and calm, and they were disappearing. They were always friendly and charming.

Those who saw them in the morning, no matter how long they stayed, they never saw them coming back before three o'clock. This used to happen every Saturday from the beginning of September till the end of November. But they always came back in the afternoon after three o'clock. Each time they came, they were smiling and people who were there didn't know who they were and what they were doing.

The swimmers get out from the sea, the boats are trying to find their way back, and by four o'clock in the afternoon the sun remains pale. The sea is now wild and deserted, the old man calls the owner and asks, "I didn't see the young couple of the handsome man and charming lady coming back, did you?" The restaurant owner looks at the sea and with a bitter smile replies, "If they did, they didn't stop for their special afternoon meal; who knows?" After this he observes the tumultuous sea. He is serious and thinking as he is looking at the vibrant waves. But the swimmers came back smiling.

One Saturday morning, five years later, an Old but brave Seaman was drinking his coffee. He watches Jason and Ismene going into the sea in the end of November. It was late in the morning. As they approach the breaking waves Ismene looks at the mountains to her left and right. She looks at the sea South and can no longer see the separation of the sea from the sky. She looks at Jason standing in front of the waves wondering. He is absorbed and thinking.

"Shall we go in Jason?" she asks. "Yes, lets go in and come back soon" he answers. "To go in with the wind will be easy; but to come out it will be hard," she whispers. Anyway, both go in with pleasure and the wind blows from North to South.

In half an hour after, both had disappeared as usually deep in the sea. But soon, the wind from North to South gets stronger and with time it gets wilder. Not long after a storm is blowing from North to South and all people have gotten out. Only Ismene and Jason are in and as usually have disappeared. Going in with the wind was a pleasure.

As they left, the Old Seaman calls the owner of the Restaurant and asks, "Are those two young people ever coming back?" The owner smiles and shaking his head whispers, "Yes, apparently they do; after three to four hours they always come back and many times after two or three hours they meet some other people comparable in charm. But you have asked me the same question many times; why?" he asks.

The Old Seaman looks inside, sees the storm rising and tears run down his cheeks. "I will not ask you anymore, but I will be praying for their health and return every time," he replies. Jason and Ismene got into the sea and disappeared. Three to four hours later, the Old Seaman gets his cold white wine with the fried fish and begins slowly eating.

He is drinking and watching the sea getting angry; suddenly for no reason by four o'clock the sea is mad and its waves are raving. The wind blows inside the sea. The young man and the charming lady have not returned yet for their late light lunch.

The Old Seaman is watching deep into the sea the foaming waves, and listens to the thundering of the clouds pouring on the crying gulf.

The wind is blowing and the rain is pouring. The Old Seaman is watching. "God save them," he whispers. He is staring into the sea wondering. The sun hides, and clouds are running fast on the sky. Something is chasing them and soon the sky gets dark. The sun has disappeared behind the clouds hiding its path.

The swimmers get out from the sea, the boats are trying to find their way back to rest, and by five o'clock in the afternoon the sun remains pale. The sea is now wild and deserted, the Old Seaman calls the owner and asks, "I didn't see the young couple of the handsome man and charming lady coming back; did you?"

The restaurant owner looks at the sea and with a bitter smile replies, "If they did, they didn't stop for their special afternoon Saturday meal; who knows?" After this, he observes the tumultuous sea. He is serious and thinking, as he is looking at the vibrant waves. They fight to rise and fall as the wind is growing. The waves are rising and raving.

They start wild deep in the sea and arrive exhausted by the beach. "Who knows?" the Old Seaman whispers. He looks at the restaurant man, two tears roll down from his eyes, gets up slowly, and goes west towards the church. He walks slowly on the promenade and soon arrives at the church of Prophet Elias. There he stops, looks east and west on Navarinou road, and when the road clears he crosses the street.

He stands to the west side of the church, looks south of the church and slowly goes in from the open west side. "I was raised in the Center, I grew up in the West, I travelled the East, and I worked in the North and South. Now I lost Odysseus but not Jason. Where am I going? Why am I afraid?" he whispers alone in the church.

One time, long ago, he had lost his son and his beautiful lady an afternoon of late November in the sea. Since then he was crying with his wife. Now for the last year he was coming alone quite often on the storming afternoons. He had lost his wife also for some reason. There was no question that she was noble and in love with him. After that, one day he was coming alone and after his late lunch he was going into the church. None knew what he was doing. He was old but still proud and respectful. His eyes were tired and looking up in the sky. He was waiting for something but it was never coming.

This time he takes two Candles and says: "This is for my real son Odysseus from Ithaka; and this one is for my adopted son Jason of the Argonauts." He is thinking as he is lighting the candles. "Let them be in peace with their beautiful women," he whispers. "But nothing from the non-existing is created, nothing to the non-existing is corrupted; to rise and fall, the same it is as changing." Tears run down his cheeks as he looks around, and slowly moves out.

The exit is looking West. He crosses the street and on the promenade he walks East again. You can not see any tears, any longer, running down from his eyes on his face, brown from the sun of the sea. He no longer hopes! He no longer expects.

For an hour there was peace. No humans were moving or could participate in the orgy of the storm except the Dolphins and the Sharks. It was an orgy of the sea. There was a natural revolution that only time was finally to master. The humans were spectators of the orgy of the sea wondering and waiting for November to embrace a new world. None else knew but the god Poseidon only. He was upset, for the disrespect of his authority.

At five o'clock in the afternoon, a young lady comes and sits at the raised platform on the beach facing the sea. The restaurant man comes out to help her. She asks a double Greek coffee with biscuits and cold water. The restaurant man asks calmly with a smile: "Do you want to be served here, Louise?" "Yes, please. It does not matter if I also go," she replies bitterly. He goes in and brings her order: Bitter coffee with biscuits and water. He sees the tears in her eyes but he says nothing.

Louise is drinking her coffee with the cold water and biscuits for an hour and a half watching the sea. That time the Old Seaman was just coming again. For an hour and a half Louise was watching the sea slightly dreaming and crying. She was probably thinking that Jason was going to come, if he does, at that place. She was going to wait till she was disappointed. She could not constrain the tears.

She was desperate and didn't know what to do. She was looking deep inside the stormy sea and was crying. Those who knew her, knew why. It was five o'clock, dark and the sea was mad. None knew why. But Louise was restless and quietly hoping, wondering and crying.

The man she loved was still in with the woman she was adoring. She knew what she was before, and what she was now. It was Ismene and Jason in her life. The storm, the rain, the winds, the waves were raving and dancing. She didn't know what to do, what to say, where to go. Tears were running down her face and she was trembling as the time was going on. If it was not the tears she would have turned crazy.

A Fishing ship came close to the beach late at six o'clock in the afternoon. The sun was now pale setting west and after that the ship continued its trip to the Kalamata harbor. Louise saw it and rose. But the ship continued its trip to the harbor right and she sat again disappointed. Half an hour later she saw a handsome man coming out of the wild waves and falling soon after on the wet sand.

He gets up again, and falls again on the sand. Suddenly, the man rises and barely walks to the beach to fall again on the sand as if absorbing the exasperated waves. Louise wakes up and seeing a young man falling again, stands up; looks carefully and runs to him. She was convinced that he was Jason, the man she was expecting. "But where is Ismene?" she cried. She could not see any woman. She could not see Ismene! She didn't know what to think. She was crying hopeless!

She runs and falls on the man; she kisses him and asks, "Jason, where is Ismene?" He opens his eyes and closes them again while tears flood them and flow on his cheeks. "Jason, what happened to Ismene?" she asks again. His eyes close and tears run out on his face. He cannot answer. Louise looks at him, kisses him and whispers, "If now I could have you instead of Ismene, I would be your slave. What I will now have to do without her or her lover?" She sat on the wet sand and was weeping. The world was the chiaroscuro of the sky. She could not hear, see or say anything more. It was too dark already.

She was crying lost without Ismene. She was in love with Jason but she wanted Ismene. "Jason where is Ismene? What we will do now without her?" The tears flooded her face and she embraced Jason. "She was eaten by a Shark," she heard him whisper and she fell on him crying. Both were crying not been able to speak. Jason was pale and Louise was crying breathing deeply and hopelessly.

That time, the Old Seaman returns and looks at Louise. She is crying and the Old Seaman sees Jason spread on the wet sand. He approaches him and whispers, "If you came; my son one day may also come." But Jason was brought by the Fishing ship, the same day. How many days have gone since your son disappeared? he was asked. "Yes, many days have passed since my son disappeared. He may have gone with his charming lady where Medea went." Tears come in the Old Seaman's eyes to keep him alive.

Jason was crying slowly with the waves. He could not say anything but cry and lament. Louise was embracing him and her warm tears were running on Jason's face. She loved him, she loved Ismene and she could not live in peace without them. She could get any man she wanted, but Ismene was her tutor; younger but more intelligent!

Ismene was not with him. The waves were whispering and Jason was crying like a child lost and left alone on the beach. He was crying stretched on the wet sand, facing the chiaroscuro sky and not knowing what to say and what to do. His eyes were looking on the sky and wondering why; why did he come alone? Why did he leave Ismene?

It was near the end of November, more than five years after the festival of freedom in Ismene's house. None now will know or understand the love that Ismene had inspired in the hearts of man and women. It was now the turn of the kind Ismene never to be Alice again. She was going to be Ismene saving the swimmers and Sailors each November, expecting them to know and be careful...

It was an afternoon and Jason was crying in his office thinking of Ismene. The sun was setting and Jason's eyes were crying watching the sun. The sea, the mountain, the sky and the sun was setting in the west. He was watching the colors, and the blue silver in the sky was magnificent. Jason as usually was watching the outline of the mountain and tears were running down his face.

Soon he was going alone again to meet his friends. Suddenly his office door is nocked. It was a year after Ismene's sacrifice and he was constantly thinking of Ismene before going alone to meet his friends Simon and Stuart in the Bar with Nicholas once in a while. He looks at the door of his office aloof and replies, "Please come in." He waits and the door opens slowly. A young beautiful lady moves in carefully.

She is serious and approaches Jason still sitting in his office and trying to hide his tears. They were tears for Ismene and the lady knew. "I know you did not expect me. But also I know that you are left alone, and many want you," replies the lady. Jason looks surprised and wonders. He cannot say anything.

"I knew that you would be alone and that you would be crying. So I came to see you and tell you that I live with you," adds the lady with tears and a smile. She moves slowly, takes a chair and sits across from him. There was a smile of pleasure on the face of the lady. She could not keep the smile and tears flooded her face. She was crying watching Jason. "I am sorry," she whispers.

Jason surprised stares at the lady. "If I am not mistaken," he whispers, "you are Flora. More beautiful now than before." "If I am now more beautiful than a flower, I will not deny it. But I was not before, that is why I never came to see you. Ismene loved you, you loved her and she was the most beautiful one." Jason wants to say something but Flora continues. "I admired and respected Ismene, and I never thought that I was more beautiful or capable. Nothing would have stopped me, if I ever thought otherwise."

Jason smiles, thinks and asks, "Were you ever married?" "Why does it matter?" she asks. "I just came here to see you. You may ask your friends to excuse you and promise them that you will see them tomorrow," she answers. Jason thinks, talks to his friends, and Flora looks at the picture of Ismene across from her on the wall while Jason is asking an excuse. "Yes, you should go somewhere for dinner tonight," he says, "and tomorrow, I want you to see me and if you wish; my friends also," he replies.

"You came that long and you deserve to see me Flora. I can see my friends any time later." She looks at Jason in thankfulness. He gets up, approaches her while she was sat, catches her face in his two hands and gives her two friendly and tender kisses in the lips. There was no resistance. She was quiet and calm. "You are easy when you kiss ladies," she replies. "Aren't you the same with man?" he asks. "It depends what you believe," she replies and her face get filled with tears. "I have never kissed other men besides you." For seven years she was respectfully staying away to give him a chance to have his child. She came only after he lost Ismene and the chance to have her child.

"For six years I was waiting for you to have your child with Ismene and be happy. And now that you lost Ismene I come to tell you that I have your son; and I want you to have your happiness, if you believe it. I am expecting nothing; but my son had to know his father. He is going now in the first grade in a private school in Istanbul." She watches him surprised and comments. "I do not expect anything but my son wanted to know his father. His mother was not a failure." Tears that she could not control started to roll now down on her face.

Jason was surprised but he could say nothing since Flora was not asking anything. She was a capable and respectable lady and Jason had his experience already. She was not to discus anything that was to question her integrity. "I am sorry that you missed Ismene. She was a noble lady." You could not hear Flora speak and question her integrity.

"Tomorrow if you please; lets discuss the progress of my investment." She opens her purse and gives to Jason a beautiful picture. "In case you are interested to know how your son looks," she adds trying to hold her tears. "If you allow me, I would like to see you tomorrow and discuss the progress of my investment." Jason is looking at the picture and asks,

"Will you like to join me tonight for something light?" She looks at him and answers, "If you are free, it will be my pleasure." "Sure, I am," he replies and picks up his telephone. He calls his friends and postpones his meeting. "Gentlemen, tomorrow I will see you in the same place; at the same time, if you can. Thank you."

After that, Jason and Flora left and went on a beach restaurant in Kalamata. Flora had never been in Kalamata before and was impressed. They sat on an attractive outside taverna facing the sea. It was a pleasure for both and the eyes of Flora were searching to find something and read in the eyes of Jason. She had talked with him many times through the phone, but they had never met after. Flora was quick enough and clever never to let Jason to meet her in Istanbul, even though she had promised to see him. Her son was still small but rising with the expectation to meet his father.

Jason had suspected that she was married and his view was approved by his friends. None could really guess the reason. Flora wanted to see Jason happy next to a noble woman. She never wished to be a cause for any unhappiness. She knew how to love the father of her son! She knew that her son would meet him one time later and ask for his excuse. She loved Jason and she was prone for any sacrifice that would leave him happy with Ismene forever. She was in reality a noble lady not wishing to blame others for her mistakes or successes.

Jason and Flora sat on an outside taverna facing the sea and they were reserved but happy. The cool night weather in the front of the sea was enchanting and the fish dinner with the wine were a pleasure for both. After a pleasant but reserved discussion that relaxed them both, Jason said, "If you like you may come with me to my home by the beach." "Left to you by Ismene?" asks Flora smiling. "Why? does it matter?" he asks wondering. "Of course not," replies Flora with a questioning smile. She was more composed and controlled than Jason.

She had not seen Jason after her second time in the hotel but she had talked to him after through the phone in a very reserved and business way. She really didn't want to see him till his son was to go to school.

The disappearance of Ismene, convinced her that she deserved him, if he liked her. She was not going to demand but know. Her respect for the woman that was making Jason happy was not to be questioned. She had to be detached and she would not have come now. But now she was free. Jason had no longer Ismene and she didn't expect him to forget.

Not long after, Jason drove to his home left to him by Ismene. It was simple compared to what Flora had in Istanbul. But it was friendlier and impressive. She really enjoyed it and from its balcony you could enjoy the view of Kalamata harbor and the mountains around. "It is amazing," whispered Flora. "Its views of the bordering mountains are charming," she added and sat in a chair by the terrace table to enjoy the spectacle. Not only the views around, but any detail was attractive and charming.

Flora was impressed. Jason offered sweet wine following his habit and whispered, "I am sorry Flora. Ismene was a charm to offer you what you wanted. But she offered herself to the sharks to save me." He felt so embarrassed that he could not avoid the tears. "I wish it had never happened" whispered Flora earnestly. "But they would have eaten you, otherwise," she added wondering. In reality it was wonder because Flora admired Ismene; and she was proud that the man she loved was loving and wanted her. She was not a compromise.

After some conversation that pleased and relaxed them both, Flora whispered, "I better go now Jason; I guess its time." Jason looks at her and asks, "Do you really want to go Flora?" She looks at him and whispers, "You know Jason that I want, what you wish. You do not know me Jason," she whispered and cried. Jason gets up, lifts Flora and kisses her with passion. She was passionate and inexperienced as about seven years ago. "Penelope was waiting for Odyseus twenty years, I can wait for you seven," she said smiling with tears.

Jason didn't understand. Then Flora whispered, "I didn't come here for you and me, but for your son. When you come for your son and me in Istanbul, then I will answer you." He smiles confused.

Flora looks at Jason in the eyes and smiling says. "I want tomorrow to talk with you my investments, and at night to meet your friends, if I can." Jason smiles and says, "Of course, they will also be pleased to know you." "Thank you Jason; you are really a noble man." Jason realized that Flora was a respectable young lady and a flower to be given not by the wind but by the will of the young lady growing it. She had shown to him how much she respected his integrity.

When he asked where was her room, she whispered, "At Haiko hotel, not far from here." "Oh, yes; I know," he replied.

———————————————

13 JASON, FLORA AND THEIR BRIGHT SON

"A wise man and a wise woman should have wiser children."

Jason met Flora on Saturday morning. He showed her the progress of her investment in six years from $50000 to about $400000. It could have being more but he had to be conservative in her absence. "Now we have enough money to let me be more aggressive, if you please," he said. He explained, Flora understood and allowed Jason to be more aggressive by using bigger portions of the funds in special cases.

They went for lunch and Jason promised Flora that he was going to be more aggressive, by trading more if she had no objections. He also promised her that his sister Irene was to come by seven o'clock and go with them in the special dinner with his friends. "She will call you to go to Ismene's house and wait for me just before seven o'clock. "Thank you Jason," she replied with a smile.

Jason called and talked to Flora and promised her to go with his sister at seven in the evening as he was going to be busy till then. He was strangely happy not because he had forgotten Ismene but because Flora was another charm; dark and imposing when there was a need. Jason never forgot Ismene but he was happy that he had met Flora.

Flora went to Ismene's house. Irene welcomed Flora with a smile but remained thoughtful and Flora looked at Irene with a surprise. Irene fixed a coffee for Flora who sees Jason's guitar and attracted as she was, she takes it and begins playing watching the Messinian Gulf with its waves, the birds and the boats raving.

At about eight o'clock Jason arrives before Flora could sense his arrival. "Do you like my guitar?" Jason asks. "Oh, yes, I love it," she replies surprised and looks at Jason's sister. Irene looks strangely at the lady trying to think where she had met her before. After while Flora whispers "It was in Istanbul; by the square. You were with another attractive lady." Irene looks at Jason and whispers, "Yes Jason, I was with Norma, and the child had whispered that he was going to go to Kalamata to meet his father when he heard that we were from here; and his mother had smiled." Then Flora, was looking at Jason and Irene was staring kindly at Flora. Then she saw two tears roll down the cheeks of Flora. She was not as charming as Ismene but she was attractive and intelligent. Irene was pleased. She liked Flora and smiled willfully. She probably remembered how nice it was in Istanbul.

"I knew who were you when I met you in Istanbul," whispered Flora. "I knew your brother; how could I miss you?" Irene was surprised. Then Flora added, "I am sorry, I had no choice to identify myself. It was your brother's right if he wanted." She saw the tears of pleasure flooding Irene's eyes. Jason was smiling wondering.

Jason understood everything and was serious. Introduced Flora to Irene and Irene to Flora. Then he said, "Ladies lets get ready and go." Jason left to get ready and Irene with Flora sat at the outside table and began a discussion about Istanbul as if they knew each other from before. They seemed to know each other for long and Irene felt more comfortable with Flora than Ismene. Not long after, Jason came out from his bedroom dressed and ready.

Jason, Irene and Flora left on feet. "We should walk to Filoxenia," said Jason. "It is not far but a pleasure," he added. With Flora in the middle, Irene and Jason walked to Filoxenia. It was a pleasant evening walking along the promenade with the sea to their right; and the houses, the shops and the restaurants all along to their left side. It was a cool and charming evening for walking along the beech.

When they reached Filoxenia, Simon with his wife Norma run to give them a welcome unexpected after the loss of his Ismene, the noble and respected by all who had witnessed her charms and abilities: quick and agile to ride a dolphin, and capable to escape the bites of the Sharks. It is hard to forget that young lady.

She was the woman of the sea. But as Norma kissed Irene and Jason, she looked at Flora and stopped. She became careful to think where she had seen that woman! She approaches her carefully, looks at Irene and wonders happily. "How did you find and invited this noble lady?" she asks Irene. "It was not I my dear, Jason will probably tell us." Jason introduces Flora to Norma and Simon and moves to the tables taking Norma with him.

"Be calm my dear, and you should know very soon," he says smiling. Norma is looking around to see what she was missing. She was missing Ismene, but confused as she was she had forgotten. Another lady, not as charming but as attractive, was taking the place of Ismene. Everyone was not as happy and Flora understood. Ismene was a charm and a queen. But they didn't know her yet.

When they reached the table, everyone got up and greeted Jason. He smiled and as soon as he sat down with Flora to his right and Irene to his left he said, "Ladies and gentleman, tonight we have with us a young lady by the name Flora." He points to all of them Flora who is a very attractive and successful flower. None mentioned Ismene but Flora sensed that they were, as she was, thinking about Ismene. Jason introduced Flora as one of his best friends and smiled.

He did not talk about the child, and Flora did not seem to mind or care. What he said was true and what she believed it was also true. She knew that as soon as they met Nikita, the name of his son, they would know whose the little boy was! She was too mature to worry. She was proud of her son. Once they were to meet her son she was certain they would love him. She knew that the seed of Nikita was Jason.

The dinner started and everyone was hungry and happy. Louise got up, went to Flora and whispered that she was Ismene's partner and one in love with Ismene and Jason. But now that Ismene left, she was going to be her partner. "Do not forget that I will love you as much as I loved

Ismene. Please, remember this." "I will," replied Flora smiling. "Should I know why!" asks Flora. Louise looks at her and answers, "It is my secret; can I keep it?" "Of course you can," replies Flora smiling.

When Louise went back to her chair, Jason whispered to Flora, "She was the love of Ismene, and Ismene loved her more than others, if you had to give your opinion. Of course, you would have to be wrong." Flora did not wish to say anything. She smiled knowing how hard it was for a noble man to say something different.

But Louise was, anyway, a hard working and intelligent young lady who loved and helped Ismene a lot. She was hardworking and thankful to Ismene without any excuses. She was not married but she was attractive enough to have what she wanted, anytime. She wanted Ismene and was hoping to find an approximation in Flora: A real kind flower; a very intelligent young lady.

By the end of the dinner Jason called the attention of the group. "Ladies and gentlemen, we are complete tonight except that Nicholas was trapped in Patra. Otherwise, we have to proceed." Everyone smiled and Jason continued. "If Flora would like; we would be happy to hear her music and songs tonight." Flora gets surprised and looking at Jason replies loud enough, "If Jason sings, I will play." Jason gets surprised; but smiling he replies, "If that is the case I will." Simon brings the guitar and gives it to Flora who was a gifted musician.

After a brief dialog between Jason and Flora, the song surprised the audience. It was a Greek song, 'Yannis the killer, son of Patrinia and one Mesolongite', which Flora was playing and Jason was singing. The audience of friends got lost in the talent of Flora: She was one of them.

It was not expected, and all got absorbed with a charming, kind and young lady. She was really more fitting the environment and passionate if not as attractive as the beauty of Ismene. But she was fitting the group as one of them. Stuart and Simon were amazed: "She is one of us," whispered Stuart smiling. They loved Ismene; but Flora was more of their level.

All were surprised and honestly applauded. Flora thanked them with tears and smiles. They were all sincere and trusted. Flora had a taste of the Greeks. Then she gave the guitar to Jason and said, "I thank you all, but now it is Jason's turn and his friends to entertain us. Jason realized that Flora was an artist but not as Greek as she wanted.

She was noble but not as skillful as Ismene. Yet, she deserved the sincere applauds of his friends. Louise got up and gave her a kiss smiling. "Jason, you know what you choose don't you?" she whispered. Jason smiled and he knew that it was Flora that was choosing. "It is not I, but Flora," he whispered. Flora responded, "Only, if I was wanted!"

After a few songs played by Jason, everyone was happy and more than everyone was Flora. The ladies said that Ismene was missing but Jason and Flora would not have regretted if she was with them or if she would not have objected, as they expected. But Ismene knew better; and Flora respected Ismene. This didn't annoy Jason who never refused anything: Flora was intelligent as well and happy.

Jason promised Flora that he was going to be with her as he loved her. She was intelligent and noble. That night was the happiest for Jason's friends for they realized that Flora was not just a woman but as well a gifted one and noble. She was an honest woman to be trusted. She was noble and accomplished: A rich artist like the others.

Jason and Flora were happy and Flora was to wait for Jason in Istanbul. Her father was to be the happiest of all, she used to say, when Jason was to visit her in Istanbul. Her friend Nitsa was excited, happy and waited. She had met Jason and she was happy as she knew that Flora was a charm: A noble lady, a charm and an independent woman. Irene loved Flora, for some reason. She was the woman of her brother.

That night, Flora was happy and fire burning next to Jason. He could not forget Ismene being close to the noble and attractive Flora. It was for him a present since he lost Ismene. Capturing the tenderness of Flora and her respect for Ismene he knew he had something more than expected: She was given to him by the Gods. She was not only gifted but also rewarded materially. The modest Jason, perhaps, for first time he was flattered. Two ladies had loved him and both were excellent musicians: Ismene gifted and Flora trained.

On Friday night Jason and Flora were again alone. They went together to a Theater play that Flora loved. She was impressed with the acting and liked to discuss the art of the people. Jason was surprised with Flora's knowledge and wondering why didn't she choose the art of Theater. She replied to him smiling, "If you had my father listening to my mother, that is what I should have been. But then my father was not that rich as he is now; and if I had done that, he would not have been as rich as he is now. Jason understood and he realized that Flora was rich.

Flora was also a business woman that had impressed her father. She had his talents. He had realized that his daughter was a business force that he was happy to take her with him since she was very young, educated and beautiful. She was a force and he was happy.

When her father learned that Jason was Greek, he whispered, "If he was also noble, he would listen to Flora." Her mother had visited Jason and she had whispered to her husband, "Terry, Jason is a noble man, and we should not cry." "Did you meet his wife?" he used to ask. "Yes, Terry, she is noble and intelligent." There her father used to shed a secret cry. Now that he learned about the accident, he used to say, "I hope that now he needs another noble woman." But he could not force noble Flora more than he did. She had decided to go with tears listening to her father. She was surprised with Jason's nobility and responsibility.

She was a noble woman not to be embarrassed by questions that were only for irresponsible men. She let her father know. "My child is his child, and if he doubts the least I do not want him the most," she used to say to her parents each time they were wondering about Jason's response. She was amazed with Jason's intelligence and responsibility!

Jason took Flora to the airport in Messini early Saturday afternoon and with tears in the eyes she whispered to him, "I will always love you, but if you are with me, I will be also happy. I will be waiting for you as long as I live. Don't forget that I lived for seven years with your child dreaming about you." Jason looked at Flora with sorrow and thought of

Ismene with tears. He knew that Flora was to be loved and trusted. She was a trusted diamond more worthy of his manly virtues.

He was a noble young man, but she was a virtuous young and capable woman also. What virtuous women do not deserve to have? Medea had taught Jason not to play with women. He could betray her, but she could punish him. Flora was not Ismene, but she could be a miracle in the things she was trained. She loved and wanted Jason with prudence. She was happy with Louise when she saw her in her flower shops. She was a faithful Hellenic woman. She knew how to love.

"Don't forget Jason that Istanbul is a Greek city. Even thou the people do not speak Greek, the spirit of Istanbul is Hellenic. You have to come and I will show you," Flora whispered just before she left. Jason smiled, held Flora's hand and kissed her. "Flora, remember, I love Nikita and his mother," he said. "That says that you will come and see him soon," she replied smiling. "Yes, sooner than you think," he says looking at Flora.

"Do you realize that he has your father's name?" asks Flora shyly. Jason thinks, wonders and his eyes shed tears. Flora realized the answer. "Your love for Nikita is your love for his parents," whispered Flora. Jason didn't miss Flora's smile. She was an intelligent woman.

Jason can see that she is a happy one. She gets into the airplane, sits at the window and keeps looking at the airport as she is leaving. Jason is pleased and appreciative. Flora is not just a female, she is also a real woman. She knows how to please. As the airplane is leaving she sends to Jason a kiss using both her hands behind the airplane window. He could not see. But she was giving him, the only one, the best she had: Many kisses after so long. Jason wanted to be with her. She would not have said 'no'. She wanted him to be with her!

Flora was a pleasure in everything she said and did. She was really a charm for Jason and his friends. She could play music, dance and sing, she could greet and smile. She was a beautiful woman. She was getting Jason out of his misery that pleased his friends. He was happy seeing his sister close to Flora; real and normal. "The same to the same always associates," whispered Jason smiling.

Jason was capable enough to find her. She was happy that she had the man she loved. But she was certain that she could have pleased and be pleased with the man that had a very noble lady. She really wanted to be Ismene's friend and have the same man if Ismene wanted. Her father was respected but could not govern her tastes and values. She was the liberal daughter of a conservative father.

Jason went to the house in the Harbor. He fixed a coffee, took his guitar and started playing. The money was the convenience, but the guitar was his passion, Jason often whispered. He thought of Ismene and cried; he imagined Flora and smiled hoping. He is thinking of Nitsa and wonders, 'Is she in love? Can she love two men as he loves two women?' Strange thoughts with subtle wishes. Only Gods can direct Jason's mind and temptations. His desires can make him drunk but will not govern his ways and preferences. He is alone now with Flora burning and Nitsa tempting his mind. He remembers how Nitsa was admiring Flora. She was one to be respected.

Jason wants to see his son that he has not seen him since he didn't know he had one with a noble lover. Flora was a noble woman that she didn't want to interrupt his happiness. "What a woman," he whispers thinking of Flora. But tears come into his eyes when he contemplates of Ismene sacrificed for him with pleasure!

No man will have ever conquered Ismene, and no man will have ever Flora: A flower that knows how to love and never fades. He is the winner and he knows it is luck. He knows it is fortune to be loved by such noble ladies. And when you know, it is often too late to act.

A child is waiting to go to Greece and see his father as his mother relates with tears of admiration for her son. Jason remembers her words and her tears: "Nikita is waiting to come and see his noble father," his mother said with tears and no demands. Jason's eyes get flooded when he thinks of his son; but he does not know when he will go: Perhaps when his heart will have healed from the pain left by the loss and sacrifice of Ismene. Then he will go to Istanbul. Not long after, Jason's eyes get flooded with tears. He thinks of his son waiting and loves his mother. She is more noble and more female than Jason can think. It is not so easy to read the female heart.

One day, early in the night, Jason meets his friends Simon and Stuart in their usual entertainment place and after their dinner with tears of pleasure he says, "I will drive tomorrow early in the morning for Istanbul to see my son and make love with his mother." His friends smiled and Stuart whispered, "It is time Jason that you do so."

"Flora may not have the powers of Ismene, but she has the will to love and please," added Simon. To see and hear that his friends were pleased, a smile was traced on the face of Jason who was in love with Flora and admired the lost and imperial charm of Ismene. But his heart could not be closed for ladies with hearts open like Nitsa's.

Flora was admiring and respecting Jason. Why he should be cruel with Flora? She was noble and respectful. Why he should ignore himself and punish Flora? His son and his woman are waiting for him.

He does not believe that she is not suffering. Noble people don't revolt but suffer while they love. Flora is doing the same suffering and hoping. No other man had attracted Flora. Not even after she had Nikita. She was really a female that loved her man as she loved her child. It was the child to keep her united with Jason. It was the child to make her appreciate Jason. She would not deny it, if she was asked.

One day after, Jason left for Istanbul to meet his son, and as he said to make love with the woman that he loved. It was Flora waiting for Jason and promising his son that one day he would have the luck to see his father, if he is patient and loving. "Your father will never forget you," she used to say to Nikita smiling with tears. Gods had blessed Jason who was rewarded for the honor he gave to Ismene to rise above her enemy. Flora was an educated and respectful woman.

His friends Stuart and Simon were pleased with Jason, but laughed with his decision to go to Istanbul with his car. "If you need we will buy your aiplane ticket for Istanbul," whispers Stuart smiling. Jason looks at Simon who is smiling also. Then Jason asks, "Why are you both smiling?" "Well we understand that flying is more expensive, and we think that we should buy you a ticket," remarks Stuart. Jason thinks, identifies what he said and all then laughed.

To be sure that there was no error in their conversation Stuart comments, "We think that it will be wiser if you get the airplane and you rent a car when you go to Istanbul." Jason thinks, recovers and smiles as well. "I think that our excited friend lost his brain," comments Simon. Anyway, the three friends agreed and left the coffee place laughing. Jason was going to get the airplane and when he gets in Istanbul he will go to a Hotel and from there, he will get a Taxi to go anywhere he wanted or rent a car. There was no problem with money!

A Friday night Jason took the place for Istanbul. He reserved a place near the residence of Flora and he decided to call on Saturday morning after breakfast. He was really excited to see his son before lunch. He was certain that Flora was a woman to be pleased and not be annoyed, anyway. If he was not lucky to see his son on Saturday, he was certain to see him on Sunday. He was not certain but hopeful.

He decided to be a surprise and see the reaction of Flora. He did not have in this case the required composure. He was going to see his son and he was afraid how to face the unexpected. As he was thinking about the fact, he was feeling really nervous. He could not hide his tears and the love that the mother of the boy had inspired.

Jason wanted to see his son and he was wondering. No matter how you love the mother, you adore your son. He was 6 years old and Jason had not see him yet! His friends were wondering how he could do it.

On Friday early in the afternoon Jason takes the Airplane from Messini and goes to the Athens airport. From Athens airport he goes to the Istanbul Airport. From there he takes a Taxi and goes to the a Hotel near Flora's house. Jason had Flora's address. He decided to visit Flora's house early on Saturday morning. He is really nervous but there is nothing better to be done. He takes a room in a Hotel and stops after at the reception place. He orders a glass of wine to rest and reflect. He was really thinking and wondering: Will his son recognize him? Will talk to him? It depends on the mother and the boy.

It is a situation that Jason is really inept to handle. But this is the case that he has to face, better than any other he had so far in his life. The ladies of the hotel were charming and tempting. But Jason was not in any case to do anything else but to wait and see his son, little later. To see the noble Flora: An exceptional flower with no demands!

In the morning of Saturday Jason is very nervous and after breakfast he sits in the Hotel Reception room and asks to be helped. A very pretty young lady goes to Jason and serves him. Anyone could see the attraction of Jason on the young lady. But that was not the case. He asked to be served and ordered at the end a cup of special sweet coffee. He took a newspaper and began reading, hoping to relax.

At about in the middle of the morning, he called a taxi, gave the driver the address where he wanted to go, and in no more than ten minutes he was at the place where he wanted to be. The place where he was driven was really pleasant, and the single family house attractive.

Jason was really nervous. He composed himself and rang the bell. A young lady comes out of the house and checks on the visitor. Jason gives his name and she asks him to wait. In five minutes, the inside door opens and a lady comes out.

She cannot see who is the guest and moves at the outside door left open by the young lady. It was Flora who came out and as soon as she recognized Jason, she run towards him, took his hands and kissed them reserved. "Jason," she whispered, grabbed his hands and kissed them passionately. Then, holding his hands yelled, "Nikita; Nikita," and asked the young lady to bring Nikita out. As she was guiding Jason in, the young lady came out with Nikita: A small boy, healthy and attractive; intelligent and thinking.

Flora catches the boy excited and stopping in front of Jason with Nikita, asks the boy with tears, "Nikita; do you know who is this gentleman?" The boy looks at Flora; looks at Jason; hesitates to answer; and finally says timidly. "Mother; this gentleman is my father!" While Jason is bending and kneeling, the boy runs on the open arms of Jason and crying whispers, "Father, do you know for how long are we waiting for you?" "Yes Nikita, since the time your mother told you that you have a father." The clever boy smiled and replied. "Yes, I knew I had a father. My mother was talking to me for so long that I had stopped to believe she knew." Jason and the servant girl were smiling while the mother was crying. The child was intelligent, and Jason happy. He realized that the boy was intelligent and alert with blue eyes.

"Lets go in please," said Flora crying. Jason lifted the boy and fallowed Flora. Tears flooded Jason's eyes. The young girl followed pleased and tears filled her eyes after she realized that Jason was Nikita's father. Flora wiped her eyes leading the way in the single family house. As they got into the house, Nikita was watching Jason in the eyes and said quite loud, "Father, your eyes are large, green and beautiful." They all laughed and the mother was happy to hear her child speak to his father. Her eyes were running from happiness seeing her son be happy as he was talking to his father.

The boy was so comfortable and happy that he forgot there were other people, as well, in the saloon next to the kitchen. His mother seeing him happy could not restrain herself. Jason realized that the mother was as happy as the little son.

Not long after, the door bell rings. The young girl tells Flora that it is Nitsa. "Let her come in," says Flora. At that time Jason was talking with Nikita. Nitsa comes in smiling and says "Flora, tonight we have to go to Belly Dansing so I can dance when Jason comes and plays his guitar. I hope to surprise him." Jason was sitting with Nikita talking and looks at Nitsa using his name. "Yes, when he comes, if he ever does," replies Flora smiling and looking at Jason.

Nitsa looks at Nikita and sees him talking with Jason, while Jason was looking at her after she used his name. "My God," she whispers, seeing Jason after she used his name. She goes to him smiling and greets him with passion. "Jason, when did you come?" she asks and embraces him again. "Last night," he replies smiling. Nitsa was happy and turned to Flora. She embraced her also with love. She sensed the happiness of her friend and could not hold her tears. She was happy.

In the afternoon, Jason took his son and went to the center of Istanbul. They had ice cream cake and pleasant conversation. The boy was conservative and careful. After they went to a number of shops. Jason bought for Nikita a Guitar and for his mother a flat Gun. The boy was surprised and careful. He didn't have ever a real Guitar.

"Nikita, the Guitar is for you from your father, and the pistol is from you to your mother. Do you remember that?" "Of course, I remember that father," replies the boy smiling looking at the guitar and the pistol.

"When you become 12 years old, I will buy you your gun and I will have excellent teachers to show you how to use guns. Do you understand?" The boy looks at his father and replies smiling, "Yes father, I do," replies the boy. Jason grabs and kisses the boy. He could not control his tears anymore. "After dinner, I will give you the Guitar and you will give your mother her Gun." The boy was happy smiling. He embraced and kissed his father.

His mother had told him that his father was to teach him those things when they were to meet. She was apparently looking forward to introduce Nikita to his father later. She was a noble lady not wishing to upset Jason's happiness. God had blessed her: She was not a bitch. Jason was surprised to find out that Flora had no other man conquered besides Jason. She was not Medea to Jason by killing his child.

They got home happy at dusk. The mother was pleased to see them coming laughing and she was in haven. She offered them almonds and other nuts with wine and orange juice and promised a nice dinner at home with Nitsa and Saul, Nitsa's boyfriend. Nikita was excited and wanted to hear about his Guitar and his mother's Gun.

"And when you are not here who will teach me?" asked the boy. Two tears run down from the eyes of Jason and he answered kissing the boy: "Your mother and your father will and you should listen," whispered Jason. The boy saw the tears and embraced Jason. He was happy to be with his father and embraced him crying: A communication between father and son had started! Jason was emotional and could not restrain himself. He had a sense that his child was very intelligent.

Not long after, Saul arrived, and the discussion between Jason and Nikita was to continue later. The boy was so happy to know his father and his knowledge. "First your mother and next your father will guide you on your way," said Jason to the boy and kissed him. Flora was experiencing the happiest moments in her life seeing her child and his father so happily communicating.

Jason was impressed with the intelligence of his child. He knew that Flora would have not approached him unless she knew that he was a noble and a brave man. She didn't believe that the mother could be noble and the boy spoiled or neglected. She was definitely correct but with the father along, she was certainly happy. She had kept her love for Jason hoping. She had his child to fill her life in the future.

What more, the Jews or Christ could give to Jason than what Nikita gave? Now he was Christ to the child, after thirty years will be, "Whatever will be, will be; Que sera, sera will be," sang Jason and the boy smiled. "That is my mother's song," whispered Nikita. "When my mother sings; she is beautiful; isn't she dad?" asked Nikita looking at his father. "Isn't she?" asked the boy again looking at his father for an approval, for a confirmation.

Jason looked at his boy and whispered, "Yes. She is not just beautiful, Nikita: She is charming!" The boy was pleased and smiled. Nikita gave a kiss to his father: He knew who and what his mother was. The boy looked at his father and was smiling thinking of his mother. He had never heard a nasty word out of his mother's mouth about his father. He was happy to meet his noble father.

The boy tells his father before he goes to sleep, "Father, neither my mother is Medea of Colhis, nor my father Jason of Iolcos. Good night." He kissed his father and went to sleep. Jason was surprised to hear his son and smiled broadly wondering with tears...

BRIEF RESUME

Dr. Vasily Kouskoulas, was Professional Engineer in the United States and worked in Civil Engineering, Construction, Automotive, and Aerospace industries. In 1971 he received his Ph. D. in Engineering from UCLA in Los Angeles.

Then, he became Professor of Engineering at Wayne State University in Detroit, at Purdue University in West Lafayette, and at the University of Patras in Greece. In 1985 he left and returned to Civil Engineering and Aircraft Industries.

Till 1995 he worked and travelled all over the world in Asia, in South Africa, in Europe, and in South America. After that, he returned to the States and worked as a Professional Engineer in the Aircraft Industry, exclusively, till 2008. He was always rewarded and respected by his co-workers and supervisors.

During that period he cultivated his poetry and writing in English, and was selected as a Distinguished Member of the International Society of Poets.

The present work reflects his philosophy in life and the virtues of men and women. The level is above the normal and justice is a virtue tested when men and women view what they deserve and pursue it with responsibility.

The virtue and the evil are always present and people should be always ready to protest and fight. The noble and the capable ones should be the ones to conspire and fight away from the established bureaucrats and policemen...

CPSIA information can be obtained at www.ICGtesting.com
Printed in the USA
LVOW07s1131291215

468218LV00001B/29/P

9 781460 265109